LEE

IN THE COMPANY OF SNIPERS
Book 12

IRISH WINTERS

COPYRIGHT

Lee; In the Company of Snipers, 12

Cover design and author photo by Kelli Ann Morgan,
http://www.inspirecreativeservices.com

Interior book design by Bob Houston eBook Formatting

Editor: Lauren McKellar, McStellar editing,
http://mcstellarediting.blogspot.com

Editor: Katie Johnson, katiestefan333@gmail.com

ISBN Paperback: 978-942895-33-6
ISBN eBook: 978-1-942895-32-9
Library of Congress Control Number: 2016911305

Irish Winter's author websites are: http://www.irishwinters.com
 and irishwinters.blogspot.com

In the Company of Snipers

You can find Irish Winters on Facebook: https://www.facebook.com/author.irishwinters

On Twitter: https://twitter.com/irishwinters1

For news on upcoming releases, sign up for Irish Winters' Newsletter at IrishWinters.com.

For more information about all my books, visit IrishWinters.com.

IN THE COMPANY OF SNIPERS

This series revolves around ex-Marine scout sniper, Alex Stewart, and his covert surveillance company, The TEAM, home-based out of Alexandria, Virginia. An obsessive patriot and workaholic, he created the company to give ex-military snipers like him a chance at returning to civilian life with a decent job.

This is not a serial with each book ending at a cliffhanger. I wouldn't do that to you. *In the Company of Snipers* is a collection of passionate love stories involving women and men who are tough enough to take on the world alone. Each is a stand-alone read, where in the course of an active TEAM operation, one agent comes face to face with his or her demons. The men and women I write about are all patriots and warriors, dealing with what they've lived through or the mistakes they've made

Spoiler alert: Every novel contains adult scenes including sexual situations (some explicit), language, and violence. I don't write sweet romance, so be forewarned.

At the end of each story, it's my hope that you, along with my heroes, will come to realize...

Love changes everything.

Prologue

Four years earlier

"Bind her!"

Tess Culver fell to her knees, the crack from the rifle butt to her head more than she could bear. Whoever these Taliban soldiers were, they were nothing like the others she'd known. It took less than minutes for two of them to tie her hands together in front of her knees, to shackle her ankles with the same rope.

Tess fought to control her trembling. She shot a sideways glance to her mentor from the orphanage, but there was nothing Sister Alison could do. Not anymore. The children needed her—not that the Taliban cared about the orphans and little ones they'd maimed in their struggle for terror. The worst was yet to come.

They'd swarmed the orphanage at the crack of dawn. No shots had been fired. Tess and Sister Alison had made no attempt to defend themselves. Why would they? They had no soldiers, no weapons, and no means to fight back. The orphanage housed the homeless and poor, not just children and babies. How could the helpless fight these monsters?

They'd come for Omar, the teenage boy with the wide-open smile who ran errands for Sister Alison. He was the best of his country, but Omar was poorer than dirt. Now he lay bloodied and unconscious in the back of one of the Taliban soldier's trucks, but for what? Because his dream was to become a doctor? Because Omar wanted to give back to the country that beat him and people like him down? Most likely.

Tess feared he wouldn't live the day. Her pounding heart echoed the same fear for herself.

A bearded man shuffled to where she'd been forced to sit and wait. What she wouldn't give to wipe the smirk off his foul mouth but she couldn't control the tremors rattling through her whole body, much less come up with enough saliva to spit in his face. Male chauvinist bullies—that was what many of these men and their self-proclaimed prophets were. They didn't believe in a cause. They just needed a reason to kill.

He'd dragged a wooden pole behind him. It looked solid. *Good.* One hard hit with it and she'd be dead. At least her end would be fast and merciful. She hoped. Steeling her resolve, she prepared to die more honorably than most of these guys lived. God, she hated them and the lies they spewed under the guise of Islam.

"You infidels," he growled when he crouched at her feet, but not like a brave and powerful tiger might growl. No. More like a conniving jackal, whining his thanks for the demeaning task he'd been given. He had the nerve to settle his dirty hand on her knee. Brave Afghan warrior, nothing. This weaselly excuse for a man might as well have a bandana wrapped around his head like the gangbangers back home in America. He was there to make a name for himself, to beat women and children because it made him look tough.

Her heart pounded so hard she couldn't think. Fear and panic had control. Death was imminent. Her mother's sweet smile flashed to mind, then her father's steady gray eyes.

They'd be sad to hear their daughter had been killed on what they honestly believed was a humanitarian mission. At least they'd think she died for a noble cause.

Tess closed her eyes, prayed one last prayer, and willed the deathblow to come fast and hard. The end of her short life might have come too soon, but death would be welcome now. She'd lived a good life. The truth may not come to light today, but it would eventually. Her quest would be revealed. Since she'd come to this beautiful country less than eleven months ago, she had singlehandedly stolen several of Afghanistan's ancient relics from the very thieves who'd looted the National Museum in Kabul. The relics and artifacts were safe now, reserved for the real heroes of this beleaguered country—the simple, honest people.

She'd truly believed in something greater than herself, but if she took her secret to the grave, that she was the cat burglar of Kabul, she was fine with it. What mattered most was that she'd helped the innocent children at the orphanage, innocents like Jamaal and Mina. They would remember the silly, impetuous American woman who had read them Disney stories of princes and princesses and happily-ever-afters. She scanned the grounds, hoping they were safely hidden inside. They didn't need to witness more cruelty.

The ugly man with his hand still on her knee grunted. Instead of striking her with the pole, he shoved it under her knees and into the small triangular space created by her bound arms and legs. Not what she'd expected. Her heart thumped wildly in her chest at this unexpected turn of events. Damn. This might be worse than death.

"That wicked mouth of yours must be taught a lesson, American," he muttered with a salacious sneer. "You cannot spread your lies and get away with it."

Hidden from his comrades by his thick, dark hair and beard, his lying eyes skated to her breasts—not that he could see them through all of her required heavy clothing. But all men knew what lay beneath a women's garb. There weren't enough layers of cotton, linen, or silk in the world to change the filthy mindset of a pervert like this guy.

He dipped one dirty finger inside her shirt collar and tugged out the crucifix her brother had given her when she'd graduated college; not that Clint was religious, but it meant something to her, a Christian in an unforgiving land. She wore it as a sign of her individuality. Her free will and her spirit. Her belief in a God who loved all of his children, not just extremists, terrorists, and jihadists.

"You think your Christian god will save you now?" One bushy brow lifted along with his lip.

"Get your hands off me," she hissed, struggling to show defiance instead of fear.

He let the chain drop to her breasts and pushed off the ground, his hand pressed to her knee for leverage. Tess caught one last terrified look from Sister Alison as two men lifted the pole and Tess along with it. Instantly, her head tilted backward, her body swinging upside down. There was no escape. She squeezed her eyes shut and hoped for a beating instead of the total degradation of gang rape in the center of the orphanage playground.

Another man stepped forward through the throng of bullying illiterates with AKs. While the others were charged with testosterone and their twisted idea of religious zeal, he seemed eerily calm. Businesslike. The scent of sandalwood approached with him. Tess couldn't miss his expensive leather loafers, crisply pressed black linen trousers, or his matching blazer.

The others quieted. They seemed to respect him. Was he there to save her? Hope flared—until he crouched to her level and softly stoked her cheek. The sensation of his skin against hers curdled her blood. He lifted her head until she had no choice but to look up at him. A cruel smile wrinkled his upside-down face, and then she knew how bad this was going to be.

"You think you can do whatever you want in my country, Miss Culver," he said quietly, the pad of his thumb rubbing a gentle circle beneath the black eye she'd gotten when she'd punched the first creep who'd laid a hand on her.

This guy could've passed for a gentleman. Suave, clean-cut, and recently bathed, he spoke with the clipped inflection of a civilized man with a British education. Yet there he was, in the most uncivilized country in the world, in charge of this death squad. She should've known.

This was him, Hasim Nizari. Banker to the Taliban. Vile molester of women and children. The man she'd rightly accused of raping a young woman before she'd realized how blind justice was toward women in this part of the world.

"You and your buddies are the ones defiling your country, not me," Tess hissed. If this was the end, she intended to die with a curse on her lips for him and all men like him. "You defile it by breathing the same air as the good people you grind under your boots. You raped that girl. You and I both know it."

He shook his head, an odd smile on his face. "You only think you know, my pretty little friend. Tread gently from now on," he whispered, his eyes lifted to the men gathering around her, "or we will meet again. I have an appetite for beautiful women, but you won't enjoy it nearly as much as I do. I can promise you that."

Tremors seized her soul, squelching her pithy comeback to a man so cruel. He rose from the ground and snapped his fingers. The cowardly Taliban warrior in charge of the attack uttered a fervent curse to all infidels. The lesson commenced.

After the first hit Tess only saw black.

"You sign. I let you live."

Yeah, right. I'm not signing that confession, no matter how many times you shove it under my nose. USMC Corporal Lee Hart swayed forward, his legs too weak to support his battered six-foot-five frame. No sooner did he tilt off axis than the two stout Taliban soldiers at his sides jerked him backward. They forced him to kneel on the wooden canes spread parallel to each other on the floor—not that kneeling hurt less than falling on one's face. There was no part of his battered body that had not been tested by these bastards. Everything throbbed. Some places just hurt worse. Others bled. Life in the day of a captured Marine sucked to hell and back.

They never leave a man behind. I'm not alone. My guys are coming back for me. I know it.

They'd better hurry. The chats with his one-eyed Taliban were getting shorter. More vehement. Bloodier. If Lee's men didn't find him soon, there wouldn't be much left when they did. The day would come when that one last brutal conversation would end with a bullet to his head.

For days, Cyclops had tried to persuade Lee to betray his country on video, to confess to the world how the degenerate United States came to oppress and destroy innocent Afghanistan women and children, and of course, Cyclops always demanded Lee reveal U.S. troop movements and strategy. Lee had feigned ignorance. Over and over again, he'd refused to comply. No matter what they'd done to him, he'd honored his vow to protect his country.

"Geez," he muttered one last time. "Don't much feel like... signing today."

The guard at his left stomped his boot down on the back of Lee's calf, grinding bone against wooden canes and concrete. Lee caught a sharp breath and grimaced while his kneecap shrieked in agony. He gritted his teeth, panting for enough air to breathe and the strength to endure. He hadn't always been able to breathe through the torture. Drowning in a bucket of dirty water and having rags stuffed down his throat for nothing more than his captors' entertainment had taught Lee a hard lesson. Air was a damned dear friend.

They never leave a man behind. They're coming. I know it.

"You will sign!"

"You see..." Lee began, but the lunacy of his intended answer overwhelmed what remained of his common sense. He chuckled at this one-eyed moron. "No. Guess you don't see, do you, Jack Sparrow?"

A fist hit the back of his head. An angry stream of Arabic rhetoric spewed from the leader's bearded face. Lee bowed his chin to his chest, spit and blood dribbling off his lip. Arabs in Afghanistan? Interesting. He would've expected Pashto or Urdu. The things a Marine had to find out the hard way.

"Today you will die," Cyclops hissed.

Heard that one before. Just do it already. Stop talking and do it.

"Take him back to his cell," his ugly warden muttered.

Lee tried to stand, honest he did. Standing made better sense than kneeling, but he wasn't fast enough on his already tortured feet. Roughly, his Taliban buddies dragged him back to the tiny cell. More like a concrete broom closet, it boasted the lovely accommodations of a tin bucket to piss in and another to drink out of. Some days, he wasn't sure which was which. They tasted the same. Dry bread might get tossed in occasionally, but he couldn't remember the last time that had happened. The room had other occupants, too. Bugs. Rats. A hook. A pulley.

They dragged him to the corner beneath the hook where he could be raised to his feet for another fun day in Kabul, or Kandahar, or wherever the hell he was. Too soon that other man would join the party. He always did. Hasim Nizari. He made the one-eyed goblin look like Winnie the Pooh.

When he showed, he was always immaculately clothed, his soft hands clean, and his nails trimmed. Why wouldn't he be? He owned the estate this pit of torture and death was on. But he carried the stink of a truly twisted mind with him, masked by some expensive men's cologne. Nizari was a master at torture and pain. He needed to die.

Lee's too battered brain mused at the ugly metal hook dangling off the ceiling. If it had been placed in the center of the room, it would've turned his hanging body into a punching bag, but in the corner like it was, they had more control. That was the ultimate humiliation of torture, the loss of control over your own body.

Lee forced his mind back home before the games began in earnest. Back to where greater powers than the barbaric bullies let loose in Afghanistan were at work in the universe. He summoned them now through the words of age-old magic. Quietly. Reverently. Hoping to God his squad was on its goddamned way!

Amazing grace, how sweet the sound...

Chapter One

Spring in Kabul, Afghanistan

"Keep it low. Keep it tight."

Well, duh. Junior Agent Eric Reynolds ignored the astute observation of his spotter, one annoying-as-hell Junior Agent Seth McCray. Instead of replying, Eric blew the dirt off his lens and took careful aim again. It was night, dark and dusty. He was invisible, camouflaged in desert cammies behind the only flat rock for miles around in the flat, dusty valley outside Kabul. Ex-Army, Seth lay next to him, his rangefinder stuck in his eye sockets like the good spotter he wasn't.

One klick away, their bearded target, Mohammed Turik, lay flat to the ground, his weapon of choice aimed toward the roof of the dilapidated and bombed out Darul Aman Palace. The only movement between the three of them was the black-and-white checkered keffiyeh wrapped over Turik's head and around his neck. The end of it lifted with the wind, giving the Taliban assassin prone position away. If Eric had his way, that keffiyeh would soon become this sniper's death shroud.

"Bastard's got NVGs," Seth reported, a twinge of disbelief in his voice.

Eric let the implied hint to hurry roll off his shoulders. Seth blew out a big sigh, spiking Eric's irritation further. If he made this shot, it would be the biggest miracle ever given the mental state of the man beside him.

Seth hadn't been himself since that last firefight—in his hometown of Chicago, of all places. He'd never gone through the hell of combat during his single rotation in Afghanistan. No. He'd waited until he was back home to get caught in the middle of a gang war in the murder capital of the United States, the Windy City itself.

The worst part was that he'd been an innocent bystander, out with his buddies at a local bar at the wrong time. The only thing that went down right that night was that he'd been armed. Illegally, yes, given Illinois' no concealed carry permit law. Yet somehow, that good thing turned into a really bad thing. He'd shot one of the gangbangers, a teenage girl, out of self-defense. She'd meant to kill him, the painted-pink pistol in her hot little hand proved it.

Seth seemed to have forgotten that one little detail. All he remembered was the look on her face when he'd ended her. Now his nerves were shot. None of the other agents on The TEAM wanted to work with him, not on a hot op like this one. They needed someone reliable. It damned sure wasn't Seth.

Eric pushed his opinion of his junior agent out of his mind and let the nature of his soul take over. The breeze had died. No movement caught his eye, but Turik was still out there. Eric could feel him.

That this particular Taliban soldier had become as good a sniper as one trained by the United States Army didn't equate to a hurry-up-and-die situation. It still took time to position, draw that steadying breath, and line up the tango in the crosshairs. A sniper was an animal unto himself and able to draw on the calm of the universe when needed, sit in the dirt, muck, and weather for days to get the job done if necessary, and save a few buddies and brothers in doing so. Eric called on that inner calm now, squeezed the trigger in one, slow, sweet—

Whoosh! A covey of birds exploded around him, followed immediately by a falcon soaring low on its nighttime hunt. Wasn't that just great? Apparently, Eric and Seth had surprised the raptor as much as he'd surprised them. Flap and feathers dipped too close. At least the damned bird didn't squawk and give their position away. At least Seth hadn't screamed like a girl and run. But could he keep still? Not on your life.

No matter. Eric had fired. The Taliban sniper now knew he wasn't alone. The round hit short, spiking a puff of dust next to Turik instead of knocking him down and sending him to his just reward in paradise.

"Damn. You missed," Seth muttered, his rangefinder up to his face where it should've been all along.

No kidding! Eric sucked in a slow, deliberate breath, willing the biting words away. As angry as Seth made him, he knew the kid was trying. Seth just needed to know when to shut up.

Turik had the audacity to simply turn toward Eric. He should've run home to his mother, but no, he lay as calm as if an annoying mosquito had just landed nearby. The man beneath that scarf had nerves of steel.

Eric rolled the knot out of his shoulder. Turik thought he was invincible. Rumor was he also had an American wife. A *willing* American wife. How the hell did that work?

"Yeah, I see you," Eric muttered under his breath, not relinquishing his post, either. Another round slid into place. He sighted Turik again. The jerk turned his eye back to his scope, paying no mind to the shot that had barely missed him, taunting Eric with his insolence. His cocky confidence in himself.

Five people had fallen to this particular enemy warrior in the last month. Well, no more. This second chance was a gift from the universe. Today was Turik's day to meet all those virgins the terrorists were always bragging about.

Eric calmed, recalculated in his head the dynamics of this shot that his spotter should've offered up, but didn't. The day's heat rising up from the ground invited a small variation. The soft breeze caressing the earth offered yet another. Eric stilled, did the math, made the adjustments, and it was time.

I've got you now.

But just that fast, Turik dropped out of sight. Of course, Seth noticed that. "Damn. You lost him."

Eric shot a loathing glance to his junior agent, the newest member on The TEAM, and the only one with a big mouth. No sense scolding the kid. He knew better. But damn it to hell!

Eric placed his eye to the scope again. Turik must've dug a depression in the ground next to him, a good idea now that Eric had time to think. A disquieting whisper persisted in the back of his mind that this Taliban sniper might have somehow known he'd be both target and assassin tonight. How could he have known? Who told? Was the man just that good that he'd prepared for all possibilities, including that he might also be hunted?

Seth shifted to his knees. "It's hot out here, bro. Let's go."

"We're in Afghanistan," Eric bit out without looking at him. "It's hot everywhere. Sit your ass down before someone takes a shot at you, and don't call me bro."

"What? Do you think he's still there?"

Seth wanted to argue? "I think if you don't shut the hell up, I'm going to shoot you instead of Turik."

Seth grunted, but hunkered down, his belly flat to the ground.

For three months now, Turik had made a laughing stock of the American soldiers sent to end his war game. The way he moved easily throughout the country reminded Eric of his SERE training in the hills of southern California. Turik was one damned good fox at survival, escape, and evasion. Of course, his success had more to do with the conflicted loyalties of the Afghan people. Somehow, despite the terror the Taliban brought to town with them, most of the local people didn't believe all Taliban were evil, mostly because, well, not all Taliban were evil.

Case in point, Mohammed Turik. Homegrown in Kabul, known by many as a neighbor and friend—heck, he was a family man. Interestingly, he had only the one wife instead of two or more, and he had a son. Eric knew where the man lived, just hadn't caught him there yet, not that he would've killed him in front of his family, but once—just once—he'd like to get his hands on the cunning bastard.

Turik had no problem hitting American and NATO targets, armed or not, and lately, he'd taken out five civilians for no apparent good reason. The French Ambassador, two American nuns, and two assistant curators at the local museum. He had to be stopped.

"Do me a favor." Eric hugged the butt stock of his rifle and fixed his scope on the last known position of his savvy target.

"Yeah, what?" Seth bumped Eric's shoulder, meriting another dark look when the rim of the scope dug into Eric's orbital bone. Either man on a hunter-killer team should know damned well better. Never touch a man engaged on target. *Never!*

"Watch the palace." Eric gritted his teeth and bit back his impulse to beat the living shit out of his partner. "He's aiming that direction. Tell me what or who he sees that we don't."

Silence meant Seth might be doing what he'd been asked. Eric hoped. He breathed a shallow breath, his eyeball once more on target. When he finally caught a flicker of Turik's keffiyeh skimming the ground at the same position as before, Eric allowed a small smile. *I've got you now.*

He aimed. Let go a calming breath. And... he kept waiting. The rest of Turik's head never showed, and there was no reason to shoot a scarf. Eric waited for thirty minutes, steeled to take the shot. The keffiyeh was there, but no head. No man. Damn.

"You think he's still there?" Seth asked finally.

"You were supposed to tell me why Turik's laying out here," Eric ground out. "What's going on at the palace?"

"Nothin'," Seth answered grumpily. "That's why I kept quiet. You were busy, and I didn't see anything much to mention. We should go."

"Then go!" The heavenly calm evaporated. Eric turned on Seth. "You're killing me here. Shut the hell up when I'm working. Damn it, man, you're supposed to be on my side."

As if he hadn't just gotten his butt reamed, Seth looked calmly toward the palace and exclaimed, "Wow. Look at that guy run."

Eric pulled his night scope up and followed the action on the rooftop beyond Turik's location. An individual raced across the dimly lighted roof at the northern end of the palace. A pack of uniformed men appeared behind the guy, their flashlights bobbing as they gave chase. The runner kept going. Looked like he meant to fly off that roof.

Eric looked closer. That wasn't just any runner. He was slender. Ran like a girl. "That's Tess Culver. What the hell's she doing here?"

Tess Culver. Notorious cat burglar. The gutsy American gal with big brass balls who'd stolen ancient artifacts from the very men robbing their country blind. She'd become a local legend and a heroine for this beleaguered country. So she was the one Turik had been waiting for.

Seth tapped Eric's arm again. "Hurry, bro. Turik's back. Same place. Do your thing."

Several gunshots popped from the direction of the palace. Eric hurried. He leveled his scope back to the assassin between them and Miss Culver. Sure enough, the Taliban's mighty sniper was back on target, his rifle aimed at the roof of the palace. At Culver.

"If she's there, Lee's got to be close by," Eric muttered, worried for that daring woman under fire. "Cover her. See if you can spot him."

"You bet." Seth snapped his rifle to his shoulder, finally acting like the soldier he used to be.

Eric zeroed in on the Taliban assassin once more. Pressure could make a man sloppy. Not Eric. Turik had settled his head and shoulders above the dirt this time. Putting his angst aside, Eric aimed low, going for body mass instead of a headshot.

"Shit. She's running off the roof. No wait. She stopped," Seth reported.

Shut up, damn it. Eric focused the crosshairs between his arrogant opponent's shoulder blades and fired at the same moment Turik got a shot off.

"Oh, my God," Seth cried out. "Did you see that?"

Eric ignored him, the last of his calm down that Leupold scope mounted to his rifle. *I hit him. I know I did.*

"She's gone," Seth exclaimed.

Damn it to hell! Seth might as well have told the whole world! No keffiyeh ruffled in the wind, and Eric bet Turik had been lying in a shallow ditch that led to a culvert big enough for escape. He bit down his anger and pivoted his scope to the palace roof where six men stood at the edge, looking down. "Did they shoot her? Where'd she go?"

"I... I... don't know," Seth whimpered.

Eric dropped his forehead to the butt of his weapon, stifling a tsunami of frustration. Seth had no business being in this fight. He was dead weight. A liability.

What the hell was Alex Stewart thinking?

Chapter Two

Get me the hell out of here.

Tess Culver exploded through the roof door and ran, her boots hitting the flat concrete surface like her life depended on it. Truth was—it did. She had no time to worry about consequences now. The deed was done, the die cast. Either Clint was where he should be or he wasn't. *The jerk better be.*

"There he goes!" an angry voice bellowed behind her. "Hurry! Catch him!"

Ha! The fools still thought she was a guy in her black cat burglar outfit. Next, there'd be shooting, and all those tough guys could kiss her—

Zip! Ping!

Right on schedule, two shots whizzed past her and splattered against the low brick wall that edged the roof. Her Adrenaline ramped up higher—like she needed more of it flooding through her system. Fire burned in her lungs. That familiar out-of-breath taste of copper, sulphur, and bile rose at the back of her throat. A sharp right turn ahead, and she'd be home free—if Clint was there.

She hit the corner and aimed her feet north to the circular front of the bombed-out palace, the best point for her most daring getaway yet. While her heart pounded incredibly loud in her chest, her feet pounded louder on the rooftop. And faster. Too quickly, the edge approached. She might not have enough time to hit her target as perfectly as she needed to. That could be bad.

Closer.

Faster.

She vaulted to the end of her road, dead center of the curved exterior wall where all could see. Back when Darul Aman Palace was built, this might have been a primo place to take in a romantic view. Not tonight.

Zip! Ping!

Whew. That one was close. *Jerk better damned well be waiting for me.*

Ignoring the bullets popping around her, she scanned the ground below. These buffoons wouldn't hit her. They couldn't risk it. If she fell now, she might break the prize in her hand when she hit the pavement.

No brother in sight. No truck headlights in the near distance, either. *Damn him. Where is he?*

With the prize still snug in her left hand and a sneer blossoming on her face, she whirled to face her pursuers. She might be sweaty and a teensy bit worried for her life, but these fools would never get what they wanted from her. They would, however, remember this day.

For months, she'd been on the prowl. Listening. Watching. Connecting dots as to exactly what was happening to all those ancient Afghan treasures suddenly missing from the National Museum, the prestigious building to the north of where she stood with the desert breeze at her back.

One artifact had eventually surfaced, a lovely golden necklace of inestimable value, now in the private collection of Prince Kalim Abdul Hazzan—in Saudi Arabia. Like that did the Afghan people any good.

Then another treasure, a simple carved knife handle of ivory, inlaid with lapis lazuli and emeralds, turned up at an auction in, of all places, Sotheby's in Paris. Nothing said "love of country" like stealing its ancient history and selling it on the black market.

Tess had decided right then and there. The plundering of Afghanistan by greedy men had to stop. That was the day the cat burglar within her arrived like a witch summoned from another world.

She hadn't realized she had a knack for thievery until the Sotheby story broke, but the exquisite treasures and relics needed to be saved. Someone had to do it. She knew so many of them by name and loved them all. The gold coins from the Yuezhi Chieftan, Hellenistic tritons, Scythian gold artifacts, and more, all bartered on the black market because of a few greedy buyers and sellers, all of them hypocrites and liars who'd proclaimed national loyalty to the country they loved. *Yeah, right.*

She spat her disgust to the palace rooftop. The six museum guards behind her screeched to a halt, the two in the rear bumping into the others they'd stopped so quickly. Uniformed and sweaty after chasing her up four flights of stairs from the basement, they looked like the pigs they were. Dumb. Bumbling. Stupid, if they thought the edge of the roof would stop her. It might if Clint didn't show in the next few seconds, but they didn't need to know that.

She stalled. That these pompous security guards participated in the demise of their country made them accomplices worthy of the same disgust she felt for that prince in Arabia. She had enough disgust to go around.

"Give it back, boy." The one with a thick black Manchu moustache approached cautiously, his fingers beckoning toward the bag in her hand.

Ha. Her ruse had worked. They still didn't know who they were up against. Wouldn't they be surprised?

"What? This?" she growled hoarsely, her throat ragged from the run, lending credence to her ruse. The bag dangled off her index finger like it meant nothing to her. The best part of this heist was that these guys didn't know if she was still armed or not. She wasn't. She'd accidently lost her pistol when the final door hadn't opened as easily as she'd expected. A girl could only hang onto so much when she was running for her life.

Fortunately, the roof was dark. Not knowing who else might be up there with her, combined with shadows, kept the guards nervous. Wary. Off balance. It also gave Clint a few more seconds to show up, damn him. She cocked an ear for the sound of his truck engine. *Where is he?*

Mr. Manchu seemed to be the bravest of the six, since he was the only one who took another cautious step forward. He scowled in that patronizing way Afghan law enforcement officers did when they thought they had the upper hand, or when they assumed their quarry was just a dumb kid they could intimidate.

"You must return what you have stolen, boy." He nodded knowingly while he spoke, as if she'd agree just because he'd told her to.

Guess again, tough guy.

"Come." He curled his fingers at her, urging her to repent and give up. "You're young. My boss will go easy on you. I'll make certain he does. I'll protect you."

"You mean Sherazi?" she taunted, keeping her voice deep and masculine. Assistant Museum Curator, Abdul Sherazi, the lowest of the low, had yet to make his appearance on the roof—not that she'd expected him to climb all those stairs. He could have. The man was svelte and athletic, but a thieving scoundrel like him had to keep a low profile, at least as low a profile as a thief like her. Only their motivations differed. He stole the treasures of his country for greed and gold. She stole for honor and the future of that very same country.

A thinner guard stepped forward, his gun clasped in both hands and aimed at her head. He actually smiled. "You'll never get away with it. There are six of us and only one of you."

Yeah, but you're all fat and stupid. She panted for more air, analyzing alternatives instead of telling him what she thought. Six armed men on a roof? Her back to the edge? These idiots still believed they were up against a boy? A girl couldn't get any luckier. Still...

She glanced to the barren road below. Clint had better get his ass in gear.

But since he wasn't there yet, she had time to give these guys a taste of American one-upmanship if only to stall. Tess shook the knitted beanie from her head and let her other accomplice—the wind, the one that had shown up—catch the length of her hair. She stripped the gloves off her long delicate fingers to reveal her richly painted nails. She might not have been wearing her brand of scarlet lipstick, but it was important she let these guys know they'd been beaten by the best, and her name was—

"He's a woman! An American woman!" Mr. Manchu hissed. Another guard spat in disgust. Yeah. She got that a lot from the macho guys in this country.

At last, a truck engine rumbled below. Relief washed through her. She scanned the wall's edge, searching for her mark. The letter X she'd scratched into the wall during her previous visit meant life tonight. Any deviance spelled *splat* in bright red below. Three stories down was a helluva drop when you're falling backward. She slid her boot heel over the X.

"You'll die in prison," Mr. Manchu growled. "I'll make sure of that now. A thousand lashes will not be enough for a filthy infidel like you."

"I say kill her now," Skinny Guy declared while he crouched to a firing position, one knee on the ground, licking his lips like he couldn't wait to end her. Another guard stepped forward, his lip curled in a sneer. Suddenly, everyone turned brave, like they all wanted a piece of her. "No, wait. We must rush her. Catch her. Then she'll be ours to do with as we please."

"That ain't never gonna happen," she taunted as she glanced down and verified her landing zone. Thank God. Clint. Truck. Airbag. Good to go.

Ping.

Damn. That bullet hit way too close.

"No, no, no." Still holding the bag where they could all see it, she waggled her finger, scolding the man who'd fired. She loved this part of the game. Risky. Reckless. But still alive and the one and only female cat burglar of Kabul. "If you shoot me, this little golden trinket will be destroyed in the fall. You don't want that, do you? What will your boss say when you fail to return it to him in one piece? Will he let you live? Any of you? I doubt it."

Tess tossed her head, daring them to risk their lives on the slim possibility she'd proposed, that they could hit her and not lose the prize. Sherazi was not known for his forgiveness. If anything, he was as evil as the man he worked with, the man known simply as Dark Man—Hasim Nizari. A shiver scuttled up her spine at the memory of the touch of that monster.

Skinny squinted down the barrel of his pistol. Closing one eye, he lined her up again.

Men. They never listen. Oh, well. Time to go.

She blew him a kiss over her fingertips. Spreading her arms wide, the bag still in her possession, she tipped backward and fell. It was a short, exhilarating-as-all-get-out trip, but one she'd planned thoroughly. The crush of the air bags when she landed whooshed a very welcome "gotcha, girlfriend." She could have crowed at her success in the face of such odds.

You're damned late, but I love you, Clint!

Tess rolled a backward somersault onto her feet, dancing off the inflatable bag to the wooden rail. While the truck swung northwest along the palace grounds, gears shuddering and headed to Char-Qala Road, she went feet first over the railing and angled her svelte frame into the open passenger window.

"You made it!" she exclaimed excitedly, her body thrumming with the adrenaline rush of her latest daring theft and too busy to acknowledge her baby brother. He *had* showed. That was all that mattered, darn his lazy ass.

Clint grunted like that was a no brainer.

She would've kissed him out of sheer excitement, but that could come later. The bag in her hand felt incredibly sweet. The safety of the passenger seat at her backside didn't feel too bad, either. She'd done it. Again!

Raking a hand through her hair, she pushed the tangled mass out of her face and over her shoulder where it belonged. No need for that windblown look now. Sex appeal had served its purpose tonight. Those idiot guards were probably wondering how a mere woman could've outsmarted the likes of them. *Ha! Men are so dumb.*

"You were late enough," she muttered while securing the prize beneath the seat. "You need a better watch, Clint. One that tells time. The right time."

Stunts like this only worked with precision planning and timing. Besides, this theft wouldn't go unnoticed. She'd actually been surprised there were only six guards tonight. She'd expected more. Glancing out her side window, she watched for trouble. So far, so good. No one followed, and she heard no sirens, but what if Clint had been any later? This could've gone bad in a big way.

He hadn't answered—not like she cared. Her brother was like that. Weren't most men? Sullen. Moody. Easily irritated by women smarter than them, or always too tired, too hungry, forever complaining because they couldn't get laid. Whatever. Who cared? Let him sit there and want. As long as he drove fast now and got this big rig of his undercover, she didn't really care what he did or thought.

She pulled the visor down, adjusted the mirror and slicked on a coat of her favorite lipstick. Victory Red. Her power color and her reward for a job well done. It matched her painted toes and her fingernails.

Still, his moody silence irked her. He should be happy at her success. He should be proud. He should at least say something. She'd just pulled off the heist of the century and risked her life to do it, while all he'd had to do was sit in his truck and show up on time. Now that she'd thought about it, he should be damned happy.

"It wouldn't hurt you to show a little enthusiasm." She turned and snapped, finally seeing the stranger sitting behind the wheel.

"Oh, baby. I'm damned enthused," the stranger with the sexy baritone rumbled.

Her heart leapt to her throat. "Who the hell are you?"

Chapter Three

Junior Agent Lee Hart grabbed her wrist at the same time as Tess Culver latched onto the door handle and simultaneously reached for her bag of ill-gotten booty. He'd expected she'd run, but there was no way this little gal was getting away from him.

"Back off," she snarled, shoving her door open with one booted foot and ready to jump to the gravel road.

"Not going to happen, Miss Culver." He yanked her back into the cab. The door slammed like he meant it to when he executed a hard right. Tess Culver was every bit as determined to exit stage left as he was to keep her. She hadn't let go of the handle or the prize—not like that bag in her hand was his first priority. Still, it was priceless and if he lost it, Alex Stewart, his boss, would have his head.

"I said let go!" She turned on him with all of one hundred and twenty pounds of feminine fury. What a sight. An angry blush coloring her cheeks. Ruby red lips that begged for a good hard kiss. Firecracker blue eyes, throwing off sparks within the flurry of dark, silken hair that never failed to get a man's attention. His natural instinct to delve all of his fingers into that mess and hold her head still while he kissed her fear away caught him up short. He shut the inclination down. She was his client, unwilling at the moment maybe, but untouchable. Like him.

He endured the ensuing clawing, scratching, and pummeling. It made driving a straight line a little tough, but not enough he'd let go of the wheel or her wrist, though. The one-on-one contact with the woman he'd only surveilled from afar until then was another thing altogether. A knockout clap of thunder rumbled in his heart, and his blood boiled like steaming, molten lava through his veins. All five senses had sprung to life with her finally up close and personal. Breathing took a sudden effort.

This woman packed a feminine charge he hadn't seen coming. Pure energy, it commanded every speck of his masculinity. Streamlined like a sleek desert panther, she'd turned all claws and hiss, one helluva brawler. Tossing her head, strands of ebony silk whispered over his bare hands telling him lies and inciting feelings he had no right to listen to.

He'd seen that hair floating on the breeze before when she ran unfettered by veils and local garb in the desert. He'd been surveilling her then. Just watching. Just wishing. Long and shiny, she used it now as a whip, but one handful, that was all he wanted. Lee resisted the temptation.

Every last speck of her dauntless spirit had been consumed with speed, agility, and good old American grit back then, not focused on him. His body stirred beneath that fierce feminine focus. Smitten. His nostrils flared to life at the allure of coconut and lime. Infatuated. *Yeah. I'm in trouble.*

Tires screeched around another corner, a trick for a big rig going as fast as this one. Easing off the gas, he let the truck right itself while he continued onto the designated location, not necessarily the one she'd intended to end the day at, but one ten times safer.

"Let. Me. Go!" the spitfire behind that whirl of hair and those blood red nails screeched. She'd released the handle to beat on him more efficiently, but still held the bag away from him. Not a problem. Being assaulted by one little female hand and two size-seven boots wasn't lethal. He'd been in tighter spots before, been hit by tougher and bigger.

"Give it up, princess. You're caught." He kept his voice calm and just a little condescending, but his grip stayed extra secure. Miss Culver knew a lot of tricks; he had to give her that, just not the right ones to break his grip.

Sideways in her seat now, she twisted, kicked, and spit. He didn't care what she tried until she aimed one heel at the side of his head, her knee cocked and loaded to deliver.

"Aw, don't do that," he said nicely. "It's just going to hurt—you."

A split second before she followed through, he exerted pressure on her wrist, which naturally radiated up her slender arm to her shoulder and—

Snap. Crackle. Pop. Dislocated. Just that easy, a little maneuver he'd learned in the Corps.

"Ouch! Damn it!" she shrieked, sagging back into her seat, her tongue licking over her wide-opened lipstick-red mouth, her tangled hair hanging in spirals over her angry, sweaty face. She clutched her injured arm with the hand that held the bag. Thunder clappers reverberated beneath long, thick lashes. "You jerk," she rumbled, blowing her hair out of her eyes with a big breath. "You broke my arm."

"Told you it was going to hurt. It's not broken, though. I wouldn't do that to you." He spared her a quick glance, not sure why he'd felt the need to explain. Damn, even mad, she was pretty, all the more dangerous in Lee Hart's book. He always was a sucker for brunettes.

Recording and studying reconnaissance videos of this particular American vixen during the past few months hadn't cured him of that particular ailment, either. Made it worse was what it did. Her long legs eating up the desert roads before she began these heists were a joy to watch. He'd timed her when she'd worked out. She was a go-getter from the ground up. Relentless. Fast. She should've joined the Corps. Tess Culver could run like the wind—an angry, devious wind. But when she chanced running in the open in just a black sports bra and workout pants? *God bless America.*

She might be sullen at the moment, but Lee knew her rep better than anyone else. Just when a man let his guard down, this girl would be gone. He'd been watching her for weeks while she'd snagged one Afghan treasure after another from the country's best crooks, the Taliban. Tess Culver, aka the best cat burglar in Kabul. *Well, not tonight, sweetheart. You've met your match.*

"Feels like it's broke, damn you. I can't believe you really hurt me, you big bully." Those red lips stuck out in a pout that made him do a double take. Okay. That was more like it. Right on cue, this twisted sister had deployed her vulnerable, I'm-just-an-innocent-little-girl routine. All that sexy, mussed hair only compounded the effect. The long, lush eyelashes, too. It could've worked—not. He'd studied her enough to know better.

"Calm down, Tess Culver," he said sincerely. "I'm not here to hurt you. Honest. We just need to talk about the mess you've gotten yourself into." Steering the heavy truck onto the dirt road, he proceeded toward the industrial section of town.

"Who are you?" she asked politely, like the good kitty she wasn't. The hissing and spitting might be out of sight, but he knew better than to answer with real facts and details. She'd just twist them, use them to suit her endgame. How she'd survived in this risky business for months was an amazing feat. He gave her that, but no more. Tonight it all ended. For her sake, it had to.

"I'm a friend. Let's leave it at that," he answered honestly.

She huffed through her nostrils and wriggled that broken-but-not-really-broken shoulder. It had to hurt. He'd dislocated his shoulder once during a fast-roping drop out of a helicopter on his first deployment. Dropped fifteen feet and landed on his ass that day. He didn't know which had hurt worse—his dislocated shoulder, his bruised butt, or the wise cracks from his buddies.

A stifled whimper sounded from the passenger side. Yeah. She'd be quiet for a minute or two. That gave him time to slow to a stop, crank the wheel left one-handed, and gauge his distance to the loading dock behind him in the side mirror. Time to back this rig up without losing his prize.

Unfortunately, it also gave her time to catch her breath, maybe her second wind. She straightened and glanced out her window. "Where are we?"

"Some place safe." This was where things could get dicey. Backing up a rig this size without a rearview meant his attention had to be focused outside the vehicle. He'd have to shift with his left hand because he still had a good grip on her.

She'd eased slightly toward him on the bench seat, lessening the tension on her supposedly broken arm. This girl was smart. She actually thought that maneuver would distract him enough she'd get away? That he'd loosen his grip? *Let her think that. Good kitty.*

He groaned as if maneuvering the rig was difficult, reached over his knee, grabbed the stick shift with his left hand, and pushed past neutral into reverse.

The minute the rig's wheels began to roll backwards, she let him have it. He saw it coming when she'd balled her right fist up nice and tight, and a pretty good punch headed his way. Not good enough. He released the shifter with time to spare and caught the blow solid in the palm of his left hand. All those years of baseball paid off. Silly woman. A man doesn't need two hands to back up a vehicle. *Line drive. Good catch. You're out!*

The damn little thing had her feet in motion again, like that was a shock. Lee turned to take the brunt, thinking he'd have to recalculate exactly when she'd snapped her shoulder back into place. She was going all out. In the ruckus, she'd balanced sideways on her right elbow, the bag still in her hand, the heels of both boots headed his way.

She's going to buck at me like a horse? This chick doesn't give up.

Admiration sparked deep within him. That was one thing he truly appreciated about Miss Culver. She threw herself into her work, but this time she'd presumed too much. He had a solid hold on that left wrist, despite the fact she meant to use her right elbow for a fulcrum. With a quick jerk, he punched their combined fists into her solar plexus just enough to— *oomph*—knock the wind out of her. She collapsed, straddling his arm, her face pressed to the upholstery, gulping for air.

"Told you not to do that," he scolded. "Now you've gone and hurt yourself."

"Shit... I... hate you," she wheezed.

He let her lay there. It wasn't entirely an uncomfortable position for a man to find himself in, the thighs of a beautiful woman wrapped around his forearm, her backside so nicely displayed for his viewing pleasure. He allowed a single moment of manly reflection. She did have a nice ass beneath her jeans. Taut. No panty lines. The body heat emanating from her was nice, too. And hot. Damned hot. His mistake.

Arching that attractive butt upwards, she took another quick aim. This time, he was a bit preoccupied. Her left boot connected with the side of his head. His rock-solid grip on her wrist slipped. Lee turned his shoulder as another kick glanced off his jaw.

The cat burglar of Kabul was still face down, but free. She hadn't connected as solidly as she'd wanted though, probably because it was really hard to aim facedown to the upholstery when she couldn't see her target.

She shifted her weight. This little minx still thought she was getting away? Lee wasn't seeing stars; he wasn't even dizzy. He fended off another volley of badly aimed kicks before he took his foot off the brake pedal and launched himself across the seat. He tackled her, flattened her, his palms splayed on the upholstery and his body trying like hell not to notice her curvy hips or the flowery perfume wafting up from her hair. A man in his line of work didn't often get this much pleasure bringing a common thief in.

Quickly, he snagged her right wrist in his right hand, leaving the bag intact, then secured her left wrist and brought it alongside her face. He could've twisted it behind her back, but he truly didn't believe in hurting women. She might not agree with him after their continual tussle, but this night wasn't about coercion. Not really.

Lee Hart, junior agent from The TEAM out of Alexandria, Virginia, the elite covert security company on the East Coast, was in Kabul at the behest of a protection order to get Miss Culver out of the country before she got herself killed. Her unknown benefactor had apparently tried to get her to leave, but she always thought she 'knew better.' He'd insisted her latest escapades had gotten riskier, but that the people of Afghanistan truly needed this particular heroine alive. The fly in the ointment was that unknown someone had demanded complete anonymity until the job was done. Lee didn't even know the guy's name. Alex had played that hand close to his chest.

"Do you honestly think you can best me?" he growled, listening to Miss Culver's heavy breathing beneath him. There was a day when all that panting meant pleasure had been given and received. He might have offered her a cigarette if he'd still smoked. Today wasn't one of those days, and who was he kidding? He hadn't been in the dating game for years. Still, playing with a sweaty gal who thought she could triumph over a guy the size of him had a definite impact on his dormant male libido.

He eased away from her before she noticed how quickly his body had responded to hers.

"Soon as you get your fat ass off me, I can... I can take you." She grunted into the upholstery, another feminine sexual sound he had no resistance to.

I can take you, too. Definitely the wrong thought at the wrong moment. Women were a delightful mystery of silk and sex and opportunities lost. He closed his eyes against the fire building in his gut, the echoing ache down deep in his groin. He was in a compromising position to say the least. It had to end.

But her hair... ahh. He closed his eyes and drew in a long deep breath. Whatever shampoo she'd used that morning rose up like heaven into his nostrils, coconut and lime, a heady brew of temptation for a man who'd been on too many remote ops to count during the past year. Just the nature of their current position was bad enough, but those ebony tangles were silky, soft, and cool, a touch of paradise in the cab of this older-than-dirt one-ton.

He stifled the feral call demanding release at the back of his soul. This woman might be Medusa and Odysseus's sirens all rolled into one, maybe with a shot of Bonnie Parker of the notorious Bonnie and Clyde thrown in for good measure, but she was Just. A. Client. Bad-assed and ready to rock and roll maybe, smelling like heaven, but nothing more than a mission to walk away from. A job with a definite return-to-sender date.

The still-rolling truck bumped gently into the loading dock with a soft jolt, but parking the rig was the last thing on Lee's mind. She thrust her head back sharply. He'd already anticipated that maneuver. Tilting sideways, he dodged her hard skull. She'd barely bumped his collarbone.

"You tired yet?" he asked patiently, still very much in control.

"Get. Off. Me."

"'Cause I'm just getting started if you want more." He lowered his voice and teased at the curl of her ear. The physics were simple. He outweighed her. He'd practiced and delivered hand-to-hand combat during his military career. There was no way could she win this wrestling match. "Tonight has been kind of fun," he whispered closer. Lower. More intimately.

"Shut up and let me go!" she screamed, and the mighty Tess Culver's mean-girl façade slipped, revealing a truly frightened woman for the first time. Her heart hammered hard and fast through her body. She was shaking. Gasping for air. The game had taken on a different tone. What had begun as a physical contest between enemy combatants suddenly felt more like—assault.

Damn it. Not what he'd intended. Not at all. Lee backed off, his throat tight and dry. He was no predator, but in the power struggle, he had crossed the line. He *was* bigger. He *did* outweigh her, but no woman, not even rough-and-tumble Miss Culver needed to fear him. "Things got out of hand," he said earnestly. "I'm sorry."

She lay still, panting into the seat, her hair spilled over her head. "Wh-what?"

"I said I'm sorry." He needed her to know she might be caught, but she'd never been in safer hands. Reaching to his belt, he brought his cuffs forward and carefully secured her left wrist.

"What? You can't!" She wriggled, but immediately stilled. A scared little girl looked sideways at him from under shiny, dark tangles, her eyes too big for her face. She bit her lower lip. A tremble raced up her left arm. "Please. D-d-don't."

Her breath hitched, and he had to look twice at the mixed signals rolling off this woman. Was she scared or not? Baiting him? If this was an act, it was a really good one. He almost fell for it until her thigh muscles bunched, and she shifted her position just enough to get on her knees in a hurry. No doubt about it, scared or not, Tess meant to win this contest. With one knee still between her legs, he pushed away, shifting back to his seat. "Don't make this any harder than it has to be."

She scrambled to her butt, the bag once again tight in her grip, the I'm-so-scared routine gone. "You can't have it."

"I don't want it." Left-handed, he pushed the stick shift into park and turned the truck off. Disgusted with himself at his less-than-professional handling of his client, Lee opened his door and tugged her across the bench seat to exit with him.

"Let me go," she growled, clutching the gearshift and then the steering wheel as he pulled her slowly toward him. He didn't want to disrespect her any more than he needed to, but damn, this was up close and personal work. He kept brushing over the breasts, thighs, and ass of a seriously gorgeous gal who could still hurt him. She needed to settle down. As if to prove his point, she twisted away from him the second her boots hit the dirt, her ass firmly planted on his thigh while she held the bag away from him.

"Knock it off." He slammed the door, spun her around, and cuffed her wrists behind her back. "You won't be needing this," he said as he removed the bag from her grasping fingers.

The bucking, kicking, temper tantrum began all over again. He ended it just as quickly. A person had no choice but to comply once their cuffed arms were forced upward. That previously dislocated shoulder still had to hurt. He continued the pressure to keep her arms straight and her sexy body a sufficient distance from his. "Why do you keep it up? You're just making this more difficult. I don't want to hurt you."

"Then let me go," she demanded over her shoulder, the one he hadn't popped out of its socket. Not fair. Two frightened dark eyes brimmed with her plea. She batted her extra-long, incredibly thick lashes. *Oldest trick in the book.* God, this woman knew all the moves.

He looked away and slammed the truck door behind them, her in one hand, the bag in his other. "This way."

Up the five steps to the warehouse dock they went, his prisoner leading the way because that was where he steered her to go. The end of the line waited inside, and he needed to get her delivered before she gave him another one of those looks.

The notion nagged that maybe this gal really was afraid of being cuffed and restrained. That lack of detail in his intel bothered him, especially since he'd been the one who collected most of it. He'd been restrained before, chained like a dog. He'd fight it if it ever happened to him again, no holds barred. Lee looked at Tess with different eyes, a glimmer of empathy seeping through his tough-guy routine.

"You don't understand," she said. "I'm not keeping this treasure, and I won't sell it either. You have to give it back. It's not what you think."

"It never is." Like he hadn't heard that before. Every thief in the whole world said that, especially the ones with big blue eyes.

"No. Really."

She seemed intent on explaining, so he halted in his tracks. He gave her his most stern look, evil eye and all. "What is it you think you need to say that I don't want to hear?"

"I'm not getting rich off this stuff. It's not like you think. It's—"

"Yeah, right." What a waste of time. He'd almost believed she'd come up with something more inventive, as smart as she seemed to be.

She tried another tactic, her sharp eyes still on the bag. "Where's my brother? What'd you do to him?"

"You mean the guy who was supposed to catch you when you fell tonight? Clint? That his name?"

"Yeah. Him."

"Don't worry. He's safe. Now move."

She balked. He lifted her cuffs an inch or so, just enough to help her remember who was in charge.

"Stop doing that!" One more time, she let a boot fly in his direction.

He was fed up with the drama. Forcing her sideways through the warehouse door, he made his way to the inner office door where the only light in the whole warehouse gleamed. This was where it all ended or began, depending on which way she wanted the night to play out. So far, Miss Culver had been lucky, but even the best cat burglar fell off the ledge eventually. If she was smart, it was her turn to take that fall and do it willingly.

He swung the office door open and waited for her to enter. She blinked as the bright light spilled onto the dusty concrete floor, and he didn't mind that she took a minute to get her bearings. This place always creeped him out. It was a distribution warehouse by day, but a good place to conduct covert business at night. His boss rented it on an as-needed basis when he came to town. Too gloomy for Lee, it was also reminiscent of another dark place with men in baggy pajamas and shaggy beards who were cruel for cruelty's sake. Those days were long behind him. Only the memory lingered. And the scars...

He nodded her into the room. "Go on. It's safe. No one will hurt you."

"You already have," she murmured, her eyes hooded and scared.

About time—if it wasn't just another act. Miss Culver should be scared, at least enough to listen for a change. She'd racked up enough lethal enemies during her time in Afghanistan, especially with her daring raids on the Taliban. She trembled, but by then, he'd already been duped ten ways of Sunday. He wasn't falling for that feminine ruse, either. That was the problem with a person as devious and as underhanded as this gal. A man never knew when or if he was seeing the real deal. He doubted he'd see it yet.

A chair scraped across the wooden floor in the office, but no one had made himself known yet. Lee let Tess have time to stew. The man inside that room knew all the tricks to breaking a person down. Waiting was sometimes the most effective tool in the war chest.

The lack of sound from the rest of the warehouse made the moment stretch out. He nudged her elbow forward. *Come on, Culver. Take the hint. Move it. I'm tired. Either you're in or you're out.*

She elbowed back, defiance a-plenty. Sucking in a breath, she made her move, and he avoided yet another kick, this one aimed at his crotch. The tip of her boot hit his thigh instead, and impatience got the best of him. *Damn, this girl just didn't quit!* He placed a palm to the middle of her back and shoved her through the door.

The guy waiting patiently inside turned from behind the wooden desk. "It's about time."

"Evening, Alex. Sorry I'm late. You know how she is."

"Miss Culver?" Alex rose to his feet in perfunctory politeness as he deliberately scanned her from head to foot, sharp appraisal in his eyes. "Are you okay?"

"What's it to you?" She tossed her hair out of her face, still all piss and vinegar. "Who are you guys?"

Lee stepped back, his arms crossed and the bag still secure in his grip. Tess Culver was a looker from a distance, but up close? Lush red lips. Full breasts, definitely more than a handful. Curvy hips, her waist tucked in small and feminine. Daintily athletic. A little sweaty. Definitely perturbed. She made it difficult for a man to swallow. She might not know it yet, but she'd just met her match and his name was…

"I'm Alex Stewart." Alex took his seat. "You've already met my trusted agent, Lee Hart. Come in. Join us."

"Like I have a choice," she spat out, her head high and her fear at bay for the moment.

Alex shot Lee an appraising nod, his brow raised. "Had your hands full?"

"Not so much," Lee countered. There was no sense in letting this gal think she was any smarter or tougher than she already thought she was.

"Who the hell are you? What have you done with my brother?" she demanded, still standing, cuffed, and sassy. If looks could kill, she'd just handed Alex his head on a platter with that chin lift of hers.

"I already told you I'm Alex Stewart, ma'am; I run a security business stateside, and as for your brother, Clint's most likely safe in bed with a bottle of booze by now, but that's not what you're worried about, is it?" Alex answered smoothly.

"Your so-called trusted agent…"she glared at Lee with more authority than a woman in her precarious position had a right to, "took something from me and I want it back."

"No. What you took tonight belongs to the National Museum, not to you nor to your brother."

"So?"

"So you stole an ancient artifact valued in the millions."

"I didn't steal it. I rescued it, you moron." She spat more defiance.

Lee took that for his cue. Stepping away from his volatile friend, he unwrapped the treasure, the Crown of the Dragon Warrior of ancient Afghan legend. Gold-leaf-covered medallions and coins glistened on golden wires around inlays of emeralds and rubies at the base of the crown. Branches over the base supported a pair of solid gold twin dragons and the ancient Dragon Warrior, also solid gold, seated cross-legged between them, his hands pressed together as if in prayer.

She eyed it greedily, biting her bottom lip as he held the tinkling artifact out to Alex. The ornament was valuable beyond compare; more so since the Taliban thought they'd destroyed it. Their insane decree of 2001preceded the destruction of the two colossal Buddhas in the Bamiyan Province. The Taliban's rape of their own country's archeological treasures still amazed the rest of the civilized world, Lee included.

So who'd had the Crown of the Dragon Warrior all this time? Who'd stolen it from the museum and who needed it transported out of Afghanistan? Tess knew who the real thief was, and that was where Alex came in. He needed to know who wanted her dead besides the Taliban sniper who'd attempted to kill her. The very capable Mohammed Turik had to be working for someone.

Alex folded his arms over his charcoal gray business suit. The man always looked sharp, and his choice of a dark suit for a late-night op? Priceless. The man was a genius at mind games. "Miss Culver, you're in no position to demand anything right now, but you are in a position of great opportunity. Are you interested at all in hearing what I have to say?"

She breathed steadily through her nose as if she had calmed, but Lee knew better. All she was doing was biding her time and gathering strength, playing it cool. The minute he unlocked those cuffs, she'd be gone, the crown, too, if she had her way.

"Interested in what?" Her chin stuck out like she dared Alex to convince her.

"Security, for one thing. The Taliban has put a substantial price on your head, and they don't care if you're dead or alive when they pay it out. You've stolen four artifacts from them, five counting tonight's theft. They've offered a bounty of four million American dollars for your head. That puts you at more risk each time you try a stunt like this."

"Is that why you're here? Because the animals who destroyed the rarest treasures in the world are after me? Ha! They're the thieves, not me. Why don't you hunt them down and leave me alone?"

The girl had spunk.

"No. I'm here because I have a customer who's interested in your well-being and nothing more," Alex countered. "For some reason, he wants you to live a long and happy life. He knew you wouldn't accept the offer to leave the country or to forget this crusade, so he asked me to convince you. If I can't, he still wants me to take you back to America. I'd like that not to be under duress, but either way, I'm willing."

She blinked one good blink, like his words had finally gotten through that hard head of hers. "Who?" she snapped, still as belligerent as ever.

Lee sighed. Yes. This would take a while. He shifted to her side again and gently grasped the cuffs while still holding the crown with his other hand. Those pretty violet blues shot daggers up at him.

"Please." Alex motioned to the chair closest to the desk. "Sit, Miss Culver. Let's discuss this like civilized people."

"Then let me out of these things first." She twisted her arms for Lee. "Now."

Oh, this woman. He grinned. Did she honestly expect that those cuffs would come off that easy?

"Let's talk first," Alex insisted. His tone brooked no discussion.

Tess clenched her jaw. Lee tightened his grip. A she-leopard like this one didn't change her spots so quickly. Just to be safe, he turned sideways to protect his family jewels.

Reluctantly, she took a step toward Alex.

Lee's radar spiked, his hand still at her wrist. *Watch out, Boss. This one's tricky.*

But Alex had already taken his seat, his disinterest obvious. He adjusted his tie, as if he had no clue what she was capable of. Lee almost wished she'd take Alex on. That'd be a contest worth paying good money to see, his once Marine scout sniper boss wrestling with a voluptuous and very naughty cat burglar.

"Do you mind?" Tess glared up at Lee, jerking her arms away from him and spoiling a perfectly good fantasy. "I can walk by myself."

She could also run by herself. He kept his hand shackled to the cuffs.

"Might as well take a seat, Lee," Alex offered. "We've got what she wants. She's not going anywhere."

Bet me. Right on cue, she scanned the high rafters overhead. This inside office space had no ceiling, just four walls and a door. The warehouse had only two exits—the one they'd entered through and the other at the extreme far end at the loading dock. No way could she make it to either, even if she grabbed her treasure and took off at a sprint. He'd run her down in seconds, and this time, he wouldn't be so polite about it.

The more she stared at Alex, the more she pursed those luscious red lips, concentrating. The girl had so many tells, she should never play poker. Plus, she wore lightweight, steel-toed military boots known for their traction and fast-paced maneuvering.

Lee released her wrist, giving her the chance to bolt or sit. That she finally accepted the chair meant nothing, not with her back erect, her body tilted forward, and her weight on the balls of those work boots. Tess meant to run. No doubt about it.

"What do you want?" she hissed with barely concealed disgust.

"To offer you a proposition." Alex was smooth.

"I want it back first."

Lee handed the Crown of the Dragon Warrior to his boss. Alex accepted it gently and set the golden treasure on the desk where Tess could see it. "What do you intend to do with it?"

"Why do you care? It doesn't belong to you."

"Agreed. Neither does it belong to you." Alex waited.

She glared, and this was where the rubber hit the road. If she'd stolen it for the reason she'd previously declared, she'd be an easy girl to turn. If not...

Chapter Four

Her fingers itched. The Crown of the Dragon Warrior lay within inches of her—again. At least it was out of the reach of that liar, Abdul Sherazi, and his despicable buddy, Hasim Nizari. That was what mattered most, but it still wasn't in her possession like it should've been.

Tess deliberated her options. There were only two of these guys. Hadn't she just stolen that priceless item from several others who'd thought they were just as smart as this Alex guy? Had those six bumbling guards been smart enough to stop her? No way. They hadn't even slowed her down. Neither would these two.

The one called Alex seemed concerned for her well being. Kind of. The other guy? Agent Lee Hart? Not so much. He definitely radiated a predator vibe, one that cranked her feminine instincts to run and hide like a prey animal. A frightened little bunny rabbit. *'Never!'* her rebel heart declared in no uncertain terms. Tess Culver would *not* be beaten again.

He had gotten to her for a second there in the truck, though. Almost reduced her to tears. The guy was built—she had to give him that. Big hands. Massive chest muscles stretched his shirt. Powerful thighs led to long legs. Those same feminine responders that screamed, *'Run!'* had also picked up his scent during their tussle. Burnt amber with a twist of citrus, possibly orange. Clean, manly sweat. Soap or deodorant, she couldn't decide which—she only knew she'd enjoyed the contact of this stranger more than she should have. He was one walking, masculine pheromone that nearly took out her common sense. How the hell did that work?

Yet she had to give him credit. He was big enough. He could've easily broken her arm instead of just dislocating her shoulder. That old injury of four years ago had left her with two dislocated limbs she'd since learned to use to her advantage. She rolled her shoulder, testing the remaining tenderness of the one he'd popped out of its socket. Could be better. Could be worse.

A tiny whisper worried at the farthest recesses of her clever mind. Did he know about that injury before tonight, and if he did, how could he have known? Did he simply exploit a known weakness in his enemy or was it just a lucky coincidence? *What's going on here?* And who was that arrogant man behind this insane protection order in the first place? It couldn't be her parents. Certainly wasn't Clint. It had to be a man though, some macho tough guy who thought he knew better than a woman like her, but who?

It was cute how Agent Hart had apologized to her earlier, though. Cute in a little boy way. Like he knew he'd scared her, which he had. As if she cared what he thought. The bottom line was that these two men had to go down, and she had to get that treasure back.

"Let me get this straight. You kidnapped me, nearly broke my arm, and handcuffed me because you want to *help*?" She tilted her chin upward, imperious and sarcastic to the end.

"You could say that." Alex cocked a brow. He was good-looking, in an arrogant sort of way. Hooded, steely blue eyes under a close military cut. Salt and pepper mingled with dark at his sideburns. Clean shaven, not scruffy like Agent Hart. Just the fact that he'd chosen a business suit instead of more casual clothing told her he was the boss before he'd ever opened his mouth. That and he seemed to think he held all the cards, that he had something she wanted. *As if.*

Agent Hart was another kind of man all together. Not subservient, but respectful, obviously an employee, maybe a trusted employee. Or a friend? He was a construct of lines and angles, flat planes and corners. Edges. Heat. Even now, his eyes slanted a trustworthy green fire at her that wasn't afraid to reach out and brand her. It flustered Tess to look at him. He might not be in charge, but he definitely radiated a raw masculine power that made her sit up and take notice.

She hated that, too. She'd been under the macho boot of the all-male Taliban for too long. Her father had never been strong. Her brother gave all men everywhere a bad name. But this guy? A shiver raced down her arms. Lee Hart was something else all together.

He was big in the way of weight lifters, but handsome. The unruly mahogany hair shadowing his face enhanced the glow of his eyes. He could be deadly, but he'd chosen gentleness in handling her. And he was strong. She'd noticed the steel in his body when he'd tackled her. The measured grip of something more than just the rough handling of a dim-witted soldier following orders. Agent Hart seemed to have read her mind and anticipated her best moves like he already knew her. She hated that in a man. They thought they were so much smarter than women. Ha.

She dropped her lashes and let her gaze drift covertly back to the crown. The only thing Alex had going for him was that he possessed the Dragon Warrior. *For now.*

"And you would call what you did to me something else?" she demanded, sure she could set his plans off balance.

"I'd call it apprehending a thief in the middle of a crime." Alex placed both palms to his knees, as cool as a cucumber. Icy blue stared her down. "I'm sure that's what the Ministry of Antiquities would call it, too."

She drew in a deep breath and mimicked his position, her palms to her knees. "They'd have to catch me first, wouldn't they?"

He cut her short. "Let's stop dancing around each other, shall we? I'm here to offer two things—protection while you're in country and safe passage home. My client's in a position to preserve all the artifacts you've—"

"I don't need your help. I've already got a partner."

"Who is at this moment sound asleep in bed and oblivious of your predicament. Look around, Miss Culver. Your brother could care less about this little adventure of yours tonight. The only reason he offers the use of his truck for these excursions of yours is the pittance you pay him, and you give him so little because you know he'll blow it on drugs. What's he using? Hash? Coke? Horse? All of them?"

Tess glared but didn't answer. Alex sure knew her brother. Clint might be a pitiful partner, but he was all she had.

"And why the hell did you take your cap off tonight?" Alex kept going, like he had any right to judge her behavior. "That was a very stupid move on your part. You know better."

She bit her lip—hard. Somehow, he'd been watching. He'd seen, and he knew too much, but he was right. It was a stupid move. Her ego had gotten the best of her, that was why she'd removed her cap. She'd wanted to show those imbecilic guards how much smarter than them a simple woman was. It was a knee-jerk reaction to their male arrogance. Not one of her best decisions.

"You had the perfect ruse, but you blew it. No one knew you were a woman except us. You're getting cocky, Tess. You won't last another day with that bullshit attitude."

"I've done fine without your help, thank you." She kept her tone aloof.

"No, you haven't. You've been damned lucky. That's all. Who's going to give a shit when you drop off the next rooftop with a bullet in your head? Clint?" Alex's hostility rose as he fired one shot after another. "I hardly think so."

She bumped the back of her boots against the chair legs. This interrogation was a waste of time. She had a French ambassador to meet and a drop to make. Commitments to keep. There had to be a way out of there, preferably with the crown.

Agent Hart had taken the chair next to her. Straddling it with his arms folded over the back gave him a casual air, but the chair spindles put a barrier between them. She couldn't kick him where she wanted to. Tess huffed, her patience running thin. These guys would never understand why she did what she did. Nobody loved Afghanistan like her, not even the fierce tribal people who lived there.

"I have to use the bathroom," she stated emphatically, daring them to argue.

"Of course you do." Alex glanced to Agent Hart, his eyes hooded and his lips tight. "Show her where it is."

"No way," she protested. "I can—"

"You're not going anywhere without him," Alex cut her off, his brow spiked. "Do you need to use the restroom or not?"

All she could offer was another glare. This annoying guy had bested her at every turn. So far. Well, she'd show him. "Yes," she hissed, "or I wouldn't have said I did, would I?"

Agent Hart tugged her to her feet and steered her out of the bright little office and into the dark warehouse. "Come on, princess. Let's go. The head's a little primitive. Hope there's TP this time. There wasn't any before."

"Don't call me princess," she hissed, twisting away from his touch.

Now it was his turn to blow out a patient sigh. "Yes, ma'am."

"And stop calling me ma'am. I'm not your mother." She shuffled along, letting him think he had the upper hand while her eyes adjusted to the dark. Truth was, he didn't. He'd have to remove the cuffs to let her do her business. There might be a window. The moment she got behind that bathroom door, she'd be gone.

"There it is." Agent Hart aimed a pencil-thin flashlight toward the absolute minimal requirement for a device to be called a toilet. "Hope someone cleaned it. It was pretty gross last time I was here."

She smelled it before she saw it. *Ewww!* A urine-encrusted, stainless steel commode hung off the wall in the farthest, darkest corner of the warehouse. No door. No curtain. No freaking window, and no chance at privacy. The beam of light from Agent Hart's hand cast silvery shadows that made it look more stained and incredibly disgusting. A shiver crept up her back and over her shoulders, stopping to tap dance at the base of her skull before it coursed up over her scalp.

"There you are. Have at it." He might have the upper hand after all.

"I can't use *that!*" she snarled, looking past him for two civilized doors marked Men and Women, anything but this—*this*—monument to venereal disease, crawling germs, and filth.

"I figured this was just another trick," he muttered, satisfaction in his tone.

"Was not," she bit out before common sense engaged. Now she was stuck. She'd have to use it, or at least pretend to use it, or... *ewww.*

He pulled a key ring from his front pocket. Man, those jeans fit tight. It took him a minute to get the keys up and out. She hadn't noticed until then, but he was wearing cowboy boots, the kind with the pointed toes and stacked heels, all tooled and decorated like expensive cowboy footgear. Only these were worn, creased, scuffed, and dusty. His long legs bowed just a bit. She'd missed the dark glasses tucked inside his shirt pocket, too, but secretly hoped they were broken. And why hadn't she seen the western shirt stretched tightly over his massive chest until then, complete with silver snaps instead of buttons?

Oh, wait. He was assaulting me. That's why I missed those details. Of course I didn't notice what he was wearing. I was busy trying to get away.

"Here you go." He slipped the key into the bracelet on her left wrist and undid one cuff. She stood against him, her arm shackled in his big, manly hand, forced to look up to meet his eyes. Her breath hitched high in her throat. Damn. He seemed so much taller and bigger in the dark. Wider. Sexier. *Was it the b-b-boots?*

A gentle glimmer in his darkened eyes connected with her nerves, lessening her fear. For a second. "Now we can do this easy or hard, Miss Culver. Are you going to be civil and take care of business by yourself, or am I going to have to cuff you to the pipes behind the toilet, pull your pants down, and help wipe?"

He'd said that just to intimidate her into behaving, the jerk.

"Leave. Me. Alone," she hissed, but when he cocked his head, she caught the intended warning. This guy didn't give up easily. Oddly, all those very intimate suggestions he'd just made fired an ember in her belly she hadn't expected. She doused it with cold disdain. He could *want* to embarrass her all night long. It wasn't happening. She lived with Clint. What Agent Hart was getting was nada. Not one little peek of compliance. Zip. Zilch.

"You didn't answer my question, and you know it." He peered through those gorgeous green eyes glittering in the dark, one brow arched, his lashes fluttering and waiting for a better answer. "Do you want easy or hard? There's no sense running in here. There are only two doors, but I'm faster than you any day of the week. I'll catch you before you get to either of them."

Her heart stalled in her throat. Hard sounded damned inviting. She was suddenly looking up into masculine danger. The only way he could've enticed her more would've been if he'd used a down-home country drawl with that threat. She'd always been a sucker for southern boys.

Gah! Snap out of it, Tess. Why couldn't she catch her balance around this guy? He wasn't even smart enough to be the boss. He was nobody, an employee. The goosebumps lifting the hair off the back of her neck begged to differ.

"Fine. I'll be civil. Do you mind?" She stepped to the stainless-steel nightmare and unzipped her jeans to end the interrogation. "Turn around. At least try to act like a gentleman."

"Yes, ma'am," he said, as he set the flashlight on the floor beside her, the beam pointed to the ceiling instead of at the toilet seat. Turning away, he didn't go far, just far enough to stay within that small circle of light—with her.

She dropped her jeans and lowered her backside toward the seat of that so-o-o disgusting and insanely unsanitary bathroom appliance. Didn't the guys who owned this warehouse believe in disinfectants? *Ewww!* When the cold metal hit the back of her legs, she jerked her butt away. *What the hell? I don't need to pee. What have I done?*

This was all Lee Hart's fault. He'd distracted her, and she'd stupidly complied when she'd never meant to. Damn him! But there she was with her rear exposed and her backside hanging over a truly disgusting commode from hell. She shifted her weight at the ridiculous predicament she'd gotten herself into. *Ewww! Damn it, just ewww!*

"How are you doing back there, ma'am?" he tossed over his shoulder.

"Fine," she snapped. He didn't care. Not really. Conversation kept them linked so he knew she was still there. So she couldn't sneak up behind him and knock the smirk off that rugged face.

Crouched over the toilet like she was gave her time to think. She glared at the back of his head, wanting to smack it hard enough to knock him out. Agent Hart did have wide shoulders and muscular arms beneath that black striped shirt, though. It tucked nicely into the leather belt at his trim waist. This view of his rear wasn't so bad, either. He looked more like a cowboy than what she thought a covert agent should look like. Denim fit him. He had nice—pockets.

A leather holster crossed his back to reveal two guns tucked under his arms, but it also enhanced that inverted triangle thing he had going for him. The holster was a surprise. He could've pulled one of those guns on her and gotten instant compliance from the moment she'd slid in through the truck window. He hadn't. Why not?

Her hostility for this guy and his boss slipped a notch in their favor. Maybe they were exactly what they said they were—trusted agents sent by someone who honestly cared about her. Maybe this wasn't kidnapping. Maybe someone really was looking out for her. It could happen.

Too late she realized Lee had stepped sideways to a nearby work sink. He cranked the screechy faucet. The sound of running water—no! She cringed even as her body betrayed her. There was no way he couldn't hear the tinkling sound echoing out of the toilet in this cavernous building. *He did that on purpose.* "Enjoying belittling me?"

"No, ma'am," he answered promptly, but rocked onto the balls of his feet like he was holding back a chuckle. "Well, maybe. A little. Come to think of it, hell yeah."

"Pervert." She glanced around the dark little corner for toilet paper. Again—*ewww!* A roll lay on its side next to the disgusting toilet, right on the dirty floor where it looked like every male from this part of the world had dribbled, peed, or splashed forensic evidence and germs galore over, under and around it. *I can't use that!*

Disgusted beyond belief, she snagged the roll with just her fingertips and ripped off a long string of the filthy tissue, hoping some germless area existed deep within the roll.

Throwing that banner of her stupidity away from her, she squinted in the dim light to see if any clean sheets still existed. Another long banner hit the floor before she was satisfied.

Finally, Tess finished the job she'd never intended to do in the first place. Nothing had gone right since she'd taken that dive off the palace roof. She'd had the crown, she'd lost the crown, and now she sat humiliated with her bare ass completely exposed. Could things get any worse?

"Is it okay if I turn around now, ma'am?" Agent Hart was still trying not to laugh, despite sounding polite.

"I'm not finished," she sniped, her fist clenched as she stepped away from hell on earth and zipped up her jeans. This guy was asking for it. He kept calling her ma'am. Maybe it was time to remind him she was full of surprises. "Okay, I'm done now," she said semi-sweetly, the wrist with the cuff still dangling on it stretched out in front of her, the other clenched into a fist behind her back. One surprise shot to that straight, masculine nose, and he could keep the Dragon Warrior. She'd be gone.

He turned with a smirk, and that did it. The second he reached for her cuffed wrist, she let him have it with the other. She would've connected if he hadn't leaned backward to avoid her. Her fist barely skimmed the tip of his chin. He easily grabbed her wrist and spun her around.

Before she knew it, her back was to that broad chest, the steel belts of his arms wrapped around her, her feet lifted off the floor, and his chin was tucked into her neck. Worse, her backside was firmly against the bulge in his denims. Tess flung her head back and kicked, but could gain no leverage. He was too close and that bulge enticed rather than put her off. An odd compulsion to rub against it rose up in her frazzled head. She couldn't breathe. There wasn't enough room to move much less hit him hard enough to hurt him.

The worst part was his warm breath wafting through her hair. It smelled like a delicious combination of cinnamon, amber and orange, mingled with clean male sweat. The fragrance tantalized. It filled her nostrils while the very masculine sensation of stubble scraped the tender skin in the crook of her neck. Instead of clenching her muscles tighter to squeeze him out, she'd instinctively turned her head, giving him greater access to more skin. More unexpected pleasure in the dark. He was inside her tangled hair, inhaling her essence as if she were—edible.

Oh. My. God.

Tess wanted to be edible. For him. She closed her eyes, her heart a pounding bass drum as the feel of that strong male wall of sheer muscle infiltrated her every wish. A maelstrom of conflicting emotions raged at the intimate contact. He'd lifted her off her feet like she weighed nothing, like he could've had his way with her if he'd been so inclined. Like she might enjoy it if he did. She couldn't fight him. Didn't want to.

His breath came in short, sharp spurts, but he hadn't said a threatening word. Not one. Neither did she. She couldn't, not with her heart pounding in her throat. Their previous struggles hadn't felt like this. Back in the truck she was scared, but now she went limp with anticipation, wondering what would happen next.

No man had ever evoked such a strong feminine response in her before. He held her very still, his heart thundering against her back. She couldn't move, and she didn't want to. A wave of sensual warmth invaded the insides of her legs, washing up her thighs and up over her belly, tightening her breasts with need until it ebbed up her neck and inflamed her cheeks. Her scalp tingled under the onslaught of all that fire in her veins. She was caught in an incredible tide of steamy desire, burning with the oddest sensation of consummate submission at the hands of the gentlest alpha she'd ever met. Her. Tess Culver. The woman who scorned men. All of them.

How extraordinary.

An out-of-control quiver pushed her head back to his shoulder, as if she sought him out. As if she needed him. She should've been fighting him with all her might, but she wasn't and she didn't know why.

"Let me down," she whispered hoarsely, her voice suddenly trembling with a need she hadn't known before. She cleared her throat, hoping to dislodge the idiot stuck in there. Oh, wait. It was her heart.

"Yes, ma'am." He complied instantly, but the moment he released her, her traitorous body arched back, seeking the warmth his had offered. His wide male hands dropped to her shoulders to steady her. She stood frozen in the moment, her head bowed and him waiting, her wondering what the hell had just happened.

Tess honestly couldn't decide whether to turn around and climb back into his arms, or run and hide from embarrassment. The amateur in her was back, and her heart thumped recklessly in her ears. She shook it off and pulled herself away from him, but damn. When his hands lifted, her shoulders missed his touch.

He's committed another act of assault. That's all. First he kidnaps me. Then he handcuffs me. Then he manhandles me. Only... Tess bit her lip at the lie. Assault had never felt like this before, and she would know.

Then why am I breathing so hard? Why's my heart pounding like an Arabian mare on the sand dunes running from her stallion? Why did I—like it? She swallowed hard. *An Arabian mare?* What an idiotic thought. *Like it?* Where'd that come from? *A stallion?* Hardly. More like a wolf. A proud alpha wolf that wasn't afraid to take on the world even there in wild and lawless Afghanistan.

Without thinking, she'd become what he'd wanted her to be all along—compliant. Nearly submissive. Flustered, she held out her wrists, ashamed at the blatant sexual flavor to the thoughts spinning through her mind. Her tongue slid over her bottom lip, wondering after a kiss from Lee Hart's tightly pursed lips

He cuffed her wrists, but not behind her back this time. Neither did he tug her to follow or steer where he wanted her to go. Agent Hart didn't touch her again as they walked side-by-side back to the office.

"I need to wash my hands," she said when they were nearly there. "That sink back there was too dirty. I didn't..." She paused, ashamed of herself for sounding so much like a helpless woman.

"I've got hand sanitizer in my gear bag," he said, his voice extra low. "It's in the office. You're welcome to it."

A smirk curled Alex's lip when they came into view. "Took you two long enough."

Chapter Five

"What exactly do you want from me, Mr. Stewart?" Tess asked the moment her butt hit the chair. At least this time, her feet were flat to the floor, her back firmly against the chair spindles.

Lee went to the gear bag he'd previously left with Alex and pulled out a small bottle of hand cleaner. Toilets in third-world countries were always an unpleasant surprise, so he came prepared. He handed Tess the bottle and resumed his place. The universe had shifted during that brief encounter with her in the dark, and he didn't like it. Not one bit.

She might look all prim and proper, squeezing the clear gel onto her hands like she was, and she might act agreeable for the first time tonight, but he knew better. This woman was like every other he'd known, a master manipulator and good at it, a person who said one thing but did another.

He didn't like being used, but he did like looking at her. All dressed in black like she was made for a damned attractive package. Although she'd smoothed her hair off her shoulders, it continued to twist in ebony tangles that glinted with hints of brown, blue, and red under the harsh fluorescent tube lighting overhead. The pleasant fragrance of coconut cookies lingered in his nose. She kept licking that lush bottom lip, her tongue pink but those lips definitely moist and red. Ruby red. Tender-looking, too. The only way they could possibly look better would be if they were swollen and wet after a good hard kiss.

His breathing hitched just imagining his mouth on hers, easing those tender, stubborn lips apart until she let him in. Would she push him away? Jerk him in closer? Resist? Fight? Or would she surrender to him and hold on for dear life? He knew he could please her. He could make her wiggle and groan, maybe scream with female satisfaction.

God, it had been a long time. He scrubbed a quick hand over his face to erase the erotic images flashing in his hard head. This woman evoked primal instincts in him, a wild call to dominate her, to fight anyone who got between him and her. His hackles lifted with the caveman instinct to bend her over that desk, but God. Lee wasn't that kind of a guy. Ever. He simply did not fight a woman for sex. Either she wanted him, or she didn't, and he walked.

Damn it to hell, he needed to get his mind out of the gutter and back on target. She was a client, an unwilling one at the moment, but still just a job with a definite expiration date—the day he got her safely back to America. With thoughts like these spinning him up, it couldn't happen soon enough.

"I want you to agree to our protection," Alex answered, "but first let's get those cuffs off."

Lee jumped to his feet, glad for something to do besides watch Tess Culver. She'd gotten under his skin in ways he'd not expected. Like a hit of crack, she'd rewired his male brain at first contact. Shit. If the truth were known, he'd been hooked at first sight.

He removed the cuffs and refastened them to his belt. Miss Culver looked surprised, but didn't bolt as he'd expected. "Thank you," she whispered, blinking up at him through those long, lush lashes and sparking the fire in his gut all over again.

"I... I really do hate restraints." Carefully, she handed him the hand sanitizer.

There seemed to be no air in that big warehouse. It was all Lee could do to tear his gaze from hers, locked onto her like he was. "Me too," he mumbled hoarsely, like some brain-dead jock while he tossed the sanitizer back into his open bag. He blinked to break her spell, then pulled out a bottle of water from the ice chest Alex kept near the desk. "Here. Looks like you could use a drink."

She accepted the dripping wet bottle and blinked those big wide eyes again like a little girl who couldn't believe the neighborhood bully could be nice. Guilt poked at him. Maybe he had been a little rough.

"I need to know a few things," Alex continued like this was nothing more than another business meeting. Like the priceless Dragon Warrior wasn't sitting on his desk—a couple million dollars of stolen property that could put him in a deep dark Afghan prison.

"Like?" Tess almost sounded honest. She ran her tongue over her full bottom lip. Lee looked closer. He hadn't taken his seat, needing to be prepared for another gamble on her part. He'd seen the scared look before, but damn. If this was a trick, she was good. Would Alex fall for it? Lee brushed a hand over his face at his doubt. To hell with Alex. Was Lee falling for it?

Maybe...

"Why do you do this?" Alex asked. "Why do you steal?"

"I don't just steal," she replied firmly, her fingers wrapped tight around the plastic water bottle. She had yet to open it and take a drink. "I reacquire what the Taliban have stolen. It's different. Regardless what you think of me, I'm not a common thief."

"I get that. You only steal artifacts from the Taliban. Why?"

She took a deep breath, gulping when she exhaled. "Is it stealing to take back national treasures from the thieves pillaging my country?"

"But it's not your country." Alex's eyes narrowed as his voice softened, puzzled.

"What you're doing is dangerous," Lee said bluntly. He didn't care which country she pledged allegiance to. Stealing from the Taliban was just plain stupid.

Tess wrinkled her nose. Alex's calm scrutiny annoyed her, Lee could tell. One minute feisty and the next deadly calm, she was simply winding up for her next shot at home plate. "Do you realize what that crown is?"

Lee nodded. "A three-thousand-year-old artifact worn by the priest during the sacrifice of the lamb. Discovered at the Tillya Tepe dig. The Golden Hill. Up north near Sheberghan."

A glimmer of respect shifted over her face. He couldn't resist winking at her. *Yeah, lady, I know a thing or two.*

He crossed his arms over his chest and continued showing off. "Does the name Victor Sarianidi ring a bell? The Bactrian Hoard?" Lee only knew all of this very precise information because he'd studied the treasures of Afghanistan intensely before this operation. Wikipedia always made him look good, but it also helped him try to figure her out, why she felt the need to become the Robin Hood of this particular country, to steal from the thieves and then to safeguard her treasure for some future day when the poor were strong enough to reclaim it. And why the hell risk her life trying to save Afghanistan? What was so great about this godforsaken country and its hordes of tribal despots?

Another violet glimmer twinkled in her eye, and he couldn't help himself. The need to impress her with more than just brute strength overrode his common sense. "Six tombs. Five female mummies. One male. Thousands of gold ornaments worth millions. An archeological treasure to defy all others."

She leaned forward, admiration aglow in her eyes, the water bottle clenched in her hands between her knees. His sniper eyes shifted beyond that plastic barrier to the intersecting seams at the crotch of her black pants, worn and lightened from too much wear and washing. Funny. They came together in a perfect X, like the X that marked buried treasure. *Big mistake.*

A raging fire burned through his belly, lighting his body up as it surged into muscles and tissues left dormant and unfeeling for too long. Tonight was not a good time to bring them back to life.

Just being around this woman rattled him, and he had no business looking at her crotch or thinking of her like he was. Of bending her over that desk and stripping her bare, slapping that ass just to see his red handprint on her creamy skin. His handprint. His brand. No one else's. To hear her mewl with pleasure when he did it.

Gah! He jerked his eyeballs back to her face, wishing his all-male mind knew when to quit while it was ahead. She brought out the animal in him. When the hell had she gotten the upper hand?

"Over twenty thousand million," she purred, a sensual smile tugging her lush red lips.

He stared her down, ignoring the sizzling sexual energy arcing between them. She had to feel it, too. The feral pull and tug of two bodies enflamed. The hunger. Else, why the scarlet blush creeping up her neck and blossoming over her cheeks?

She cleared her throat. "I'm impressed, Agent Hart. Not many people understand the Bactrian Hoard. Many of those artifacts date back to the first century. Some to the Bronze Age. I take it you're a scholar of archeology?"

Busted! Train wreck. He couldn't lie, so he hedged. "No, ma'am. Just an interested party." *And a dumbass to think I could fool an expert like you.*

Just that fast, he lost her attention. She straightened and returned her gaze coolly to Alex. "Do you know how many Afghans have even heard of that treasure, much less understand how rich and respected their country once was in the eyes of the world?"

"Damned few."

Tess nodded. "The few in power shouldn't dictate the legacy of the masses, no matter if the masses might be ignorant at this unfortunate moment in history, Mr. Stewart. That is why I steal. To keep the future within reach of these people. Afghans deserve the chance to learn how great they once were, to see their rich ancient heritage, but it's being shuttled off to the highest bidder instead of safeguarded and protected for their future. Most of it has already been stolen right from under their noses for paltry silver and gold."

"But the curator at the museum was guarding these treasures," Alex said firmly.

Tess leaned forward, her weight once again on the balls of her feet.

Here we go. She's going to run. Lee gripped the back of the chair in front of him in case he needed to throw it out of his way the second she made a break for it.

"It's not the curator I'm stealing from," Tess said softly. "It's his assistant, Abdul Sherazi. The man is a liar. He's hidden some of the greatest treasures from the Taliban inquisition, and now he's selling them piece by piece to line his pocket."

Alex's brow lifted at that astounding piece of intel. "To who?"

"To the Taliban banker, Hasim Nizari," she said it with authority. "Do you doubt me?"

The name stole Lee's breath. He hadn't expected to hear it again. Not tonight. Not from her. The room just got unbearably stifling. His throat drew tight.

Who didn't know the psychotic pedophile or that Nizari seemed Teflon-coated? That he'd escaped all attempts to apprehend him? That he still aggravated the US military to no end because they'd searched for him, but couldn't apprehend him? The man was too well connected. He had a penchant for dressing in linen business suits. His victims said his eyes were dark and soulless, like the blackest night of no stars and no promise of a sunrise. Worst of all—no hope.

But Lee knew him from another time, before the man's appetite turned to children. Another blackest night that had nothing to do with ancient treasures.

A wave of nausea struck. Lee reeled at the force of the memory. He gripped the back of the chair, his fingers tight between the spindles, and he swallowed hard. That other dark room swelled around him once more, offering sights and smells he wanted desperately purged from his soul. He fell back on the only thing one of his many counselors had taught him to do. The only thing that worked.

He summoned the serene image of an innocent little boy with green eyes tossing the fallen stars and dreams of his youth back up into the night sky where they belonged. Lee drew in a long, deep breath to instill control. To keep the rising panic at bay. With all his heart, he concentrated on the starlight reflected on that sweet kid's face, his eyes still filled with wonder for the good in the world, because there *was* good in the world, damn it. Dreams still *did* come true.

Lee clung to that scene, the only thing that kept him from falling into outer darkness. One by one, deep breath by deep breath, the child he once was forced every fallen star and dream back into the universe where they belonged. Despite men like Nizari, the world *was* worth fighting for. The child proved it, standing there and tossing stars like he had faith. Smiling. Offering hope. Bringing peace.

That Lee could create this vision in his mind proved he was in recovery, that he could overcome the torment that had been visited on his mind and body. He drew in a deep breath, knowing damned well that Alex hadn't missed his reaction to the mere mention of the madman's name. That Alex had his back. That he'd covered this misstep like the good spotter he was by keeping Miss Culver's attention on him and off of Lee.

Lee swallowed hard and calmed. The power of that ungodly devil faded yet one more time. The present night with Alex and Tess materialized back into focus. Breathing became easier. Lee's heart rate paced evenly. The suffocating thunder in his head stilled. He could think clearly. The days of living hell were long behind him.

To prove it to himself, Lee studied their captive cat burglar closer. Tess's voice had wavered when she'd spoken of Nizari. He had detected fear in her, but it was impossible to see through her mask. Whatever her thoughts were on the subject, they seemed as deeply buried as Lee's. He dismissed her reaction as just another aspect of this mission that he'd soon forget. He'd already given Alex his two weeks notice. This was his final op and when it was done, Tess Culver would forever be nothing more than a name on his final report.

"Can you prove it's Nizari?" Alex asked.

"Yes." She moved the water bottle to her left hand and pulled a thumb drive from between her full breasts with two long, delicate fingers, and a lift of her chin that declared her total superiority to the world of men.

Lee couldn't help the smile that tweaked his lips. She'd kept that little item hidden well, not that he'd have strip-searched her to find it. Still, he should've thought of that. Women had all kinds of interesting hiding places.

Alex took the USB drive. "What's on it?"

"A video of Abdul Sherazi meeting with Hasim Nizari."

"Are you sure it's him?" Alex cocked his head in disbelief, his eyes narrowed. He shot a flash of concern to Lee.

"Yes." Tess followed Alex's glance to Lee, then settled on Alex again. "Sherazi moves the artifacts he's stolen from the museum under cover of night. Nizari finds a buyer or passes the treasures onto the black market. That is one way the Taliban is being funded. Watch the video. You'll see."

Alex slipped the thumb drive into his inner suit jacket pocket.

"So now you believe me?" Tess asked, finally removing the cap from the bottle and lifting it to her lips, her head tilted back and swallowing as she kept her gaze on Alex.

Lee succumbed to her charm, watching her lips purse to accept the cool drink, her throat working as she swallowed gracefully. The way the hollow at the base of her throat pulsed. The way her hair hung in a shiny riot of black curls off her shoulders and down her back. Only when she finished the drink and licked her lips did he snap out of it. He was thirsty too. Just not for water.

"Not so fast," Alex interrupted the magic moment. "Now I'll verify. Then I may believe. Until I do, you'll remain in Agent Hart's custody."

Say what? Damn it, Boss. Lee rubbed the day's stubble on his chin. He hadn't seen that one coming. Custody meant cuffs, which she seemed to fear. He didn't want to use them.

Tess glanced at him, her jaw clenched, looking none too happy with this new development. "When you verify that information, and you will, what will you want from me? Enough of the bluff and bluster and the big talk. You're not here to protect me. What's this really all about?"

Alex uncrossed his legs, his hands on his knees. "I have come here for one purposes only, to save you from yourself. My instructions were to extricate you from this country while there's still time."

She stared at him.

"You're damned good at what you do, Miss Culver, but you're doing it with inept help. Believe me, you're a marked woman. Your ignorance isn't heroic—not in this country. It's foolish. Believe me, Sherazi, Nizari, and the Taliban will catch you, and when they do, they'll use your dead body to end the honest efforts of others who are more diplomatic at saving relics and artifacts, at safeguarding this nation's history. You're right. No one has the right to steal a nation's cultural heritage, but to fight back with reckless disregard for your own life is nothing but arrogant pride. In the end, you'll only give the Taliban more fodder for their propaganda machine."

"So you want me to walk away from this country and let the Taliban win?" She hurled the accusation with vehemence, her fingers twisting that half empty plastic bottle into garbage.

"Partially. I'm also here to protect what you've already acquired. I have a trusted agent who is willing to legally transfer what you have stolen to a museum for safe keeping until this war is over. My source claims you've stolen more than this crown, is he right?"

"Possibly," she hedged. Her lashes fluttered as her gaze drifted up to Lee with a hint of mischief, a sparkle of a dare. Damn. She was still playing the smarty-pants cat burglar. She just didn't get it.

Alex called the game. "Miss Culver, let me make myself perfectly clear. You are now in my custody, per the terms of the contract. Like it or not, you will not steal another item. You'll be returned to America on the first military transport out of here, where you'll be placed in protective custody. Only then am I authorized to reveal who signed this contract for your safety. Then you'll understand. Until then, I'm under a strict confidentiality agreement. You have to trust me and my men."

"Give me a break. You can't sign a confidentially agreement that infringes on my rights as an American citizen!"

Alex's gaze narrowed. "Want to bet? You forget. You're not in America."

Lee held his breath.

Tess blew out a barely suppressed sigh between pursed lips. She flounced her hair back with a wave of her hand, her jaw clenched tight, and her nose in the air. "Fine, but who is your trusted agent? Who will you deliver the crown to? It must be kept safe."

"You'll have to trust me on that one," Alex replied dismissively.

Bam. The shutters slammed shut. Tess pursed her lips, biting the bottom one hard.

"Who's your trusted agent? Who's accepted the artifacts you've stolen before tonight?" Alex asked the same of her.

Her nose twitched. Barely. Tess threw his words back in his face. "Guess you'll have to trust me on that one, won't you?"

Chapter Six

Alex gave Agent Hart a silent guy-signal, and the cuffs came off his belt.

"Excuse me?" Miss Culvert protested when he tugged her to her feet, but neither man seemed to be paying attention to her. "I want the crown back," she insisted before she lost her freedom.

"What's next?" Agent Hart asked his boss while he followed those invisible orders without answering her. He pulled one arm behind her back and snapped the cuff to her right wrist.

"You don't have to do this," she pleaded, apparently not very convincingly. "I thought we had an agreement."

Alex chose to answer his employee instead of her. "I should hear from Eric and Seth soon. In the meantime, get some rest."

Agent Hart grunted, Alex smirked, and Tess got angrier at the unspoken implication that it was unlikely Agent Hart would get a moment's rest in the near future. "I want the crown back," she ground out while he wrestled her other wrist into the cuffs.

Once again, she stood with her hands behind her back, at his convenience with his big left hand shackling the chain between her wrists. Apparently trust was a one-way road with these jerks. It had vanished the second she'd refused to disclose her source, which was really unjust. Alex had yet to reveal his. He wasn't cuffed.

They'd left the inner office as a threesome. Alex caught the light, but the men paused in the shadowy doorway for more guy talk. The exit beckoned. Tess knew she could best Agent Hart. She sized him up, planning how to take him down. He was definitely bigger, but not so wide around the middle. *Hmmm, what a body.* The night hadn't been a complete waste. The manly hand between her hands didn't feel so bad. His thumb kept rubbing circles on her wrist that felt—good.

"Eric and Seth need to finish this," Alex muttered. "I might have to sanction a home invasion if they can't catch him any other way. This guy's racking up kills too fast and too easy. Remember Hathcock? This guy might be as good as Cobra."

A burst of aggravation ignited in her gut. Who cared about some guys named Hathcock or Cobra? She didn't. The bag with the crown now dangled off Alex's fingers instead of hers, while they stood chatting likes a couple of idiots.

"Eric's damned good, too. He'll get him, Boss. Don't worry."

"Maybe he needs a better scope," Alex said, a twinge of sarcastic humor in his voice.

"More like a steadier spotter. Seth's still damned shaky. He's gotten better, but he still has a long ways to go."

Alex pursed his lips. "Understood. Eric's got a helluva job ahead of him, but he'll pull Seth around."

Tess had no clue what these guys were chatting about, but audacity spiked an idea. She might not be able to grab the artifact, but one sharp twist of her body followed by a kick or two, and she could be out of sight. She mentally accepted

Agent Hart's challenge. *Let's see if you can really run as fast as—*

"Hey." He wiggled the cuffs. "Pay attention. You might learn something." Dark green smirked down at her. He'd read her mind. He'd caught her, and of all things, she wondered what her hair looked like. *Argh!* This guy was driving her nuts.

"Can we just go?" Again, she was ignored.

"This op might still take a day or two. Hope I didn't put you in a bad spot." Alex sounded apologetic—to Agent Hart.

"Been in tougher spots. I'm here as long as you need me."

"Sure wish you'd reconsider leaving The TEAM. I hate losing a good operator."

Lee Hart was quitting? Interesting. Tess's ears perked up.

"I've got to get my head straight, Boss. Give me time. I might be back."

"We'll know which way to proceed once I know what's really on the thumb drive," Alex muttered.

"You staying at the presidential palace?"

"Not exactly."

"Don't know how you do it." Agent Hart chuckled. "You're as bad as Turik. Seems like you and he both go anywhere you want. That's saying something in this city."

Tess shot to attention. Turik? That name she definitely knew. What did Mohammed have to do with these guys?

"Keep in touch." Alex extended a hand, which Agent Hart grasped up to his elbow. "Will do."

Tess caught the drift of loyalty between the two. These men were much more than just a boss and his employee. She blew out an exaggerated sigh to show her disgust with the whole guy moment taking place while she stood cuffed and dying for it to end.

"Sure thing," Agent Hart answered, once again in charge as he angled her toward the exit, which she no longer intended to utilize to her advantage. That moment had passed. Wherever he was headed, she was going, like it or not. Alex didn't venture out of the warehouse, at least not that Tess noticed. And he still had her crown, damn him.

"Where are you taking me?" she asked when Agent Hart escorted her to a dusty, camouflaged Humvee parked in the shadows.

"Home." He opened the passenger door at the same time as he pulled her against his hip. Their bodies collided. Standing next to him brought a rush of feelings she didn't expect. Her body reacted in ways she wasn't proud of. Dripping ways. Clenching ways. Wanting-him-doing things-to-her ways.

Thinking she could shut out the sight of him, she closed her eyes, but that activated her nose. The smell of cinnamon and orange mingled with a hint of sweat on the midnight air didn't help. Her nostrils flared to take in another whiff. How could he still smell this good after all she'd put him through? But he did. Musky. Manly. She closed her eyes and drank it in. Good-smelling men were hard to find in this country. Case in point—Clint.

"Hey." Lee nudged her elbow with his. He stood close looking down at her, and all that height did crazy things to her heart rate and her head. Dizziness twinkled at her peripheral. It could've been stars. "It's a big rig. You want a boost up or can you climb in yourself?"

"Back off," she snapped, annoyed with herself more than with him. It was time to hop out of fairytale land and remember she was his prisoner, not his date, for hell's sake. Even as she did, her devious mind licked its lips at the prospect of him laying his hands on her again. The moment stretched, and she very nearly forgot what to do next. Was he going to kiss her? He stood close enough to. Was he going to hug her? She held her breath and waited him out, daring him for a change.

A small smile tugged the corners of his mouth. "I get it. You're too damn short. I'll boost you up."

She shivered and prepared to be boosted.

"You gonna do this or what?" he asked, crouched at her knee with his hands interlocked together, making a step. *Oh. That kind of a boost. He wasn't going to lift her into the vehicle.*

Out of sheer embarrassment for her dumb thinking, she stomped her boot into his proffered boost and was hoisted up and inside the Humvee in no time. Of course she ended up sprawled across the seat because she had no way to support herself when she landed, not with her hands cuffed behind her back. He was polite enough to pull her into a sitting position and fasten her seatbelt before he closed her door like the gentleman he wasn't.

I'm so stupid.

He climbed into the driver's side, started the engine, gunned it for good measure like most guys, and away they went. Whatever he was doing to her brain, it had to stop. She had no intention of falling for some jock in cowboy boots. Not with important work to accomplish in Afghanistan. No way.

"I'm hungry." At least he could feed her now that he'd kidnapped her.

"For?"

"A cheeseburger would be nice. Fries."

He cocked an eyebrow. "You like American food?"

"Duh. I'm an American."

An appraising green eye drifted over her dark hair. "I thought you were a local girl come back home to play Robin Hood."

"You didn't even know who you were kidnapping? You thought I was Afghan?" Sheesh, how stupid was this guy?

"I didn't say that. I read your file. You grew up in New Jersey. I just figured you had family here, that's why you love this country, and that's why you came back."

"Actually, I do have family here. My great-grandfather on my mother's side left Afghanistan years ago to give his family a chance at freedom. He didn't keep in touch with his family though. Those were dangerous times. If I have relatives here, they don't know me, and I don't know them."

"Hmm. Interesting."

"You thought you could fool me about the treasures of Tellya Tepe, didn't you? You don't really know anything about the digs, do you?"

"I know a little. Archeology's a hobby of mine," he admitted. "Of course I know more about dinosaur digs in Utah than ancient Persian artifacts."

"A natural history buff then?" She calmed. Despite the cuffs, this conversation felt normal. Even though she'd been snippy, he'd continued responding courteously. Tess cast a sideways glance, taking in the sight of the very capable man at her side. Lee looked tired, his face drawn and his laugh lines subdued. It had been a long night.

That she was still this stranger's captive should've frightened her more, but it didn't. The scruff on his cheeks and chin made her wonder if that was one day's growth or two. His hair had been recently trimmed, the neckline neat. He'd never fit into Afghanistan looking like that. The insight told her a lot about Agent Hart. He didn't plan to stay.

"Guess so. I've only been to the one site in southern Utah. Found a fragment of a fossilized dinosaur eggshell." He turned to her with a glint of pride in his eye. "Best day ever."

She couldn't suppress a grin. "I know, huh? The second you touch something from eons ago—it's like magic, isn't it?" There was that wink again, as if he and she shared something deeper than idle chat. She changed gears. "Who's Hathcock?"

He took a moment to answer, driving in silence north to Kabul. "Carlos Hathcock was a United States Marine Corps sniper and a true legend," he finally answered proudly.

"Then who's the Cobra guy?"

Lee cast an appreciative smile her way. "You were paying attention. Good girl. Cobra was a damned sharp NVA sniper. NVA is North Vietnamese Army in case you didn't know. The NVA offered a thirty-thousand-dollar bounty on Hathcock's head for killing so many of their guys. He and Cobra finally came face-to-face—at least as much as snipers could get in the jungles of Vietnam. Cobra and Hathcock fired at each other at the same time. Hathcock's round went straight through Cobra's scope and into his eye. Killed him dead." Lee shrugged one shoulder. "Cobra missed. Hathcock lived to tell about it. End of story."

"Yeah, right." She sniffed her disbelief at the outright exaggeration. Men lied; like Clint, The guy couldn't tell the truth if it walked up to him on the street and slapped him in the face. Agent Hart didn't offer further argument so she moved on. "Who's Eric?"

"One of the men trying to save your sorry ass," he muttered.

"I told you I don't need help," she ground out. This guy didn't have a clue what she needed. She had everything under control. Mostly. Sort of—not. Okay, so she'd screwed up at the palace, but she wasn't about to admit it to this guy.

"You keep saying that, but you came damned close to dying. My buddies usually wear helmet cams when they're on ops. Let's see if they were there tonight, and if they caught the shot that damned near knocked you off that five-story wall you were parading across."

"It's only three stories and I wasn't parading," she hissed. "I was stalling because Clint—I mean, you—were late. You're the one who nearly got me killed. You and those stupid guards who thought I was a boy." None of this mattered. She wasn't dead.

"How about I make you a deal?" he asked. "If I can prove that you nearly ate a bullet out there tonight, will you at least listen to what I'm trying to tell you?"

"I already listened. Didn't I shake hands with your boss? So why the cuffs?"

Agent Hart smirked, not taking his arrogant eyes off the road. "You did say all the right words."

"Trust goes both ways, you know."

"It does," he replied smoothly. "I'm just not up to chasing you down again. You're smart, Tess, but you're cocky. For some reason, my boss doesn't want you dead before we can convince you we're the good guys."

She huffed at his typical, I-know-better-than-you, condescending male attitude and looked out the side window, biting her bottom lip hard. The truth was that Alex was right. Agent Hart, too. Clint had been trustworthy—at first. He'd followed her to Afghanistan, but only for the lure of easy money and adventure it seemed. The liar claimed he wasn't using drugs, that he had an enterprising business, but one had only to look at his hollowed cheeks and drawn face to know better. If anything, he was the one who needed to be shipped home like a spoiled child and locked up in rehab until he kicked his habits, not her. He was the one who needed Agent Hart's help. Their goals had never been the same anyway, but if he left, she'd have to locate another accomplice, no easy task in this particular part of the world. Maybe it was time to trust this guy and his boss.

"Then prove it to me," she challenged. How on earth could he do that?

"Okay. Good." That seemed to satisfy Lee. "Soon as I get hold of Eric and Seth. Who knows, maybe I'll order popcorn from room service so you can see how close one of those guards came to ending you."

She had to smile. He'd turned into a little boy again, all excited about a stupid movie that was maybe five minutes long and worthless in her estimation. It almost sounded like a date. "Who's Seth?"

"Another sniper buddy of mine."

"A what?" She straightened in her seat at that word. "You're a murderer, too?"

Agent Hart offered a deep sigh, his eyes glued to the road as a flock of a dozen or so sheep and goats swarmed around the Humvee on the outskirts of Kabul. "No, ma'am. I'm more like those guys over there."

He nodded at the two young boys urging the sheep into the narrow alley, no doubt on their way to the morning market. The sun hadn't yet cleared the steep mountains to the east. For the moment, the country was bathed in pinks and golds. The boys and sheep were peacefully tinted by the sun's early salute to the world.

She didn't understand. "You're what? A kid with a loaded staff?"

Lee shot her a gentle smile. "No, ma'am. I see myself more as a shepherd guarding his flock from the wolves in the world. Damned proud of it, too."

She huffed through her nostrils at that ridiculous comparison. A man with a gun was nothing but one man's hero and another man's terrorist. A shepherd? Ha! Shepherds took care of sheep. They were gentle and kind. This guy was just another predator—who smelled like cinnamon—who knew how to lift a woman off her feet without hurting her—who had to-die-for green eyes and gloriously thick, rich hair the color of nutmeg, hair she wouldn't mind raking her fingers through if she got the chance. Hair she wouldn't mind dipping her nose into.

Tess huffed again, trying to remember when she'd hit her head hard enough she'd lost her mind. That had to be the problem. She certainly wasn't herself. Too many enticing pictures of Lee's hands on her and the way his pockets moved when he walked kept popping into her mind.

It had to stop.

Chapter Seven

"Where are you from?"

Lee offered Tess a sparse glance. *Women.* Always up to the same old tricks. First, they tried to make conversation like they were interested in you as a human being. Next, they wanted to know how you were feeling. At least this one was predictable. Crabby and nosy, but predictable.

"East Coast." That was indefinite enough. She didn't need to know his real hometown.

"New York? Boston?" she asked, still prying.

Yeah. She was a natural, but he wasn't going to let her lead him down the garden path, not after that surprise encounter back at the warehouse. The feel of her slender body tucked into his still lingered like a luscious warm brand on his hip. Somewhere during the night, they'd entered the twilight zone of intimate, physical feelings. He needed to stop that freight train before it became anything else.

"You ever watch the Red Sox play? The Yankees?" she probed.

Right again. Bet she played a mean game of chess, too. Tess certainly knew all the moves, but he didn't respond. The less he told her about himself from now on, the better off they'd both be when this operation ended. He didn't need female entanglements.

"Not talking to me anymore, huh? 'Fraid I'll figure you out and murder you in your sleep while you're supposed to be guarding me?"

No. I'm afraid I'll start to like you more than I already do. He kept a stiff upper lip and let her watch the scenery for a few more blocks. His hotel was just up ahead.

"It's sure going to be quiet the rest of the day."

Yep. Damn quiet. Shut up already.

She let out one of those lingering sighs women employed to prompt a man to ask how she was doing or what was wrong. He didn't. Lee turned into the subterranean parking garage at the Ambassador Hotel. Appropriately named, since it was located in the heavily guarded ambassador's section of Kabul, this hotel provided twenty-four hour surveillance and extra-tight armed security. Twice, suicide bombers had been stopped dead on their feet outside the hotel front doors—as in literally, dead on their feet. Lee had seen the intel. Two pairs of bloody feet in shabby boots had been all that remained both times. Aside from the Camp Eggers, the hotel was the only truly safe place for non-military Americans in Kabul at the moment, and he was glad for it. He could sleep the rest of the day there and maybe half the night. It also ought to keep Tess in as well as keeping trouble out.

He parked the Humvee in its assigned spot next to a sporty Land Rover. Man, those things always looked like they were ready for a jungle safari, especially painted in camouflage like this one. The Brits sure knew their vehicles.

Grabbing his gear bag from the back seat, Lee snagged his denim jacket too and slipped it on to conceal his holstered pistols. There was no need to frighten the other guests. He walked around the rear of the Humvee to the passenger side.

This time, Tess made no move to kick him when he opened her door. No matter. He was still on high alert. If she'd tried it once, she'd try it again. "Time to go."

"What did you really do to my brother?" She slid off the seat, nearly landing in Lee's arms.

He straight-armed her and stood her on her feet. No way was he falling for that sneaky tactic again. The exotic scent of her hair still lingered in his nose. Hell. It lingered all the way down to his boots. The soft feel of her breasts hadn't left his fingertips, either. He hadn't meant to grab a handful in that last struggle at that disgusting toilet. It just happened.

Instantly shifting his hands off her very firm, underwire bra hadn't stopped that other world from materializing though, that world where he and Miss Culver might actually enjoy each other in the very best sense of the word. Even now, the damnedest ideas kept sprouting up inside his stupid male brain. They all had to do with sweaty, naked bodies—hers and his.

"Sorry," she muttered, her hair falling over one shoulder to hide half her face. She tossed her head. Dark blue eyes shadowed with early morning violet shone up at him. "Didn't mean to touch you."

He snapped his mouth shut and looked away. This woman was pure evil, casting a sensual spell with her web of deceit, those sexy blue eyes that were too big for her face, and all that silky hair, splashed with highlights. This op had taken a decidedly risky turn, one he'd have to be extra careful maneuvering through. He focused on the way forward.

"You don't like me, do you?"

"Don't really care one way or the other." He snagged her elbow and pulled her toward the elevator, his gear bag over his shoulder and his bed calling his name. It would sure be good to shower and shave. Sweat and sand were never a good combination on a man's skin.

"I don't like you, either." Now she sounded just plain childish, but it was good to know. The less she liked him, the less danger there was of anything stupid happening.

"Where is he?"

"Who?"

"Clint. My brother."

Lee hit the elevator call button. "Home sleeping it off, I guess. I really don't know. He went one way, I went the other."

"Oh, that's right. You hit him."

"No, ma'am, I didn't, but I did give him a fifth of Jack to let me drive his truck. I told him I was his relief driver, that you knew all about it. Baby brother never asked a question. He sure as hell surprised me when he grabbed the booze and hightailed it out of there like he did. That boy moves fast."

"You were waiting for me at the palace?"

"Sure. You're easy to follow, which is something you ought to think real hard about. If I can find you that easy, so can anyone else. You could be dead right now."

"So you keep saying." She grunted, missing the point of his warning completely.

"You've got balls, I'll give you that," he admitted, still waiting for the elevator. "You all but walked into a trap tonight. Someone was waiting for you."

"Of course someone was waiting for me," she hissed, her fists clenched behind her back. "It should've been Clint, but you're wrong. I was the one who set the trap. I was the last person Sherazi expected to see there."

"I'm not talking about Sherazi. Someone else is in this game, Miss Culver, someone who wants you dead. I'm assuming Nizari was there, too?" That was the only thing he hadn't figured out yet. When had Nizari, the Taliban banker, gotten involved with stealing museum artifacts from Abdul Sherazi, a man known for butting heads with the ruling imam? "How'd you get the crown away from Sherazi and his men?"

She grunted. "They thought I was a young punk. I held them up at gunpoint. What else?"

He had to look closely to see if she was lying. Judging by the cocky tilt of her chin, she was proud of what she'd gotten away with. "You're telling me you waltzed into a clandestine meeting with a known murderer who is also a sexual deviant, a thieving curator, and six guards, with just you and your little gun?"

She offered a condescending smirk with her swagger. This woman was proud of herself. Stupid, but proud.

"Then what? You ran like hell?"

"Yeah." The air whooshed out of her and just like that, the bravado was gone. "They were right behind me. I've never run so hard in my life. I thought they had me for sure."

"Where's the gun?"

She had to be lying. He hadn't found a gun, and he'd been all over her—well, almost. He had missed that pesky USB drive, but there was no way she could've hidden a pistol in her bra.

"I dropped it," she said in a hushed voice, and he looked twice. That second confession revealed a bit more of the mystery that was Tess. She was over-confident, clever, and pigheaded. All those attributes made her dangerous, but—she had pulled off the heist of the century all by herself. And it definitely scared her. Maybe there was hope for her after all.

"How many times have you done this?" He had to know.

"Your boss was right." She nodded, her eyes on the ceiling of the parking garage. "This was the fifth, umm, yeah, the fifth artifact I've recovered."

Lee blew out a breath of disbelief and a little awe. She wasn't telling the truth, no doubt about it, but five was an impressive number. He just had a feeling there had been more along the way. A gal didn't just wake up one morning and decide to become a cat burglar out of the blue. No, she had to have practiced with smaller thefts that led up to these phenomenally huge but stupid ones.

The elevator finally arrived, the door opened, and she entered without assistance, which was nice for a change. Just his grip on her elbow was enough physical contact to set his heart pumping overtime. He didn't need another wrestling match with the woman his body seriously wanted to get better acquainted with.

"So, umm." She rocked back and forth on her toes "We're sleeping together while I'm in cuffs? That'll be fun. Kinky too."

"No." That deserved an immediate answer. Not only no, but hell no.

"Hmm." She kept rocking, "Just wondering. Sounds like we'll be in the same room if you're supposed to guard me, though. Right?"

The darn minx bumped him with her elbow, like they were a couple of high school kids on prom night. "You'll have your own bed, but you'll be handcuffed to it."

"Oh," she purred. "Handcuffed to a bed. I haven't done that in a while."

The image of her in six-inch heels and a black leather corset slithered into his head. He focused on the control panel and resolutely counted the floors until the tenth. Two to go. It was still early morning. She might need a gag over those ruby red lips for the rest of the day so he could get some sleep.

The elevator pinged and two men entered at the ninth floor, both Afghan businessmen. Lee pulled her into his side and back against the rear wall to hide the cuffs. That wouldn't do.

She rubbed up against his thigh. "I'm still hungry."

He stepped a half-foot away, just enough to give her space and to squelch the heat rising in his gut. At the tenth floor, things had to change in order to step around the men and exit the elevator. Lee pulled her along with him. Keeping her flush to his side, he stayed between them and her to keep the cuffs out of view.

Instantly, she capitalized on the move, leaning in way too affectionately. "Hmmm. I like this, honey."

"Knock it off," he muttered as he nodded to the gentlemen. One of them spiked a brow, casting a curious look toward Tess. Lee cleared the door, exited the elevator, and took a sharp left, tugging her with him. He needed distance from this woman. Just one more step and—

She stuck her boot between his feet and tripped him. *Damned liar.*

He only fell to one knee, but she'd bolted by then, and she'd gotten away. She had a good head start down the hall. For one second, he actually enjoyed the view of her backside pumping energetically away from him. The girl was an athlete, no doubt about it, but dumb. Even with handcuffs, she believed she was invincible. She thought she could escape. Still, half the fun was in the chase.

Pushing off the floor, he sprinted after her. Man, she was quick. Clearing that hallway, she turned left into the next. At the same corner, he had to think fast in order to vault over the cleaning cart in his way, still watching her ass move faster away from him than he'd anticipated. He should've remembered. This gal could run. Well, not today. He was going to catch her and—

A cleaning woman backing out of one of the rooms collided with Tess. She tried to right herself, but down she went, and the poor woman with her. The morning's exercise was over, and Lee's heart was pumping for more than one reason.

"Are you okay?" he asked the cleaning woman while he helped her to her feet. She smoothed the hair out of her eyes and readjusted her veil and her clothing, muttering what Lee didn't know. At least she didn't sound too angry.

Quickly, he snagged Tess by the elbow and hoisted her to her feet. Of course she barreled into him and knocked him over, falling on top of him when she lost her balance. "Let me go," she growled, banging her head into his hip as they sprawled on the floor.

"No, ma'am, I will not," he groaned. This time he didn't extend the courtesy of letting her walk to his room. He circled her waist with one hand and lifted to his feet with her tucked over his hip. She was facedown and backwards, her cuffed wrists where he could keep an eye on them. Her backside, too.

She squirmed, trying to turn in his arms and kicking both feet. "You can't keep me handcuffed forever."

"Yes, I can." He blew out a big breath, taking long strides down the hall. The last thing he needed was to have to explain to hotel security why he was carrying a struggling woman to his room like this.

"Help!" she called out. "Help! He's—"

Smack! He brought his hand down hard on her backside. "Quiet you."

"Ouch, you hit me!"

"Yes, ma'am, I did," he muttered, turning the corner with an armful of sass. Finally at his door, he pulled his key card from his shirt pocket and slid it through the magnetic lock, still wrangling the obnoxious woman on his hip. Before the door opened, he caught the puzzled look from his Afghan neighbors just leaving their room.

Tess turned to them, but he never gave her a chance to speak. Lee slapped her ass again and grinned at the friendly folks while he did it. "Newlyweds. Just playing. You know how it is. Sorry if we disturbed you." To prove his point, he gave her another loud spank.

"Knock it off," she declared angrily, "and we're not playing."

The gentleman pantomimed another spank with his hand, his face split in a mischievous smile, so, for good measure, Lee grinned and landed another one to Tess's very wiggly bottom. That made four. She deserved a lot more for the trouble she'd caused.

"Help me," she squealed, but Lee was home free. The neighbor chuckled and walked away with his wife, the door lock blinked green, and Lee angled Tess feet-first into his room. But he wasn't done with her. She had a lesson in counter-terrorism coming, and he meant to give it to her. He dropped his key card to his nightstand and headed straight for the bathroom with her thrashing like a damned fish.

"No," she groaned, still trying to ram his leg with her head.

"Can't you be good just once?" he asked politely. Her last chance.

"Can't you let me go, you jackass?"

"Hoped you'd say that." He turned on the bathroom light and flipped the shower on. One faucet for cold. One for hot. He deliberated using both for half a second, but warmth and comfort weren't an option. He cranked the cold spigot.

"Don't do this!" She arched her back. Pulling the shower curtain aside, he dropped her on her pretty little butt and into the cold spray. She scrambled to her knees and barreled into him with her shoulder, still fighting with everything she had and still not getting it through her hard head. She couldn't win. No way. No how.

"You're an asshole!"

"So you say," he muttered, "and you, my dear, are a pain in the ass." Straightening his arm, he easily restrained her beneath the cold water, making sure to keep her inside the tub while she sputtered, struggled, and cursed. There was no sense getting water all over the floor.

"I hate you! Let me out of here." By then, she looked like a wet dog, her hair streaming over her face and black mascara smudged around her eyes. Make that, she looked like a wet raccoon. Only her ruby red lips weren't smudged. Probably waterproof. Hmmm.

He would've done what she wanted if she hadn't taken another kick at his thigh. He pushed her off balance when her boot came up, and down she went again, sputtering all the way, her hands still behind her back and the entire bathroom floor getting soaked.

"You've got to," she wheezed, "let me … up, damn you."

"No, Miss Culver. I don't *got* to do any such thing." He crouched alongside the tub, still holding her under the cold-water treatment he knew would finally knock some sense into her.

"B-b-but you're drowning me."

"Am not. You can breathe just fine. You're just getting a cold shower. That's all. I'm not hurting you; I'm just teaching you a lesson."

She spat at him and coughed, shielding her face from the water while he made sure she caught the brunt of it. Darn, she was a pain. At last she bowed her head, water dripping off her nose and chin, her hair running like black silk over her back and shoulders. Damned if the tips of her nipples weren't displayed like marbles through her sodden black blouse. He averted his eyes, not doing this for sport, only as the last line of discipline in a long damned day.

"Had enough?"

"I'm going to kill you when I get out of here!" she spat as she lurched over the edge of the tub to ram him with her head. Crazy woman would've knocked him over if he hadn't been on guard.

"Guess not." He snagged her shirt collar and turned her around, forcing her face-first into the spray where she'd get a mouthful and maybe a little sense in the meantime. Silly woman had no chance. She was shivering plenty. It was just a matter of how long she wanted to challenge him.

"I hate you," she sputtered, her eyes squeezed tight against the steady spray. "I. Hate. You!"

"Yeah well stand in line," he muttered. "You're not the first. Won't be the last."

"But I..." She sagged, all that beautiful hair draped in a drenched curtain around her face, and the fight finally gone out of her. He hoped. "I really hate you. I'm fr-freez-z-zing."

"Are you done acting like a prima donna?" He let the cold shower continue for another minute until he was sure she'd had enough. Of course, there was no telling.

"Please." She sighed, spitting water. "Let me out of here."

Lee cupped her chin so she had to look up. She had a way of not answering a direct question. "I asked if you're done acting like a prima donna?"

She shook her head, but didn't open her eyes.

"Look at me, Tess," he ordered, his fingers firm on her jaw and his thumb on her chin.

She lifted her eyes, blinking to see him through the stream of water sluicing over her forehead. "What?"

"I asked you a direct question. I expect an answer."

"I'm done," she answered quickly, shivering and covered with goose bumps, those delectable nipples on point.

"Are you going to need a come-to-Jesus meeting every time we disagree? Because I promise, I can do it."

She shook her head vigorously, panting. "N-no."

"Do you understand that every time you run, I will catch you? Every time I catch you, you'll go under a cold shower. Next time, I might just paddle your ass, too."

Man, she looked pitiful in an adorable way. She sat there drenched and blinking the water out of her eyes. His eyes drifted over her breasts. She didn't need a padded bra, but it might've disguised the very sensual beast he'd captured. Two perfect pebbles embossed her sodden shirt exactly where a man was prone to look. Dressed in black and soaking wet like she was would've made for a helluva temptation if he'd been another kind of man.

Nonetheless, disciplinary action was quickly turning into something he hadn't intended, and he needed to end it. Lee turned the water off and pulled her to her feet, letting her stand in the tub while the water drained. He snagged one of the extra thick Turkish towels off the rack behind the door. That was another good thing about this place. The towels weren't two feet by six and transparent like a lot of the ones back home.

If not for the cuffs, he'd have tossed the towel at her and walked away. But she was restrained, and now she was wet. He hadn't thought this far ahead. She'd have to get out of those wet clothes. He debated. Uncuff her? Damn woman couldn't be trusted. Leave her cuffed? That meant he'd be undressing her, and she'd be naked and then—

He stared at her, all soggy and unintentionally seductive. She'd turned submissive, keeping her eyes on the floor and her mouth shut. He put it to her. "Listen up, Tess. Either I uncuff you so you can get dried off and dressed all by yourself, or I'll do it for you. You decide."

She turned her cute, dripping-wet ass to him and wriggled her fingers. "Uncuff me. Please. I'll be good. I promise."

He doubted that, but he had no choice, not with the bulge in his pants begging for attention it wasn't going to get. He had his own problems to deal with and removing one article of clothing from that very chilly, goose-bumpily hot female bod would only cause more. Breathing hard, he pulled his key ring out of his pants pocket, fingered the smallest key, and unlocked the cuffs.

"You try anything," he rasped, his voice suddenly gravelly, "and so help me you won't like how the rest of this morning goes. Cold water ain't nothing. I can promise you that."

"Okay," she whispered. If he hadn't already heard that little-girl routine of hers a couple times, he would've believed it. He stared at her for another second, the back closure of her bra outlined beneath her wet blouse. Shaking his head at the predicament he'd gotten himself into, he removed the cuffs.

She didn't move, other than to lean her head against the tile shower wall while she rubbed her wrists and her shoulders and shivered. "Thank you."

There were no windows in the room, but he didn't want to leave her alone. The woman was as devious as the day was long. Somehow, he was sure she could find a way out of a bank vault.

"You've got ten minutes. Hear me?" he asked gruffly to mask the tender feelings creeping up on him for this obnoxiously tempting woman. "Any noise in here besides the toilet flushing, the blow-dryer, or the faucet, and I'm back and you won't like it. Next time it'll be worse for you."

She nodded, still panting, and her heaving breasts calling him on. He did an abrupt about-face and stepped out of the bathroom, shutting the door only to stand on the other side and try to get his head on straight. There was nothing in there with her but towels, toilet paper, toiletries and the blow dryer. He'd purposefully never left his shaving bag in hotel bathrooms when he left for the day, so she had no access to a razor. Drinking glasses were on the desk by the coffee pot. She might be able to break the mirror, but he'd hear that, and then there'd be another go round with her.

It shouldn't take Tess long to get dry. The sound of her clothes hitting the floor, and the image of her standing naked and shivering spiked his sex-deprived body. He shook it off. Yeah, she'd already hit all the marks on his imaginary play-bunny scale of what to look for in a hot babe, but that day was never, never going to happen. Not with this chick.

She flushed the toilet. The shower came back on. When she opened the door fifteen minutes later, a very meek Tess Culver stood there, her eyes on the floor and the towel wrapped around her. His heart thudded to a screeching halt. Damn, she was incredibly sexy, her wet hair shiny and hanging straight down her back, her red lips bitten and swollen and lush and...

Gah! What now?

"I, umm, need a robe or something. My clothes are wet. I have nothing to wear."

Oh, yeah. Dry clothes. Damn. He swallowed hard and pulled a white fluffy hotel robe from the closet. "Here. Put this on," he ordered, trying like hell to sound like a drill sergeant to get his mind out of the gutter. She was wearing nothing but a towel, after all. "Hand me your wet clothes when you get this on. I'll send them to the laundry. They'll be back later this afternoon."

"Okay, sure," she said meekly.

Still not buying it.

She slid into the robe and let the towel fall to the floor before she turned back to her clothes. "There's stuff in my jeans pocket I need."

"Then get it," he muttered, trying real hard to keep this stern routine up. Right then she looked pretty subdued, and by hell, he shouldn't have had to go this far, but she'd pushed. She'd asked for it. Some guys would've done a lot worse to her in this situation.

Tess crouched to the floor long enough to retrieve her things.

"Show it to me," he ordered when she stood, wondering how far she'd let him push her around.

Obediently, she opened both hands and offered them palms up. Four things lay there—a now waterlogged cell phone, a soggy purple nylon wallet, a tube of lipstick, and a silver crucifix on a gold chain.

"That's all?" He had to play the bad ass. She might have already secreted something in those robe pockets.

"Yes," she said meekly.

"Show me your pockets. All of 'em."

She blinked at him like she didn't know what he meant, and damn it, she had the thickest fringed lashes. *The tough-guy routine is getting more and more difficult to pull off.*

He leaned in to check the deep robe pockets with his own fingers. Finally. She'd told the truth, but he was in trouble. Every molecule in his masculine body had tuned to Miss Culver like pigs on grain.

Before he could step back, she leaned into him, her fingers on his chest—not what he'd expected. The damned woman was trembling. "I'm sorry," she whispered with a sigh.

He stifled the impulse to wrap his arms around her and tell her everything would be okay, afraid she'd hear the freight train in his chest if he did.

"No, you're not," he threw back at her. *But I sure as hell am.*

Chapter Eight

"I won't make any more trouble for you."

Lee tipped her face away from him, but the moment had happened, and he'd been a sucker for her from the get-go. Since the first time he'd seen her run, he'd worried about the attraction he felt for her. He just couldn't let anything else happen.

"Tess," he ground her name out.

"Yes, Agent Hart?" For once, he detected no deceit in her expression.

"I'm calling room service. Get in bed."

She pulled back, and he was damned glad. One more second of close contact with this enticing woman, and he'd be answering to his boss for something unbecoming of a trusted agent.

"Which one do you want me to sleep in?" she asked. He could only hope the fight had finally gone out of her.

"Take the one by the window." Lee usually got a room with two racks in case one of the guys dropped in unannounced and needed a place to drop, but no one in their right mind would escape from a ten-floor hotel room, would they? He eyed her suspiciously. She'd gotten awfully tame in the last few minutes. That spooked him more than her cocky attitude had. Did he dare relax? Hell, no.

Lee called room service and ordered two American-style cheeseburgers with lettuce, pickles, and the whole sesame seed buns thing, as well as two large orders of fries and catsup, a rarity in most foreign countries. Two bottles of Coke and two tall cups of ice completed the order.

When she crawled under the covers, he turned the television to BBC's twenty-four-hour news channel. It had the most non-partisan reporting of American news he could stand, but he was wet from the bathroom escapades and tired. The cuffs had to go back on, or he wouldn't be able to shower or get some rest. He unsnapped them from his belt and held them up for her to see.

"Can you put them in front this time?" She didn't argue, not even once.

"I'll do you one better." He sat on the bed opposite hers and fastened one cuff to her right wrist. "I'll leave one hand free so you can eat. Sound okay?"

"I guess." She sighed.

Lee made quick use of a hot shower. When done, he changed into a comfortable pair of gray running pants and a simple gray T-shirt with USMC stamped in bold block lettering on the chest. And gray socks. Always socks.

He ran a quick hand over his hair before he left the privacy of the bathroom, going for the casual look of a man who had no one to impress. For once, she was where he'd left her and looking sleepily at the television.

But her hair was wet. That would never do.

Turning to the steamy bathroom, he snagged the last dry towel and the blow dryer. "Sit up," he ordered, not sure if he was worried about her hair or if he needed to make a point. He was in charge. She needed to comply.

Without a single word of debate, she rolled to her side and placed both feet to the floor. When she reached for the blow dryer, damned if an idiot didn't show up and say, "Here. Let me. I'll do it."

He cringed. *Why did I say that? What the hell am I doing?*

Her hair was a damp mess of tangles and curls, and Lee was in more trouble. He'd never dried a woman's hair before. Didn't even have a brush to do it properly, but he'd started this, and he'd finish it. Otherwise, she'd think she had the upper hand.

He plugged the drier into the outlet behind the nightstand between their beds. His heart commenced a steady drumming, and, if he'd really been smarter, he'd have changed his mind and rescinded his order. But no. Lee kept going.

He sat next to her, his knee pulled up on the bed while he pretended he knew what he was doing. With the first handful, he relaxed. This work wasn't all that hard. He aimed the nozzle of the blow dryer from her scalp to the ends of each silky handful, holding it away from her head to provide the most airflow. That seemed to do the trick.

Layer after layer of black and brown tresses came to life with shimmering highlights of reds and blues mingled in with the dark. It was actually soothing how his fingers combed those tangles away until her curls were smooth. Sleek. Sexy. By the time the left side was dry, he was wishing he'd worn something a lot heavier than cotton running pants.

"Turn around so I can dry the rest of it." He kept his tone tough, like this was just another boring job, like he wasn't turned on when she tipped her head into his palm and sighed. Like he didn't want to bury his fingers and his nose at the nape of her neck and kiss the hell out of her.

Once again, she obeyed. With her robe smoothed beneath her, she curled her legs under her and faced the headboard, the remaining hair just as long, damp and...

I am such a dumb ass. Man, she's gorgeous. Why'd I start this?

He grasped another wet handful and the endurance test began anew. If Tess noticed the effect she had on him, she didn't capitalize on it. She didn't have to. Just the fact that she sat peacefully, enjoying the service he foolishly provided was enough to push him over the edge. Her butt ended up against his knees. He worked quicker and more efficiently before his mistake got any larger. Or thicker. Or harder.

Whew. At last. Mission accomplished. He smoothed the final handful of dark silk into place, letting it slide between his fingers as he turned the blow dryer off. One thing was sure. He'd never make this mistake again. Wrapping the cord around the blow dryer, he unplugged it and turned abruptly. The job was done, and so was he. Their breakfast of burgers and fries couldn't get there fast enough.

He'd no more than stretched out on the other bed and pulled the blanket across his lap to conceal his frame of, umm, mind, when a knock at the door told him breakfast was served.

"Aren't you going to get that?" Tess asked quietly when he didn't immediately jump up and answer the door.

"Of course I am," he barked back at her, wishing like hell it were that simple. Women didn't understand how difficult it was for a guy to strut around the room once his manhood was alerted to a sexy female in the vicinity. A guy's body just didn't work that way. "Besides, they'll leave it outside my door. I'll get to it. Hold your horses."

"Whatever," she whispered.

He squeezed his eyes shut and mentally field-dressed the mule deer he'd shot in Wyoming during his last hunting trip out west. He mentally hiked the Grand Canyon again like he did the year before when he'd searched out Havasu Falls with a good buddy of his. He very methodically pictured cleaning his tactical sniper rifle, then field-stripped it, oiled it, and polished the damned imaginary thing.

Finally relaxed enough he could get on his feet, he retrieved the dining cart, and situated it between the beds. Tess swung her feet to the floor. She licked those full red lips, and two things dawned on him. He'd calmed down enough to eat, and this girl hadn't eaten in a while. Why not? He lifted the silver cover off her plate. "You hungry?"

Silly question. As soon as she one-handedly snagged the burger, it hit those sexy red lips and mayonnaise and catsup dripped down her chin.

His mouth dropped open.

"Oh," she moaned, licking those sinfully wicked lips. Her tongue swept over them, a luscious wet invitation he had to deny. "This is so good. So. So. Good." She moaned again, rolled her eyes and chewed, and he was compelled to watch because, well, he was a guy, damn it. His stomach clenched. A rush of molten lava pooled in his groin. His problem sprang back to—attention.

That sassy, impertinent, sexy, red-lipped mouth of hers had him mesmerized, and his body hardened all over again. Tess wasn't the daintiest eater. She made short work of her breakfast, moaning and grunting so much it sounded like she was having sex instead of a burger.

Lee bumped the backs of his legs against his mattress before he closed his mouth. He was certainly in the mood by the time she stuffed one dainty index finger along with the last bite of burger nearly all the way into her mouth, catching the dribble of catsup before it got away from her. He licked his lips just watching. Who would've guessed catsup could get a man hard? He bunched up the blanket on his lap again.

Tearing his eyes away from Tess, he grabbed his plate from the cart. The cheeseburger was decent. The fries weren't bad either, but watching her? Priceless.

"I was so-o-o hungry," she growled, her voice more a feline purr of pure satisfaction. "Mmm, mmm."

He leaned back onto his pillow, hungry all right, just not so much for that burger.

"What? You're not going to eat?" she asked, her eyes lit up with surprise.

"I am eating," he retorted, then shoved the burger into his big mouth to prove it.

She'd moved onto fries and more catsup by then, dipping and sucking and making the most erotic noises with that mouth and—

Argh! He choked on the dry bun.

"You okay?" she mumbled over a luscious mouthful. "Need a drink?"

He nodded, still sputtering to clear his airways. "Fine," he rasped, and then coughed some more. After gulping half of his Coke, he was able to breathe again. Thinking was another problem. Watching this gal argue with Alex had been an all-nighter, but now that he knew the secret, he made a mental note. *Do feed this wild animal—but don't hang around to watch her eat.*

"You gonna eat all those?" she asked, her brow raised and her eye on his plate of fries.

He held them out to her. "I'll order more. Want a chocolate shake to wash it down?"

Those pretty eyes rolled again, and he was sure he'd died and gone to heaven. Damn. She was sexier than hell when she ate, the way she chewed, and the way those red lips turned prehensile when they got close to food. She moaned and sighed all the way through his order of fries, so he ordered another burger for himself, two more baskets of fries, and two large chocolate shakes with whipped cream and cherries on top.

"Could you, umm, get one more thing?" She hesitated before he hung up the phone.

"What else do you want?" *What else was there?*

"I'd die for a beer." Those dainty brows crinkled and her shoulders ducked with the plea, and damn, he was in trouble.

"Heineken?"

Again with the died-and-gone-to-heaven eye roll. "Yes, please."

Okay. Make that two beers on top of two chocolate shakes—not his usual way to drink beer, but okay. The alcohol might put her to sleep.

The waiter was quick with this order. Tess seemed as eager for this serving of carbs and protein as she was the last, sucking down the chocolate shake like it was water. It did a man good to see a woman eat like this, but caution lights began to flash at the back of his mind. There was a reason she was eating so much. There had to be. Was she baiting him into believing she was really this hungry or—was she really this hungry? And why hadn't she eaten? Furthermore, how the heck could she possibly eat so much? Where was a tiny little thing putting all that food?

He twisted the bottle top off his beer, offering her his chocolate shake. It went as quickly as the first. This gal was a lean, mean, eating machine, no two ways about it. At last, she opened her bottle of beer and took a swig, leaning into her pillow with a drawn-out and very satisfied sigh.

"You had enough yet?" He had to ask. The way she'd inhaled everything in sight was phenomenally amazing.

"Yes. Thank you, Agent Hart. I needed that."

"Why so hungry?"

Smiling shyly, she waved his question off, offering a small burp instead. Wrong answer.

"Tess. What's going on? Why were you so hungry?" He eyed her sternly. She should've known better than to blow him off like that. The shower wasn't far away.

"I, umm..." She licked the salt or something off her index finger, then stuck that red nailed finger all the way into her mouth and slowly drew it out. Darn her tempting ass. He looked away and counted to ten. Did she have any idea how hot all of her innuendos, lips, tongue, and fingers movements were to a sex-starved man? And that mouth. Those ruby lips. Nothing but wickedly sinful, a tad prehensile, and—just the way a woman's lips should be.

"It's just that it's kind of hard to eat when you're..." Apprehension shone in her blue eyes.

"When you're what?" *Get on with it, Miss Culver.*

She sighed in that timid way she had when it suited her. "You wouldn't understand. You're a man."

Like him being male had anything to do with anything. Everyone had to eat. He waited, tired of all the showdowns and mind games with this tenacious woman. Nodding toward the bathroom door, he arched a brow to get his point across. "Swim or spill."

"Oh, all right. It's not like it's a secret or anything. I work part-time at an orphanage in downtime Kabul," she said quietly. "It's just hard to eat when starving children are standing in front of you."

He sat up straight and focused on her. "You work at an orphanage? Really?" *Why did I not know that?*

She nodded without looking at him. "You didn't think I spent all my time on rooftops, did you?"

"When? I mean, how many hours do you work there?" His throat went dry. He'd been to Afghanistan two separate times just to surveil this woman, and yet he'd missed this, another sign he needed to quit the covert surveillance world. That little detail explained the food addiction and her lithe figure, but going without food so children could eat? He hadn't seen that coming and he should have. "Which orphanage?"

"Saint Raphael's. It's outside the gate at Camp Eggers. I go in whenever I can."

He knew it well. "What do you do when you're there?"

She shrugged. "Whatever the director wants me to do. Sometimes I teach, but most of the time, I work with the kids who've been injured by IEDs. I bathe them and feed them. I help them readjust to life without limbs or sight. I handle grief counseling with their parents if they have any. Whatever I need to do," she shrugged again, "I just do."

He sighed. The reminder of all those poor children dampened his joy of having just watched her eat.

"There's a six-year-old girl named Mina." Tess turned talkative. "She and her little brother were walking to school one day, only the Taliban had buried a bomb the night before.

Jamaal stepped on it. He lost a leg and part of his arm, but Mina…" Tess paused, still not looking at Lee. "She lost sight in both eyes. Of all the kids there, she and her brother are my favorites."

A twinge of guilt shuddered off Lee's shoulders, even though the sensation that he was being played persisted. Was this woman actually willing to use injured Afghan children to further her cause? Was she softening him up so she could catch him unaware? Darn. She was good, but the conclusion didn't set right. She might be audacious with the Taliban, but he couldn't see her being cruel with children. He couldn't decide what to believe.

"I tried for days to find their mother," she said wistfully, "but they only had their father, and he couldn't keep the children. He was elderly, and they were too much trouble. He still comes to visit, though, and they love him."

Lee studied her profile from his bed. There was one way to find out if this was true or not. He dialed Mother all the way back in Alexandria, Virginia. Morning in Afghanistan meant late night on the East Coast, but the lead techie for The TEAM was always on call. "Hey, Mother. What are you doing in the office this late?"

She answered, just as he knew she would. "Working, Lee. How about you?"

Tess spiked a wickedly sharp brow. "You didn't believe me?"

Lee shook his head, trying to listen to both women in his ears, but mostly to Mother. "Boss has me working on a video he just sent. How about you?"

"That wouldn't be the video of Hasim Nizari, would it?"

"Sure is. Why?"

Lee stalled. Damn, Alex was quick. "Could you double-check an alibi for me before you go home?"

"You betcha. Whatcha need?"

"I need to know about an orphanage outside Camp Eggers here in Kabul. Saint Raphael's. Could you find out for me if there's a little boy there named Jamaal and a little girl named Mina? They're brother and sister. She and Jamaal might need medical aid. I'd like to get that started."

"Anything else?" Mother was always at her best when she was involved in everyone else's business.

"Not right now." Lee kept one eye on Tess. She'd heard the whole thing. He'd expected a stronger reaction, but she looked like she was asleep, another response he didn't trust.

"I'll call back when I find out. Don't go too far."

"I won't. Good night, Mother."

"Night."

Lee disconnected the call. Tess was asleep. She should be. The woman had on a definite carb overload. Not a fry had survived her prehensile lips and the two chocolate shake glasses were sucked dry, the beer bottles, too.

He was feeling a little sleepy too, but several chores remained. Lee pushed the dinner cart out into the hall and hung the *Do not disturb* sign on the doorknob. He gathered Tess's clothing from the bathroom floor and rung each piece dry. After stuffing her black jeans, shirt, black bra, and very sexy black lace panties into the laundry bag, he placed a quick call to the front desk for a pick up. Into another bag went his dirty laundry, with orders to please avoid starching his underwear this time.

It didn't take long before a young boy knocked politely on the door, asking after the laundry. With that chore taken care of, Lee turned the light off, returned to his bed, and turned the volume on the television to low. As quietly as possible, he placed another call.

Eric answered at the first ring. "How is she?"

"Sleeping," Lee replied. "You must have talked with the boss."

"Yes. Sounds like you've had more fun than Seth and I did last night."

"You have no idea." Lee glanced at the other bed. Tess had turned away from him, the curvy dip of her waist and hips defined beneath the robe.

"Damn," Eric muttered. "Wish we'd known you were already standing by to catch her when she dropped."

"You were there? Where were you guys situated?"

"Yeah. East side, facing south. Between the museum and palace. Didn't expect we'd be working a joint op with you tonight, though. Seth damned near blew a gasket when she pitched over the edge like she did. Everything happened at once. We couldn't see you or the truck over the palace wall, just the roof."

"Damn, I wish I'd known. Were you wearing helmet cams?"

"Seth was. He was spotting for me. Why? You want to see the video?"

"Yes, and so does Miss Culver. She's got the idea she's invincible."

"That girl's nuts."

"Speaking of Seth, how's he doing?" Lee avoided Eric's correct observation of Tess. Overall, Eric had the more difficult part of this two-pronged operation. He had to deal with Seth.

"Good."

"You can't talk, can you?"

"Got that right." Eric's succinct answer was explanation enough.

"Could be worse, you could be here," Lee muttered softly as he glanced at Tess again. She'd groaned in her sleep, her cuffed hand over her head and her clean hair mussed and shiny, cascading off the pillow. No doubt about it. She was out like a light—and sexy as hell. Soft and hard at the same time. Sweet and mean. Shit. He was in way over his head.

"We're hearing a lot of Taliban chatter about a big meeting going down in Kabul, maybe tomorrow. Did Alex mention anything about it to you?" Eric asked.

"Haven't talked to him since early this morning. Been kinda busy. If I know Alex, he's still backtracking everything she's stolen and who's buying it."

"Like I said, she's nuts."

"What's up with you guys? Where will you be tomorrow?"

"Unless we get more intel on the next Taliban move from the Army, we'll be around the museum. Turik's hit all of his victims in that general area, and he's done it late afternoon every time. We were lucky today. Seth spotted him coming out of that orphanage by the base."

"Saint Raphael's?" That surprised Lee.

"Yeah. That's the one. We were gonna drop off the shoes Seth brought. You know how he is. No kid should go barefoot and all that."

Lee knew. Since the incident in Chicago, Seth couldn't buy enough shoes for little kids. It stemmed from the fact that when he'd hit that girl with the pink pistol, his shot blew her backward and out of her shoes. Lee really wanted to talk with

Seth. He knew what the guy was going through, but he couldn't. Not yet. Lee needed enough help all by himself.

"What was Turik doing there?"

"Playing with a couple kids. A little girl and a boy. They looked like one big happy family."

"Tess works there," Lee muttered. "That could explain where she's getting her intel on the museum thefts. Maybe she's working with Turik."

"Could explain why he tried to kill her." Eric yawned. "That whole honesty among thieves thing, you know. Is that all you wanted?"

"You guys need to take Turik out of the game, buddy. Do it now before he kills anyone else."

"No shit," Eric hissed. "You do know he took a shot at your girlfriend tonight, don't you? That's why he was there."

"Seriously? You got that on video? I was hoping for a close-up of the guards. This is better."

"Hell, yeah. Turik would've had her if she hadn't dropped off the edge when she did."

"Maybe he's working her for information. How else could he have known where she'd be?" Lee blew out a slow breath at the thought. It felt true, but damn. He could've caught a dead body instead of the very sexy one sharing his hotel room. Tess scrunched her nose in her sleep, then reached to rub it with her cuffed hand, growling when she couldn't stretch far enough. Even in her sleep, Tess Culver was petulant as all get-out.

"Can you drop by later this afternoon? She needs to see that video."

"Can do. Listen, we're headed out to look for Turik again right now. We can be there at fifteen-thirty. Will that give you time to catch some shuteye?"

"Good enough. See you then." Lee signed off.

Shuteye implied he'd have to sleep with one eye open, a very distinct possibility with Miss Culver in the same room with him. He went to her bedside for a moment, content just to look down on her while she slept.

Alex had a helluva lot of nerve charging him with guarding this hot-blooded, hot-tempered woman. Odd, though, how Lee's empty hotel room felt cozy—or soothing—or something since he'd dragged her ornery butt over the threshold.

There were no two ways about it. She was a gorgeous woman, one who should be doing anything but mixing it up with a bunch of terrorists who'd proved over and over again they had no qualms demeaning women. He'd surveilled Tess often enough to know how she looked running, climbing, and just plain walking down a busy Kabul street. But to be standing this close to her was breathtaking. Her eyes were shut. Coal lashes fanned over mauve-tinted cheeks, lending a certain exotic mystique to her Central Asian ancestry. Full red lips, still not smudged, pinched together in a little-girl pout as if she was dreaming, maybe kissing someone in her sleep.

His gut clenched at the notion that she'd been with another man, one she was dreaming of. He wanted to be the one who smudged that lipstick, damn it. He wanted his hands on her and her mouth on him, and shit. He shut the inherent protective streak in his nature down before he lost his mind. It served him well in this covert surveillance business, but not today. Miss Culver was just a client. Just another job. Nothing more.

The collar of her fluffy white robe had parted to reveal just the pillowy top of her right breast, not showing much skin, but beguiling as hell. It didn't help one bit knowing she was naked and warm beneath that fluffy robe or that he could heat her up if she were cold.

The automatic instinct to lie beside her and partake of that tender body threatened his last ounce of good sense. It had been a long time since he'd let his defenses down to become so vulnerable—or so dumb. He reined his horses in, dragged his eyes off of her, and stepped back and away. No sense in getting worked up about a thing that wasn't meant to be. Tess wasn't his type. He'd already got the hint, loud and clear. Never the two would meet.

Besides, he wasn't ready for a woman in his life. Nizari had made sure of that. The marks he'd left on Lee's body were the ultimate turn-off to the feminine persuasion. One didn't survive the barbarism of a cruel man without scars and the lingering demons that went with them. Just the thought of the brute brought the damp, dank smell of that tiny cell back to Lee's mind. It hadn't been big enough for a man his size to lie down and stretch his legs, but the smell was the stuff of nightmares. Filth and blood. Sweat and fire. Fear...

Lee rolled his shoulders, shrugging the demons off yet one more time. The irony of having lived a healthy, pure life before that nightmare, of having avoided drugs, cigarettes, and booze through his teenage years and even boot camp, only to be saddled for the rest of his days with a psychological addiction to a nightlight and outright fear didn't escape Lee.

He'd lived his time in Hell. Because of Nizari, each day was another twelve-step challenge to let it go, move on, keep positive, and never let Nizari win. And every day, Lee got up like any other alcoholic or drug addict on the planet, and he started all over again. He performed his mental ritual of picturing his younger self, throwing stars and dreams back into the sky.

He brushed his teeth and pushed the blackness away for another day. He showered and shaved while he invited the light to enter and to stay. A man's brain ought to work the other way around. He should wake up energized and full of life, ready to conquer the world instead of jolting out of the same running nightmare from which he could never get away.

"Hey." A soft touch on his wrist startled him out of the past. "Are you coming to bed, Agent Hart?" Tess asked sleepily, her hair tousled and tangled, her lips full and wet, and her free hand feathery light on his skin.

Lee's heart stuttered. Coming to bed sounded a helluva lot like an invitation he shouldn't refuse. *Could it please, just for once, be that easy?* But he knew better. If he were dumb enough to fall for her, she'd see. She'd cringe. She'd pull back in disgust, and she'd come up with a very reasonable excuse never to look at him again. She'd turn away, and that one fatal mistake would turn the rest of this op into misery.

"Go to sleep," he said softly, lifting her fingers off his arm and placing her hand on her pillow.

"'Kay," she whispered groggily, her cheek mashed to the pillow again. "I's just asking."

He pulled the light blanket up to her chin, covering her robe, and he sat on the edge of his bed watching her drop off to sleep. Client or not, he very much wanted to climb into bed with Miss Culver.

He just never would.

Chapter Nine

Her eyes popped open. She'd heard something. A child out of bed at night? An animal in the orphanage? An assassin come to murder her in her sleep? The Taliban? A shudder raced up her spine.

Nothing but the hush of the empty hotel room and the man snoring softly in the opposite bed came back to her ears, but her heart wasn't hammering for nothing. Tess ducked deeper into her covers. She *had* heard something. Someone else *was* in this room.

Quietly testing that her cuff was still locked brought another wave of panic. She was trapped with no way to run and shaking like a leaf. Not her usual exit strategy. Her nightmares always started like this, trapped, restrained against her will. The muscles in her throat clamped shut, restricting airflow, making it hard to breathe or calm herself.

Why wasn't Agent Hart protecting her? He'd said he would. Wasn't that the deal? He'd promised. Panic crept over her shoulders at the deadly snare he'd trapped her in. This was all his fault.

Er-r-r. Ar-r-rg.

There it was again, that sound, a guttural groan, deep and tormented from the other bed. From Agent Hart? She shot an annoyed glance his way, relieved and irritated at the same time. At least there was no murderer come to get her, but growling like a bear? Really? Snoring she could deal with. Clint did plenty of that. Growling? Not so much.

Slivers of the bright afternoon Kabul sunshine filtered through the closed slats of the wooden shutters, just enough to offer the dimmest light. Damn, what was that man wearing? Agent Hart looked overdressed with gray running pants and a T-shirt, the sheet draped over half his body. Funny. She'd expected a bare chest. Hairy legs. Maybe boxers. But this man even wore gray socks to bed. How odd. She smirked at the sight. Ha. Why not pajamas? They'd make as much sense in this desert climate.

With a small sigh of relief, she relaxed. At least, the racket she'd heard was just—him.

"No-o-o," he growled, straightening both legs, his hands stiff at his side and his fists clenched. His thick chest heaved.

She leaned up on one elbow to better see what was going on. He was restless, his head shaking back and forth in continual grunts and denials. The veins in his neck bulged. Agent Hart was dreaming. That was all. He looked like a little kid about to have a temper tantrum, his face sweaty and his hair mussed. Maybe that was all this was about. He was hot. He should be with all those clothes.

"Knock it off, Hart," she ordered. "I'm trying to sleep over here."

"Won't," he muttered darkly as if in answer, his right hand brushing over his chest in short rapid strokes like he was brushing bugs away. Only he hadn't answered her, and he didn't stop scrubbing his chest. The brushing turned frantic. He arched to one side, his face contorted, and his back lifted off the mattress. "Corporal Lee Hart," he ground out, following that odd proclamation with what sounded like a series of numbers she couldn't quite distinguish. Name, rank, and serial number?

Tess looked closer. Agent Hart was red-faced, rigid veins visible on his forehead, his lips tight and his brow furrowed in—pain? This was some serious nightmare.

"Corporal Lee Hart," she whispered louder. "Wake up. You're dreaming, and you're making a lot of noise. I can't sleep. Stop it."

He bared his teeth to her, hissing as he jerked to a sitting position and shook his head, his eyes still closed. One hand raked viciously over his head, his fingernails scraping his short mahogany hair all the way to his neckline and back again. His other hand went to his stomach, clutching his shirt, pulling it away from his body, stretching it until the seams creaked in protest.

"Can't. Won't do it," he declared between sharp panting breaths, his eyes still closed, his voice more rumbling growl than tone. "Never. No. Won't... do... it!"

"You're ripping your shirt. Will you lay down and just relax?" she muttered, coaxing him awake.

Even annoying, he was a rare sight to behold. His biceps were sheer muscle, thickly veined and coated in a sweaty sheen. Those broad shoulders were ropes of solid musculature, and a definite rift defined his pecs, the left from the right, even through his T-shirt.

When her nose twitched, she turned completely on her side just to watch his antics, her head pillowed on her bicep. He must've splashed aftershave on after his shower. She hadn't noticed it once the food showed up, but she noticed it now. Cinnamon and orange, her new favorite men's fragrance.

He groaned with whatever internal torment visited a man his size, but honestly. What could a big guy like him be afraid of? She scoffed at the tough image he'd projected. Maybe he was scared of spiders. The desert was known to produce some big ones, like camel spiders. Ha. Wouldn't that be funny?

The sight of that clean-shaven chin made her smile, though. A cleft divided it neatly, or was it a scar? A dimple? She'd need a closer look, but for now, she drew in a long, slow breath of that delightful, clean man-smell and let it fill her lungs. Let him growl all he wanted. He wasn't hurting anybody, and a man who obviously took care of himself was easier on the eye than what she usually woke up to.

Agent Hart groaned again, a whine crawling up from deep inside his chest. "Never betray my... country. Stop it."

Tess bolted upright. Despite his words, a hurt little boy had just spoken. *Betray his country?* This was no normal nightmare. This was deeply rooted terror speaking, a nightmare he'd lived. She would know because too many nights she'd screamed herself awake. He was—her.

"Agent Hart." She reached for him, her bare feet flat to the floor between their beds, but her fingers couldn't even touch his knee. "You're having a nightmare, Lee. That's all. Wake up, honey."

His eyes popped open, and for a moment, it seemed he'd obeyed, until tremors rattled from his head to his gray socks. It looked as if he'd had a seizure. He stared at nothing, those once kind greens gone zombie dark with barely any light in them and no whites either. His mouth worked like he was a fish gasping for air, but he wasn't choking. His fists knotted inside the bottom of his shirt, still pulling it taut away from his stomach.

"What's going on? You're scaring me. Come on. Snap out of it," she said more kindly, reaching as far as she could for him. "I'm right here. Take my hand. Grab hold. Come on, you can do it. I know you can."

"Don't... touch me, Nizari!" he growled. "It hurts."

The name reached out and punched her straight in her heart. She couldn't draw a breath. *Nizari? He did this? Too?*

The little boy in Lee was gone. Coal black eyes glared at her, full of shadow and loathing. With one fist, he reached behind him and jerked the shirt over his head and tossed it to the floor like a challenge. He commenced scrubbing his chest and abdomen frantically, tearing long thin gouges and bellowing, "Don't! Don't! Don't!"

Tess panicked. He was hurting himself, but she couldn't get to him. He'd already marked his handsome body with ugly scratches that—

God, no. Her stomach lurched up her throat. She stifled a cry. He wasn't hurting himself. Those scratches weren't fresh. They weren't bleeding. They were—scars. Deep. Red. Ugly scars. Some longer than others. Some that outlined the curve of each rib he'd exposed. Small black, circular pockmarks marred his perfect stomach muscles, but they didn't stop there.

"Agent Hart," Tess called to him, desperate to help. She stretched closer. The black marks rounded his sides and descended below the elastic of his pants. Cringing awareness tightened her breath at the pain he'd endured. She looked to his feet, wondering what lay beneath the gray ribbed cotton socks. Suddenly his clothes weren't so much an attempt at propriety as they were camouflage. Agent Hart wasn't dressing properly. He was hiding.

"Lee, honey, I'm here." Her panic turned to tears. "Please. Grab my hand. Let me help you. It's only a nightmare, honest. Nizari's not here, only me. He's not real, but I am. You're safe now, I promise."

"No! No! No!" He shook his head. "He... won't stop! Every day! Every night! The dark man comes!"

The dark man, what locals called Nizari because they were afraid to speak his name.

Panic lifted up Tess's dry throat. She had to do something. "Lee, listen. I'm right here, baby. Open your eyes and see me. There's no one else in this room but you and me. It's just a bad dream. Reach for me, Lee. Let me help you, for a change. Take my hand. Please."

He hissed even as a whine travelled up from his gut. "I can't," he choked. "The stars... don't... work. Don't you get it? I throw them up, but they keep falling down!"

His anguish overwhelmed her. This was a man deeply tormented, fighting demons every time he closed his eyes. Tess choked, her hand to her mouth. "Lee," she sobbed, blinking tears out of her eyes, her body stretched to him as far as she could make it reach. "Please. Take my hand. I'm real, honey, and I know just what you're talking about. Please, baby. Let me help. Come to me. Please, Lee, come to me. Look at me. See me."

His chin dropped to his chest, his lashes lowered, and his body covered in sweat. "Hoo-rah," he growled savagely, saliva dripping off his lip to dribble onto his bare chest. "I... win again... not... you..." Breathing heavily, he patted his belly with his palm instead of gouging at it with his fingernails. "Boss is right. Living's... best revenge..." he mumbled incoherently. The blatant hatred in his eyes faded. His cheeks filled and hollowed with every deep breath he sucked in and blew out. His chest heaved. Sweat glistened over his exposed body, so much that his waistband was dark with it.

A desperate plea lifted up from the depth of her heart. "God, oh God, Lee. Please, please take my hand. Let me help."

He seemed oblivious. Gradually, his head lolled to the side and Lee went limp. His eyes closed, and ever so slowly, the poor guy pitched forward. Tess hit the carpet between their beds before he could, offering her body as a cushion. He never woke up—just dropped onto her thighs and circled her waist with one strong arm, his fingers clutching her hip. He pushed his face into her stomach and growled as he succumbed to sleep again. Tremors still jerked at his fingertips and feet, but the worst seemed over. Only the deep pulls for more oxygen remained. Only her tears.

"My poor sweet baby, what did Nizari do to you?" she sobbed quietly, her fingers in the deep, lush thickness of Lee's sweaty hair, needing to comfort him. She knew exactly what Nizari had done, the evidence stark and clear. Tess was shaken to her core, the damage inflicted upon this strong man now laid bare to her. The tables had turned. Suddenly, she was glad he'd caught her at the palace. She was glad he'd chained her to the bed and made her stay with him, if only because she of all people knew what he'd lived through. He needed never to wake up alone to that kind of a nightmare again, at least not while she was with him.

Gently, she smoothed her free hand over Lee's head and down his neck to his muscular shoulder and bicep, thankful she could reach any part of him at all. With her one arm stretched as far as she could make it reach, she cradled the battered warrior against her. "How could he do this to you?" she cried quietly, eternally aghast at the depths of man's depravity against his brothers and sisters.

While Lee lay panting in her arms, his face and body drenched with sweat, her heart hurt. She looked at this handsome body differently, trembling at the knowledge she possessed that he would surely not want her to know. How could an American man as big and strong as Agent Hart have met this kind of fate? The Taliban must've captured him when he was a soldier. They'd turned him over to Nizari who'd tortured him.

That explained both Alex and Lee, why they dressed the way they did and spoke to each other like they did. They were ex-military, U.S. soldiers come to right a country full of unspeakable wrongs. They knew the cost if they got caught, yet there they were again. Taking chances and all because of—her.

She'd seen plenty of their kind before on the streets of Kabul—US Marines, Army, SEALs, and Air Force. They'd all seemed astoundingly respectful, handsome, and professional, in such sharp contrast with the Taliban who had no problem beheading mothers and fathers in soccer fields, hanging mutilated bodies from bridges and buildings, or maiming innocent children on their way to school.

No wonder he'd told her he was sorry when he'd cuffed her. He was stronger than her, yes, and maybe more determined, but he might have unwittingly recognized a kindred spirit. He'd never been cruel, not even when he'd held her under the cold shower. All of his actions were only reactions to her bullying.

Tess shuddered as his breathing steadied. He relaxed and nuzzled, his nose moved to the corner of her hip, and she very much wanted him to stay. "You poor baby," she muttered, wiping her tears on her shoulder. "How can I ever help you?"

Of course he didn't answer, but her heart did. *You're helping him now. Just. Don't. Stop.*

Chapter Ten

Damn.

The last way a man wanted to wake up was with his face in a strange woman's lap and her fingers playing with his hair, tracing his ear, and sliding down his neck to his collarbone. Lee opened one eye and fell into a pool of deep blue with a tinge of violet. Instantly, he knew what had happened. *Freaking nightmares.*

If that wasn't bad enough, his shirt was gone, no doubt ripped to shreds and hanging off the chandelier. Lee gritted his teeth. The damned *Green Hulk* had emerged again, and now Tess Culver knew what a monster he was. He clenched his jaw and steeled himself for another round of hurt. Why did it have to be Tess?

"Good afternoon, Agent Hart," she said softly, her fingertips tracing the edge of his ear all the way down to his jaw again. He shivered at the very intimate touch that somehow registered in his groin. Man, she smelled good, but why was she being nice? Oh, yeah. She'd seen. Now the pity party would commence. Then she'd have to leave. Then he'd get mad. *Goodbye and good riddance.*

It had to be late afternoon judging by the lack of direct sunlight in the room. Maybe early evening. Still light outside though. The stars in the twilight sky back home had never been so pretty as the ones in her violet-blue eyes. This was definitely a first, but the last thing he wanted to share with this cantankerous woman. That they were both flat on the floor didn't bode well. That she was sitting against her bed and cradling his head in one arm the way she was felt awful damned odd, too. This was new, a very different experience with this particular half-naked woman.

Maybe she didn't know it, but her cleavage was plenty visible through the loose collar of that robe. So was her crucifix. Poor Jesus. He looked smothered between those pillows of soft, silky skin that Lee shouldn't have been ogling. He wasn't sure how to proceed, so he didn't do anything, just closed his eyes, played like an ostrich, and wished the floor would open up and suck him and Jesus back to the States.

"I thought I recognized you," she said quietly, her finger tracing his ear again.

Huh? He shivered under the gentle touch and blinked that same eye open, not sure what she was talking about. Of course she recognized him. They'd just spent most of the night and half the morning wrestling, arguing, and eating together. Another shot of fire raced from his ear to his groin. He wished she'd stopped teasing.

"We have a lot in common, Agent Hart. When the Taliban came to the orphanage," she said quietly, "I thought they'd kill me for sure."

He rolled to his side so he could see her better, but he didn't his head move out of her lap. It had been a long time since he'd been this close to a sexy woman, and Tess was definitely sexy. She smelled of soap, shampoo, and that intrinsically feminine scent that had the same effect on him as her tantalizing fingertips did. Why, when a man had been on the starvation diet from hell, did this woman smell so—damned—edible?

"They made Omar go with them," she whispered, "but they had to make an example of me before they left. I made them mad when I stood up to them, so they beat me with sticks and rods, with rifle butts. Thank heavens they left the children alone."

He held his breath. He knew all about Taliban discipline. It never ended well.

"Omar was just fourteen," she said softly, a glimmer of moisture welled up in the corner of her eye. "I still don't know what happened to him."

He reached a palm to her cheek, offering the only thing he had to give. Connection.

She seemed unable to speak, so he said the hard words for her: "They hurt you."

"They might have hit me, but Nizari was the one who ordered it. He was there." She squeezed her eyes tight, and his heart opened wide. It had been too long since he'd cried for anyone, but he wanted to now. Instead, he scrambled to his feet and scooped her into his arms, settling close to the headboard so her cuffed arm didn't have far to stretch. Protecting another was always better than being protected. Or pitied.

"Please don't be lying to me," he murmured. "Not about something like this. Not about that bastard, Nizari. I couldn't bear it."

"It's not," she squeaked, her voice tiny and timid, not this cat burglar's usual modus operandi. "That's why I said I recognized you. I see the same pain in your eyes. He hurt you, too." Sliding the robe off her shoulder, she covered her breasts with her palms while she revealed the ugly lash marks across her skin.

Lee turned her in his arms, needing to see it all. The robe pooled at her hips, but the hash marks of a wicked beating covered her back, even her arms. He didn't look farther. The marks continued low, no doubt to her backside, too. Damn it to hell. She'd been thoroughly thrashed. How could men do this to a woman as small as Tess? How could they do this to any woman? Anyone?

He helped her slide back into the sleeves and tugged the robe to her neck, concealing the terrible secret of her lush body along with the lovely temptation. A groan escaped his gut at the pain she'd endured. Breathing hard, Tess turned back around and leaned her head under his chin. Lee fought the wave of tender emotions for this woman curled up against him.

How could this have happened? What had God been thinking? This common thief, this crazy woman knew exactly what he felt. She not only knew, because many people knew what he'd gone through—she understood. She'd lived through the same kind of experience. She'd been there.

"You were lucky," he rasped, his arms circling her while he breathed deeply of her warm feminine scent, completely disarmed. "They usually kill foreign aid-workers they don't like."

"You were lucky, too," she said quietly, her fingers soft and tender on his scarred, bare chest, the place where no woman had touched him in a very long time. "They usually kill soldiers."

"I was lucky," he agreed, half-afraid she'd stop the gentle massage over his heart and half-afraid she wouldn't. *Lucky I met you.* The warmth of her palms and fingertips soothed with a power stronger than all the balms and ointments he'd used over the years to erase the scars and heal the memories. "Took 'em a few days, but my USMC squad hit back. Hit 'em hard. My guys dragged me out. Medivacked me to Bagram. Their team of trauma surgeons saved my life."

"I'm so sorry," she whispered.

"Yeah. Me too, but I'm good now." *Except for the nightmares.*

He wrapped his arms around her and held on tight. Sorry was such a small word. So was hate. It didn't come close to the depth of ugly feelings he carried for his tormentors.

The night of blessed noise came back to him, not the screams of other men being tortured for a change, not even his own screams, but instead, the *hack-hack-hack* rotor slap of Air Force choppers coming in low and deadly, laying down hellfire as they did. The God almighty vibration of heavy USMC APCs, Humvees, and MRAPs charging to the rescue. Nothing sounded better than the very welcome rapid-fire challenge of M16s and fifty-cals to AK-47s and bullshit Russian rifles.

Light 'em up, he'd thought that night, *and light me up with them. Please. Kill me now with friendly fire so that my time in Hell can end. Kill me with them if that's what it takes to send these bastards back to the deepest depths of Dante's fucking inferno.*

But the Corps' aim was true. No Americans died that night, and the sweetest sound he'd ever heard came to him in the guise of a battle-hardened gunnery sergeant with a pinpoint laser on his rifle rack. He'd come straight for Lee after he'd shot the lock off the cell door. Lowering him from the ceiling hook, that tough old leatherneck had cradled Lee as gently as a father might his brand-new baby. Lee's own mother had never sounded so tender or so sad. Lee still cried when he recalled the best words uttered that night. "I've got you, boy. Don't cry. You're going home."

Other men had died that night, and they were called Taliban assholes. Only one had escaped, the wickedest of all—Nizari.

Lee blew the ugly thought away with a deep breath and focused on the angel in his arms instead. Tess seemed content to be there, almost like she didn't want to leave. Like she was done fighting. "Where did you go? Who took care of you after they...?" He couldn't finish.

She rubbed her cheek against his scarred chest. "My brother."

The need to absorb this wild woman into his soul confounded Lee. Of all the people to have come into his life, why her? Why now? All he could do was breathe while he calmed himself at what they'd both endured. But he was angry she'd suffered, angrier than he was when Hasim Nizari had tortured him.

"I'd like to try something," he whispered. She lifted her eyes to his, and he had to ease her off his lap before he tried something different than what he intended. Those tender lips begged to be kissed, if not in thanks for sharing her secret, then just because they were close and looked as sweet as hell. Not much lower, the soft, creamy pillow of two seductive breasts begged for the same attention. He had to move away before he moved in to stay.

Locating his torn shirt on the floor, he tugged it over his head to cover his ugly body, and retrieved the handcuff keys from the nightstand at the other side of his bed. Without any hesitation, he gulped and unlocked her. "There. You're free to go. I won't keep you here anymore."

Lee took a step away from her, his hands at his side, still breathing hard and fully aware that Alex would have his head for this insubordination. Lee just couldn't do it anymore—couldn't hold Tess prisoner, not now that he knew what she'd lived through. No wonder she hated being cuffed. Hell, he did, too. "Go on." He nodded at the door. "Go. Just go."

She demurred. "I can't."

"Yeah, you can," he encouraged her. "I won't run you down. I won't hold you back. In fact, I'll call a cab. I'll help you get away."

She ducked her neck into her shoulders, and *damn*. A feminine blush danced across her cheeks. Genuine embarrassment glistened in her eyes. She wrinkled her nose. "I'm naked, remember?"

"Oh. Yeah." A flame of heat rushed him. He knew that. Really, he did. It was hard to miss that robe she had mostly on, but kind of off.

"Besides…" She took a step toward him.

He gulped and took a step back, but then he caught himself. She was all of five-feet-six in bare feet. Why was he running?

"I'd like to try something, too. You know, just to see what happens."

"No, Tess." He stopped her cold, breathing hard and wanting to try that exact same thing, but damn it, he was messed up beyond the norm and uglier than sin. No gal as beautiful as Tess should ever settle for less. For him. It wasn't fair to her, but deep down he knew better. Fear was a powerful deterrent, and he was plenty scared.

A shadow of hurt crossed her face, but still she advanced, tugging the sash loose on that very fluffy robe. The tiniest slice of her tasty body revealed itself as she took another step, the perfect line between her breasts, down her stomach, and all the way to Never-Never Land. He couldn't hear over his heavy breathing, and his heart had just launched itself into hyperspace. The reverberations of all those wonderful possibilities she'd just hinted at rattled him to his toes. Blastoff would definitely commence in Lee-minus-ten.

He shook his head to reaffirm his spoken denial. "No," he repeated weakly. "Just—no. I can't."

"But I think you can." By then she was directly in front of him, and his body was aimed in the right direction like the dummy it was, thick and hard and throbbing for her attention. That she was trembling didn't help. That she wasn't afraid of him or running in the opposite direction, or worse, kicking him in the crotch like she'd tried to before, confounded him. Women were such a mystery.

Slowly, she lifted to her tiptoes and reached one hand for his neck. His breath stalled. She was going to touch him, only this time he had a choice in the matter. Did he dare take that kind of risk again and let her? Did he have the guts to face the loneliest possibility in the world? Rejection? Worse, rejection by a beautiful woman with lovely eyes and a sinfully tempting body that he wanted to run his hands and lips, his fingers and his tongue all over?

Those damn violet-blues enticed him, and he succumbed like the weak man he was. There was no way to resist this woman. Slowly, he stooped to allow her to do that very foolish thing—to touch him. She was his client—in a way. He was her armed escort—in a way. Never the twain should meet. Until now. *In a way.*

Her slender fingertips at the back of his neck brought a world of warmth and comfort, feelings that had been foreign to him for too many years. Just those silky soft fingers on his bare skin poured the oddest sensation of peace over his scarred, knotted body. It felt like the sweetest, kindest rain edging over the toughened lines on his chest, running in sensual rivulets over the gnarled skin where Nizari had worked his red-hot blade like an insane artist.

Lee's heart thudded to a halt. How could he let her do this knowing how damaged he was? How could he allow her to get so close? Truth was he couldn't stop. She'd held all the power the minute she'd lifted to her toes. He stooped lower, his hand suddenly at the very warm small of her back, still outside her robe and afraid as hell to enter.

She no more than tilted her chin upwards when he fell. An enormous ball of fire ripped through him, blowing his negative opinions of himself into the universe with all those other fallen dreams and stars now restored to heaven. She moaned, her lips pressed against his, and a fire ignited—a fire that needed one outlet.

Her name was Tess.

Chapter Eleven

A solid knock at the door startled Tess, but she was lost in the warmth and hunger of Lee's arms. His mouth. His tongue. She'd never tasted a man as sweet as cinnamon honey. She curled her fingers in his hair and opened her lips, needing more of the tenderness pouring into her. More of his taste and his strength. This—*this!*—was heaven, a sensual feast she could never get enough of.

"Hey, Lee. You in there?" a man called from the other side of that damned door.

"Go away," she mumbled around the masculine tongue dancing with hers, tangling and untangling, probing and tasting. Needing her as much as she needed him.

Lee didn't budge, and Tess didn't dare. She maintained the contact, her bare breasts flattened to his T-shirt-covered chest. She couldn't let him go. Kissing him had started a nuclear reaction she didn't want to shut down. Not yet. He might be worried, but she'd felt the trembling, ropey muscles beneath his skin. Rock-solid shoulders descended to sculptured biceps and forearms that circled her in steel as if they'd never let her go. She burrowed into him, wanting under that shirt he'd just hidden behind. Wanting inside of his heart. Skin to skin. Soul to soul.

"Hey," he muttered into her mouth, his teeth softly nipping her lower lip as he ended the kiss. His tongue kept savoring, lingering on her lips and groaning even as he withdrew, almost like he couldn't get enough, like he couldn't bear to separate himself from her. Breathing heavily, he pressed her under his chin, his hands flat to her back, still not letting her go.

"I'm naked," she murmured, not sure why she'd said that other than she wanted him to tear the robe off and take all she had to offer. Whoever was on the other side of that door could wait. This opportunity might never come again.

"Believe me," Lee ground out, his voice deep and rumbling beneath her ear, "I know."

"Yo, Lee. Open up, man." The guy at the door was persistent.

"Damn it, Eric," Lee muttered softly. "Not now."

Tess turned, her arms still circling his waist, and her ear listening to his hammering heart. Intentionally, she spread her fingers up under his shirt and stroked those very strong back muscles as far up as she could reach, letting the constellation of scars on his back become her map, her universe. He growled, the sexiest, rumbliest sound she'd ever heard. In that instant, he'd transformed from a battle weary soldier into a Himalayan snow leopard that hadn't been petted in far too long. And she intended to handle every last inch of him until he purred.

"I have to answer the door," he explained, his breath coming in short, quick huffs. "Eric and Seth are here. I knew they were coming."

"Your sniper friends?" She remembered, still stroking, still gentling the beast beneath her fingertips.

"Yes," he breathed hotly, the smell of cinnamon reminding her of another close encounter in a dark warehouse. Was that all she was ever going to have with this man—close encounters?

Slowly, he extricated his hands from her until she relinquished him only because she had to. She stood there with her arms at her sides, unwilling to step away from the tender light radiating down upon her. Green had never shone so warmly. She placed both of her palms on his chest at each side of his sternum. A small murmur escaped his lips, but he didn't step away.

"Tess," he whispered, trembling beneath her touch, his palms covering her hands.

"Yes?" she asked breathlessly, not knowing what life-changing words he might utter next, but preparing herself for all possibilities. *'Love me,'* she commanded his heart. *'Want me,'* she ordered his soul. *'Take me,'* she wished with every fiber of her being.

"You're not dressed. Go hide in the bathroom," he whispered.

She blinked. Okay, that wasn't exactly what she wanted to hear, not now with her romance thermostat set on high. Make that hot and climbing, but what else could she do? "'Kay," she said softly. If he wanted obedience, she would give him that. For now. She closed her robe and stepped away.

"They won't stay long."

That made her smile. At least he had the good grace to sound hopeful.

"Coming," he muttered while he undid the chain lock and the deadbolt, offering her one last tender smile over his shoulder as he invited his buddies inside.

She closed the bathroom door quietly and turned to her reflection in the mirror. A very flushed but strange looking woman with bright dark eyes smiled shyly at her. With a toss of her head, Tess smiled back. When the woman in the mirror grinned, Tess giggled quietly to herself. That really, really happy woman was her. She touched the glass, her fingers to the outstretched fingers of that other person. "Hi," she whispered. "It's good to see you again."

"You got the video?" Lee asked from the other room, his voice nearly back to normal.

"Yeah. This was on your doorknob by the way," another deep voice answered. "Looks like the dry cleaners brought your lady friend's clothes back or something. Wonder what's in the brown paper bag. Should we check it out, Eric?"

"Damn, Seth. Give it to me." Tess smiled. Lee sounded protective.

"Look. It's lady's underwear. Where is the sexy gal this belongs to? Taking a shower?"

"I said give it to me."

Tess wanted to giggle. Seth was definitely given to profound understatements. She flushed the toilet just to provide a little authenticity to her activities in the bathroom, but then she couldn't hear the men's conversation. As soon as the toilet ceased gurgling, she pressed her ear to the door.

"I have another copy so go ahead and keep this one. You got a way to view it?" That husky male voice had to be Lee's friend, Eric. Tess listened, her ear flat to the door, trying to differentiate voices and personalities. Seth seemed playful, almost boyish, Eric more serious.

"Grab a seat. Let me see if there's a DVD player in the television cabinet." Definitely Lee.

"Brought one with me just in case." Seth. "Here's the cable. Should be easy to hook up unless your TV's too old."

"Good thinking." A deep, throaty chuckle. Eric again. Tess smiled to herself. That guy had to be a character. His sexy baritone oozed personality. "You're one surprise after another, buddy."

She listened as the three men tried to load the DVD, cussing when it didn't work. Someone flipped a few buttons to get the player to play. Seth wanted a beer. Lee told him to check the refrigerator in the corner and get it himself. Eric muttered about another hot day in paradise. The oddest sensation persisted. Here she was, half-dressed, a room away from three men, two of whom were total strangers, all of them snipers, but she felt not one bit of worry. Was it because Lee was there? And why did she suddenly trust him? Because they shared common experiences and a common enemy? Because she'd been given the privilege of seeing another side of him? Those seemed like good enough reasons to her.

The men quieted. They must've gotten the video loaded. Garbled voices and static at last evolved into Eric's tense voice. Then Seth's. A shot rang out. Then another, followed by an anguished cry from one of the men, she couldn't determine which.

"I figure," Seth said quietly, "that someone told Turik she'd be up there. How else would he know where to set up his rifle and which way to aim? I mean, really, he was positioned perfectly, his butt to Kabul and his scope on the palace rooftop, just waiting for her."

Tess's heart stopped. *Mohammed Turik? He tried to kill me? No, no, no. He's a friend. He wouldn't do that.*

"He knew exactly where she'd show," Eric muttered, "and the guy was prepared. He'd dug a shallow trench. He meant to stay there all night if he had to."

"Like he knew we'd be there too," Seth cut in. "He dug his hide alongside a drainage ditch, then hightailed it out of there when he missed Culver. We never saw him after he took that shot."

"But who told him?" Lee asked.

The men were quiet as the video ended, but Tess wanted to scream. *Clint! That's who! Damn him.* Was it possible? Had her own brother betrayed her? Lee said he'd split with a fifth of booze. Was he also low enough to get her shot? How much had he received for that cowardly act? It was nothing compared to what he was going to get from her. A flash fire called temper annihilated her common sense. Clint was going to die. All she had to do was catch up with him. And to think she'd paid him in advance to drive his truck? To catch her when she fell? He couldn't have hurt her worse if he'd missed her and she'd fallen to her death. He'd better run. That explained his unexplained absences over the last few months. He'd been hanging around with Mohammed, maybe the Taliban. *The jerk! The nerve!*

"It's not her brother," Lee declared as if he'd overheard her mental rant through the bathroom door. "It couldn't be. No way."

"Who else then?" Eric asked.

"Yes," Tess whispered to the closed door. "Who else knew I'd be on the palace roof last night? I only told Clint."

"Turik was at the orphanage where she works. You said so," Lee explained. "Maybe he overheard something."

"I never told him," she replied softly, but Lee was right. Mohammed did frequent the orphanage. He usually brought treats for the kids, not intrigue and deceit. Or did he? Her foot set to tapping. Come to think of it, he was also at the orphanage the day before that creep Nizari had her beaten. Was Mohammed behind all of this?

"She's just like her goofy brother, Lee," Eric muttered. "You can't trust her. Sounds like you're getting involved with—"

"You guys haven't spent any time with her to know what she's like," Lee snapped. "She's a lady. She's not like Clint Culver at all."

"And you have?" Eric shot the accusation.

Tess stilled, straining to believe she'd heard right. Lee thought she was a lady? What was he? Blind? She was no lady. If anything, she was more of a swashbuckling pirate. The kind opinion brought tears to her eyes. *He really thinks I'm a lady?*

"Hey," Eric groused. "You're the one who wanted the video. Show it to her. If nothing else, you can prove she's on somebody's radar. Let Miss Culver figure out who's trying to kill her."

She listened to the DVD being expelled from the player and the sound of a zipper, probably the camouflage covered bag she'd seen in the closet.

"I will," he answered, "but she's been through enough."

"Sounds to me like she's turned into your girlfriend pretty damned quick," Eric mumbled.

"She's not my girlfriend. Just a client. Any one of us could've drawn this duty. You want to trade?"

She stiffened at the door. *He wants to trade me?*

"No, I don't want to trade." Eric chuckled softly. "Don't get your knickers in a twist, Hart. It just looks real comfy in here with her in one bed and you in the other. Whose idea is that?"

"Shut it, Reynolds."

Eric chuckled. "There might just be hope for you yet."

Tess smiled. She agreed. There was hope for Lee. But not for Clint.

Maybe not for Mohammed, either.

The door had no more than shut behind Eric and Seth when Tess exited the bathroom, her face masked. One glance and Lee held his breath. The bossy woman was back in full force, the seductress gone. *Here it comes. Back to reality, dumbass.*

"I was listening," she said. "May I see the video?"

"Sure." He acquiesced quickly. The sooner she saw it, the better. Then they could get back to being nothing more than client and bodyguard.

He stuck the DVD in the player. Hitting the play button, he stepped back, his chin to his knuckles. She sat on the coffee table as the dark video played. Figures were hard to make out, but Seth had done a decent job capturing Eric's perturbed face over and over again. The view panned to the palace rooftop. Once again Seth exclaimed, "Wow, look at that guy run."

Lee observed Tess's reactions carefully while Eric and Seth decided she was that guy. The helmet-cam followed her to the edge of the roof. It panned back to Eric laying on his belly to the ground, his eye to his scope and a dark ball cap backward on his head. Just before he fired, Seth switched back to view the palace. There she stood on the edge of the roof, Tess Culver, the heroine all Kabul talked about, the infamous lady cat burglar who'd dared defy the Taliban over and over again. The sexy silhouette ready to plummet to her death, her arms spread, her hair billowing, and the bright floodlights behind her. God, what a sight.

Lee shifted his gaze from the screen back to Tess when the camera angle dropped to the ground. The spark from those two distinct shots Turik had taken cracked in the dark. Tess's hand lifted automatically to her tight lips. A tiny groan rose from the back of her throat, but there was the proof, damn it. Someone else was out there last night and that person was Mohammed Turik. She might as well face the facts. She'd been marked to die that night, and the only reason she hadn't was because Eric and Seth had busted Turik's ass, making him miss.

The pain in Seth's voice when he cried, "Oh, my God, she's gone," was difficult to miss. Lee turned the video off at that point, ejected it from the player, and waited for his client to make her move.

Tess turned on him, her hands on her hips, but her eyes glimmering. It struck Lee hard. This Mohammed Turik guy was no casual acquaintance. Miss Tess Culver had feelings for the bastard. What the hell was that about?

"How did Mohammed know I was going to be there?"

"You got me," Lee answered, stuffing the video back into his bag, annoyed that she could care for someone like that murdering assassin, Turik.

"But he knew where to set up his position. He knew right where to aim, didn't he?"

"Yes," Lee admitted. "He's good like that."

"I never told anyone what I planned, but my brother might have shot his big mouth off when he was drunk," she proposed. "He might have said something he shouldn't have."

Lee avoided her eyes. Their conversation could only go two ways, and both were uncomfortable. Either she delved deeper into the possibility that Clint was worse than a deadbeat, or she defended Turik. He went to the phone to order room service and to get back to business. "You hungry?" he asked, trying like hell to change the subject.

"My brother betrayed me," she mumbled somberly.

"No, he didn't," Lee said with conviction. "Someone else did. Probably Turik."

"That doesn't make sense. He was the one shooting at me, so someone had to have told him."

"Trust me. It wasn't Clint."

"But you said so yourself. You bribed him with a fifth of Jack." She crossed her arms over her chest and her toes set to tapping.

He shut his big mouth on the verge of sharing confidential information. "But he's not the one trying to kill you, Tess. Turik is. He's the one who took that shot, not your brother. I can't reveal how I know that it wasn't Clint who set you up; I just do. Trust me."

Tess nodded, her expression bleak while she contemplated the video.

"Pizza okay?" he tried again.

She nodded. "Yeah, I guess."

Clint seemed to be forgotten, at least, for then. Food was a definite hook for this sexy fish. Lee rolled the stress off his shoulders. Good enough. Pizza would work.

"What kind do you like?" She rose from the coffee table, glancing sideways, her body all kinds of slinky. Definitely slinky. "I'll bet you're a combination guy, heavy on the ham, Italian sausage, and pepperoni, maybe bacon, too. No anchovies. Extra cheese? Mushrooms?"

His gut clenched at the way she sidled toward him. Damn. She'd hit all his culinary weaknesses, except for the anchovies. He actually liked them.

Her tongue slid over her bottom lip before she headed his way. "Do you like a thick crust? A stuffed crust? Dripping with cheese? All moist and tender and succulent? Huh?"

Damn. This woman changed gears quickly. The way she drawled out succulent stopped him cold—ah, hot. Definitely hot. Violet-blue eyes held him with a black magic kind of a spell. She was still a couple feet away, but damn, he was frozen in place and going nowhere fast. All the intel in his top-secret mental vault was in danger of being revealed. "Or do you like it thin and hard? Crispy? Crackly?"

Man, everything off her tongue sounded just plain naughty. A man's heart should be smarter, but even his breathing seemed impaired. His brain sure was.

"And beer. I'll bet you're the kind of guy who likes a schooner of ice-cold draft with your steaming slice of hot, melting pizza. Lots of it in a frosted mug. Always Heineken? How about Dos Equis? Coors?"

Honestly, all he heard was steaming—hot—sex.

The phone clattered to the floor. Heck, it could've floated to outer space for all he knew. She made pizza and beer sound erotic as hell. She might be talking food, but her body was saying something else. The sash on her robe hung loose, revealing another meal. The thermostat in the room must've failed. Lee fought the urge to strip his shirt off again.

"Umm, yeah. Beer." Not one of his more intelligent statements.

"And garlic bread, all buttery and salty?"

He licked his lips. *Buttery. Salty. Sweaty.*

She took another step, her voice low, and her lovely hips swaying. Heck, all of her swayed and tantalized. She'd turned fluid, warm and inviting, buttery and salty. The svelte seductress was back, and damn, she was already on top of him and rocking his socks off. He licked his lips again before it dawned on him that his mouth was hanging open. He shut it.

"I like pizza,'" he admitted hoarsely. There was no way to sound smart. She stalked him, but he had yet to take one step back.

Her hand lifted to his chest, and he let her touch him again, square on the thin red line that went from below the hollow of his neck to his navel. Nizari had never cut deep enough to kill, only enough to make a man bleed, cry, and suffer. Tremors roared up his legs, over his butt, and on up his back. Client/agent rules flitted around his head like they might be important to someone, somewhere.

"Don't," he offered quietly, trying to salvage his tattered professional persona. "You're my client. Let's just eat and call it good."

"I bet it'll be more than just good," she whispered, her breasts on the verge of spilling into his hands. He'd catch them, oh yes, he would. "You don't have to do anything you don't want to, Lee Hart."

And when did a guy refuse that kind of offering? Once again, she was up on her tiptoes, and he automatically did the gentlemanly thing. He crouched to her level like a dumbass that said one thing and did another. He warned her off even as he pulled her forward, his body and his hands on automatic pilot. "This isn't a good idea."

"I think it is," she coaxed, her fingers shooting unseen sparks all the way to his groin. "You're my Alexander."

Whatever that meant. Alex Stewart was Alexander—not him. The scent of this woman filled him, and he was losing ground fast. Too fast. The pizza had better get there soon. Oh wait. He hadn't ordered it yet. Lee gulped. He was a dead man.

"Tess," he whispered, because his commanding voice had turned tail and run, the coward. "Stop. I can't do this. I'm not ready." *And this isn't real. I'm still dreaming. No woman wants a guy like me.*

She stopped, but by then she was inches away, and his brain was dying from lack of oxygen. Thinking was hard, umm, difficult, oh hell—everything was hard.

"Besides, you're in my care. My professional care," he emphasized, knowing he needed to step back. Wishing he could.

She nodded, her eyes still fixed on his. The light in them changed from predator to beguiling. "I understand," she whispered with a small nod. The rivers of ebony curls nodded, too. "Really, I do. Some days I don't feel like I belong anywhere, either. It's like everyone knows what happened to me, like the whole world stood there and watched while they beat me nearly to death, but no one was brave enough to lift a hand to help. Like no one cared. Like what those cruel men did to me was insignificant." Her long fingers trembled on his chest. "And I'm angry and hurt all over again. I don't understand cruelty or war or... anything. Some days I don't know who I am. That's why I steal from them. I can't let them win. I have to be me again. You understand, don't you, Lee?"

Once again—direct hit. He lost the war right then and there. This crazy, foolish, risk-taking woman knew him inside out. She'd read him like she'd written his playbook. His hands slid down her arms to her slender waist. He took possession of her body and pressed her under his chin so he didn't have to look into those compelling violet blues. Her robe had parted, her bare breasts pressed against his T-shirt again. Against his chest. Her heart pounded, hot and steady. He squeezed her so she couldn't feel him shaking.

"You're taking yourself back by just being here," he said as the lovely smell of shampoo filled his nostrils. "It's a slow process. Just don't stop being brave. Keep yourself safe and alive. That way they can't win."

She wrapped her arms around him, her fingers splayed on his shoulder blades. "I'm not that person they left behind that day. I'm stronger. So are you. It's been four years for me."

"Me too," he acknowledged. That she and he had tangled with Nizari and both survived around the same timeframe was a freakishly bizarre coincidence. "May," he pinpointed the month.

"Yes," Tess whispered, her breath feather-soft on his neck. "The end of May, four years ago." A shudder raced over her shoulders, the kind of shudder a guy like Lee instantly smothered with his big hands. Logic gently nagged she might still be playing him, but he couldn't deny the scars on her back nor that she seemed to know what he'd suffered on a fundamental, maybe even an elemental level. As if she'd been there in the cell when it all went down.

"Tess, I'm sorry. I'm really not ready for... whatever's going on between us this evening," he repeated. What an odd thing for a man to admit, but it was true. Lee Hart didn't do one-night stands. Ever. As difficult as this was, he would walk away from this tempting offer. He would lift his mind out of the gutter, take his mental hand off her ass, and be a good and decent man. Any minute now.

She let him off the hook even as she hugged him tighter. "I feel like I already know you, like we've done this before."

"We do have a couple things in common. That's all," he rationalized. It made sense. Were all trauma survivors linked like he and she seemed to be? Could they read each other's minds like she seemed capable of doing to him? *Maybe...*

Minutes passed and his heart calmed. Having something so uniquely tragic in common with Tess helped. He couldn't explain it, but holding her and knowing what she'd lived through was a powerful balm. She wasn't disgusted to touch him any more than he was to touch her. He could almost believe he was human again. Maybe even worthy.

She looked up from her very secure place in his arms, pulling him in with just the blink of her lashes. "You order the pizza. I'm going to wash my hair before it comes. Sound good enough for now?"

He nodded. She had to go. He had to let her, so, he did. He released her slowly and took that all-important step back, his heart not pounding quite as hard nor hurting as much as he'd expected. She offered that smile again, that soft lift at the corners of her mouth.

"I'll order pizza," he growled to confirm his wavering conviction.

And then I need a cold shower.

Chapter Twelve

Lee might not be ready for sex, but she was. The moment she doffed her robe, Tess stepped under the warm shower spray and let it caress the parts of her back and sides where his hands had just been. She didn't need to wash her hair. It just seemed that he needed space, so she gave it to him.

The hot water felt good, soothing all those too-eager parts of hers back into normalcy. Not climbing up that handsome rugged body had taken every last shred of her willpower. Never before had she wanted to assault a man for purely sexual reasons. The stark reality of all that longing and sexual tension she'd stifled for way too long swept through her like the water sluicing over her shoulders. Everything about Lee Hart declared him an honorable man. He might see himself as damaged. She didn't. Not. One. Bit.

Tenderness for him welled up inside along with a powerful dose of wanton lust. How she could feel two such powerful feelings for this stranger amazed her, but he was right. They didn't really know each other. She needed to calm down before she got herself in trouble.

With her hands to the tile below the showerhead, she gathered her wits and let her mind wander to his nightmare and the scars on his back. Nizari had been methodical in his torture. It must've taken days. The very real possibility that the same perverse madman linked her and Lee stole her breath. Hasim Nizari. The most evil of the Taliban.

The thought of his cold-blooded cruelty brought shivers even in the steamy shower. Tess scrubbed her arms. She'd never get clean enough or far enough from the memory of that awful day. For all her tough determination, that shattered part of her still remained, tucked inside and scared to death it could happen again, that he could order her bound and beaten anytime he wanted.

She comforted the weaker person she once was. *Take a deep breath, Tess. Think of something else. Fight back. Steal another treasure. Prove you're smarter than he is. Never let him win.*

Another deep breath in and her thoughts shifted to Agent Lee Hart and the adorable look on his face when she'd tried to seduce him. Ah, the man's willpower was stronger than she'd expected, probably the best thing given their circumstances. She didn't need the complications of a good man in her life. And Lee Hart was a good man, an honorable man who just happened to be her bodyguard. Nothing more. They had an amicable situation between them. That was all. She'd stay on her side of the room. He'd stay on his. They'd eat pizza and watch television together for the rest of the night. Nothing else. It just wasn't meant to be.

She blew out another soul-cleansing sigh, poured a dollop of shampoo into her palm and began to wash her hair. The clean fragrance of Lily of the Valley soothed her anxious spirit. Only one thing worked better to center her soul. She opened her mouth to sing. A gospel song came out. The words of the hymn filled her private sanctuary of steam, and once again, she was saved.

The worries of the day slipped away. She was Tess Culver again, the cat burglar of Kabul, the invincible, a troublemaker to the notorious Taliban, a woman who'd found a way to strike back at the tyrants who pillaged and raped the weak. She didn't have to prove anything to anybody but herself. The weight of past memories lifted. She raised her voice to God. "I once was lost, but now I'm found. Was blind..."

Tess sang the first verse of the beloved hymn through as she washed and rinsed her hair. Slippery suds slid down her body and into the drain. She pictured that wicked day and all the sadness of it going down the drain with the suds. The steam and heat felt good, easing aching muscles from her adventurous night before. When she applied the last of the crème rinse, fresh lavender and mint filled the room. She took a deep whiff and began the song again, belting out, "Amazing... grace..."

Tess paused. Had the bathroom door just closed with a quiet click? The shower curtain revealed a shadowy figure beyond her sanctuary. Lee? She peeked around the curtain, keeping herself covered and blinking the water out of her eyes. It was him all right.

He stood there, his arms crossed and his chest heaving. "You're singing." His voice was tight with accusation and some other emotion she couldn't identify. How that big strong guy could look so vulnerable ripped her heart out. It seemed Lee still floundered through the muck inside his head where his past reality had been viciously jerked away from him. He was still trying to catch hold of the person he used to be. Half of him was Peter Pan, the other half, that annoying shadow he'd never be able to stitch to the bottom of his feet again. He couldn't step forward while that elusive part of him was stuck in a past that didn't exist.

Extending her hand, Tess gulped, but offered him the company of her steamy sanctuary. "I like to sing when I'm happy. Join me?"

He looked so angry standing there glaring at her, his chin to his chest, licking his lips like he was. She waited. Did he want to shower with her or not? Did he want her to shut up and stop singing? Tess couldn't tell. She curled her fingers urging him forward. "Come on, Lee."

Of all things, a wave of fear sliced through her brazen confidence. The man honestly commanded the space around him. He was dressed. She was not. Not a good combination. Angry energy filled the tiny room. He looked fiercer than before, as if confrontation with a naked woman took all of his courage. Dark emerald eyes skated over her breasts and down her belly to the juncture of her legs.

She bit her lip and gulped, waving him forward instead of covering her nakedness or crossing her legs to hide what he'd already seen. "We could sing together," she offered timidly. "The song could use a good, strong baritone. Come on in. The water's fine."

The crazy man pushed the curtain aside, and just like that, he was in the shower with her. Fully dressed. Gray running pants and T-shirt. Gray socks. Staring at her, the water dripping down his face, over those hostile brows and off his nose. His brows spiked and veins etched his forehead. Fiery green eyes scorched her naked body down to her bare toes.

"You look a little overdressed," she murmured, suddenly more shy than she'd expected to be and more than a little afraid. Hadn't he just very definitely said 'no'? Then why was he there? What did he really want? Intimidation? He had it in spades. Was this when he might hit her?

"Sing," he ground out, his nostrils flared as the shower drenched that tousled head of reddish brown hair, darkening the fire in it, but not the flames burning in his eyes. Silvery rivulets ran down his face, sluicing off his cheeks and dripping along the hard edge of his jaw.

"Okay, umm, is 'Amazing Grace' okay?" She used her softest voice to calm him as she took back her control. The line about music taming the savage beast came to her. Lee definitely had the savage beast routine down, but she was willing to bet this entire tough-guy act was one big bluff. Darkness coiled beneath those thick, tensed muscles, but Lee hadn't hurt her before. He wouldn't hurt her now. He was just tormented by devils he couldn't wrangle, emotions he hadn't come to grips with.

So she sang, quietly at first, moving him directly beneath the shower as the first verse rolled out. He'd moved like a wooden soldier, stiff and resistant, and "Amazing Grace" sounded a little squeaky, but not for long.

At the second verse, she lifted the bottom of his shirt and held it, letting her eyes ask the question as the song and warm water worked its magic. He tensed, and she would've obeyed if he'd hinted that no, this wasn't what he wanted, but with a quick, curt nod he gave her the go-ahead. He blew out a breath that caressed her breasts when she eased the fabric up. He raised his arms to let her pull it over his head and off.

Without asking and still singing, she dropped the shirt and reached for the bath wash while she started the next chorus. Filling her hands with soap, she began a slow, soft scrub across his hair-roughed chest and abdominal muscles. His scars.

The man had some serious power beneath his anxious panting. His shoulders rippled all the way to his elbows. The cords of his neck were clenched so tightly, she wanted to throw him down to the tiled floor and massage the heck out of him. Sheets of water sluiced over that wide chest, rippling between his pecs and down his furrowed six-pack.

Tess kept her touch gentle and her voice sweet. A world of latent anger lay beneath the tortured surface of this savage beast. She'd never wanted to tame one—until now.

His poor ribs had taken the brunt of Nizari's knife. Thin scars. Razor thin. So much pain and agony had been etched on his body. All his scars were healed, but she knew the truth. Each angry mark was a portal back in time to that ugly day. He could run from it all his life and never get away, because he took it with him. Every lash. Every hit. Every cut.

Without asking, she lifted up on her toes and planted a row of kisses along the scar that ran from collarbone to collarbone. Her breasts skimmed over the roughness of his chest. His breath hitched. So did hers. But this wasn't about sex. Foreplay, maybe. Not sex. Not yet. This gentle man required hands-on therapy first.

Despite the noisy cadence of her heartbeat, she lowered her lashes and resumed singing. At the third verse, she'd washed as much of his skin as she'd bared. It was time to get brave, but when she slid her fingertips along his waistband, Lee stiffened. A groan grumbled up from his gut. He clenched her hand. "No."

She lifted her gaze to meet his, and the same fierce green stabbed at her. She hesitated. He looked angry, but confused. Climbing into her shower fully dressed was his idea. He had to lead—or let her.

He drew in a deep breath. Again came the quick nod, and she faltered. Drops of water clung to his eyelashes, giving him a little-boy quality. This wasn't therapy any more. She wasn't helping just him. She needed this next step, too. The order of the verses jumbled in her mind. "'Tis Grace that brought me safe thus far..." she sang timidly.

Very slowly, she slid her fingers beneath the waistband at his hips and let them rest there. *What on earth did this have to do with Heaven's almighty grace?* Tess worked massaging circles over his hipbones, the pads of her thumbs pressed into the inner crease of his thigh. She girded her loins and pressed on.

Never in her life had she felt more exposed or so unsure. This was uncharted territory; this "Amazing Grace" therapy that seemed to be helping a man brimmed to overflowing with his wretched past. He stared down at her, his tongue skimming his lower lip as his eyes flickered over her nakedness. The fierce angry green had softened with another, more dangerous light. Darker. Ominous.

Her heart lodged in her throat, constricting her airflow with its every pulsing beat. "And grace will lead me home..." She let the song linger, humming the melody because she could no longer remember the words, and her voice had grown too tremulous to project anything close to confidence. Her heart pounded with the audacity of her actions. *Why do I always have to push one step too far? Why can't I leave well enough alone? Why is he here?*

Slowly, she knelt and eased the gray pants to the floor, leaving him only in boxers and socks. Looking up at him, past thighs as big as small tree trunks, brought the oddest sensation. This man whom she barely knew exuded shuddering waves of raw masculinity. He was damaged, yes, but what a sight, him standing over her like some angry god, his fists clenched, his bulk shielding her from the spray. Lightning might flash at any moment. Thunder might boom. He shoved the soggy pants behind him with one quick kick.

She'd already seen the black pockmarks on his stomach. They seemed sporadically placed, but she recognized them for what they were. Burns. Her heart pitched. The frightened voice of that little boy from the nightmare revisited her mind. Did he scream when they'd tortured him? Did he grit his teeth and writhe and hold it all inside when they carved into him and burned his skin? Did he cry? Suddenly, she needed to know.

Still crouching before him, she rested her fingers on his feet, not sure she had the strength to continue. The shape beneath the socks appeared normal, so he had all his toes. That much was good. Without asking permission this time, she unrolled the socks to his ankles. He flattened his palms to the tiled shower walls and lifted first one foot, then the other as she bared his feet.

Her heart stopped. Discolored rings revealed where the flesh had been burned nearly to the bone from electrical wires. All his toenails were gone. His toes were black. The kind of blackening that would never go away. The kind of torture the Taliban was known for. *Damn.* Suddenly, her brazen decision to seduce Lee Hart seemed more cruel than helpful. She'd pushed too hard this time. He'd been hurt and trying to hide it, but she'd egged him on.

The spray hid her tears but not the pain rising up in her throat, tearing her heart out. How could she look him in the eye? How could she not?

"Tess," he whispered hoarsely, his hand cupping the back of her head. He tugged her to her feet and pulled her close.

The moment her cheek caressed his bare chest, the tears fell. She bowed her head, not letting him see. It wasn't pity she felt. It was something else—something that truly scared her. She wanted to give her heart to him—all of it.

"I sang that same song," he said quietly, "the whole time I was held prisoner. I sang it every day and all night. Before and after. They came and they went. It was all that kept me sane. When you started singing, I don't know what came over me. I had to hear—more."

She listened and tried very hard to breathe normally without sobbing. This brave warrior was a survivor. He didn't need pity, and she had none to give.

"In my head," he whispered. "I couldn't let them hear me, so I sang it in my head. Over and over. Every day. All day. All night, too."

She wrapped her arms around his waist, fully aware the only article of clothing between them was his drenched boxers, ready to be gone but only when he decided. She would've settled for simply sexually assaulting him before. Now she wanted that same more.

Large masculine hands caressed her back, smoothing over her shoulders and neck to sink lower to her hips and her backside. At last, they cupped her bottom. So gentle. So strong. The paradox of the world of men puzzled her. She knew the strength of this man who held her now. Lee Hart was big enough to take the world apart if he wanted to. He could hurt her. He just wouldn't.

"That song saved me." He nuzzled his nose into her wet hair, pushing it aside to reach her skin. Soft nibbles graced the line of her neck. The sensual warmth of his tongue outlined her ear, and she shivered all the way to her toes. "It saved me then like you're saving me now," he whispered. "I couldn't before, but I'd like to sing it with you now."

"Yes," was all her squeaky voice could muster.

He pressed her ear to his chest, his big hands on her back, and Lee began the first verse again. How odd. He wanted to sing at a time when most other men would've wanted sex. Odder still, Lee's deep rich voice didn't drown her soprano out, not even when he lifted his face to the ceiling and the song felt more like a prayer of truly amazing grace.

She wept openly, her voice hoarse, and her heart full for this incredible man. There they stood, singing in the rain, only each verse rang differently now. Each truly spoke of being desperately lost and then amazingly found. Of being valued. Of being loved even during the worst of times. A ragged sob caught in her throat. The song was her wretched story come to life. Finally found. Finally safe. Home at last.

When the duet ended, he tipped her chin, his mouth so close the water ran from his lips to hers, a trickle of life-giving, soul-saving grace. "May I?" he asked, his deep voice resonating through the sins of her willful soul. Claiming her. Redeeming her.

She blinked, not understanding what he was asking permission for, not needing to know, either. The trust in those green eyes encompassed her in a shivery kind of warmth that had nothing to do with the now cold shower. Her soul trembled. Her faith.

"Yes," she answered meekly. *Forever. Yes.*

He leaned down, lifting her into his arms as easily as he would a child. "I'm ready now, Tess."

"Me too," she whispered, her voice suddenly too soft for the tough woman she was.

He turned the shower off and parted the curtain. She didn't remember him opening the bathroom door, only that he wrapped her in a towel. When he placed her on his bed, he did it so carefully she felt like one of those stolen museum artifacts of immeasurable worth. Like she was priceless.

Like Agent Lee Hart might love her enough to stay.

I once was lost, but now I'm found.

The line of the song filled Lee with the strongest feelings for the woman in his arms. Tess rested sweet and seductive alongside him. He'd dropped his waterlogged boxers to the bathroom floor before he'd joined her on the bed, and now they lay together, the pizza still unordered, but his appetite about to be satisfied.

Was this love? He held her in his arms and prayed it was. Could he wait to find it in his life? No more. The fire between them drew him onward. Somehow, an ember had always existed between him and this rare exotic creature, a link he couldn't deny. Not one made of gold, but of something more priceless than time itself.

"Tess," he breathed, closing his eyes only to mentally whisper her name again and again, an echo he didn't want to lose. She halted further conversation, her hands on the sides of his face, pulling him into her mouth. Fire swept through him, up from his toes, his thighs, his spine.

Somewhere in the back of his mind a voice whispered that an agent shouldn't engage in sex with a client, but somewhere else in his heart, the forces of nature conspired to do just that. Tess Culver wasn't just another client. This was the woman he was going to make love with for the rest of his life. This was Tess. His woman. His soul. And if it wasn't the right time to tell her, he could at least show her.

Her hands roamed freely over him, never pausing a second as she stroked and petted his ribs and waist down to his hips. She had no problem touching his skin or his scars. Never flinched. Never grunted with disgust. Just covered him with what his body craved—her sweet touch. Her tender kisses.

The animal inside him flexed its unused lustful muscles and growled in compliance. Her eyes lit with that same fire. All that wet hair turned into writhing fingers that pulled him onward as they tumbled together, caught in the rhythm and beat of a song of lust as old as life. Like threads, it weaved a silky connection, binding them together in passion and fire.

He let his fingertips explore the silky softness of her breasts, to feel the weight of those plump delights that surely craved his tongue as much as their tips peaked and hardened. He savored both, nipping and suckling to arouse her body the way she had done with his.

One knee found its way between hers, and soon, he was wrapped intimately inside the tight, silky sheath of her sexy body. The movies always showed fireworks, but this pleasure felt more like piled-high-in-the-sky thundering storm clouds that lifted Lee to the stars before they crashed him down. Down. Down into ecstasy. Down into Tess. Again and again. He clutched the cheeks of her sweet ass, pushing all his love deep inside of her. Claiming her.

I love you, Tess. The words escaped the filter of his heart, but not his mouth. He cringed even as he gave her all he had to give. *Too soon to think like that, dumbass. Way too soon.*

Yet it felt right. This was no temporary thing, no one-night stand. He pushed himself deeply into her again and offered more, proving the depth of his love in every physical way possible while she opened her tender body wide to receive him. She'd so willingly offered herself as a gift. The perfect gift.

When the storm was spent but the thunder still hummed loud and strong between them, his large body covered her smaller one. Their hearts pounded as one, a synchronization of souls taking place. A definite realignment in the universe. He had no more to give, and yet the temptation of her luscious body tantalized him. Still enticed and teased. He nipped her earlobe, enjoying the taste of her silky skin on his tongue, the scent of her feminine fragrance in his nose.

Her fingers laced around his ears and pushed him back. He didn't want to look into her eyes, not yet. He didn't want to read in them how dumb an idea this was, how she didn't really know how to jump from hot, steamy sex to saying goodbye.

"Lee," she whispered, the tip of her tongue soft at the end of his nose.

He groaned. Hell. He might've just gotten her pregnant for all the pre-planning he'd put into this very important moment in their life. Even that thought stabbed him with remorse. *Their life?* Was there such a thing?

He should've been more careful. There was no "their life" yet. There was only her and him, two strangers who'd gotten carried away. A smarter man would've been more careful. Agent/client privilege didn't include jumping the client's bones at the first opportunity. *What have I done?*

She bucked softly against him with her hips, not enough to dislodge him but enough to get his attention. "Will you open your eyes and look at me?"

He couldn't help but smile. Tess was the sassiest, bossiest, most determined woman he'd ever known. He lifted his head just enough to stare nose to nose into her eyes. Violet-blue light bathed him in tenderness. Not one speck of indifference or disgust glimmered there. Only the bathroom light behind them shone on their feet and backsides. How could she glow in the shadow of his love like she was?

His doubt fled. He tunneled his fingers into her dark curls to brace her head as he kissed her deeply.

"You're amazing," she whispered, her breath mingling with his. He inhaled deeply and slowly, breathing her into the vast emptiness that until then was him. Arching her body against his, from bone to bone and heart to heart, she kissed his mouth with sudden ferocity. "I... can't believe you're here. With me. L-like this."

That sounded promising, but it also sounded as if she'd caught herself before she said the L word, too. *Not yet, Tess. Let's slow down. Let's not say it yet. Just show me. I'll prove I love you and you prove you love me.*

Another ember glowed, this one the deepest amethyst in her eyes, and he was hungry all over again. Nipping her bottom lip, he began to feast again on delicate feminine flesh that outdid pizza any day. Her ruby red lips were finally smudged and bruised. Branded.

He trailed a path of heated adoration down her chin with his mouth, the urge to devour her ramping up again. She lifted her head allowing him fuller access to her neck, and he obliged, his nose full of her sensual fragrance and his tongue in foreplay heaven. She stiffened beneath him when he buried his nose in her hair, kissing the edge of her ear and working his way slowly down her jaw and neck only to return to her lips again. Everything about her body called to him, but for now, he wanted the joy of consuming those beautiful, sassy lips.

Her hands roamed over his back and down his ribs while he concentrated on a way to get enough of her. There wasn't one. She'd become his drug of choice, a sweet addiction of coconut and vanilla now steeped in cinnamon and the scent of two bodies already joined—the scent of sex and sweat. He returned from a foray of licks along her throat to her mouth again, nipping, tasting, and hopelessly in love with her lips. With all of her.

He shouldn't have been. The emotion was too soon and so sudden, but here he was, nibbling sweetness from a woman who somehow knew him inside out. Her fingers stretched soft and warm over his back and down his backside, digging her nails into the cheek of his ass and asking for more. The heat between them lurched into fire. He rained kisses, hotter and hotter on her cheeks and forehead, on her tender eyelids and softly pulsing temples. In his mind, every touch from him to her was a brand that marked her, while every touch from her to him felt like life itself. His heart was full.

When he framed her face with his big hands and tipped her chin up with his thumb to begin another assault down her neck, he heard her coming undone. Amazing. The feminine growl of this woman's unleashed passion bestowed though the simple act of kissing pleasured him beyond belief. He restrained himself from interrupting her moment with his needs and simply held her close while she stiffened and shuddered through the waves of another climax. How terribly sweet that just his kisses brought her to the peak of joy? He grinned, proud of himself for remembering how to please a woman. This woman.

She panted beneath him, the softness of her overheated body clutching him tightly while aftershocks rippled through her. There was much he didn't know about this exquisite treasure, more he wanted to do with and to her. He licked his lips, and then he licked hers, tracing the circle of her sensual mouth as her tongue followed suit. Sinking against her, he cradled the head of the very beautiful Tess Culver, the notorious cat burglar of Kabul, in his big hands.

Nose to nose, he breathed in the sigh of a satisfied woman. She filled him more than his body could ever fill hers. She was his, only his and all his.

So he started again.

Chapter Thirteen

The pizza finally came. It was good. The conversation was better.

"You have a boat? Really?" Tess asked. They were cross-legged on the bed, the pizza box spread beside them, and discussing any subject that came up. He hadn't put another shirt back on, and that alone was a significant first step. She'd snagged it when he didn't use it. For now, that was all she wore over her freshly laundered underwear. He wore a clean pair of boxers, but his hairy legs were still bare and hard to keep her hands off of. The compulsion to touch and pet him persisted. It took all of her self-control to not. He insisted on replacing his socks, though. The sheets and blankets were somewhere on the floor.

Lee shrugged. "It's no big deal. It's not a fancy yacht, just a rugged little sailboat."

"Is it very big?"

"Nah. Twenty-seven feet. Six berths if you forgo storage space. It's got an enclosed head. A built-in shower. Lots of deck space. I think you'd like it."

"That sounds big to me," she said, her eyes on his legs again. Lee was sculptured granite with a few nicks that only added to his appeal. Muscular calves expanded when he moved. He was eye-candy in motion. Her respect for him just kept growing. He was a survivor the same as she was. That meant he was tough, but fragile. Maybe a little crazy. Her heart flip-flopped. They had an awful lot in common for two people who'd just met.

"Hey, you." He tapped the tip of her nose. "Where'd you fade away to?"

She jerked her mind away from her introspection. "I was imagining you out on the ocean. You have a seafarer look about you."

"I look like a pirate?" He arched a wicked brow. "Aye, aye, Matey."

"Not exactly." She looked into the gentle green eyes of the man who'd kidnapped her. How had this happened? Last night she'd hated him, but now? He'd become important in a way she couldn't explain. "You have that far-away look sometimes, like you're thinking too hard or watching the horizon. Like you have somewhere else to be."

"I do, huh?" He rolled his eyes and wiggled his brows. "You ought to come with me some day. I'm sailing the Atlantic when I'm done with this op. You'd like it. It's... sufficient."

That odd statement made her realize how little she knew about Lee. "Sufficient? What's that supposed to mean?"

He winked. "It means I'm not looking to be the richest, the most powerful, or the smartest guy in the world. It's something my mom used to say. I am what I am. I want just enough that I can comfortably live my life. I want to die a happy man with my boots on."

"Wow," she murmured. "That's kind of deep."

"Nah. It's just life." That far-away look had just skated across his face before he ripped another mouthful from his fifth slice of pizza. The man could eat, and it made Tess smile.

It was late evening. Three bottles of beer were already gone, and he seemed relaxed. All that sex hadn't hurt, either. Neither did the fact that he now knew she was on birth control. Tess smiled to herself. She should've told him earlier. He might have been able to enjoy himself a little more.

She had to admit, never before had she craved kissing a man like she did Lee. That he'd been able to shatter her merely using his lips on her mouth was the best surprise of all. His fingertips worked wonders, but his mouth? To die for. Tasty. Persuasive. So damned delectably hot.

"What'd you mean when you said I was your Alexander?" he asked.

She reached her index finger to his mouth and traced pizza crumbs to the tip of his waiting tongue, wondering which of them craved the other more. He'd ignited an insatiable part of her soul. "You know, Alexander the Great. The conqueror of the world."

Lee cocked a devilish brow. "What you talking about?"

"You don't know about his great love?"

"Wait a minute. Was he great or was his love great? Which is it? It can't be both." He teased, and she giggled. Lee Hart was a funny guy. His hair, curled and messy after his impromptu shower and their ravishingly good sex, gave him a boyish charm. Now that his guard was down, he was playful. He hadn't lost that serious core, but neither was he focused on his shortcomings.

"Do I need to tell you a bedtime story?" she asked demurely.

"Yes, ma'am, you do." He grabbed another piece of pizza, set his beer on the nightstand, shoved the pizza box away, and flopped his gorgeous head onto her lap, his knees bent.

"Well..." She combed her fingertips into deep, deep mahogany, smiling at the charming man chewing pizza and grinning up at her like he didn't have a care in the world. It was hard to believe he'd made love to her as thoroughly as he had. As gently. "A long time ago in a galaxy far, far away..."

"Give me a little credit," he interrupted. "Alexander the Great was never on *Star Wars*."

She kissed his forehead, an ache beginning to build deep in her soul for this incredible man. "But it *was* a long time ago—more than two thousand years."

Lee nodded and chewed, talking with his mouth half-full. "Around 300 B.C., maybe a little sooner, right?"

"Ahh. You're smarter than you look." Now it was her turn to tease.

"Keep it up and you'll see just how smart I am," he rumbled. "You ready for more?"

She put a fingertip to his lips. "Behave. Story first."

He growled petulantly, and she started again. "When Alexander first came to this part of the world, he wasn't much older than us, and—"

"Wait a minute. How old *are* you?"

"You dare to ask a woman her age in the middle of a bedtime story?" She pretended offense.

"I'm just thinking I should've asked sooner, too. I might've committed a crime against a minor and—"

"Oh, hush." She ruffled her fingers through his hair playfully.

"You're over eighteen though, right?"

"Yes, sir, I'm twenty-nine. And you?"

"Thirty-one." He finished that slice of pizza and licked his fingers. "Good. My information was correct. You're legal. You may continue."

"I may, huh?" She took a deep breath and started again. "Alexander was determined to rule the world. He'd already beaten the powerful Persian King, Darius the Third. Spring had come to the Bactria, but the stone mountains were still covered with snow. A fierce mountain people lived there, very wealthy and arrogant. They scoffed at this audacious young general named Alexander despite his reputation for conquering nations and the massive army he'd brought with him. Their pride proved their undoing. Alexander's bravest soldiers worked night and day to scale the steep mountain walls. At last, the proud mountain people's defenses were breached. They had no choice but to surrender and submit to his will."

"Sounds tactically smart to me." He finished his pizza and lay peacefully twisting a strand of her hair between his fingers, pausing to lift it to his nose. Every time he did, he closed his eyes and breathed deeply like he couldn't get enough of her scent.

"One morning, Alexander saw the beautiful daughter of one of the noblemen he'd taken captive, Roxana. The legend says her golden hair gleamed brighter than the wheat fields of the Kunar. The precious beads and golden ornaments dangling over her face and head were nothing in comparison to her exotic beauty." Tess smoothed her index finger over his lip. "You see Alexander was smitten. He told his closest generals Roxana had stolen his soul with one breath, that he couldn't regain it until he made her his."

Lee lifted a hand to her cheek. "I know how he felt."

Tess rubbed her cheek into his palm, craving everything about this man. "On the day Alexander and Roxana were wed, more than ten thousand of his men also took wives from the mountain people."

"Whew," Lee sighed. "That's a lot of 'I dos'. Does this mountain kingdom have a name?"

"Sogdiana, the ancient land that is now Tajikistan and Uzbekistan. But it wasn't an unwilling marriage for strategic influence, as historians have portrayed it. Oh no. Alexander and Roxana's love was a thing of destiny. It is said the larks in the meadow gathered in chorus when he and his beloved walked by. The great eagles of the sky offered aerial escort. Even the lonely wolf became more loyal guardian than beast, trailing behind them like a pet dog to do their bidding. All of nature bowed to the much-loved warrior and his lady."

"That's a nice fairytale, but I've studied Alexander and his push for world domination, Tess," Lee said. "He wasn't a nice man. He killed his father and murdered his brother. It took him eighteen bloody months to conquer Sogdiana and Bactria. He only needed Roxana to seal the political alliance between him and the rulers of that part of his kingdom. That was all."

"Possibly," Tess hedged. "Did you know he didn't allow his armies to pillage the countryside of the lands they conquered?"

"True. He wanted to be lord of the land. He wanted subjects, not slaves."

"He was the ultimate politician. A genius."

"He was that," Lee agreed, "but he also became paranoid. Some historians think he was a bi-polar genius with ferocious mood swings that resulted in him murdering his closest friends."

"Shh. Who's telling this fairytale?" She grinned down at him. "Do you want to hear about Roxana or not?"

His cheeks crinkled into the warmest smile when his chin tilted up. "Yes, ma'am," he whispered. "Your wish is my command. I will obey."

"Okay, so maybe he was nothing more than a brilliant military strategist and a great general, but his love for Roxana was legendary, and..." Tess paused to run her fingers through Lee's hair, watching it ripple as her hand moved over his scalp. He closed his eyes, and a sexy masculine rumble escaped his lips. There was no way to resist this man resting so intimately close to her.

Tess leaned into those tempting lips and let her tongue caress his again. His hand circled her neck, pulling her gently into his open mouth. Their tongues tangled. The story faded away as their combined body heat built. With a sexy groan, he flipped her over his hip and into his arms, growling, "I'm ready for dessert" as he nibbled her bottom lip between urgent kisses.

"Me, too," she muttered with every beat of her heart.

He slid his hand down her body and peeled her panties off. Before she knew it, she was beneath him again, her bare body open for him and his mouth working her over-stimulated nerve endings. The sappiest moans escaped her throat, more feminine whine than intelligent communication. Lee seemed able to turn her inside out with one touch. He drove her crazy with his mouth and his fingers. Her soul vaulted up into dizzying pinnacles that stole her breath and left her gasping for more... and more.

His mouth trailed fiery sparks down the line between her breasts, cleaving her in half with his tongue, and she climbed once more to the heights of forever. This was the boost she'd wanted, his knees pressed to the backs of her thighs as he offered her a view of eternity. She fell, clinging to him and panting her exhilaration away, his own spent energy purring in her neck.

"Have I known you in another lifetime?" he muttered, his voice rough and gravelly.

"Yes," she breathed, her heart clamoring in her chest. "Remember? You're my Alexander and I'm your Roxana."

He sighed heated shivers into her soul. "Were they half as good together as we are?"

She shook her head. "Never. No one could ever be as good as us."

"Hoped you'd say that," he said, rolling to her side. She turned to him as he gathered her into his arm, her head comfortable on his chest.

"I feel like I have known you before, too," she admitted, "but it isn't possible."

Lee sighed deeply. "Same with me. I don't know about all that Alexander and Roxana stuff, but you definitely do something to me."

Her heart expanded. Life was crazy. Love more so.

"I didn't do anything." Tess placed a kiss on his whiskered jaw, her eyes brimming with sudden tears. This man had brought a forgotten part of her to the surface as well. She felt that same sense of restoration taking place in her heart, as if she'd found something she'd lost. As if she'd been found in the process.

Her brash and reckless side had taken a step back, the same as it did in the warehouse when he'd first embraced her. Was this what true love felt like, to want another person's happiness more than yours? It felt right, but it scared her. Love stories ended badly. People always lied or cheated. Worse—they left. Like Alexander did to Roxana. Like so many other men did to the women they claimed they loved.

"So how's this fantastical love story of yours end?"

"He died," Tess said simply. "At nearly thirty-three years of age, he died, leaving Roxana behind and heavy with child. Alexander never saw the son of his great love."

"And then they were murdered," Lee whispered. "This isn't a good way to end a fairytale."

"That's what historians want us to believe."

"Right. His kingdom was spread so far and wide across the known world it couldn't be controlled by one man. His enemies forged alliances to ensure that his son would never become the ruler that Alexander was. Roxana was sent to Macedonia to live out the rest of her days. The boy and she were murdered there."

"That's what historians want us to believe," Tess repeated.

Lee peered down at her. "Are you telling me you're smarter than historians?"

She batted those not-so-innocent violet-blues at him, her hand seeking the crook of his neck as she pulled herself on top of him again. "Yes. I'm telling you there's a legend that is truer than history. Roxana may have been a foreigner, but she had many loyal friends. In her darkest hour, she wasn't alone. When her enemies came to assassinate her and her son, they found nothing. She and her child were already spirited away to the high mountains of the Hindu Kush. Historians insist she was buried in Persia, but that was a lie spread by Alexander's enemies. Even today no one can prove it. They have no grave or body of Roxana or Alexander's son."

"Then who'd they kill in Macedonia?"

"How do you know they killed anyone? They didn't have to. The lies started then because Alexander's enemies couldn't admit his heir still lived. That they'd failed."

"Then what?"

Tess sensed Lee didn't necessarily believe her, but he wasn't going to argue. "Roxana and the boy, Alexander IV, lived the rest of their lives among the mountain people. He lived to be a great leader and a noble chieftain. He had many wives and children. When Roxana finally died of old age, the people couldn't bear her passing. Her son had her body mummified in the way of the ancient Phoenicians."

Lee didn't answer, so she continued, "According to the legend, the village holy man removed both of Roxana's index fingers after she died, and he secreted them inside a golden reliquary. That way he and his monks travelled the region to share the memory of their beloved queen. People came for miles around to pay homage and to seek her immortal blessings when they touched her blessed remains."

"Kinda like the relics of saints in cathedrals and churches, huh?"

"Yes." She traced the outline of Lee's lips with her index finger. "Kinda like."

"Interesting theory," he mumbled, snatching the first knuckle of her finger between his teeth and sucking. She smiled to watch his eyes close while he enjoyed the taste of her. Again there was that feeling he didn't believe her story, but he wouldn't argue.

"What if I told you I have proof?"

"Mmm," he mumbled around her finger, his eyes still closed "I'd like to, mmm, see that."

"I have the golden reliquary, Lee," she said softly.

Both eyes popped open. He pulled her finger out of his mouth, one brow spiked. "You what? Say again?"

She couldn't help but smile. He looked so earnestly perplexed. "I said I have the ancient reliquary from that village high in the Hindu Kush. I have the blessed fingers of Roxana."

"No way." Lee straightened against the headboard, pulling her into a sitting position with him. "How'd you get it?"

"I stole it from Sherazi after he stole it from the museum when the Taliban ordered all ancient idols destroyed. He planned to give it to Nizari as a gift." Her joy in her stealthy achievements knew no bounds. It felt good to share her wonderful secret with Lee.

"Are two fingers still in it?"

She nodded, wiggling with uncontrollable excitement. "Yes! Roxana's! I contacted an archeologist friend of mine, Monsieur Favreau, and he offered to have the DNA testing done for me. We should get the results back any day now. He's the one who discovered the truth of the legend before he went into French politics. Isn't that too good to be true?"

Lee's face blanched white. "The French Ambassador? You knew the French Ambassador? He's your trusted agent?"

"Yes, why? Do you know him?"

Lee blew out a small breath between pursed lips. "I hate to tell you, but he's dead, Tess. Turik shot him the day before yesterday."

"No." Her mouth dropped. "But I just... but then... What about Musa? Yusuf?"

He took both of her hands in his. "Were they the assistant curators at the museum? One with a heavy gray beard, the other young and—"

"Yes." She clutched his wrists, pleading. "Tell me, Lee. Please. Are they okay? They have to be okay."

"Oh, hell." He pulled her into his side, his heart pounding in her ears and the lovely moment destroyed. "They're both dead. Turik shot them, too."

"What have I done?" she murmured, her perfect world coming undone. The sweet, kind face of Yusuf and those of his family came to her mind. His wife, poor Miriam. Poor baby Benjamin. "They helped me secrete the reliquary out of the museum. We thought we'd covered our tracks so well. What have I done?"

"That explains a lot," Lee said. "I hate to ask, but—"

"Who else? Tell me!" she demanded, pulling away from the safety of his arms. "Who else has Mohammed murdered because of me?"

Lee bit his lower lip and Tess's heart sank.

"Oh, no. Not Clint," she begged. "Not my baby brother."

"No. Two nuns. Did you know—?"

Tess crashed back into his arms, the breath knocked out of her and her heart broken. The strong man wrapped around her couldn't diminish the weight of the world burying her now. Sister Alison had a friend visiting from the states. She'd told Tess this friend might be joining her to work at the orphanage.

"Sister Alison. My friends," she groaned. "What have I done? I've been so busy stealing the crown, and now they're all gone."

"I'm sorry," Lee murmured into the top of her head. "I'm so sorry."

"Please," she sobbed, the pain in her gut relentless. "Tell me the children at the orphanage are safe. Mina? Jamaal? They're still alive, aren't they?"

"No one's hit the orphanage," he assured her. "The kids are safe."

That much was good, but all Tess could do was hold on tight to Lee and cry.

Mother called to confirm what Lee already knew to be true. Tess did part-time work at the local orphanage when she wasn't running across rooftops spitting in the face of the Taliban and their adept assassin. Jamaal had lost both legs, and his sister Mina was blinded, both hurt by the same IED left by a rabid, fanatical countryman. Their father was sick and elderly.

The orphanage was in disarray since the administrator, Sister Alison of the Maryknoll order out of New York, had been killed, along with another nun. Another aid-worker had stepped in to handle the needs of the children. Sweet little Mina cried for her missing friend Tess, but Lee couldn't bear to tell Tess that.

"I did a little more research into your client," Mother announced brightly.

Lee gazed into the sad face of said client. Tess had cried herself to sleep. The pizza and two beers hadn't hurt, but all those unexpected deaths were more than she'd seemed able to bear. She lay in the crook of his arm, her face splotched with red, and her poor eyes swollen. When she moaned in her sleep, he felt useless. There was no way to shield her from this tragedy. She blamed herself while he planned a hundred different ways to kill Turik.

"What did you find out?" he asked quietly.

"The Taliban made an example of her four years ago."

"Already know that. They roughed her up pretty good. What else?"

"Well, did you know she's been in contact with the French—?"

"Yes. Monsieur Favreau and Tess were working together before he was killed."

Mother huffed through the phone. "Then I guess you know her brother flies a helicopter. He's been back and forth between Kabul and the high Hindu Kush the past three months. I've got him on a satellite-recon photo meeting with a fellow named Iskandar Kadir."

"Who's that?" Lee asked, keeping his voice low.

"You tell me," Mother said. "You're the one who already knows everything."

Lee waited. Mother might get her dander up, but it wouldn't take long before she'd spill the beans. She was OCD that way. Knowledge was her power base. She had to know more than the next guy, but thankfully, she was also compelled to share.

"He's an arms dealer," she said, right on cue. "Meets with Clint Culver every month."

"Clint buying or selling?" This news surprised Lee. Clint hadn't struck him as a fully functional member of the human race the one and only time he'd met him. The idea of a doped-up punk behind the stick on any aircraft was just plain scary.

"Doesn't always look like Clint Culver's gunrunning though, Lee. He's not always unloading. Sometimes he's picking up."

"Picking up what?"

"Guess you're going to have to find out, aren't you?" she came back at him.

"Thanks, Mother." Lee signed off, ignoring her jab.

He'd already intended to do just that.

Chapter Fourteen

Alex looked grim. "I'm cancelling the op."

"Why?" Lee asked. "What's going on now?"

After a long, sad night, Alex had summoned Lee and Tess to the hotel's main level restaurant. They'd dressed in a hurry and now sat at a comfortable circular booth waiting for their server to bring coffee and breakfast.

Tess sat stone-faced and solemn. Her eyes were puffy and red, her pretty face drawn and pale this morning. She'd slipped back into her black cat burglar get-up. The woman beneath the stoic demeanor was doing all she could to keep it together.

Lee could only hope he and Tess didn't look too chummy. That whole fraternization-with-clients rule could cause a problem if his boss caught wind of it, more so if Alex turned confrontational. It wouldn't take much to push Tess over the edge, not as tightly strung as she was.

"The news isn't good." Alex sipped his coffee, boiling hot and black as always. He turned to Tess. "How did you get the videos and pictures on that USB drive?"

Her chin came up, surprising Lee. Instead of sorrow, she'd chosen to lead with anger. Impressive. "People talk. I listen."

A hint of annoyance crossed Alex's brows at her evasive answer. "Do you know everyone on that video and in those still shots?"

"Sherazi. Nizari. Why? Who else should I care about?" Again, she radiated insolence instead of grief.

Alex pulled several photos from his inner pocket and handed them to Lee. "Anyone look familiar to you?"

Lee looked at the black-and-white four-by-six photos. Tess had caught several transactions taking place between the assistant museum curator, Abdul Sherazi, and Hasim Nizari. Some of the parcels passed to Nizari were large enough to require both hands, but many appeared quite small. It was the man in the background shadows on two of the shots that caught Lee's attention. Mohammed Turik.

"He's a busy guy," Lee muttered, debating how much he should let Alex know about the Taliban assassin and their unwilling client. Tess seemed to understand that Alex expected insolence from her. Lee reached for her hand under the table to let her know she wasn't alone. She spared a quick dismissive glance in his direction, nothing more.

"Or he's targeting professionals who've caught onto the museum thefts." Alex already had a full head of steam. Talking to him would take some finesse. "Think about it. Turik killed the French ambassador, an expert in Bactrian artifacts who was only in Kabul to offer his government's protection and assistance to anyone willing to work the archeological digs. And those two assistant curators Turik offed would've known if any artifacts had gone missing from the museum. This contract is not what I was led to believe. I don't like it. Something else is going on."

"Who are you talking about?" Tess asked, craning to see the photos. "Oh. That's Mohammed. He used to be one of my sources, before... yes. I knew he was there. I just..." She turned away, biting her lip.

Lee caught the desolation in her tone. Alex noticed too, his brows furrowed with scrutiny. Not much evaded this apex predator. He turned to Lee, his nose already out of joint. "What the hell is going on with you two?"

Lee met his boss's hard blue eyes, giving nothing away. "We think Turik is hunting everyone involved with the disappearance of a certain artifact from the museum. All those people he's killed in the last two days were Tess's friends. The problem is that Turik was also her friend, at least she thought he was. Only now, she could be the link between the murders."

"*We think*?" Alex's eyes narrowed. "What artifact?"

"Turik also took a shot at Tess last night just before I snagged her. Eric's got it on video."

"I saw the video. What artifact?" Alex demanded again, his tone tighter.

"I thought Mohammed was my friend," Tess said sadly, "but he was just using me."

"What son-of-a-bitchin' artifact, damn it!" Alex slammed his palm to the table, his demand ground out between clenched teeth.

Tess startled and jumped. Lee grabbed her wrist. A whisper of caution flitted across his neck, pinging his sniper sense and causing him to look twice at the breakfast crowd. None of them looked out of the ordinary. There were a lot of US military faces scattered through the restaurant, some booths full of other uniforms. Some men sat alone. Some with families. Nothing looked out of place. A knot of dread had settled in the pit of his stomach. It wasn't Alex he had to fear. Someone else was watching.

Lee faced his boss, a man not known for patience or understanding, then turned to Tess. "Boss, Tess is in possession of a priceless—"

A tiny red laser dot danced over her face.

"Shooter!" Alex roared. "Everybody down!"

Lee didn't think, just body-slammed Tess full force to her side onto the padded bench. His weapon automatically in his palm. Turik had to get through him first. Not satisfied with the bench, he went to the floor with her and shielded her with his body. The table post was hard in his back, but he needed all the cover he could give her. He lowered his head and peered once more into that now terrorized breakfast crowd.

Chaos erupted. Men's voices rose angrily around them. Women screamed. Dishes crashed to the floor. A baby cried. But no gunshots sounded. After the initial frenzy, the dining room had grown oddly silent. Everyone seemed to be holding their breaths. Lee glanced across the bench for Alex, but the man was gone.

"You're not leaving too, are you?" Tess asked, her voice shaking as much as her fingers on his chest. "Don't go, okay?"

"You know better than that. I'd never leave you, Tess." Lee relaxed in order to instill calm in her. "Alex will be right back. He's scouting the perimeter. Maybe someone saw the shooter. He's a sniper too, remember? Maybe he can end this before someone gets killed."

Her heart pounded against him, flattened to each other the way they were. He could feel it clearly through her shirt. And that lacy black bra.

Lee shook the distracting thought from his head. They could make love later. Right then and there, they needed to survive, because they weren't dealing with just a shooter anymore. He tucked her head closer as the air rippled and vibrated. A familiar whoosh headed their way. That only meant one thing—a rocket-launched grenade was in transit. People were going to die. *Not Tess.*

Lee hunkered over her with his whole body, bound to protect her if it meant his life. The rocket skimmed across their booth and blasted the opposite wall directly over the breakfast buffet, tearing through tables and people on its way through infrastructure and onto detonation. The explosion threw debris, fire, and smoke on impact. Sirens went off along with the sprinkler system. The cries of the wounded and terrified melted into one shrieking lament.

"Lee!" Suddenly, Alex gripped Lee's shoulder, pulling him and Tess from the floor. "There's a damn Taliban army outside. Move it."

That must have been the chatter Eric was concerned about. No further encouragement was needed. Lee dragged Tess with him, scrambling in the direction of anywhere but where they were. Another explosion slammed the outside wall of the hotel, shaking the walls with its vibration. *Rat-a-tat-a-tat* automatic fire sounded too close and personal.

"Where to?" Lee asked.

"Eric and Seth are—" Alex paused, leveled his pistol, and shot the AK-47-wielding man who'd just rounded the column at the restaurant's elegant entrance. The idiot dropped dead to his knees, and they pressed forward.

Lee followed with Tess sandwiched safely between Alex and him, his hand in the middle of her back to keep contact as much as to offer assurance. They ran as a single unit into the hall. When Alex flattened his back to the wall outside the maître d's abandoned post, so did Lee and Tess, with Lee closest to the entrance.

Another rocket shook the floor beneath them. The walls rattled. That blast was closer. Sirens screeched out front of the building. The local authorities were responding to this brazen assault and no doubt hotel security was fighting back, too. A group of five heavily armed and tactically protected Marines stormed by on their way out the door.

"Eric and Seth are across the street," Alex yelled above the noise. "So's the U.S. Army."

BLAM! The front entry exploded. Lee ducked, grabbing Tess, his hand pressing her face into his chest. He looked over his shoulder, his heart pounding and his ears ringing. The Marines who'd run past him were gone. Nothing remained of those poor men and women but—nothing.

Tess looked up at him, her mouth moving, but he couldn't hear. She reached up to the back of his head and pulled her hand away to show him. Blood covered her fingers. Damn. He'd been hit. He felt his scalp. Sure enough, he had a good-sized divot just behind his right ear. No pain yet, but it didn't matter. He wasn't dying, and they needed better cover. Right damned now.

He pushed her away from the hellish scene, and once again they followed Alex. Moving swiftly through the hall, they passed the front desk to the elevator and stairs. Only emergency personnel and military first respondents scurried past them.

At the stairwell, Alex opened the door and peered upward, while Lee instinctively took the lower-level view. He shook his head to clear the persistent ringing in his ears. Alex looked angry, his jaw working and probably swearing, if Lee knew his boss. The man could curse more than most, and his lips were moving plenty, but Lee couldn't hear a damned thing. He pointed to his ears to let his boss know he'd been compromised. "Can't hear. What?"

Alex pointed up, so Lee nodded an affirmative to move in that direction. Like most stairs in large buildings, these scissored back on themselves with a small landing between each level. Alex led quickly, but they only moved to the interim landing between ground level and second floor. He crouched to one knee and gestured for Lee to let him check his wound. Lee bowed his head. He'd been hit, but he wasn't worried. Head wounds tended to bleed profusely. He just didn't want anything else going on back there—like his brains falling out.

Alex thumped his shoulder, giving him a thumbs-up. Good enough. He returned the sign.

It looked like Alex was talking into his earpiece again, so Lee kept a lookout below. He didn't need hearing to take out any enemy soldiers coming through that fire door on the first level. Tess leaned into him, shaking.

Gradually, Lee's hearing returned enough that Alex's voice became audible. He still sounded like he was talking underwater.

"Say again?" Alex cocked his head. "Pull back. We're in the stairwell, center of the building. Between the first and second floors."

Tess hadn't asked, just reached her hands to the side of Lee's neck and pulled him down to her level. She worked quickly to compress the bleeding with the heel of her hand. Lee caught the frightened shadow in her eyes, but there was a lot of determination, too. She was lovely to watch, her concern for him a nice touch in the middle of mayhem. And face it, a man liked a woman's hands on him over a guy's any day.

"Am I going to live?" he teased to lighten the mood. She still looked so sad.

"I've seen worse," she whispered, biting her lower lip as she dabbed at his head. Her fingers were drenched in red by then, but he wasn't worried. The hole in his head didn't hurt. "I'll clean it better when we get back to your room. You'll need ice. There's a big bump back here."

"Negative," Alex interrupted. "We're moving to a safer place. Anything in your room you can't live without?"

"My gear bag would be nice," Lee answered. "It's got all my ammo and weapons in it." He took over holding the makeshift compress at the back of his head.

"He needs ice and a wet towel," Tess added. "Can you do that?"

Alex lifted a brow at that question, but got to his feet and headed up. "Eric and Seth are on their way in. Soon as I'm back, we move out. Keep our girl safe."

The noise from the battle at the front of the hotel seemed to have died down, so Lee relaxed. Other people staying at the hotel came and went in an anxious rush, but he and Tess maintained their position on the landing. She'd planted herself against him, her hip rubbing his.

"This is crazy," she muttered. "Why is Mohammed after me? Just because of a two-century-old artifact?"

Lee grunted. "You've tossed the ultimate challenge, Tess. You're a woman, and you're stealing from the Taliban. I don't guess they like that very much."

"But you don't understand. Mohammed's always helped Sister Alison and me. He's brought food and medicine when supplies were low. The kids all love him. It doesn't make sense."

"Tess, you saw the video. He tried to kill you."

She bit her lip, still not believing what she'd seen with her own eyes.

Lee looked away. She was right. It didn't make sense that Turik had tried to kill her, not unless he'd been using her for information the same way she'd used him. That smacked of a closer relationship between her and the Taliban's best man than Lee wanted to think about. Something was going on between Tess and this Turik guy.

Lee understood that she'd been on her own for a while, a damned dangerous position for a single woman in Afghanistan working as a foreign-aid worker. None of those humanitarian organizations offered much security, and her brother was no help. Had Turik been the reason she'd come to Afghanistan? How on earth had she met up with a man the likes of him? Better question, was it only the kids who loved him?

She reached to dab at his head again, but Lee shrugged her away, his nerves on edge. They'd just shared something incredibly good and wonderful. He'd felt an intensely intimate connection with Tess that rattled him to his core. Hell, he'd even thought he loved her, and not just because she'd gotten to him, either. No. Their lovemaking felt right at every level. Had he just made the ultimate fool of himself?

He'd only said that word once before. Veronica's perky smile taunted him. She'd been another strong-willed woman, the curse and bane of his life before the Corps. Only Veronica was one of those love-the-one-you're-with gals. When he'd gone to boot camp, she'd quickly moved on despite the five-thousand-dollar engagement ring on her finger. That was his first real lesson in how cheap talk was. Was it just as cheap with Tess? Was she in love with a Taliban assassin, the damned jerk who'd tried to kill her?

Gah! How stupid was she? He couldn't wrap his mind round that one—that an intelligent, beautiful woman like Tess could fall in love with a cold-blooded terrorist who had no problem shooting down unarmed men and women on the street. How the hell did that work?

"How do you know this Turik guy?" Lee had to know the truth.

"I just told you." A glint of hurt welled up in her eye. "Mohammed stops in at the orphanage sometimes. I know he's Taliban, but he's a good man, Lee. He's a father. He cares about the children there."

Lee studied Tess, hoping they'd passed beyond all the subterfuge and lies—that she wasn't playing him. She'd done it so well before. It was hard to know if she was telling the truth now, and he had to face it. He'd jumped her bones in the heat of passion. He didn't really know her.

"Lee," she said quietly. "What's wrong?"

He turned away, not ready to ask if she was lying because he didn't want to know the answer. Besides, he didn't need to understand the human-interest side of the guy who'd tried to kill her. It sure as hell wouldn't matter the day Lee killed him.

Chapter Fifteen

Tess clung to Lee's hand as they made their way down to the parking garage. He hadn't rejected her completely, but she sensed a definite barrier between them. When Alex returned from Lee's room, Eric and Seth were already there, and they were moving fast. Lee carried his backpack over one shoulder, his rifle in one hand, her hand in the other.

Knowing capable ex-military men had her back provided a small degree of comfort, but the sporadic bursts of automatic gunfire from the hotel and angry shouting from the street meant the battle wasn't over. Alex still carried the plastic bag with a damp hand towel and some ice. As grouchy as he was, he'd done what she'd asked.

"Sit rep," Alex demanded as they walked down the basement steps of the hotel and through the garage.

"Maybe fifty to sixty Taliban," Eric replied. "They've got RPGs and are hitting the front of the hotel with all they've got. A few of them made it inside, but were repelled. The Army's pushing back. Marines are already deployed and engaged in hand-to-hand with the enemy."

They were covered in grime and sweat. Eric and Lee were dressed entirely in tan, from their desert-colored boots and camouflaged pants, to their shirts and baseball caps. Even their T-shirts were the same color. Weapons, too. Right down to their holsters, they were dressed to fade away. Alex, too, was in desert-colored business suit. Only Lee stuck out in relaxed jeans and a western shirt. Blood trickled down the back of his neck again.

"Where we going, Boss?" he asked.

"My place." The power emanating off this man called Alex startled Tess. He seemed angry, coiled like a snake and ready to strike. He led. His men followed and she with them, the lone woman in a fast-moving group of soldiers with long legs. She had to run to keep up.

The Land Rover was gone from the parking stall next to Lee's. Alex halted in that empty space and turned on her. "No more games. What the hell aren't you telling me, Miss Culver?"

Tess stopped in her tracks, surprised at his vehemence and not sure what he meant. All the men faced her. Despite his earlier coolness, Lee clenched her hand in encouragement.

"What?" she asked.

"The Taliban specifically targeted you," Alex growled. "You're valuable to them. Why?"

"I might have something Hasim Nizari wants." She shot a glance Lee's way, not ready to trust his boss, but not ready to die, either.

"What?" Alex spat the one-word command. "Is that the artifact you two alluded to earlier?"

"Yes. It's a reliquary," she replied, suddenly timid and her throat dry.

"A what?" Eric asked.

"What's a reliquary?" Seth asked.

Lee intervened, stepping between Alex and her. "It's an ancient artifact that holds—"

"Bones," Alex hissed. "Relics. Whose?"

She hesitated long and hard before she could form the words. "Roxana's."

"Who's Roxana?" Seth asked.

"Alexander's Bactrian wife?" Alex replied, a whip of scorn in his tone. "Son-of-a-bitch."

Another siren sounded too close. Heavy trucks rumbled overhead.

"Do you have her body, too? Her son?" Alex asked, his blue eyes like sharpened ice. He'd certainly connected the dots quickly. "Do you have Alexander IV or not?"

Tess nodded, powerless against the fury of the sudden desert storm called Alex. She'd underestimated him. He seemed to know the history of this land quite well.

"Boss, what's going—?" Lee tried to speak.

"Are they mummified? Desiccated? Cremated? Ashes? What?" Alex didn't let up.

"Mummies," she whispered, her confidence shattered.

"You've got both Roxana and Alexander IV's mummified remains? Are you absolutely certain?"

"I believe so, yes," she admitted, her eyes meeting his despite her trembling. "Monsieur Favreau offered to match the DNA to—"

"That's why Turik killed him," Alex snapped. "He's playing me, the son-of-a-bitch. Where are the mummies now?"

Lee positioned himself more fully between her and Alex before she could answer, but she caught the disbelief rolling off Alex's tongue. *Who's playing you?* Lee still seemed to believe he could help, but she knew different. She was the reason her friends had been murdered. Her arrogance had left a wake of sorrow she'd not seen coming.

"That's why Turik shot the two curators," Alex bit out. He didn't ask. He told. "They helped you steal the reliquary, didn't they? Turik wants it back. That's why the Taliban are storming this hotel. They know you're here. What'd you do, call him?"

"No, I would never," she whispered as her heart broke all over again for the families her thoughtless actions had hurt. "I wouldn't endanger you. Musa and Josef only told me Sherazi intended to give the Crown of the Dragon King to Nizari. Josef overheard him setting up the meeting. That's why I was at the palace last night. I had to steal the crown from Sherazi before it was lost forever. This is my fault. I shouldn't be here. I've put you all in danger. I need to go."

"How'd you get the reliquary?" Alex bit out.

"Enough!" Lee roared, an angry finger stabbed at Alex. "Lay off, Boss! She didn't kill those people, damn it. That bastard Turik did. This is his fault, not hers."

The second Alex stepped forward, Lee's shoulders squared, and he faced off with his boss. Tess cringed. Lee would fight because of her. Not good.

"And the nuns?" Alex snarled at her despite Lee's protective stance. "Did you know them, too?"

"They worked at the orphanage," Lee answered as he clenched her hand and intertwined their fingers behind him. She leaned into his back, hiding from his very intense boss. "Tess worked with them, but they weren't involved in the heists. None of them were."

"Son-of-a-bitch!" Alex cursed again. "He's targeting everyone she knows to get at her. Do you have any idea what that reliquary means?"

She wept. The children had to be next. Poor Mina. Poor Jamaal.

"Leave her alone!" Lee roared. "Of course I know what this means. Turik's scared shitless that there's a damned slim possibility one of Alexander's descendants still lives today. Big deal! Every conqueror from Adam down to Joe Blow spread his seed at every two-bit village and camel dump along the way. It doesn't mean anything."

Tess couldn't speak. She'd turned into the coward she normally wasn't. The deaths of her friends had sucked the nerve out of her. She'd wrought havoc wherever she went. It had to stop. "I need to leave," she mumbled, but her voice was lost to a loud boom overhead that shook the concrete garage, sending showers of dust onto the friendly enemy combatants in the parking garage. She clutched Lee's fingers. "I have to get to the children."

He tugged her into his arms. That not-so-gentle reminder they were caught in a fierce battle seemed to calm Alex. "It means three things. The whole world of science and media will jump on the slim possibility that a descendant of Alexander lives today. Hope will once again blossom in this godforsaken country, and lastly..." He stepped around Lee to glare at Tess, "the Taliban will do everything in their power to destroy anyone stupid enough to rally behind the cause. Whoever those unlucky descendants are, they won't last a day, and neither will your girlfriend. You already know that, don't you, Miss Culver?"

"I do now," she murmured, closing her eyes to shut him out. "Just let me go. I have to get to the orphanage. The children..."

A strong hand gripped her forearm. It was Alex. His anger was gone. "Lee's right, this isn't your fault, but now we know who Turik's after and why. Hey, I brought what you asked for."

He handed her the bag of melting ice and the towel. "Are you ready to work with me now?"

She didn't know whether to cry or—cry. His sudden kindness stuck in her throat. "The orphanage. If he's killing everyone I know, the orphanage will be next. He knows how much I love Mina and Jamaal. Please. I have to get to them."

Alex answered with one quick bob of his head. "I'll take care of it. Don't worry. The guys and gals from Camp Eggers will protect those kids." He'd changed in the twinkling of an eye. Stabbing a finger at Lee, he snapped, "You and me need to talk later about what the hell fraternization means." Then he turned to Eric and Seth. "Go with Lee, and you'd better damned well keep her safe."

"Yes Boss," Seth muttered.

Alex pivoted on his heel and scrambled into the Humvee parked behind Lee's. "Follow me."

Lee tossed Eric the keys to his Humvee. "You got this?"

"You bet." Eric caught them handily, trading his rifle as he opened the driver's door. "Put this where I can reach it. Might still need it."

Lee secured the weapon next to his seat while Tess set the bag of ice on the floor and fastened her belt, her fingers shaking as the buckle clicked. Seth rode shotgun. An engine roared and tires screeched behind them when Alex took off.

"Hang on," Eric growled as he gave chase. The darkened windows were up and the air-conditioning on, making their escape from the hotel anonymous and half comfortable. Pulling out of the parking garage driveway, he exited into the back alley, following Alex instead of taking the main road.

"What's got him so hot under the collar?" Seth asked as the Humvee bounced into traffic.

"Just keep your eyes open and your rifle ready. This might get ugly," Lee muttered. Leave it to Seth to not comprehend all that just went down.

Tess leaned back into the seat, her world out of balance again and her head spinning. Just last night, she'd been the one to reach out to Lee. She'd been the comforter, and it had been a very good night. Suddenly, they'd traded places. She didn't know who she was, brave crime fighter or simply a selfish fool who'd gotten everyone she loved murdered.

Her mind drifted to Clint. Where had he gone after he'd handed her over so easily to Lee? That had turned out to be a good thing, but he hadn't known that then, had he? Was he so deep into drugs that he was helping Mohammed behind her back? The awful thought took her breath. She stared out her window, fighting tears and grief. Every evil thing that had happened circled back to her. Did Clint hate her so bad that he wanted her dead?

Lee's head tilted toward hers and her body automatically responded, sidling closer. He pulled her into his side; his hand around her ribcage felt intimate and warm. Safe. The last thing she wanted was conversation, but he muttered against her cheek, "I can't help if you won't let me, Tess. I've come all this way for nothing."

She caved. Lee was honorable to the core. She decided to trust him, and in doing so, Alex, Eric, and Seth. It was time to stop running.

Eric's sharp eyes in the rearview mirror winked back at Lee. It didn't matter who knew now that Alex had already figured it out. Lee cared about Tess. She was more than just a client.

"I didn't know you had the mummies too," he murmured into her ear as Eric tried to keep up with Alex's speeding vehicle.

"I was going to tell you," Tess whispered back, dashing her hand over her eyes and sniffling. "I got distracted. This whole day's been… awful."

Her voice was tight. He'd caught her crying, and she was trying to disguise it. He kissed her forehead, offering the only encouragement he could. He was the one here for her, not Turik. "You doing okay?"

She brushed his question off, reaching for the bag Alex had given her. "Let me take another look at your head."

He obliged, bending over and leaning closer. "Is it a hole or a slice?" he asked, going for cavalier.

"It looks like something sharp hit it, but nothing is stuck in the wound as far as I can see." Tess took the damp washcloth and wiped his neck and head, gently dabbing the wound. She ended by pressing a handful of ice into a towel and giving it to Lee to hold to the back of his head. "It doesn't make sense. That reliquary has been in the museum for years. Why is it so important to the Taliban now?"

"Maybe it has to do with the mummies. Where have they been while the reliquary's been under lock and key?"

"That must be what happened," she whispered, more to herself than anyone else.

"What?"

Violet-blues looked up at him through fluttering lashes. "There's something else." She gulped, uncertainty shifting across her features. "Monsieur Favreau worked for WAR. I do, too."

Lee leaned in closer, thinking he'd heard wrong. "What war?"

"No. WAR. It's an acronym for Worldwide Archeology Rescue. We are a group of concerned archeologists, history buffs, and regular people trying to save the treasures of Afghanistan before the Taliban destroys everything."

He relaxed. That kind of war was okay. "Which are you? Archeologist or history buff?"

She rolled her eyes. "I'm nobody. Monsieur Favreau was the archeologist. He actually worked some of the digs in this part of the world. He visited our orphanage one time. He loved the people of this country, especially the children. After the Buddhas of Bamiyan were destroyed, he was determined that depth of mindless destruction must never happen again. He was a charming man."

Lee kept one eye on the road and the other on Tess. Alex seemed to be driving through every back alley in Kabul, heading north in a gradual circuitous route. No vehicles appeared to be following, but he'd caught Eric and Seth's backward glances. All of them remained on high alert. Anything could happen, even away from the war zone they'd just escaped.

"Do you have the mummies or not?"

"Oh, yes." She nodded, biting her lip like she was thinking hard. "At least I know where they are. Jacque took me to see them. Not only have I seen the mummies, but I've seen the hands with the missing index fingers, and as I've told you, I know where those fingers are."

"Wait a minute." Lee stopped her. He'd caught the familiarity in her voice. "Jacque?"

"Yes. Jacque Favreau." A mischievous twinkle sparkled in her eyes. "The French ambassador. He asked me to go with him into the Hindu Kush, and I said yes. I wouldn't have missed it for the world."

"How long was this trip?" Lee shook off the stab of irritation that cramped his neck. She thought this guy was charming? How the hell old was this Jacque dude?

"It took seven days. A week." A sparkle still glinted deep in her eyes. "It was fun. I met a tribe of very interesting people. You would've liked them."

"Would I?" Lee bit his bottom lip a little too hard, doubting he'd have been as enthusiastic as she was.

"Are you jealous?"

"No," he answered quickly. *Hell, yes.*

"You're funny. Monsieur Favreau was very spry and energetic, but he was in his mid-sixties. Hardly my type. Besides, he's dead now so it doesn't matter."

Bet me. Spry and energetic didn't discourage the image forming in Lee's mind. Older men molested younger women every day. "How'd you get there? Where'd you sleep?"

"You're jealous of a sweet old man who Turik killed?" She had the nerve to argue.

"I am not." He pulled her into his side despite their seatbelts and changed the subject. Yes, the ambassador was dead, but still. The thought of Tess alone with a Frenchman in the very primitive Hindu Kush for a week irked the shit out of him. "So you're fairly certain you can make a DNA match?"

"I was," she mumbled, "but now I'm worried about Jacque's assistant. Mohammed may be after him, too."

"What's his name?"

"Pieter Marchal."

Lee tapped Seth's shoulder. "Contact Mother. An assistant to the murdered French ambassador needs protection ASAP. Pieter Marchal. Make it happen." Seth gave another backward glance before he started punching numbers into his satellite phone.

"Where are the mummies now?" There was no sense asking how young this Pieter guy was. Age didn't matter when it came to a pretty woman, and Lee didn't want to know.

"Would you like to see them?"

He nodded. "Sure. If that tribe kept the mummies safe all these years, maybe they can keep you safe, too."

"Hmm." She considered the idea. "That might be the solution."

"It still doesn't make sense though," Lee admitted. "So what if you can prove these mummies are who you think they are? Does that mean this country is going to pin their hopes on some guy who's been living in the mountains all his life, drinking yak milk and praying to Buddha, just because you tell them he's a descendant of Alexander the Great? How will that save the world? It sounds more like you're signing his death sentence."

"You know about the Buddha?" Of everything he'd just said, that was what caught her attention.

"Ah, yeah."

She wasn't about to let this go. "You're Buddhist maybe?"

"Me? No. I'm Catholic," he insisted. "I used to be. It's just that, well, I kinda believe a little of everything and most of nothing right now." He sighed, his hand still very much connected to her ribs. "Guess I'm trying to figure everything out..." His words trailed away with his gaze. Now wasn't the time to get psychoanalytical. He had a doctor back home for that. And a priest. And an old Indian medicine man. Hell. He even had a fortuneteller.

They'd all missed what Tess had nailed the moment he'd met her. The second they'd touched. Her singing "Amazing Grace" in the shower had all but done him in. She'd gotten under his skin and into his heart pretty damned fast.

Tess brought his gaze back to hers with a gentle finger against his jaw. "Tell me," she ordered softly.

Lee grunted. "Tell you what?"

"Do you believe in the teachings of Buddha? You do, don't you?"

He looked down on her, which wasn't hard at this close proximity, their noses nearly touching, and her breath soft and warm in his face. Only the Humvee's steady engine noise filled the space between them.

"I'll tell you what I believe." He nipped her lower lip, his other hand smoothing against her cheek to shield them from those dark observant eyes in the rearview mirror. "The Taliban is scared you'll unite the tribes of the north with this descendant of Alexander, maybe the entire country. The last thing they want is someone with that kind of mystique and perceived power to stand up and challenge them and what they're doing. You've got them running scared right now, and they don't like it."

"But think of it. Bringing an age-old legend to life would make this country take notice. A great warrior could offer this proud people hope if he's the right man for the job," she whispered. "And hope is a powerful magic."

"These *proud* people have had centuries to rise up and save themselves. They always end up killing each other," he said sarcastically. His mouth on hers ended the argument, savoring her sweet lips. She all but fell into his arms. There was something about kissing Tess Culver that felt like the first kiss all over again. A man could get lost in her body. Lee surely wanted to.

Eric interrupted as the Hummer lurched to a sudden stop. "Hey guys. We're there."

Chapter Sixteen

Lee looked into Eric's worried eyes in the mirror. The man had something to say, but Lee gave him no time to say it. Instead, he pulled Tess out the door right behind him, glancing at the morning landscape for trouble. Out of Kabul didn't mean safety by a long shot. If anything, they were more exposed in the open than in the city. A decent sniper didn't have to get close to kill them.

"Where are we?" Tess asked.

"About to get our butts kicked if I know Alex," Lee muttered.

Eric had parked alongside an Army-green eighteen-wheeler, a single trailer hooked behind it. The rig was running, but no driver sat in the cab. It had been situated off the beaten road between the crests of two small hills, one sheer stone, the other covered with scraggly pines and brush. More of the same trees downhill shielded them from view.

Alex motioned them forward as he climbed out of his Humvee. "You men okay?" he asked, those damn sharp eyes not missing the fact that Lee still held Tess by the wrist. "Any trouble?"

"No, we're good," Lee answered. "Is this your idea of a hotel?"

Alex nodded toward the side door of the rig. "Inside. Now."

Lee couldn't have been more surprised. Inside was an Army-style hotel, as in six bunks attached to the walls at the back of the rig, and a head-shower combination near the bunks. High-tech communication equipment dominated the entire front half. Several satellite recon images glimmered from computer monitors in choppy black-and-white contrast. A map of Central Asia covered the wall opposite the desks. The centrally located kitchen area completed the living quarters.

Rugged Junior Agent Hunter Christian manned one bank of computer monitors while easy-going Jordan Hannigan offered a half-salute from the other bank. "Hey guys. 'Bout time you got here."

Hunter scrambled to his feet, cuffing Jordan as he reached past him to shake Tess's hand. Hunter was the latest bad boy Alex had hired, a hardcore Marine who commanded others with a voice of steel. Dark-haired and tattooed from his wrists to who-knew-where, he gentled his normally harsh voice for the lady in the house. "It's very nice to meet you, Miss Culver. I've heard a lot about your exploits. You're quite a famous woman."

Hmm. He'd said that without one expletive, an effort for the foul-mouthed repertoire he usually led with. Maybe there was hope for Hunter after all.

"Is that good?" she asked quietly, and Lee had the sudden urge to punch Hunter in the gut. For no reason. He just didn't appreciate the longer-than-necessary handshake and the hungry look in the guy's dark eyes.

Fortunately, Jordan was on his feet and extending a handshake by then, so Hunter had to release Tess's fingers. "Morning, ma'am. Sorry 'bout that," Jordan apologized. "It's just that we've been twiddling our thumbs waiting on you and the guys to get here."

"You have?" Alex slanted a wicked glare at his junior agent.

Lee pulled Tess out of the line of fire while Jordan choked up his big foot and explained—quickly—how busy he'd been while the boss was gone.

"I need your cell phones," Hunter announced with an apologetic nod toward Tess. "Sorry, ma'am, that means yours, too. I need to make sure no one's tracked you here."

She shrugged and handed hers over. "It doesn't work. It got wet."

Hunter frowned. "What'd you do? Drop it in the bathtub?"

Lee caught the smile tugging at Tess's lips. "Something like that," she murmured.

"Nice place you've got here, Boss," Seth muttered as he wandered into the back room and dropped his gear on the lowest bunk along one wall. "Not as nice as the hotel. Are we staying with you?"

"No," came the definite answer. "You and Eric still have work in town, remember?"

Jordan relieved everyone but Alex of their weapons and gear. He stored the assortment inside a metal cabinet at the front door within easy reach. Lee allowed a twinge of relief. Knowing Alex, that cabinet would also be loaded with ammo and additional weapons, all readily available. Excellent.

"Where are the mummies?" Alex asked the moment Jordan secured the gear.

"Where's the Crown of the Dragon Warrior?" Tess shot back, and Lee grinned. They were back at square one again. Showdown. He couldn't decide who'd just met their match.

"Let me show you something, Miss Culver." Alex stabbed a finger into the screen Hunter had just resumed monitoring. "Do you know what that is?"

Lee peered over Hunter's beefy shoulder with Tess. Hunter worked his keyboard to bring the image into better clarity. Obviously a satellite feed, it depicted what looked like a campfire with several figures hunched nearby. Two rectangular objects in close vicinity might have been jeeps or trucks. It was an obscure image on a grainy background at best.

"Looks like some kind of a camp. Who are they?" Lee asked.

"You tell me," Alex answered, nodding back to Hunter and Jordan. "As soon as I learned of the mummified remains of Roxana, I had these guys pull a week's worth of recon photos from specific areas along the highest habitable mountain ranges. You're only seeing one shot. Look at the wall map."

Tess's breath caught, but all Lee saw on the map were the multitude of red stickpins in one specific area of the southern Hindu Kush.

"Every one of those pins is a camp full of soldiers just like these guys," Hunter said. "They weren't there a week ago, but now, this quadrant of the mountain's western face is crawling with them."

"That's a major Taliban neighborhood," Eric said, his finger in the middle of the pins.

"And it's high in the mountains. Sheer rock," Seth added. "There are no passable roads up there. They've all been shelled. Only goats live up that high. Goats and Taliban."

"And it's damned near in Pakistan," Lee breathed. The grand scale of the Hindu Kush was bad enough. Sheer stone mountains with lush hidden valleys offered nothing but a hard place to live and no way to travel unless a man planned to fast rope in. Getting out was another problem all together. Seth was right. Roads were few and rugged, more likely full of bomb craters.

This particular area straddled the border of Pakistan. The people living there were descendants of the same fierce tribes who'd resisted invaders for centuries, including the equally fierce bringers of Islam who'd forced conversion at the edge of a sword. The locals were known to kill trespassers at first glance, especially foreigners.

Tess had kept silent so far, but her face betrayed her. That area was important to her. Lee could tell.

Alex watched her intently, too. "Is there something you'd like to tell me now, Miss Culver?" he asked, a hint of sarcasm in his voice.

When she didn't speak, he did, his index finger tracing a small trail on the map. "A group of three men climbed this trail two days ago from this village." He tapped the map an inch from his finger on the trail. "That was the day Monsieur Favreau met his death outside the museum. By all appearances, the men were local tribesmen. I don't believe they were Taliban, but they could've been. They reached this point..." he turned to Tess, "and they disappeared. We could get no thermal readings. No satellite imagery. Nothing. Approximately, two hours later, they reappeared in the exact same location. At the same time, a helicopter landed at this point." He indicated a precariously narrow ridge that in no way looked like it could support a landing pad.

Tess watched with wide eyes, holding her breath.

"I take it you already know who was in that helicopter," Alex insinuated.

"Who?" She shook her head, all of her over-confidence on hold.

It appeared Alex finally had the upper hand. His eyes narrowed as if he were deciding whether to believe Tess or not. Lee felt the game shift. Alex might be a tough charger, but he also knew when to take a step back when his assumptions were wrong. He appeared to be doing just that. "You really don't know, do you?"

Tess met him head on, her eyes full of questions but not deceit. "I need to speak with you and Lee alone."

Alex didn't have to ask. Eric, Seth, Hunter, and Jordan excused themselves and made a hasty exit. Only when the door had closed behind them did Tess blow out a deep breath. She shot Lee a tender glance. "How would I know who was in that helicopter? The only time I've been up there was with Monsieur Favreau. Jacque and I rode donkeys as far as we could, but then we had to climb the rest of the way on foot. And yes, there's a cave hidden on the face of that mountain, Mr. Stewart. That's why you thought those men disappeared. The entrance is impossible to see unless you know where to look, and it's extremely difficult to reach. The mummies are hidden there, but no one else can know. I only trust you and Lee."

"So this is where you believe the mummies of Roxana and Alexander IV are?" Alex asked. A look of awe settled on his features as he traced that trail again with the tip of his finger.

"No. That's where I know they are," Tess said, stepping to Lee's side as she corrected Alex. "Roxana and her son's mummies are both there, many other mummies, too. Only a handful of the village elders are entrusted with this secret. That's how they've been able to hide the mummies from the rest of world for more than two millennia. We cannot let this cave fall to the Taliban. They'll loot it and destroy everything."

Lee blew out a slow sigh. "It's damned rugged terrain, Tess. You'd have to be a mountain goat just to live in the valleys."

"That's putting it mildly," Alex agreed. "These tribes are tough. They have to be to survive on sheer stone in some of these mountain valleys. They build their homes on vertical terraces, one on top the other. Even trees hang on for their lives at that altitude."

"You've both been there?" Tess asked.

Lee couldn't answer. That Alex didn't either meant he wouldn't. Black ops were black ops forever, and operators never told. As it was, they'd both said too much.

Lee offered an acceptable answer to pacify Tess. "We study a country's topography in our line of business. There's something you need to know. That pilot in the helicopter..." He let his sentence hang, wishing he didn't have to dump another shock on her. Five deaths were enough. She didn't need proof of her brother's deceit, too.

"Yes?" Those violet blues lit up with anticipation.

He reached for her hand to lessen the shock. "It's Clint."

"My brother? No. He doesn't know how to fly." Her brows furrowed with disbelief. "Even if he did, there are no drug runners that high in the Kush. You can't grow poppies or marijuana on solid granite. Why else would he go up there?"

Lee didn't argue. It didn't make sense to him either, but he knew Mother's reputation for accuracy. If she'd said it was Clint Culver behind the stick in that chopper, then it was. Mother only offered definitive information after she'd verified, validated, and well, definitized. That Tess didn't know this side of her brother was a puzzle Lee hadn't solved yet.

She cocked her head, glancing at Alex then back to Lee. "You guys are full of shit. Clint's not bright enough to fly a helicopter. He's a dweeb. He's... he's Clint. You've seen him, Lee. Did he look like he could handle anything more complicated than his truck and a bong?"

Lee shrugged and let it go. He'd get to the mystery of Clint soon enough. For now, he had his hands full keeping Tess alive. "What's the game plan?" he asked Alex.

That his boss's icy blue eyes were hooded should've been a clue there was another power struggle coming. Alex turned on Tess. "Where's the reliquary?"

"Safe," she answered.

"As safe as those mummies?" Alex nodded toward the map.

"Yes," she declared evenly. "There's no way—"

Alex flipped the switch on another monitor that portrayed an army of Taliban soldiers thundering down a dilapidated staircase. "I had Eric and Seth plant a few of Mother's Tattle Tales after your first little heist," Alex said by way of commentary. "Remember where you hid the reliquary?"

Lee recognized the location. He'd been inside that building years earlier. Those stairs led to the lower level of the derelict Darul Aman Palace. The soldiers on the screen all carried handguns and rifles. Lee recognized the man leading the charge, too. Turik. Shit. She'd hidden the reliquary where Nizari and his soldiers wouldn't think to look for it, only now—they were.

"Is this live?" she asked, the tips of her fingers tight on Lee's forearm.

He glanced at his boss's somber face. This wasn't a live feed. Turik already had the reliquary. *Damn.*

"No! No! No!" she growled, but the answer was emphatically yes. She shoved away from Lee and whirled toward the door. "I'm leaving. I have to..."

Alex let her go, not missing a beat. "This is how we'll get the reliquary back, Lee," he said, while he retrieved a roll of architectural blueprints from the side of Hunter's desk and unrolled them for Lee to follow along. "It's now in a safety deposit box at the Central Bank of Kabul. Our friend Turik stashed it there. By midnight, I'll have the box number. Come daylight, we'll go in and retrieve it."

Lee nodded. Looked like he'd be robbing a bank instead of mountain climbing.

Tess glanced over her shoulder, her hand already on the doorknob. "He put it in a bank?"

Lee caught a smirk flitting across Alex's face as he kept ignoring her. "You won't be going in through the front door." He pointed to the plans. "You'll enter through the neighboring building, here, at this shared wall. It needs to be quick and dirty. Jordan's your EOD guy. He'll handle the explosive charge that will put you right inside the downstairs vault."

Lee nodded to confirm his agreement, one eye still on Tess. "Right. Got it. Jordan's damn good. Should be a quick in-and-out."

"Fine. I'll go," Tess ground out as she stalked back to the desk. "You're not doing this without me."

Alex didn't spare her a glance when she peered around him to the blueprints. "Meanwhile," he continued, "I'll run interference and maintain vigilance topside. Have I missed anything?"

Just the violet-blue daggers that Tess is throwing at you, Boss.

Lee lifted the blueprints off the desk to study the architectural design of the bank building. It didn't look like a tough job. The shared wall ran the length of the north side of the Central Bank of Kabul. It wouldn't take much SEMTEX. Once the wall was breached, they'd be inside the vault. Then it was just a matter of removing the right lockbox and disappearing before the locals showed up.

"Just keep the police off our butts," Lee answered, sure that Tess was dying to take charge. "There'll be an alarm inside the vault. Jordan will need to use a light touch so we don't make too much noise. Do he and Eric already know about this?"

"I have a better idea," Tess said, like either of them was listening.

Alex continued ignoring Tess. "Get ready, Lee. You'll go in before sunup."

"Can do," Lee answered, thoroughly enjoying the cat-and-mouse game. Alex did know how to play off Tess's pride.

"Will you two pay attention? I said I have a better idea, guys," she demanded. The cocky cat burglar was back with a vengeance, and she was pushy, too, especially when Lee lifted the plans over her head and out of her reach. His height made for one aggravated, but determined short woman.

He leveled a stern eye at her, enjoying how he and Alex had reeled her in. "You'll join us on one condition, Miss Culver. I'm running this op. Me. Only me. You'll follow my orders every step of the way or you're grounded, is that clear?"

When her eyes changed to flashing cobalt with sparks of amethyst, his heart stuttered. That she managed alluring and belligerent at the same time reeled Lee in, too. Damn. How was he ever going to get control?

"Why should I join you? Your plan sucks. I have a better way inside that bank," she declared saucily. She couldn't have acted more like a brat if she'd stuck her tongue out after that bold declaration.

He egged her on, running his gaze up and down her very sexy body, the blueprints still out of her reach. "Seems to me you're a little *short* on manpower and explosives."

"Seems to me you're a little short on brains," she shot back, her hands on her hips, and her swagger back in full force. "How many times have you been inside that particular bank? Huh?"

She had a way of bobbing her head and shoulders when she was over-confident. His dumb heart flipped. Alex was standing somewhere in the same room, but Lee only had eyes for Tess with her chin jutted out and licking her lips like she was ready to fight. An I'll-show-you, tough-as-nails survivor had replaced the sad lady in mourning.

He couldn't resist the challenge. Bring it on. "What's it matter? A good operator only needs one shot."

Her nostrils flared and he was in heaven.

"Just because you play with guns does not make everything a target," she hissed. "I, on the other hand, have been inside that very vault. I also know the layout of the entire building, not to mention that I'm the only person in this room with enough talent to make this theft happen without making a sound. I've filched five treasures from the National Museum. What have you stolen, tough guy?" The gauntlet was thrown. She had him there, and she knew it. With one half-step forward, she was under Lee's chin and glaring up at him. "Who do you think has the Star of Persia?"

Lee cocked an amused grin. This girl was damned seductive when she had her dander up. This was another coup she hadn't yet told him about. Anyone who'd heard of the Hope Diamond also knew of the famed Star of Persia, a natural cluster of emeralds so large they were said to look more like green crystal fingers than precious jewels.

The story of their theft was the thing of legends amongst the media—no doubt the defrauded insurance company, too. But she hadn't stolen it from the museum. Not reckless Tess Culver. She preferred doing things the hardest way possible, and she had.

A jewelry heist in far-off Darfur had recently brought worldwide attention to the fact that the one-time prize was no longer in the National Museum of Afghanistan where it belonged. Go figure. The Sudanese rebel who'd acquired it in a clandestine black market transaction and just as quickly lost it, screamed foul. He wanted vengeance upon the common thief who'd lifted it out of his very impressive treasury where he'd kept his mostly ill-gotten booty.

The embarrassed National Museum curator had demanded redress, although he hadn't realized it was missing until the story broke. Meanwhile, the talking heads of the world had expressed varying degrees of outrage. The daring thief had never been apprehended. The media had a field day. And Tess Culver had gotten off scot-free.

"That was you?" Lee asked with more than a hint of admiration in his tone.

"I also have the Sultan's collection of rubies. It truly is the finest in the world."

Again with the chin tilt, and Lee wanted to kiss the sassy lips she kept sticking in his face. But he was also impressed. That particular collection of rubies was an equally rare treasure that Alexander the Great had brought back from his failed foray into India, another theft Lee hadn't known about. What other treasures did she have? And where was she keeping them?

"You two need a room?" Alex muttered behind him.

Actually, not a bad idea, but Lee got the hint. He stepped back from his very audacious client. Business now. Room later.

"Let me guess," Alex poured on the sarcasm. "You stashed those treasures at Darul Aman Palace, too."

"No," she retorted. "They're... safe. Safer."

"Then why the hell didn't you keep the reliquary just as safe?" he demanded. "Why'd you hide it where Sherazi and Nizari planned to meet?"

"Did you ever consider that just maybe I didn't know they were going to meet there?" she hissed. "When Musa and Yusuf handed it off to me at the museum, one of them tripped the alarm. I had to hide it some place close by or risk blowing my cover, so I stashed it at the palace. Monsieur Favreau still needed a DNA scraping from the fingers to run his test. We hadn't enough time to remove it to a safer place."

Lee caught her word choice. *Safer?* He'd studied her for weeks before this operation, yet he'd still missed the fact that she worked at an orphanage. Her last two revelations declared the nerve of this audacious woman—and that he was in over his head. "That's why you and Jacque visited the mummies. You're keeping all of these jewels and artifacts in the crypt with Roxana, aren't you?"

She didn't have to answer.

"That is a damned good hiding place, if you think about it," Alex muttered. "I can't see that particular tribe giving up a secret they've kept for more than two centuries."

"And the treasures still belong to the people," Tess insisted. "Everything I've stolen I've returned to Afghanistan. It's all there where it will be protected. I can show you."

Lee mused. "Sherazi and Nizari seem to conduct a lot of clandestine business at the old palace. It might be a good idea to see what else is stashed there, Boss."

"You do realize you've broken quite a few international antiquity laws"—Alex rolled his eyes—"besides stealing."

"You do realize nothing will be left of this country if we wait for the Taliban to recognize your precious international laws?" Tess bit out sharply.

Lee sighed. Alex and Tess had just summed up the plight of Afghanistan—caught between a rock and a hard place.

Alex extended his right hand to Tess, his palm up and his fingers beckoning. "Give it up."

The most beguiling smile blossomed on her pretty face as Tess reached between the two lowest buttons of her tucked in shirt and retrieved his gold and silver watch. Instinctively, Lee checked his back pocket. She was a pickpocket, too?

"Did you realize I'd taken it?" she asked Alex coyly.

He pulled her silver crucifix and chain out of his sleeve and dangled it at the end of his fingers. "Did you miss this?"

She clutched her now-bare neck. Another challenge sparked deep in those violet-blues. "You stole my cross," she hissed.

Lee checked his back pocket again.

Chapter Seventeen

Tess won the argument.

Early the next morning, she was none other than the notoriously wealthy Cashmere bin-Awa, supermodel and totally *spolt bratsksi,* the daughter of Russian oil-tycoon, Zoe Zurat, and Arabian Prince bin-Awa, owner of the worldwide oil conglomerate, Awa Petroleum. Based in Dubai, it boasted subsidiaries in South America, Russia, and as far north as the Mongolian-Manchurian steppes.

Tess kept her stride long and her chin high, in keeping with the energy of the temperamental Cashmere as she marched into the Central Bank of Kabul. Marble columns guarded the interior aisle that led straight to the manager's desk. Three on the left, three on the right, all fitted with security cameras. She glanced neither to the left nor the right as she bee-lined through the busy bank, her head held high. Her steps were sure and true. Her heels clicked on the smooth marble floor.

Cashmere had a reputation of making outlandish demands for paparazzi to attend her every move. She loved the press, and, mostly due to her billionaire father's money, the press adored her. Tess intended for every move she made to prove that Cashmere truly was in the bank this morning. What a show.

She'd disguised herself beneath a mantle of luxuriant red hair that matched Cashmere's, and a navy blue, floor-length, pencil skirt that barely hid her three-inch open-toed heels, courtesy of Alex's expense account. She had to give it to him. Once convinced she knew the bank inside out, he'd gone all in. And he had the money and resources to do it.

Not only had he outfitted everyone overnight, he'd also contacted someone clever enough to provide combinations to the bank's lower level vault where the safety deposit boxes were securely maintained, as well as a few other indispensible items to insure the ruse went off flawlessly. He'd also kept her up half the night practicing Cashmere's handwriting—just in case.

She couldn't believe the reach of Lee's boss. It was early morning when a carrier arrived at the rig with, of all things, a complete set of the wealthy supermodel's fingerprints. Tess very much wanted to know how he was able to come up with them, and how he did it so quickly. She just might have to check into his holdings when this heist was through.

Tess fingered the violet hijab at her shoulder, projecting an air of tolerance for the old ways while expressing a flair for the modern. She had no intention of expressing submission, a quality neither Tess nor Cashmere subscribed to.

Except when it came to Agent Hart. Tess had been pretty submissive with him.

The memory of their lovemaking flamed to mind and blazed her cheeks with her favorite indiscretion. She shot him a quick glance out of the corner of her eye. A momentary smile tugged at those manly lips, almost as if he'd read her mind and planned a little more submission in her near future. No other man had gotten beneath her skin as fast as he had. Ever.

Both Lee and Alex liked her idea of walking through the front door of the prestigious Bank of Central Kabul in broad daylight better than using SEMTEX, with its over-the-top, testosterone-filled ramifications. They trotted at her heels like trained Rottweilers on short leashes, Lee on her right, Alex at her left. Just the way men should be, submissive and at her beck and call. She could get used to this.

Tess allowed a throaty chuckle to bubble up, drawing Alex's annoyed brow and Lee's adoring smile. There was no doubt about it. Alex and she were cut out of the same cloth while Lee wasn't. Hence, she'd never get along with Alex, but Lee? She chuckled again. He believed in her. He had faith. And because of that devotion, she loved him more all the time and she wouldn't let him down.

Eric and Seth were somewhere across the street supplying Alex and Lee with intel via their carefully hidden Bluetooth earpieces. Neither Alex nor Lee acted as if they were receiving, but she knew they were. She'd seen the miniscule devices they'd both hidden deep in their right ear canals. No wires. Nice touch.

Both men also wore slim-fitting tactical vests beneath their dark gray business suits, two holstered pistols under their arms, and at least one lethal-looking knife with serrated edges in their boots. They exuded wealth and class when they were actually men of war. She was as humbled to be walking between them as she was proud of them. She made them look good.

That the paparazzi weren't in attendance should've been a clear signal to the shocked and unprepared man of finance that something was amiss. The bank manager should've noticed Cashmere bin-Awa didn't sport her usual entourage of a dozen bodyguards, and that she dropped her flamboyant designer handbag to the floor the moment she stepped up to his desk. The real Cashmere didn't bother with purses. She had staff.

Mr. Hussein looked up from his computer. A flicker of relief raced across the deeply etched worry lines on his forehead when he peered around her and caught sight of only two escorts. In that split second, Tess knew she had him. She'd banked on her close resemblance to the celebrity heiress to get her through this tricky operation. Now she could also count on Mr. Hussein's desire to be rid of her before the cameras showed up. It really was all about timing.

"Mr. Hussein! So nice to see you again," she gushed with her best fake Russian accent, air-kissing his sallow cheek while he did the same to her. "You've been well?"

"Miss bin-Awa," he acknowledged, his fingers weak and flimsy on her hand. "Y-yes, I am fine, but I wasn't expecting you today. Why are you here? Is there a problem?"

She waved her hand at him with a dismissive, I-could-care-less flutter of her fingertips. "Why would you say that? Just because I arrived with only two bodyguards this time? I thought you would like that for a change."

Immediately, Lee and Alex stepped to the side of Mr. Hussein's desk in rigid synchronized formation. Both in matching Oakleys, their dark glasses added an element of anonymity to their chiseled jaws and chins that clearly declared, *"Stay out of my way."*

"Oh, no, no, no. It's just that you usually send advance notice before you arrive," Mr. Hussein chirped, a sheen of sweat on his upper lip as he glanced at the two men, "but... here you are."

"What you mean is that I always draw attention to your fine bank when I visit. Ah, yes." Tess dropped into the leather chair in front of his desk, fanning herself with one hand, studying the manicured nails on the other. "My, my. It's unusually warm in here, is it not? Is your air-conditioning broken? The press will be here soon enough. I have to let them know where I'll be. They seem to find me irresistible. It may get warmer. Don't you agree?"

"So it would seem." His head bobbed in nervous agreement while his eyes scanned the entrance, most likely looking for his next heart attack. "That is exactly what you are—irresistible, very intelligent, and quite the businesswoman. Let me check on the cooling system for you. It will take just a minute." He waved a teller over to his desk and promptly assigned her the task of informing maintenance that he had a problem.

Tess caught his undertone. Mr. Hussein wasn't good at hiding his true feelings. He must work extra hard to tolerate the real Cashmere, who was known to be at least a hundred times more obnoxious than Tess was being now. That made this op all the more fun.

"I was on my way to Monte Carlo and..." Tess glanced around the lavish lobby and yawned, taking in the blinking red lights of the security cameras along the ceiling as well as the six armed guards, three at the entrance and the other three scattered throughout the lobby. Seven tellers manned the windows. Four loan officers were engrossed with clients at their desks; three were not.

The stairs to the basement vault beckoned at her left, but what she needed at that moment lay immediately behind Mr. Hussein's pretentious desk. The bank vault. An impressive, older masterpiece with linked locking mechanisms, it boasted steel-reinforced concrete walls, and the customary array of anti-theft precautions and alarms. She would know.

Her lashes lowered. Alas. Divesting that vault of the Taliban's share of Afghanis, the currency of Afghanistan, would have to wait for another day. She only needed the vault's sensitive security system at her beck and call for this job.

Poor Mr. Hussein. Shortly, the device she'd hidden in her purse would trigger the steady blare of the vault's alarm and add more chaos to his already frazzled nerves.

"Excuse me?" He ran a finger between his sweaty neck and the stiff collar of his white dress shirt. "You were going to Monte Carlo? Why did you detour to my bank? It isn't on the way, is it?"

"As I was saying," she continued airily, "I was on my way to Monte Carlo, but I had a notion to see my collection of rare lapis lazuli. The jet needed to refuel. I was here. Ha. It seemed a simple thing to do. May I see my babies?"

He breathed a sigh of relief, smiling and nodding while he removed a digital tablet from his top right drawer. "Yes, of course. Your signature."

Tess lifted her brows to her hairline, tapping the tip of her index finger to her bottom lip. "You can't be serious, Mr. Hussein. Look into my eyes. It's me, your dearest friend, Cashmere. Surely you don't need my signature on that silly device."

She watched his throat clench as he tried to swallow. Twice. He hesitated, but recovered quickly. "Of course not. Right this way, Miss bin-Awa."

"Ah, you're so good to me, but perhaps I am being a bother. Here. I will give you what you need for your, how do you accountants say it? Audit trail?" She scrawled her much practiced version of Cashmere's signature to the tablet's screen, then rose with an easy lift, beckoning for her guards to follow as she nudged her bag farther beneath the chair with her heel.

Lee and Alex followed in tight formation. Tess latched onto the poor bank manager's elbow, overloading his tightly stretched nerves with a brush of her hip against his and a suggestive wink. "Ah, you've been working out. I feel muscle beneath this fine silk suit. I'll speak to my father about your indulgence with me. He asked about you only yesterday."

"He did?" Sheer consternation was a nice touch to Mr. Hussein's already green gills. He tugged at his tie as he gestured toward the basements steps. "Your father? Me? What may I do to help Prince bin-Awa?"

"Oh, nothing," Tess rambled, her hands firmly attached to the sweating manager's forearm and elbow as she looked this way and that. Walking with long, languorous steps, she made certain her swaying hips bumped him at every other step. All she needed was to be inside the safety deposit vault within the next two minutes. Once the door was locked behind her... well, that was all she needed.

"We were just talking about the terrible thing that happened over at that other bank in the city. You know, the embezzling ring that walked out their front door with all those millions? Such a scandal! Everyone who is anyone is talking about it."

Mr. Hussein didn't choose to speak, maybe because he couldn't. It was true. Several Kabul banks had been rocked by scandal during the past year. Tess poured it on. People no longer trusted the country's financial institutions. What's a rich heiress to do? Tsk. Tsk. "But Father is pleased he can rely on someone of your financial talent. He trusts you. I think he might even pay you a visit soon. He likes you. I can tell."

"Oh, how good for me." Mr. Hussein offered a weak smile as they approached the vaulted room. "Your guards must not enter," he said sternly.

"But of course not." Tess leaned into his ear, her knee bent and her heel raised in feminine grace. "These dumb jocks have no clue what to do with my treasures. Look at them. They're all muscle, and most of it is between their ears," she stage-whispered. "Surely you know what I mean."

He cast a sharp look toward Lee and Alex, the three keys to the vault already in the three locks and his fingers at the security pad. "If you say so."

"I won't be long," she purred, tapping her ruby red lips with a recently manicured fingernail of the same color. "I just wanted to touch my beautiful babies again. They are so precious to me."

He unlocked and swung the heavy door open, and gestured her to enter. She nodded graciously and went inside the vault. "You're most kind. I truly don't know what I'd do without you."

"Your wish is my command." He couldn't have sounded more insincere if he'd bowed and scraped at the same time. "You do have your keys for your box?"

She offered a suggestive shoulder lift. "Why, Mr. Hussein, what a question to ask a lady. I have mine. Do you have yours?"

The poor man couldn't win. He hurried to Cashmere bin-Awa's several lock boxes, flustered with her suggestive tone. "Which one are your, umm, babies safely secured in?"

Tess tapped the box that matched the key in her pocket. Alex's information had better be right. Pulling the key up and into Mr. Hussein's face, she winked, then inserted it. He unlocked the second lock and... bingo. Perfect fit.

Tess released the breath she hadn't realized she'd been holding. Mr. Hussein did the same, the poor, poor man. It was so not his day. "There you are," he said hurriedly. "Most customers are allowed ten minutes, but I'll make an allowance for you, Miss bin-Awa. There's a phone just inside the vault door. Take all the time you need to examine your treasures. Ring when you're finished."

"I'm sure you—" Right on schedule, the alarm shrieked. Tess feigned indifference, raising her voice over the din. "If that is the press, please tell them to wait for me upstairs. Ah, the noise. I'm not ready to meet with them. They can be such a bother." She waved her fingers, shooing him off as if nothing troubled her. "Go on, now. You have a bank to attend to. Don't worry about me. Once I see my babies, I'll be fine."

"It's not the press." Mr. Hussein glanced nervously toward the stairs, then back to Lee and Alex, still as immoveable as the marble pillars on the first level. "It's against bank policy to leave a customer in the vault when an alarm is triggered. I'm afraid I'll—"

"You don't trust me?" Tess spiked an eyebrow, one hand on her hip and her lips pinched into a childish pout. This was where the rubber met the road. He had to believe she was a powerful brat with too much clout; that she would run to Daddy bin-Awa at the first inkling of not getting her way.

Mr. Hussein lowered his chin to his chest as he suffered through a full-on body tremor. "Of course I trust you. I have only the deepest regard for your father. Please. I will secure you inside the vault. Your bodyguards may wait here if they choose, or they can go upstairs with me." He swallowed hard. The poor guy's throat had to be parched the way he worked his throat muscles.

"Don't worry about them. They'll wait here," Tess said. "Now lock me in. Hurry. You have important business to take care of. I don't wish to be a bother."

Mr. Hussein did just that. Pushing the heavy vault door shut, he closed Tess inside.

Finally! She ditched the heels the moment the door sealed, fully aware a video camera inside the vault recorded her every move. Instead of lifting the lid on the lockbox, she feigned a fit of sneezing that took her out of the camera's line of view. Once beneath it, she pulled a small aerosol can and a pair of gloves from the folds of her hijab. With one shot of the acidic spray, the camera lens was permanently distorted.

She tugged the gloves on. Just as quickly, she scurried to the wall where Turik's safety deposit box was stored. Again, she wondered at the scope of Alex Stewart's covert surveillance business as she slid the appropriate box from its numbered location. The man seemed to have inordinate access to all manner of resources. She could learn to like him. She had the bright ideas, and he definitely had the means. They could go far.

Laying the metal box on the table at the center of the room, and using the two keys Alex had provided, she opened Turik's lockbox. There lay the most exquisite artifact in the world, the reliquary of Alexander the Great's lost love, the royal Bactrian Queen Roxana. Tess lifted it into her gloved hands, in awe of the ancient queen all over again.

Unfastening the tiny metal latch, she double-checked that both desiccated fingers were still intact. Tess had to be sure. Closely examining them, she looked for the barely visible impressions left by Monsieur Favreau's scalpel. He'd been so careful not to damage the relics when he'd taken his DNA sample, but Tess had been just as careful to observe, to memorize the unique identifying characteristics of those age-old fingers.

She breathed a sigh of relief. Both fingernails were stained and dark, both chipped with unique and delicate patterns of decay. Yes. These were the same fingers.

Satisfied but her throat parched, she set the reliquary on the table while she removed her personal lockbox. Within a minute, she transferred the reliquary from Turik's lockbox to Tess Culver's. Quickly, she replaced Turik's lockbox and hers to their proper places.

Her heart pounded and her lips were dry. Time was running out.

Although Mr. Hussein had said she could have all the time she wanted to play with her collection, once he realized the scope of his problem upstairs, she knew he'd return in quick order. As heavy as the vault door was, it could open silently at any moment. If he caught her now—

Anxiety crawled up her back like a giant spider. She hurried to the table where Cashmere's lockbox waited, its lid still down.

Click. The precision cylinder in the massive door had just tumbled. Oh my God! He was back. She wasn't done. She needed Cashmere's blue stones in her hands to authenticate the ruse. Her heart thudded. Tess ripped the gloves off and glanced over her shoulder. The vault door hissed open. Time was gone.

Panic grasped her by the throat. The lid was stuck!

She tried again.

Tick. Tock. Tick. Tock.

"Sir." Lee tapped Mr. Hussein's left shoulder before he could swing the vault door open. "I believe you dropped this."

Keeping his best *Men in Black* impression going, Lee handed the tense-looking man his very expensive Rolex watch, which Alex had successfully lifted only moments earlier. Mr. Hussein glanced at it, and did a lightning-quick double take. He snatched the watch out of Lee's hand, glaring like he couldn't believe he'd lost it to begin with. Suspicion shifted across his face.

Lee returned to a bodyguard stance, his hands clasped in front of him, his back straight, and his Oakleys forward. He and his boss were clones for the moment, two bouncers whose only duty was to protect one Cashmere bin-Awa, who had better get her pretty little ass out of that vault if she knew what was good for her.

"Where did you find it?" Mr. Hussein barked, his nose twitching in annoyance.

"On the floor, sir," Lee offered his best Tommy Lee Jones impression. "Isn't it yours?"

"Of course it's mine. You know it's—" Hussein's eyes darted up the hall, back to the stairs, and finally landed on the vault. "Thank you. You're a rare man. Most people wouldn't have returned an expensive watch like this." The heavy door opened soundlessly while he circled his wrist with the elegant piece of jewelry and clasped it shut.

Lee flashed the pretentious watch on his own wrist, hopefully a good enough fake Rolex to be convincing. "I don't need two, sir. Just doing my job."

Raucous coughing caught Lee's attention. There stood the beautifully distraught Cashmere bin-Awa, one hand caught up in the purple scarf around her neck to cover her nose and choking her tear-filled eyes out. She leaned dramatically against the doorframe, her other hand to her forehead. "Praise Allah! I thought you'd never come." She coughed and sputtered again. "The air in here isn't good, my friend. I have been suffocating this entire time. Come. You must see this."

Pulling Mr. Hussein into the room with one hand, she held her scarf to her nose with the other. She pointed to an odorous wet spot on the floor. "Don't you have enough staff to clean the vaults? Are you too poor to afford simple maintenance, or are you too cheap? How could you do this to me? Me! Prince bin-Awa's only daughter!"

Lee listened to her carrying on and Mr. Hussein's flustered apology. The poor man had just had the morning from hell. First, the royal brat had shown up unannounced. Then the electronic device hidden in Tess's purse had pinged the high-tech vault's security system upstairs. And now Miss bin-Awa was coming undone in his basement over a puddle of something Tess had deposited on the floor. Actually, it was a semi-toxic concoction of mashed camel dung and some kind of cleaning compound Jordan had come up with, its rancid odor wafted unpleasantly into the hall. No wonder Tess was hacking up a lung. It smelled nasty.

"And look at this," she demanded, her sexy Eastern Bloc accent growing whinier. She dragged the bank manager by his elbow to one corner of the room.

"What is it?" Mr. Hussein squinted at the video camera, its lens now opaque and worthless.

"How do you expect me to know what is wrong inside your bank? That isn't my problem. It is yours," she declared emphatically, gesturing to a tray of glistening blue stones on the counter behind her. "I was barely able to enjoy my lovely collection when I was overcome by noxious fumes. I looked around and I found this, this mess! You've ruined everything! My entire morning has gone sour in my mouth!"

Lee suppressed a grin. *Okay, now she was just plain overacting.*

"But Miss bin-Awa..." Mr. Hussein tried to get a word in edgewise.

"No!" Tess stormed out of the vault, still coughing and covering her mouth. "You'll have to secure my collection for me. I'm too weak to do it. I'm faint. The fumes in your vault have compromised my delicate system. Ahh! It is too hard to breathe, and your bank is still too warm. I'm so disappointed in you, Mr. Hussein. I thought you were my closest friend. I can't stay one second longer. I want to go home. I need the fresh, cold air of my country to restore my good health."

"But Miss bin-Awa..." He stood perplexed at the vault door as Tess feigned another coughing attack, leaning into Lee with her head bowed, her slender fingers covering her mouth, obviously in a shattered state.

"Get me out of here, *meine liebchen*," she begged pathetically. "My heart is broken. I must call Father. Can you dial his number for me?"

"Yes, ma'am," Lee replied stoically, not cracking a smile at the spoiled brat on his arm who'd called him—in German no less—her sweetheart. *Let's hope Mr. Hussein is too spun up to notice.*

"Wait. Please. Let me help." The poor guy had a problem, caught between Cashmere's now unguarded precious stones in the vault, and his very angry client throwing a class-A temper tantrum in the hall. Lee almost felt sorry for him as he supported the weeping phony Cashmere up the steps.

Tess let out a distraught wail. The few customers in the lobby turned at the loudly distraught woman on his arm. The security guards held the entrance doors to hasten their departure. Alex followed closely behind, his hand to his ear while he relayed specific and clear instructions to the pilot of the non-existent bin-Awa Lear jet on the tarmac at Kabul International. "Prepare for immediate take-off," he ordered loud enough for all within range to hear. "Yes, that is a go. Have Prince bin-Awa on the phone by the time we arrive."

Into the pristine black limo they went where their driver, Hunter Christian, had the engine running. He met them with a stifled grin, the limo door open. "Well done, guys."

"Sit rep," Alex barked the moment he slid into the front seat and closed his door.

"The cell phone in Miss Culver's purse is transmitting perfectly," Hunter replied. "It'll ping the anti-theft alarm on the main vault as long as it's in the building. The noise will be unnerving at thirty-minute intervals. It should provide all the distraction we need for step two."

"Are you two ready?" Alex turned to the backseat where Lee and Tess sat side by side.

"Ready," Lee answered, while Hunter pulled away from the curb. "Mind closing the privacy window so we can change?"

"Copy that." Hunter activated the dark glass, his brow lifted, the hound dog.

The smoked-glass window between front and back seats was no more than raised when Tess captured Lee in a passionate tangle of hands, lips, and tongues. "We don't have time for this," she breathed, her hands wandering over his chest, down his abdomen to his belt. "But seeing you in this suit," she moaned as she pushed his jacket off his shoulders and whipped his belt out of its loops. "You're so damned hot."

Me? Hot? Lee's blood fired at the nerve of this woman climbing into his lap and undressing him. It had been a long time since he'd heard anything close to the sexual tension or the urgency in her voice. His tie went next. He returned fervent kiss for kiss, his hands just as quickly to that annoying scarf at her neck that made it impossible to nuzzle her throat.

Common sense kicked in the second her long fingers breached his zipper and fondled him. "Holy hell, Tess," he ground out, clutching her hands before she delved any further. "We can't do this. Not now. Not here." *Not with my boss in the front seat.*

The needy moan from deep within her throat made him think twice. They couldn't grab a quickie in the back seat of this limo while Alex sat in the front—could they? His body roared, *"Hell yeah!"* but his brain offered nothing but pure, hard to accept, logic. *Be smart. Work first. Sex later.*

"But I deserve a reward for my performance," she coaxed, her breath hot against his, her tongue caressing the hell out of him, "and I want it now."

This—*this*—was why Lee craved her. Her passion. Her impulsive spontaneity. Her voracious hunger for life and for him. She made him feel like a kid again, like he could do the impossible. Manly satisfaction tweaked the corners of his mouth. With her kind of kinetic energy in his big hands, how could he lose?

Well alrighty then. "Lose your skirt and your underwear," he ordered. "This is going to be quick."

He should've known better. Tess stripped out of that pencil skirt, her blouse and—everything. *Holy Jesus H. Christ.* All Alex or Hunter had to do was accidently bump the button to activate that smoked-glass barrier, and Lee would be fired on the spot for having his hands all over his very naked client. Who cared? Not him. Not with this sultry temptress perched on his knees and fondling the hell out of him.

She giggled and she wiggled. "Your turn. This is supposed to be quick, remember?"

He hurried, dropping his boxers just enough to get the job done. He'd no more than bared himself when she straddled his thighs, her hot core dripping down on him and her body poised for action. Lee took control of her naughty propensity for risky situations, his hands firmly on her hips to hold her still before she started rocking the limo. It had been a long damned time since he'd done anything so daring.

"Gently," he urged quietly, a definite raspy timbre to his voice. "Smoothly."

He lowered her onto him, sheathing himself into the bliss of her steamy bliss, his body aching for release. The outright dangerous position they were in added to the sexual tension rippling up his spine. Tess ground her hot self against him, her hands braced on his shoulders while he controlled the ride. Breathing hard, she rocked gently, her eyes on him all the way, as in… All. The. Way.

A whimper escaped her lips at the same moment the burn commenced low in his groin, thickening him while he stretched her. The roar of the fire in his veins threatened his control, but he held fast. To her. To their incredibly hot connection. The sultry scent of their sex filled the back seat area, but he didn't care. It only added to the outrageous risk factor. The insanely foolish, adolescent stunt he meant to carry to fruition now that he had his hands full.

With a quiet whimper, Tess arched her back, filling his face with her soft, pillowy breasts. He latched onto one taut nipple, suckling her into the fiery hunger of his mouth, swallowing her whole. She mewled and lightning struck him hard. He pushed up and into that farthest recess of her core, lifting her ass with that final explosive thrust.

And damn. The risk was worth the sensual energy that struck, welding them together. It was worth every last heartbeat of her amazing ride. Before the sizzle from that magnificent arc of pure white lightning collapsed them into each other, he tugged her under his chin, his palms still splayed over her naked ass, kissing her passionately, needing that exclamation point to the end of this utterly crazy operation.

Her hands smoothed down his waist and around to his backside, squeezing between him and the leather upholstery to hold him tight. With one last passionate taste of her sweet lips, he lifted her temporarily sated body off of his and away from more risky temptation. For now. There were no two ways about it. Tess would be the death of him.

But what a way to go.

Chapter Eighteen

He'd never planned to be a bank robber. It just happened. One moment he was a junior agent for a prestigious covert surveillance company out of Alexandria, Virginia. The next he was making love in the back seat of a limo, then waltzing through the front doors of the Bank of Central Kabul with the stunning Tess Culver on his arm, and the second heist of the day was underway.

She'd traded the red hair of Cashmere bin-Awa for her own natural ebony piled high on her head with wispy tendrils dangling casually over her neck and around her ears. The scarf was gone as was the expensive get-up and high heels. He couldn't take his eyes off of her when she'd changed clothes in the back of the limo. What red-blooded guy could?

"You're going to make me laugh." She'd warned him as she lifted that sexy butt off the leather seat to slide denim jeans up and over her hips. "Stop looking at me like that."

He'd pretended innocence while he'd pulled on olive drab cargo pants and a red, white, and blue T-shirt, courtesy of Hunter. "Like what?"

"Like you're hungry again." She offered another dazzling smile, tying the white laces on her bright pink Nike running shoes. How appropriate for the cat burglar she was at heart.

"I am hungry." He licked his lips. "Can I help it if you're drop-dead gorgeous? The first minute I get you alone, I'm going to eat you up. Count on it."

That had made her wiggle. By the time they were changed into tourist-type street clothes, he was thinking of room service and a candlelit dinner to celebrate their impending one-upmanship over the arrogant Taliban assassin. Maybe a flaming dessert. Definitely flaming sex on the table. Maybe sex in the shower of some high-priced hotel. Or on the balcony. It had been a long time since any woman had made him feel this way. He wanted Tess happy from one end of her very sexy body to the other. Safe, happy and all his.

He'd doffed the Oakleys, then covered his head with a baseball cap, the brim in back, and away they went, holding hands like two kids on vacation. She'd slung a simple cloth tote over her shoulder to conceal the reliquary once she'd retrieved it. By the end of this heist, Turik would be out of luck, and Tess would have what she wanted out of her drop box and back in her hands.

"Comm check." Alex's voice in Lee's ear came through sharp and clear.

"Copy that," Lee replied, his eyes on Tess and his index finger to his earpiece to reduce the road noise.

"We'll be waiting at the corner in twenty. Be there."

"Copy that." Lee swung Tess's hand in his. An errant thought of marriage flitted through his mind. Being with Tess elicited strong feelings, but a wedding? Mortgage? Children? The universe had just shifted, or maybe it was the whole world. Whatever.

She looked different all of a sudden, her eyes brighter and her smile deeper. Even her shiny hair bounced with more energy. This woman challenged him in so many ways. Here they were on their way to complete a seemingly innocent transaction that had mind-bending implications, and he was thinking of making her his wife? Life didn't get any crazier.

"A penny for your thoughts," she said as they climbed the steps to the front doors of the bank.

He lifted her knuckles to his lips and kissed them. "I'm just thinking I'm the luckiest man alive."

The two security guards at the entry stepped aside. An alarm sounded throughout the building for a long shrill burst. Lee covered his ears with both hands. "What is all that racket?" he shouted to the guard.

"It is nothing to be concerned about, sir," the stern man announced with a heavy Arabic accent. "We are having a minor difficulty with our security system today. Please go about your business."

Lee swatted Tess's backside. "Git your business taken care of so we can get out of here, sweet cheeks. That racket's awful hard on a man's ears. Step on it."

She shot him a mischievous grin and a wink over her shoulder on her way to a teller's window. "Shouldn't take me long, dear. Are you hungry?"

"For you? Always!" Lee declared with a salacious grin. He stayed next to the guard, his arms folded across his chest, watching her walk away. "Just got engaged," he said, rocking on the balls of his feet. "Yep. We're headed to Dubai for a little private time together. You ever been there?"

The guard scowled and stepped away. Lee kept watching Tess. Yeah. Dubai would be the perfect place for a honeymoon. Or Paris. Maybe Rome.

She cast a sideways smile at him and a little wave as the teller led her to the basement vault. He tapped the Mickey Mouse watch on his wrist where the previous Rolex had once been strapped. "Move it, darling. Time's a-wasting," he called across the lobby.

Tess scrunched her shoulders as she disappeared down the steps.

"Hey." He stepped closer to the same guard. "Where are they going? I thought she was just withdrawing something out of her safety deposit box."

"That vault is in the basement," the guard muttered without making eye contact.

Lee lifted his shoulders in an exaggerated shrug. "Okay. No problem. Just keeping an eye on my woman, you know what I mean? Ain't she hot?"

The guard stepped yet farther away, and Lee was amused. Meanwhile, Mr. Hussein had appeared at the main bank vault with two men in identical uniforms, both with tool boxes in their hands. He pointed at the vault and appeared to be explaining the problem of the alarm to them. Both men nodded, and just then, Tess all but danced up the steps. Her little routine had taken less than ten minutes. She waved at the bank manager, squealing. "Oh, hi! Mr. Hussein! Hi there! It's good to see you again."

He rolled his eyes and offered a pathetically unenthusiastic hand. The man should never attend a Red Sox game. He'd never survive Boston's version of the wave.

"You got what you needed, baby doll?" Lee pulled her into the security of his side and planted a kiss on her red lips.

"I did." Her eyes sparkled. "I guess there's a problem with their security cameras in the safety deposit room, honey. The teller only left me alone for five minutes. Do you believe that? I hardly had time to get my little old lockbox open, and there she was again. Isn't that funny? Let's get a chopper out of this crazy town today. I want to celebrate being your fiancée."

He steered her toward the entrance. "Nothing else I'd rather do, little lady."

The security guard rolled his eyes and opened the door. It took them two minutes to walk to the limo around the corner. Lee couldn't have been happier. He and Tess were home free.

"Wow," Seth said for the tenth time.

Tess couldn't agree more. Successfully recovering the reliquary was the shot of optimism she'd needed. Hidden in the mountains north of Kabul, Alex's hideaway seemed the perfect place for two bank robbers to lay low. That she was surrounded by armed bodyguards eased the tension she'd felt since she'd found out that Mohammed had not only shot at her, but had also stolen her prize. That Alex of all people, was in the kitchen fixing breakfast was icing on the cake. But that golden reliquary lying on the table? Seth was right. *Wow.*

"Shouldn't we open it?" Seth asked.

"Breakfast first. Put it where it won't get broke," Alex barked.

Seth waggled his brows. "Does he think he's the boss of everyone?"

She had to smile. Alex did have a way of making everyone jump.

"Come on, bro." Eric skimmed a hand over Seth's shoulders. "Outside. Now."

Seth frowned. "Holy cow. I'm surrounded." But he followed Eric.

Tess hadn't realized how hungry she was until they'd returned triumphant from the bank. The joy of reclaiming the priceless treasure barely subdued the pain of losing her friends, but she refused to be beaten down. Lee was right. She hadn't murdered them. Mohammed had. But it still hurt every time she thought of Jacque's calm love for the Afghan people and Sister Alison's devotion to the children. Mohammed Turik seemed determined to destroy everything good in this country.

The minute the reliquary was finally safe with the mummies, she intended to visit Musa's and Josef's families. They needed to know their fathers and husbands were heroes. She needed to get back to those two sweet children at Saint Raphael's, too. The place had to be in disarray since Sister Alison's death. Who was there to read Mina stories? Who cared for Jamaal and helped him get around? If she'd stolen the artifacts for the money, Tess would have those children out of the orphanage and in a home with a good family. She'd make sure they had access to better medical care. She'd find a way to get Jamaal the best of prosthetics. She'd rescue every last child.

The smell of bacon, eggs, and pancakes made her stomach growl, reminding her she wasn't rich. She'd been on Alex's dime since Lee had apprehended her. Before that, she'd depended on Sister Alison for room and board. She might have known the bank's layout, but her bank account was as close to zero as it had been since she'd come to her land of dreams. Clint was no help financially, and she didn't dare call home to beg for just a little more money. Her parents had long ago given up on her.

Lee was right. Her days in this wild, fierce land that she loved were numbered. Once she left, she'd never see Mina or Jamaal again. That thought hurt. Adopting Afghan children was another impossible dream. Leaving Saint Raphael's would be another heartache she'd have to carry for the rest of her life. Tess swallowed hard, not ready to face that sad goodbye.

Suddenly, the trailer felt small. She couldn't breathe. Lee chuckled from the kitchen where he'd gone to assist with breakfast. Hunter and Jordan still kept watch on the Taliban soldiers who'd gotten close to the hidden crypt, reporting anything out of the ordinary to Alex. Eric and Seth had stepped outside. She decided to join them. She needed a breath of fresh air, too.

Opening the door, she drew in a deep breath to ease the tension in her soul. Already hot from the desert sun, the sky was crystal clear, bluer than she could remember it. The sound of two men's voices drifted from behind the rig.

"She's real pretty, ain't she?" Seth asked. "I like her. Lee'd be smart to keep her around."

Tess froze. They were talking about her. She backed into the shadow of the rig where she could watch and listen without being seen.

"I guess." Eric leaned against the diamond-plated steel bumper of the eighteen-wheeler, his back toward Tess. "How are you holding up?"

"'Kay," Seth replied.

"Still taking your meds?"

Tess cocked an ear at that question. *Meds? What kind of meds?*

"Gonna need more Seroquil if we stay in country much longer. I'm almost out."

"I'll call Mother," Eric said. "She'll find a way to get it to you. You did real good during that fight at the hotel. Has Alex talked to you yet?"

"Nah." Seth grunted. "He'll get around to it."

"Seems to me you're doing better."

"It comes and goes. You know how it is."

"Talking helps. Let it out. We've all been there."

"Not like this you haven't."

"Are you cutting again?"

"Sometimes." Seth's voice seemed lower, farther away. "It helps when I see her face at night. She's just standing there, and I watch the bullet hit her. And she's looking at me, and the next thing, whoosh. It rips a hole right through the middle of her chest and it blows her backward. All that's left are her shoes. I don't know why but cutting seems to let out the pressure."

"What color are her eyes?"

"What?"

"What color are her eyes, Seth? If you're looking at her, you have to remember the color of her eyes."

"Brown," he said softly. "They were big and brown, like a baby deer's eyes. A fawn's. They looked like brown liquid with a sad questions mark in the center, like she was asking me how I could've done that to a little girl like her."

"And her hair?" Eric seemed to be pressing Seth, his questions coming one after the other, as if they'd had this conversation before.

"Soft brown, too. She had a red braid hanging off to one side, kinda like those gals down in Jamaica. One gold bead on the end of it. It was swinging on her cheek. Kinda like..." Seth paused, "like a Christmas ornament on a pine bough in winter. She looked straight at me, Eric. Lots of bullets were flying that night, but it was like she knew where the one that hit her came from. Like she knew she was dead. Like she knew I killed her."

"What'd she do next?"

"Huh?"

Eric didn't let up. He kept firing questions. "Tell me what she did next, Seth. You remember. I know you do. Tell me."

"She knelt," Seth groaned. "She just kind of folded up like a ragdoll, and she knelt on the floor and she was gone. She had brown eyes," he said again. "And I shot her. I blew her out of her shoes. And she died. I killed her."

"What'd she have in her hand?"

"I don't know." Seth had that far-off sound in his voice again. "God, man, I don't remember everything. It happened so fast."

"Yes, you do. If you remember her shoes, you remember what the hell she was holding."

"I do?"

Eric kept him on task. "Tell me, damn it. What was in her hand, Seth? A doll? Flowers? A popsicle?" One of the two lit a match, probably Eric. The smell of sulphur took Tess back to the day four years ago when the Taliban overran the orphanage and dragged poor Omar away with them, never to be seen again. They'd shot a lot of ammunition that day, most of it into the air. It was always the same with them leaving noise, fire, and blood where ever they went. Maybe a battered body or two.

"I think..." Seth paused again. "Oh, yeah. You're right. I remember now."

This conversation sounded a lot like doctor/patient confidentiality might be at work. What kind of soldier was Eric anyway? A medic? A chaplain? And what kind of a sniper was on anti-depressants while he was on an active mission and carrying a gun?

"The thing is," Seth said softly, "I know she had a pistol in her hand that day, Eric. I know she meant to kill me. I was a stupid white guy in the wrong side of town, and I was in her way. I forgot how messed up the world could be back home. Me and the guys were just drinking a couple beers and throwing back tequila shooters. A guy oughta be able to do that anywhere he wants, wouldn't you think?"

"It'd be nice if it always worked that way," Eric said. "So what kind of weapon was she holding?"

"A scuffed up piece-of-shit Colt Mustang Pocketlite. She'd painted the grips pink. Least someone did. Looked like a toy. I wish it was."

"Pink or not, she still would've killed you with it, man."

Seth said something Tess couldn't hear, but Eric's answer was sure and swift. "Get your head out of your ass, McCray! You don't think that little gal would've blown your frickin' head clear off if you hadn't shot her first?"

A boot scraped gravel, kicking several rocks into the shadow with Tess.

"You pick. You choose." Eric spat angrily. "Every damn day you get up in the morning, you decide if you're to blame or if she was. You think it's any different for the rest of us?"

"I think none of you guys ain't never shot a kid!" Seth roared.

"You think wrong!" Eric yelled back at him. "Talk to Gabe Cartwright for hell's sake, why don't you? Jesus Christ, Seth.

Talk to Alex. You aren't the only one who's had to make a hard call in the middle of a combat situation, and trust me, that's exactly what you were in, Chicago or not. Look around. Stop feeling sorry for yourself. That thirteen-year-old girl you're feeling so bad about was making herself a name that day. All she wanted was her screwed-up rep, and you were how she meant to get it. You weren't the first, and you wouldn't have been the last person she'd shot. You ever think about that?"

"But—"

"But nothing," Eric growled. "Stop feeling sorry for that two-bit bitch. Feel sorry for the kid she would've shot the day after she killed you. Feel sorry for that little kid's mother and his father. Feel sorry for anyone she'd already killed, but don't waste one more second feeling sorry for her. You saved lives by putting her down that night. That's a sniper's ultimate job, damn it. It's tough but... We. Save. Lives."

Dead silence met Eric's outburst. Tess cringed, not wanting to be caught. It was time for her to leave. She took a quiet step backward before she pivoted on the ball of her foot. She just didn't expect to run face-first into Lee's muscular chest when she turned around. He cautioned her to be quiet with a finger to his lips while he pulled her to the other end of the rig. "Guess you overheard, huh?"

"Seth feels guilty. He's messed up because he shot a girl who was going to kill him. I don't get it."

"You don't get what?"

"That he's a sniper. He carries a loaded gun everywhere he goes. I've never seen him without one, but it sounds like he feels guilty that he defended himself."

Lee brushed a hand through his hair, instantly setting off a shock of red and gold sparks in the sunlight. She couldn't help but notice the quiet strength beneath the corded muscles under his shirt. This man radiated a calm center despite, or maybe because of, the abuse she'd seen inflicted on his body. He was as much a paradox as Seth. Why was he back in the land where he'd been tortured?

"This time was different, Tess. Seth and that gal were standing maybe five feet apart in that bar that night. For whatever reason, they both froze. He got a good look into her eyes before he had to decide." Lee shrugged. "Eric's right. She would've killed him. The police report knew her rep. She was a cold-blooded punk, pink pistol or not. She'd shot two other guys the night before in a holdup, but this time, it was straight up self-defense on Seth's part. No question about it. One of Chicago's finest saw it go down. The police never charged him. They just took his statement and let him go."

Tess glanced back at the opposite end of the rig. "He sounds so sad."

"It tortures him, but he's got to figure it out." Lee drew her close for a quick kiss on the cheek. His arms around her felt warm and strong. She drew in a deep breath of that hint of cinnamon and relaxed into his chest.

He dipped his nose into the crook of her neck, nuzzling. "You have to understand. Right now we're in a warzone. Most kills over here are sanctioned. A military sniper knows there's ugly work to be done when he's on an op. No one wants to take another's life, Tess, but in combat, it's a case of equivalent retaliation. The Taliban are sure as hell going to kill us, so we return the favor, hopefully before more boots on the ground are killed. Simple. We in the military follow definite rules of engagement, but when you're back home, you're in a different mindset. Seth thought his fighting days were behind him when he went home. He was safe in the land of the free and the brave. He made a mistake. He let his guard down."

She lifted her chin to look into the most amazing green eyes. Deep and gentle. So full of love. "Then why is he back here where something much worse could happen?"

A shadow darkened Lee's handsome face. "Because the boss won't fire a good man. Seth just has to remember that's who he is. He's not so messed up he can't function."

"That's why you're here, too, isn't it? Alex hasn't given up on you. You're a good man."

A rumble vibrated under her fingers. "He's a stubborn son-of-a-bitch. This was supposed to be my last mission with The TEAM. I didn't want it at first. I argued. I was done, like Seth, tired of carrying a weapon twenty-four-seven. Tired of fighting. Then I saw you running..."

"And here you are." She ducked her head under his chin and sighed, her ear against Lee's heart, his hand in her hair, combing tangles through his fingers. The scent of him and the tenderness of his touch eased the melancholy of Seth's predicament. "Eric sounds like a doctor, not a soldier."

"Marine Corps medic," Lee explained. "That's why Alex assigned them to work together. Seth might drive Eric crazy, but he's the only one making progress with the kid, and they both know it."

"Kid? You all look like you're the same age. Alex doesn't look much older."

"A year in combat can make a man old awfully fast. He's got ten years on me."

"He's a good man," she said softly. "All of you are."

Lee pressed a kiss into the top of her head. "I like to think so. Come on. Breakfast is ready. Let's eat."

Chapter Nineteen

"Not exactly. That's when Harley flew over the handlebars and landed face-first in pig slop," Alex said as he finished his last forkful of pancakes. "I've never seen a man slip and slide through so much crap to get away from a mad mama javelina."

Lee laughed until he had tears in his eyes, holding his stomach at the outlandish tale of Mark Houston and Harley Mortimer on their one and only wild pig hunt in northern California.

"What'd he do next?" Seth wiped his eyes, still busting a gut at the tall tale.

"He turned around and popped that pig right between the eyes," Alex said. "Best smoked brisket I've ever tasted."

Seth all but rolled on the floor, and Lee had to give it to Alex. He had a knack for leadership. One minute he was all hard-assed and belligerent, but the next, in the kitchen cooking breakfast like it was no big deal to wait on his men and women.

Lee had been to his boss's home near the Shenandoah Valley back in Virginia, plenty of times. Alex and his wife, Kelsey, held regular dinners, picnics, and get-togethers, transforming The TEAM into a tight-knit family like a good military leader would have done. He'd heard stories about how Alex used to be a regular hermit, mad at the world and everyone in it. Lee had never witnessed that side of the man.

Yes, Alex could get damned mad, but he usually had a good reason when he popped a gasket.

But he was sneaky. Lee knew what his boss was doing even in the middle of breakfast that was really more like a late lunch. He was diagnosing the readiness and fitness of his team. He was studying each individual team member. And he was planning for combat that might never come. The man never rested. He should've been a damned general. No doubt about it.

That he'd effectively diffused his team's over-the-top energy with something as simple as delaying opening the reliquary until after breakfast proved it. Alex was in control.

The afternoon was a relaxing change from the hectic hotel bombing and bank robbery of the morning. Damn it had been a busy day. Tess sat with him on the small couch, her legs curled beneath her and a glass of iced tea in her hand. The reliquary was safely hidden beneath a floor panel in a fireproof, explosion-resistant safe where Tess had placed it herself. Eric and Seth weren't expected to resume the hunt for Turik until the next morning. For this one afternoon, they were just a group of guys and one pretty gal enjoying a meal and having a good time together. It seemed surreal after the last action-packed days.

"I've got movement onscreen," Hunter said from his bank of monitors. He'd joined the team for a plate of breakfast, but opted to eat at his post.

Alex set his plate on the kitchen counter. "They're too damned close."

Hunter zoomed in on the image. "You're looking at around fifty soldiers in the vicinity of the crypt. They started closing in an hour ago. They're moving faster now."

Lee and Tess joined the standing room only crowd behind him. "No," she hissed quietly. "This can't be happening."

But it was happening and there was nothing anyone could do to stop it. Shadowy figures crept toward the entrance of the crypt. Foot by foot, they moved slowly but surely until, one by one, they began to disappear. Tess groaned as the dastardly deed unfolded. The Taliban had found the crypt. They were doing the unthinkable. Mummy after mummy was dragged to the entrance and tossed down the steep embankment. Lee clutched her shoulder until she pulled away from him and let loose a shrill, "No!"

A particularly brave soldier dragged one along the trail and set it on fire. Smoldering black smoke curled over the scene.

"Ahh!' she cried, voicing everyone's frustration. She pulled her hair and paced. There was nothing to be done but watch yet another diabolical deed by an ignorant breed of men. Finally, she turned on her heel and walked out the door. Lee let her go.

"Can't we get a chopper to take us up there?" Seth asked. "We need to stop this. You know anybody?"

"It'll take time. We're too far away," Alex answered. "We're too late."

The vandalism didn't take long. Within the hour, the activity at the crypt slowed. One by one, the brave bullies began their downward trek. Only the smoking remains were left behind. There were no words for the despicable crime against Afghan culture Lee had just witnessed. Even Alex seemed deflated by this senseless act.

"I say we go anyway," Seth insisted. "We've got to do something. We can't just sit here."

"We might be able to save a couple mummies," Eric said. "Boss?"

"We need to move this rig." Alex's answer seemed irrelevant, but it made sense. There was nothing left to be done at the crypt but to pick up the pieces, and even that would be difficult considering the extreme terrain.

Lee went looking for Tess. Closing the door quietly behind him, he peered toward the back of the rig and then toward the cab. She was nowhere in sight. A frisson of unease flickered up the back of his neck. He stepped off the stairs. "Tess? Where are you?"

Nothing. Unease turned to panic. She couldn't be gone, could she? He rounded the rig, looking everywhere. Nothing but dust and disappointment. "Damn. Where are you, honey?" he called.

"Up here." Her voice drifted from above. There she was, her legs dangling over the edge of the trailer. He latched onto the ladder at the back of the rig and joined her. Wordlessly, she leaned into him, her fingers on his chest. He covered her tiny hand with his, thankful for the feminine pulse under his thumb. Coconut and lime drifted into his nose, instantly replacing his distress with soothing calm.

They sat facing west, and despite what he'd just witnessed, Lee was as content as he could ever remember being. He'd grown up in a large family in Astoria, Oregon. Two sisters. Three brothers. The best mother and father a kid could ask for. With the Pacific Ocean two steps out his front door and the mighty Columbia River out the back, he'd had the perfect childhood and growing up years. Captained his baseball team. Took state. Dated a few girls. Went to college.

Then along came the war, and he'd joined the Marines. Deployed to Afghanistan. Ran smack into Nizari. Lee honestly didn't fit in anywhere after that ordeal. No place felt safe, not even inside that perfect home or with that perfect family he'd grown up with. His mom and dad hadn't understood how he could leave them again, but he'd had to. He didn't belong in Astoria any more. He'd been offered a job on the East Coast, and he didn't turn it down.

He pressed a kiss into Tess's dark tangles. The TEAM was the only place where Lee did fit until… the day came he didn't. He couldn't explain what happened, but even among a group of ex-military, most of them Marines who'd been through similar trauma, something was still missing. Not until he saw Tess running that first time did he feel whole again. Go figure.

The hot sun had settled low in the sky. Shadows of boulders and rocks darkened the arid landscape, but he had Tess. The warmth of her body against his sparked more than just a physical calm. He couldn't explain that either, he just accepted it. Somehow, she was familiar to his body and mind, maybe his soul. She was exactly what he needed.

The only outward sign that there was something going on in her mind was the way her right index finger kept rubbing over the top of her thumbnail. He'd expected her to be more emotional after watching her dreams ransacked and destroyed. She wasn't. Lee waited.

At last, she pointed to the snow-capped mountains in the distance. "I think about Roxana sometimes, and I wonder if you're right. Did Alexander really love her like the legend tells us, or was he just another cold-hearted man who had a world to conquer? Was she just another conquest? A trophy wife to exploit while he ruled the world?"

Lee let her talk.

"She lived in the mountains, Lee, not the civilized cities of Persia, Greece, or Sparta. Her ways were so different from his. When he returned to Macedonia, she left everything behind. Her family. Her sisters. The mountains she loved. The winter snows of the Hindu Kush. Her people. Everything, Lee. Roxana gave up all she was for... him."

The desolation in Tess's voice crept into Lee's heart. This was a side he hadn't seen of the woman he loved.

"She had to be so lonely," Tess whispered, her eyes cast up toward the rugged peaks of stone off to the northeast.

Lee raised her hand to his cheek, still content to let her speak. The senseless destruction of the mummies meant more to her than just the loss of priceless artifacts. Her own brand of loneliness eked out of her.

"This is the land that killed Alexander's dream of conquering the world," she said quietly. "No one knows exactly how he died. Some say he was poisoned. Some say his own men killed him. Others believe his ghost still walks the mountain tops."

Lee followed the direction of her finger. The high mountain snows reflected pink and gold in the waning sun.

"I think he died of a broken heart. Not even Roxana's love was enough for him. He had the greatest treasure a man could find, but he wanted the world, and in wanting the world, he wanted less than what he already had. He wanted chaff when he already possessed the rarest gold in his hand. He had the love of a good woman, Lee. He had a son on the way. He had everything, but it wasn't enough."

Lee kissed her knuckles one by one. He had a feeling Tess wasn't talking about Alexander so much anymore, that someone in her past had left her behind just as heartbroken and sad as Roxana. That she just might be as lonely as Lee was.

"The Taliban think they can destroy everything they disagree with. They leave orphans like Mina and Jamaal behind wherever they go."

"You really care about those little ones, don't you?" he asked, finally understanding the depth of her love for this country. It was always the children who suffered the most. They deserved a brighter future than the one staring down the road at them.

"It's time someone stood up to all the liars in the world." Her voice turned firm.

"You're just one person, Tess. You're not an army."

She nodded. "But I *am* one person. I might not be able to prove those fingers matched the mummified remains of Roxana anymore, but I can prove the DNA in that reliquary matches the living members of that tribe. I can prove there's still hope for Afghanistan."

He felt the import of her words followed immediately by the futility. One person could also be captured and worse. He opted for sanity. "There's always hope," he muttered, his fingers massaging the tense muscles at the base of her skull. "How did you know the mummy and the fingers were really Roxana's? You've got to have more proof than an old legend."

"I do," she whispered. "Actually, your boss does."

"Alex?"

"Come. I'll show you." She climbed down from the roof of the trailer, and together they rejoined the conversation inside. Tess headed straight to Hunter, still seated at the monitors. "May I have my cell phone back?"

"Sorry, ma'am. I've already removed the batteries of all those phones to disable GPS tracking. It's pretty much worthless. Besides, it was old tech." He opened his drawer and handed her a new cell phone. "I set you up with the latest Smartphone, unlimited coverage, and—"

"It's okay. It wasn't really a cell phone. May I please have it back? I really need it."

"It's not?" He looked as surprised as Lee felt. Reaching into the top drawer at his desk, Hunter retrieved her old phone. "Sure. Here it is."

"Thank you," she said when she had it in her hands again. "I wasn't worried when you took it from me, Hunter. You're a good man. I knew you'd keep it safe."

Damned if tough old Hunter Christian didn't blush like a little kid.

Now everyone was watching. Tess pressed the side of her phone, which released a spring-loaded compartment not unlike those inside a battery-operated watch. She stared up at Lee as three tissue-covered discs fell into her palm. She handed one to Lee, one to Alex, and the last to Hunter. Those violet-blues were full of mischief. "Unwrap your Christmas presents, boys."

Lee tipped the object in his hand out of the tissue to reveal a gold coin.

"Whoa," Hunter muttered at an identical coin in his hand. "I thought your phone felt a little heavy after I lifted the batteries."

Lee flipped the coin over in his fingers, definitely the right weight for a solid gold piece. The coin was barely the size of a copper penny. One side showed the relief of an elephant with an ornate letter 'A' printed beneath it. The opposite side showed a man's profile, his bearing proud and strong. No letters marked that side. An ornate coiled rope circled the edges.

"Wow," Seth said. "It that real gold?"

"Son-of-a-bitch," Alex whispered reverently. He turned on Tess. "Is this real?"

She beamed like a little girl and nodded. "Yes, Mr. Stewart. These are the rarest coins in the world. Only one has ever been located before. It was Alexander the Great's. He had his own coinage struck with his image."

"He was a narcissistic bastard," Alex breathed. "Where did you get them?"

"There's more," she answered without answering the question, a typical Tess tactic. "It's time to open the reliquary."

Lee handed his gold coin to Seth and went to the floor panel beside the ammo cabinet. He lifted the thin carpet aside, entered the security code into the floor vault, and removed Tess's tote. Handing it to her, he let Tess do the honor of unveiling her priceless treasure. Very gently, she pulled a long object from the bag and unwrapped the burlap covering it.

"Damn," Eric muttered when the object came into view.

"It's cool, isn't it?" Seth exclaimed proudly.

Lee couldn't believe his eyes. The reliquary was made entirely of gold, burnished with age. A cylinder of around eighteen inches in length, its width measured a man's forearm. Elegantly carved with the very obvious design of a Grecian warrior astride a horse at the front, it boasted two symbols on the side, one at each end. Lee recognized one as the ankh, the ancient Egyptian symbol of eternity. The other looked like a flower of some kind. Maybe a rose.

He couldn't take his eyes off Tess standing there with the century-old artifact in her hands. There wasn't one iota of pride on her face. No greed. No Arrogance. Only reverence, as if she held something more sacred than riches. His heart swelled as he finally saw the real Tess Culver and he couldn't have been prouder. She was no cat burglar. She was the light to his darkness and the light to Afghanistan's darkness, too. Anyone who looked at her could see the love in those violet-blue eyes. The tenderness.

She pointed to the ankh. "As I'm sure you guys already know, this is the symbol for eternity. And this"—she indicated the etched flower—"is the symbol for Roxana, also known as the Rose of The Hindu Kush." She moved her fingers over the embossed warrior astride his horse, caressing the image. "This represents Alexander the Great. His son, Alexander IV, had this reliquary made to honor Roxana, to unite her to his father for time and all eternity. Mr. Stewart, would you care to do the honor of revealing Queen Roxana's fingers?"

Alex was speechless, and Lee didn't blame him. Whatever spirit resided inside that reliquary, it filled the inside of the trailer like a living presence. Tess looked to Lee, their eyes meeting with a shiver. He didn't need to see the fingers to know they truly belonged to Roxana. An unseen presence from another dimension had just deigned to pay them a visit. He could almost feel the spirit of the forgotten queen in the air around them. No wonder the legend had survived for more than two centuries. No wonder the simple people up high in the rugged Hindu Kush revered Alexander and his beloved Roxana.

"Go on. Open it," Tess whispered to Alex. "You bear his name. You should be the one to reveal his beloved. You must see what I've seen so that you too will believe."

Alex accepted the reliquary into his arms, cradling it like a baby. "It's not as heavy as it looks."

"It's hollow and the walls of it are quite thin," Tess explained. "See the ridge along the side? Slide your fingernail along the edge. It will open."

He did as she directed. An entire quarter-side of the cylinder flipped outward. "Ahh," he murmured as he took a seat. "I can't believe I'm holding this."

"Now you know," Tess said quietly, her hand on his shoulder.

"Son-of-a-bitch. I can't believe I'm holding this," he repeated, his eyes riveted to the treasure in his palm. "It's his, umm, her f-finger."

The softest glow lit Tess's violet-blues as she murmured, "Yes, it's Roxana's and Alexander's fingers."

It wasn't often Alex stuttered. Lee went to his side, peering into the open compartment. Nestled within a scrap of coarse, dark fabric were two skeletal fingers. That would've been awesome enough, but more mindboggling was the item glittering from one of those fingers. A gold signet ring, one that kings for centuries had used to declare their power and authority. Their seal. Its stamp depicted a man with a spear atop a rearing stallion.

Wow. Seth's earlier word was the only one that fit the sight. Lee was finding it difficult to breathe. Alexander had loved, make that, worshipped a stallion he'd tamed as a young boy, Bucephalus, perhaps the most famous horse in all antiquity.

The only one Lee knew that had a city built around its tomb when it died. *Holy shit.*

He swallowed hard. He'd seen pictures of this identical representation in a war-strategy class. Rays of a sun radiated from behind the mounted figure. Two Greek letters inscribed below the image cinched the deal. The alpha and the omega. The beginning and the end. The first and the last. This *was* Alexander's seal, no two ways about it.

He took a seat beside Alex, the air knocked out of him at the otherworldly spirit of the rare antiquities in the room. He finally understood why Tess did what she did. Okay. Now he believed.

Chapter Twenty

"You look busy," Tess said to Hunter.

The reliquary was safely hidden again, along with her own personal reliquary, the cell phone with the three coins. Night had fallen. Despite the Taliban's latest crime of hate against their countrymen, Tess was at peace watching Hunter clean his rifle.

He sat on the floor near the ammo cabinet, his weapon in pieces on a plastic mat spread in front of him. He'd already cleaned two identical weapons, and worked on another, ramming the rod into the long barrel with cleaning patches. The man was a methodical study in motion, slow and steady as if every action was well thought out and pre-planned. His hands were large and capable; his fingers elegantly long and seemingly out of place for a hardened soldier.

A black tattooed snake extended from beneath the sleeve of his T-shirt to wrap around his forearm, the wedge-shaped head flat on the back of his hand. Red inky eyes stared forward to his knuckle while the slithering beast's red fork-tongue stretched to the end of his middle finger in a continual obscene gesture. Curiously, a tattooed knife pierced the creature's head from side to side, the tip of the blade pointed between his index finger and his thumb. The opposite end, the handle grip, declared USMC.

"Yes, ma'am. Just business as usual." He peered down the barrel before he re-inserted the rod. "Everyone else is busy. Thought I'd clean 'em all since I was doing mine."

"They look alike. What kind are they?"

"Custom-made bolt action rifles, ma'am. You ever shoot a rifle?"

"No," she admitted. "Just a pistol."

"You conceal carry?"

"I don't, but I should."

"I can set you up with one of our extras if you'd like. The boss won't mind. He'd as soon everyone was gun smart and packing."

Tess glanced at Alex. He practiced what he preached. Two pistols occupied the double leather shoulder holster he wore, and she had no doubt they were loaded. The holster looked worn, the polish thin and scuffed. He'd unstrapped a nylon ankle-holster earlier, and stored it in the top shelf of the ammo cabinet. The knife sheath at his hip sported a heavy black-handled blade.

The sight of him armed like he was filled her with a definite sense of awe. Even on the phone, he exuded power, and there was no other word for it; he was a handsome man in an elegant yet feral way. Dark-haired with a hint of silver at his temples, he cut an intense, rugged profile, not so much heavily muscled as trim and athletically fit. He seemed the kind of guy who could and would challenge everyone, physically and mentally.

The stories he'd told earlier revealed a humorous side to him, but she'd seen the other Alex Stewart, too. He'd shifted from savvy businessman to sarcastic commander-in-chief in a snap, and his team jumped to obey when he did. They were probably used to following orders. She, on the other hand, didn't jump to anyone's orders, and she wasn't going to start now. She definitely didn't want to be on his bad side, but neither would she allow herself to be bullied.

Alex seemed the type who'd push until a person shoved back. So she had. It had made a difference. Their path toward an agreeable peace accord had been one power struggle after another, during which he'd resorted to using the brute force of Agent Lee Hart. She didn't mind that so much now, but she also wished she'd been a little less confrontational. Maybe things would've gone smoother if she hadn't been so unreasonable with Lee. Alex only wanted to help. He had an odd way of asking. Make that telling. *No, make that kidnapping.*

She shrugged the paradox that was Alex Stewart away. Something was up. She could feel it in the air. He stood behind Hunter's chair, his satellite phone glued to his ear, discussing relocating the rig. It was hard to tell exactly what he was saying. Like the other men, Alex spoke in acronyms and military speak—racks, head, aft, and the forever present ma'am. It had made her feel old at first, but she'd decided it was just the way these ex-military types worked. Respect seemed automatic with them.

There were six bunks on the back wall. The upcoming possibility of sleeping in the same space with six men would be interesting. She wasn't so much intimidated as wondering what Lee thought about the arrangement. He and Eric had taken a walk earlier that had ended at Lee's Humvee. Lee looked up when he'd noticed her watching through the front window. That simple eye-to-eye contact had elicited a wiggle she couldn't hold back. The man did things to her body without even trying.

"Appreciate the support." Alex finished yet another phone call before he gathered his troops, calling Lee and Eric inside. "We're relocating. Tonight."

"Where to?" Lee asked.

"Lieutenant General Scott just offered up a parking stall inside Eggers. Stow everything. We move in ten."

"Isn't he the new NATO Commander?" Lee asked.

"And a damn good friend," Alex replied. "Worked with him years ago."

"So we'll operate from Eggers from now on?" Eric asked. "No more hotels?"

"For now," Alex answered. "The Taliban exploded a car bomb during the attack on the hotel. Like it or not, Eggers is our only safe port."

Lee blew out a slow breath. "That means we have to travel back through town. They'll be laying for us, Boss. Are we sure about this?"

Alex nodded toward Tess. "No choice. We've got what they want."

"I need to contact Pieter Marchal," she said. "He can facilitate getting the reliquary out of the country."

"So can I," Alex declared. "Why risk transferring it to a third party when we can do it?"

Her need to argue with this domineering male persisted, but Tess couldn't honestly come up with a good reason not to trust him. She'd seen the reverence on his face when he'd handled the reliquary. Even now, he was asking, not telling.

His finger tapped the edge of the desk where he stood. Blue eyes studied violet. She studied back. A different light had graced those devilish blues since she'd proven she had the artifact. He'd allowed her to return the reliquary to the safe. He'd even trusted her with the security cod, in effect respecting her ownership of the artifact. So why did it feel like everything with him was a power struggle? Was he toying with her? Baiting her? Daring her?

"Okay," she said evenly, not breaking eye contact. She'd trust him. Again. "But the reliquary is under my control. I make all decisions concerning its future."

"Yes, ma'am." He nodded, a bemused smile tugging the corners of his eyes. There was that word again, only from him it sounded more like a tease.

"Boss, Miss Culver could use a weapon," Hunter interrupted the stare down, his rifle now reassembled and the cleaning kit stored. "You mind if I arm her?"

"Not at all," Alex said, again with that same smile. "Glad to hear it. Give her one of the Rugers." He glanced at her hand. "One of the smaller ones. Extra ammo, too."

Just that fast, the confrontation was done. Lee winked across the room and gave her the thumbs up sign. Whatever just happened, he seemed to approve.

She balked when Hunter pulled the Ruger out of its case to give her a quick safety lesson, though. The pistol he meant to give her looked too small, and she'd wanted a real gun.

"Trust me," he said as he smacked the six-round magazine home with the heel of his palm, his dark eyes serious. "This baby's perfect for most ladies. You don't need a big gun to get the job done, and look…" He tapped a nearly invisible pressure pad at the front of the trigger guard. "Laser. Just point and aim. You'll get your message across."

Tess pointed the weapon at the floor, away from the guys to get a feel for the pistol and to test the laser, her slender fingers alongside the trigger guard to ensure no accidental discharge. This little baby, as Hunter called it, would've been a better choice that night up there on the palace rooftop than the bulky revolver she'd lost. The Ruger was lighter. More compact. It fit her smaller hand, and the weight of it was perfect. She could've hidden it in her pocket while she'd run up all those stairs. "Thanks, Hunter. This will do. I like it."

"Here, put these pinkie mags in your pocket." He handed her two more loaded magazines and a nylon holster for the gun. "You're right handed so strap this holster over your left shoulder, and wow, look at you. You're damned near one of the guys." He stood back as she did as she was told, the pistol now snug under her left arm. His gaze dropped to her boots and slowly travelled up her legs, flickered over her waist and breasts, but the look of approval on his face and the lazy, crooked smile on his lips took her breath. Nothing but stark male appreciation.

She snapped her fingers to get his attention. "My eyes are up here, Hunter," she teased as she cocked her head to the side. "On my face, not in my bra."

He shook his head as an embarrassed smile brightened his all too serious mouth. "Sorry ma'am. For a second there, you reminded me of someone else. I apologize for being a jerk. Lee would kick my ass if he saw me ogling you, and he should. Anything else you need?"

"I hope not."

"You take care of yourself," he said as he brusquely secured the ammo cabinet, all business and the smile gone. "I'll see you on the other side."

She stopped his hurried withdrawal with a palm to his rock solid forearm, hoping she hadn't offended him by calling him out. Man, this guy had some muscles under that shirt. "Whoever she is, Hunter, she's lucky to have you in her life."

Hunter stopped what he was doing. He looked at her hand on his shirtsleeve, then met her gaze head-on. A shadow shifted within those heavily lashed pools of deep, dark coffee brown. "No ma'am, she isn't. She got herself pregnant and married a rich guy before I joined the Corps. Now if you don't mind, let's roll."

Ouch. Tess drew her hand away as if she'd been stung. Hunter angled his shoulder and walked away. Whoever that married woman was, she was an idiot.

The men didn't need ten minutes to secure the inside of the trailer. Seth had already cleaned the kitchen, what he called the galley. The few loose items around the desks and monitors were easily secured and the drawers locked up tight. Travel commenced as soon as everyone vacated the trailer and climbed into their assigned vehicles. The sun had already set, the western sky barely aglow as darkness descended.

The convoy consisted of Jordan driving the eighteen-wheeler tractor and trailer with Hunter literally riding shotgun. She'd seen him store what looked like a sawed-off version of the weapon and another rifle beside his seat. Alex followed in his Humvee with Seth at his right, both equally armed with additional rifles. The exact names for the weapons they were now equipped with evaded her, but one she knew for sure— RPG. Seth had stowed the grenade launcher behind his seat.

Eric and Lee brought up the rear in Lee's Hummer with Tess in the backseat. All of the men were armed with the compact rifles Hunter had just cleaned. Pistols graced their hips or thigh holsters. Tension was high as they'd pulled out of the narrow canyon they'd hidden in. They had miles to go through dangerous Taliban terrain. Predominantly a United States military base, NATO Camp Eggers was located near the U. S. Embassy in Kabul, not far from the Presidential Palace. Getting there over dirt roads wouldn't be easy, but that wasn't the problem. Who might be watching those roads was.

The vehicle's headlights pierced the heavy darkness as Lee continually scanned all directions. He turned from the front seat, his hand cupping Tess's kneecap. "If anything happens, you stay with me and Eric. Stick close. Understood?"

She nodded, her mouth dry.

"I mean it, Tess. I know how you are. You think you can fight the world. Not this time. You've got some of the best snipers covering you right now. There isn't a one of us not ready to die for you. Don't make this hard."

That thought had never crossed her mind. *Die for me?* These guys she barely knew? She glanced at Eric's dark eyes in the rearview mirror. He winked as if he'd just read her mind and agreed with Lee. Tess gulped. That extraordinary sense of submission flooded her psyche once again. She was there to help these guys save her life, not hinder them. She could do this.

Lee tapped his fingers to her knee. "Okay?"

"Yes," she answered, trembling at the very real danger zone they were entering. Her quivering stomach pitched acid up the back of her throat.

"Don't look so worried." He rubbed his palm over her kneecap, the warmth from his manly touch calming her nerves. "We're only twenty miles out of town. Once we pass the airport, it should take thirty minutes to get to Eggers. We'll get you there safe and sound."

She nodded, wanting to believe it could be that easy. Turning back toward the front, he removed his hand and instantly, she wanted it back. Lee was her rock. Without him, the night seemed so much darker and the short journey into town frightening.

He tapped his earpiece and cocked his head, no doubt listening to orders from Alex. At the same time, Eric turned the headlights off, plunging them into darkness again. The convoy moved slower, but just as steady. Tess's heart leapt up high in her throat. What did Eric know that she didn't?

The sights that had flown by on their hurried exit out of town turned to indistinguishable shadows. Modern concepts like streetlights didn't exist in Afghanistan. Except for the few lively nightspots in downtown Kabul, the rest of the countryside closed up shop and went to bed after evening prayers. A single campfire could be seen for miles, halogen headlights farther.

"Are we on Kardoshman Road?" she asked.

"No. KB," Lee answered, his tone tense. KB as in Kabul-Bagram Airport Road, swung northeast of the airport before it connected with Russian Road to go west or Awali May Road to go into the city. Everything looked the same outside her window—dark and dangerous.

Eric muttered something she couldn't quite make out. When Lee leaned closer to him, she stifled more tremors. These two soldiers were discussing possible scenarios and strategies she wasn't privy to. No doubt Alex was advising them, Hunter and Seth, too. They all knew more than she did.

Tess brushed a hand through her hair, wishing they were already safe inside the Army base.

Eric slowed the vehicle to a crawl. "Just a herd of sheep, ma'am," he said quietly. "Nothing to worry about."

When a herd of wooly bodies and unexpected bleating inundated the Humvee, her heart pounded harder. Despite the cover of night, every vehicle in this convoy was a sitting duck. Even now, Mohammed might be lining them up in the sights of his rocket launcher. She rejected that thought on sight. The Taliban would never blow up the reliquary. They needed it as much as she did, if only to witness its demise. To brag how great they were, like they did when they destroyed the Buddhas at Bamiyan. That they ruled the world and no one could stop them.

The Humvee rolled slowly forward, spiking her adrenaline with the compulsion to run. "Why are so many sheep in the road?"

Lee squeezed her knee in reply. He'd rolled his window down. When his palm left her knee, she stiffened. Brakes lights flashed ahead. Alex had stopped, the rig and Eric, too. Her heart pounded. Something was wrong. Sheep didn't stroll around at night like these were. They gathered in flocks for safety from jackals and wild dogs. They settled and grazed.

"Got it, Boss," Lee said as he leaned his rifle out his window and aimed off to the right.

"What's going on, Eric?" Tess asked. "Why are we stopping?"

"Just being careful," he answered evenly, handing a pair of goggles to Lee. "I need you to get on the floor, ma'am. Cover your head with your hands and arms. Keep your face down. Stay away from the windows."

She unfastened her seat belt and sank to her knees, straining to listen to Lee and Eric's solemn chatter. Bleating sheep shielded the men's conversation even more.

"Yeah, I see him," Lee muttered, but she couldn't see anything from the floor. *What did he see?*

"Two on this side." That was Eric.

An icy chill shivered up her neck. They weren't talking about sheep. The suspense was too much. Tess lifted her head to see what they were looking at. Both Lee and Eric's faces were masked with night-vision goggles, that in itself a *Star Wars* sight she hadn't expected. She flattened her face to the back passenger-side window, willing her retinas to pick up the slightest deviation in all those fuzzy shadows that might indicate danger.

"Alex is on him," Eric whispered.

"Me, too," Lee replied. "Got him."

Got who? Tess pressed her nose to the glass trying to see. *Who is out there?*

"Hang on!" Eric bellowed, his foot to the pedal, nearly ramming their car into the rear of the Humvee ahead of him. "We're moving."

The fast acceleration shoved Tess backwards onto the seat. The Humvee shuddered. It bumped over something in the road while Eric wrestled with the steering wheel. She nearly hit the ceiling. Another thump, bump, and—oh hell. Eric was running over the sheep in his way.

She hung onto the back seat, her hands spread wide as another bump tossed her knees up off the floor. The pathetic bleating of frightened and injured sheep filled the air. They screamed when Eric ran over them. He growled back at them and kept going.

"Incoming!" Lee hurled himself over the back of the front seat, grabbing her as he did, knocking her to the floor, smothering her into the carpet even as the vehicle bucked again.

Whoosh!

The explosions heaved the Humvee upward, sending fire through the floor that burned her hands and hurt her head. Men's voices roared around her. More gunfire. Sparks flew in dizzying waves from the most brilliant sun of heat and fire. Smoke filled her nose—the smell of blood, too. Some weapon coughed out an explosive light. The night turned into blistering, dazzling stars.

Suddenly, the floor gave way to gravel and dirt, and Tess realized she was no longer inside the vehicle. Lee's angry bellow filled the air, but he sounded far away. Her head felt heavy and sick, full of fog. It seemed the damned sheep were lifting her off the ground, insisting she go with them, and she knew then she'd been drugged. Her perfect little pistol was gone, and some of the sheep were really foul smelling men beneath capes of sheepskins.

She twisted and turned, fighting back with what was left of her strength, but her senses were dulled. Her vision blurred and her head buzzing. The violence and noise faded away.

Suddenly, it was cold and so very. Very. Dark.

The incoming grenade hit low, jolting the diesel cab of the rig upward when it exploded. Another took out the Humvee. Lee fired into the flock that was full of wolves. Taliban soldiers covered in sheepskin crouched among the herd, making the flock nervous when they moved and more nervous when they halted. Lee had spotted it first, the ropes tied from sheep to sheep, linking the animals into a nervous caravan that meant one couldn't move without the others. He and Eric communicated what they saw to Alex, but too late.

Eric opened his door, his rifle pumping rounds through mutton and man as he met the enemy head-on. Lee sheltered Tess, but had no choice. Eric needed cover so he provided steady bursts of rifle fire through the open side window. As long as Tess stayed inside the Humvee, he could protect them both.

Jordan and Hunter scrambled out of the rig to his side, covering him as well as Tess. Good men. But then they flew, tossed high on a deadly trampoline of fire and smoke. Alex and Seth appeared out of nowhere, showering sheep and shadow in arcing streams of red-hot rounds that lit both night and man.

"Fall back!" someone screamed, but there was no place to fall back to. The flock surrounded all three vehicles.

Lee searched for Eric. Against the tremendous light of another explosion, he saw him, one knee to the ground and firing, the butt of his rifle tight to his chest, but then Eric's body jerked as if he'd been hit and hit hard. From out of nowhere, a man possessed screamed as he jumped over the hood of the Humvee and charged to Eric. *Seth?*

He'd transformed into Satan incarnate, running straight into the bleating sheep and Taliban, screaming profanities Lee had never heard. A wave of wicked heat and shockwaves rolled over Lee, battering his senses. The whole world shuddered, and Seth fell, too.

A deadly sting hit Lee's shoulder. He slapped at it, then jerked it out. *Son-of-a-bitch. A hypo.*

"Tess!" he called out, his heart stuck in his throat at the awful possibility that she'd been targeted. He hunkered over her to protect her, but the head in the crook of his arm was nothing more than a rock, and he couldn't recall how he'd gotten into the desert.

On hands and knees, he searched for her between rocks and sheep. The sticky sky poured something warm down on his head. It stung his eyes, blurring his way. Coppery sweet, it trickled through his hair while the morning sun blossomed overhead in the middle of the night. His strength gave out.

He fell into the deep, dark Taliban earth.

Chapter Twenty-One

Lee groaned, stretched out on his stomach like he was, a dirty rag stuffed in his mouth. Forcing his eyes open, they barely cracked, but that was enough to see that Tess lay bound and gagged in front of him, her eyes rimmed white with fear. They were both alive. That much was good. But she kept fading in and out of focus, and breathing took effort. That wasn't good.

He stretched to test his restraints. There was no way to move with his hands bound behind him. He was hogtied, a particularly nasty method of restraint that connected his feet to his neck, forcing him to keep his back arched, so he didn't suffocate. That explained why he kept passing out. He was strangling himself.

He was conscious enough to know they were in the bed of a pick-up truck surrounded by men in baggy clothes who didn't seem worried about their victims. The word clawed at Lee. There he was, victim to the Taliban again, and now Tess, too. He'd seen Eric fall, and Seth. Maybe Hunter and Jordan. Alex? He couldn't be sure. Somehow in the mayhem, he'd been drugged.

Bitterness choked the life out of Lee. His buddies were injured, maybe dead, and he was on his way back to hell. Terror clawed at him, the awful suspicion that Nizari might be behind this, if for no other reason than this damned bumpy ride. Vague memories of another truck ride years earlier surfaced. That's when he'd been captured and how Nizari got hold of him back then. Lee pushed the despair of upcoming torture out of his mind and focused on Tess, thinking only one word at her and hoping his eyes portrayed it now. *Live.*

Tess stared at him, imparting only fear. He summoned the last of his strength and courage. There in this darkest hour, he had nothing more to offer. The truck screeched to a halt. Rough hands dragged him off the truck toward a concrete block building. His gut clenched. He recognized the cells. His cell. *Shit.* He was back at Nizari's. *Damn it.*

He twisted to see where they were taking Tess, but a blinding blow caught the side of his face. He growled, writhing backward, fighting to know what was happening to her. The desperate move only cut his air supply. A scream climbed up his throat, but came out a muffled noise through the rag in his mouth. By the time he turned back around, one of the soldiers lifted the tailgate and slapped it shut. The taillights blinked and faded as the truck rolled away.

Lee's heart dropped. Tess was gone. *No!*

Tess couldn't see. After they'd dragged Lee away, one of the soldiers climbed into the truck and covered her head with a bag. She'd tried to get Lee to listen when he came to, but he seemed incoherent most of the journey. Blood had covered the side of his head, and the way he'd blinked and stared probably meant he had a concussion. He'd been injured in the battle, his face sweaty and bloodied. So had she, but the word she kept hearing from her captors brought more waves of terror.

Nizari.

The very real knowledge that these men worked for the Taliban banker scared her to death. She prepared herself for pain. What were they willing to do to her to get what they wanted? How far would they go? Sadly, she knew. They'd already destroyed the mummies. Now they wanted the reliquary, and they'd do anything to get it. She hoped Alex and his men were still alive and that they still had it.

The truck didn't go far from where they'd taken Lee, and she was glad. She was in the same vicinity as he was. Somehow, that mattered.

Rough hands pulled her off the truck bed and lowered her feet to the ground. The smell of sweat and filth surrounded her, filled her nose and seemed to swallow her alive. She gagged, trying to breathe through the filthy fabric pressed against her face. Someone loosened the ties at her feet and right away, another shoved her in the back. She would've fallen if one of the guys hadn't jerked her back to her feet, laughing and speaking words she didn't understand. By the guttural tone, they weren't compliments.

The two pushed her forward. One kept his fingers in the middle of her back, sliding down with every step as if tracing her spine toward her tailbone. She took a quick step forward to escape his creepy touch. He muttered something to his friends who snickered. Tess shuddered. She'd left the world of men and had now entered the world of pigs.

They directed her forward and slowly up a set of six steps, across a short concrete patio, still chuckling. Judging by the muted sounds around her, she'd entered a building. The smell of cleanliness and the brush of fragranced air beneath her hood let her know she was in a house.

Three distinct men's voices. Three captors. She swayed, unintentionally bumping the guy to her left. Grunts from the others ensued. The man she'd bumped grabbed her by the waist and ground his hip against hers, chortling disgustedly as one of the others blatantly palmed her breast through her blouse.

A whimper escaped from deep in her throat, but the touching and grunts only worsened. The man at her left traced a finger over her shoulder and pushed the collar of her blouse aside. She stiffened, shaking at the thought of the worst scenario. What chance did a woman, bound and blind, stand against three men?

Suddenly, the pawing ceased. Someone else had arrived, someone the other three feared. Her knees buckled at the sickening scent of sandalwood that came with the arrival. It was him. Her worst nightmare. *Hasim Nizari.*

"Miss Culver." His oily voice rumbled between them. "You have taken something of mine, and I want it back."

She took half a step backward. The bag from her head lifted. Hasim Nizari stood less than two feet away. Impeccably dressed in a black business suit and white shirt, his black tie was encrusted with a silver pin, the profile on the pin strong, fierce, and—*Grecian.*

It appeared he'd been to the crypt.

"Shall we get down to business?" he asked, his voice as slimy and thick as the coagulated blood of his victims. He cocked his head as if listening to something far away. She heard it, too. It started low, then escalated into a masculine roar of pain. Her heart stopped.

Lee!

Holy shit!

Lee gritted his teeth so hard something cracked in his jaw. Felt like a tooth. Once again, he was hanging like a side of beef in Nizari's torture chamber. A single bare light bulb brightened the stark black splashes of dried blood against whitened concrete walls. Whoever the jerk was playing with the knife, he wasn't Nizari. That bastard had skill, a bizarre talent that allowed pain to build before it overwhelmed. Bozo here was just plain cruel, and the younger man with him was there for the entertainment value. All he'd done was watch and grin like the son-of-a-bitch he was.

Already stripped to his boxers and covered with sweat, every quaking muscle in Lee's body contracted from the pain. He blew out a snort, shocked he'd let that scream get away from him. He hated when he did that. Maybe it was just the shock of being back there again, back in hell. Who said lightning didn't strike in the same place twice?

He shook the pain off, gulping great mouthfuls of air while he could get it. Breathing was all-important at times of extreme duress. He equated it to the pains of a woman in labor. Focus. Breathe. Endure. Maybe live a little longer.

Whoever Bozo was, he and his buddy had suddenly run from the room swearing at each other. The bastard left the blade imbedded in Lee's left bicep when he'd left. It hurt like a mother. Blood ran red and watery down his stretched arm and into his armpit.

A fillet knife. Seven inches long and thin. He'd used one just like it on the rainbow trout he caught in that river in Utah. Who would've thought he'd be the one being filleted?

His mind wandered back to the peace of that gurgling stream a world away. Folks in that desert state called the darnedest things a river. A stream just had to flow downstream to qualify. Didn't even have to be big. Lee blinked the pain away, took stock of his surroundings and refocused his energy. Being back in Utah sounded like heaven at that moment, but he didn't have time for recollections.

This torture chamber was pretty much the same as the last time he'd been there. No improvements. Same style of hooks in the ceilings. Same rusted pulley system. Nizari might be a genius at mutilation, but he wasn't big on innovation.

Shit! Lee's eyes stung from the sweat trickling off his forehead. *Hurry.* Angling his shoulder to the left, he created just enough spin to view the rest of the room without losing control. A dirty table stood in the corner with the tools of the trade: razors, scalpels, knives, pliers, torches, flares, and bolt cutters.

He shook the sweat and blood out of his eyes again. There they were. Battery cables. Every torture chamber needed a pair. That must be why Bozo and his sidekick had taken off. They'd gone to get a battery to go with those cables.

Shit. It's going to be a long night.

"Don't hurt him!" Tess crumbled to the ground. Her plan to spit in Nizari's face dissolved with that heart-stopping shriek of pain. It had to be Lee. They were torturing him to make her talk.

"Then tell me where my treasure lies."

"I don't have it."

"That is clear to see. Where is it?"

"It was in the truck, the eighteen-wheeler with us," she confessed all she knew, anything to save Lee.

Nizari seemed perturbed by that answer. He cast an evil glare over her head to his lackeys before he crouched in front of her. This man could make her flesh crawl just by being in the same city. Sharing the same room as him took her breath. Sandalwood rose up in her nostrils to disguise the scent of death.

"If I remember correctly, you were in a different position the last time we met, Miss Culver." He paused to smooth the back of his manicured fingernails over her cheek. "I liked you better that way. Upside down. Subdued. Powerless."

An involuntary shudder rolled through her as she turned away from his touch. He'd promised the next time they met she'd enjoy it less. She already did.

"I prefer my women dressed in more traditional garb," he murmured, the tip of his fingers tracing her jaw down to her chin then to her collarbone. "Let's get you out of these infidel trappings, shall we. Even as filthy as you American women are, your scent still attracts me. There ought to be a way to bottle your fear, especially after all the trouble I've taken to extract it."

Squeezing her eyes tight, she willed Lee's handsome face into her mind. It failed to comfort. His cry of pain had reached just once across the distance. This was all her fault. He shouldn't have to relive his worst nightmare. There had to be a way to escape.

"I'll send my men to retrieve the eighteen-wheeler, Miss Culver. If you're telling the truth, I'll spare your friend. In the meantime, let's get to know each other better."

The moment his fingers left her skin, she bowed her head. If it saved Lee, she'd do anything. *Anything.*

"But if you've lied, if you dare disobey me..." Nizari grabbed her throat, squeezing her larynx, and bringing her nose to his. His black eyes radiated cold darkness. "I'll skin him alive, and you will watch him suffer and bleed until he dies. It will take days, but I promise, you'll watch every second of his pitiful life drip away. Then I'll do the same to you."

Tess believed him. This creature was no longer human—if he'd ever been. Nizari was become evil incarnate. Depraved.

He grabbed her elbow and marched her through another doorway into a much larger room, locking the door behind her. "Turn around," he ordered.

She did, quivering from fear, but not so frightened she couldn't take in her surroundings. The room was tastefully decorated with elegant couches and chairs, the floor covered with an expensive rose and gold Persian rug. Ancient pieces of art hung on every wall. Gold and marble Grecian busts graced finely carved wooden tables and cabinets. A collection of gold statues behind the glass doors of one of those cabinets caught her eye. She recognized the ornate collection of Buddha statues, some standing, others reclining, but all supposedly destroyed by the Taliban.

This place was Nizari's private museum. He'd lied. He hadn't sold or destroyed what he'd stolen. Despite the explicit fatwa of the ruling Imam, Nizari's home boasted hundreds of idols. "Do you like what you see, Miss Culver?" he asked, his breath on her cheek as he loosed the ties from her wrists.

Gooseflesh shivered up her neck and into her scalp, but she chose to lead with defiance instead of fear. "These pieces were in the National Museum. Now they're here. Why?"

"I collect fine things," he purred. "Paintings. Statues. Women. Girls. Boys. All were meant to be worshipped, possessed, and enjoyed—like you." He stepped around her, his hands sliding over her shoulders to her arms, then to her waist until he stood in front of her again.

Her gaze hit the floor along with her heart.

He leaned forward, his mouth to her ear. "You may hate me for what I've done to you in the past, but rest assured, you'll hate me so much more after tonight."

Chapter Twenty-Two

Hurry.

Even as the four-year-old memories rose up from the grimy floor to swamp him...

Even as an overpowering gag reflex kicked in at the smell and sight of this torture chamber...

Even as he felt the draft of putrid air currents against his body, Lee knew. He wasn't the same man he'd been years ago. Back then he'd been fresh out of boot camp and wet behind the ears. Proud. Cocky. It had taken his squad six days to find him—six days of bone-cracking, skin-burning, mind-depleting torture. Only an idiot didn't learn from his mistakes taught by the shiny implements in this mad classroom. And Lee had learned.

Lesson one: Experience was a hard teacher, but a teacher nonetheless.

Lesson two: All those bloodstained instruments were only tools, not scary instruments of impending doom and death. They could be, but he'd used each of them before in other facets of his life. They weren't scary. They were just there in a deplorable place to be used by despicable men.

Lesson three: Escape from this fun house was all about upper-body strength. That was why he'd devoted hours to lifting and pumping anything and everything to increase the power in his arms, shoulders and back. He'd grown massive, his muscles thick and—sufficient for the task at hand.

Lesson four: Time was wasting.

But the best lesson of all? It was better to kill than be killed.

The Corps' steady mantra pounded in his head. *Move it. Move it. Move it!*

This particular den of torment had been constructed fairly well. The metal hooks in the ceiling were stout enough to hold an adult male's weight. *Hmm. Five/eighteenths-inch hex head, galvanized steel lag screws*—the random thoughts of an over-stressed mind.

Lee recognized that errant observation for what it was worth, his brain's attempt to divert his attention from the burgeoning hysteria of his impending terror. It worked. The simple knowledge that this playground of horror was every-day concrete, wood, and screws reduced its horror. This cell was nothing more than that of a high school gymnasium, a place where athletes were proved and tested. And Lee was in the test of his life.

Hoisting himself up, inch by steady inch, he climbed the chain until he could reach the hook with both hands. Very gradually, and because he was shaking from the exertion, he lifted his legs until he pressed into a tremendously difficult handstand, a true test of strength for a big guy like him, but one he'd made damned sure he learned back at The TEAM's in-house gym. Agent Zack Lennox had taught him this move, God bless him.

Slowly, so as not to break his shaky center of gravity, Lee extended one leg until he could hook his heel into the neighboring hook. That was all he needed to reduce the pressure on his hands and forearms. He allowed a calming breath at that miniscule success. It put him in an upside-down position, but it allowed enough slack that he was able to lift the chain binding his hands off the hook. *His hook*. Nizari would look damned good hanging from it.

Still upside down, Lee jerked the fillet knife out of his bicep. It had gone in deep and it hurt as much exiting. Clamping his lips against the scream crawling up his throat, he allowed his pain to devolve into a groan before he tossed the blade aside. Finally free and fueled by rage, Lee dropped to the floor. He wasn't able to walk the last time he'd left this wretched place. Tonight would be different.

Move it. Move it. Move it!

So far, so good. Bozo wasn't back yet, and neither was his sidekick. Lee knew how these guys operated once they were pumped up on adrenaline. They were probably still running around trying to decide which battery to rob from whose truck. It wouldn't do to steal the wrong one.

Blood flowed to Lee's starved arm muscles. He flexed, shrugged off the pain, and prepared for the next step. He needed to be free of his manacles to be one hundred percent effective. The table should hold something to cut through the chains. He saw it then. His heart plummeted into his gut. A shiny silver crucifix on a gold chain lay among the instruments of all that promised pain. Shit. Somewhere in this shop of horrors, they had Tess.

He lifted her cross from the grimy table and hung it around his neck.

Hasim Nizari had better run for his goddamned life.

Nizari prowled.

Tess plotted.

He made her undress in front of him and clothe herself in the style of the harem, her nakedness barely covered by sheer veils, her face covered in the same manner. He forced her to kneel on a prayer rug in the middle of his grand room while he stalked her in ever-tightening circles. The shiny gold medallion at the center of the rug perplexed her, but the carpet beneath her knees was soft and luxurious.

He hadn't physically hurt her yet, but he would. A vile rapist by nature, he was the lowest kind of pervert who used little girls, boys, and young women for his brutal pleasure. Why some of the Taliban suffered his deviant appetite only confirmed how they manipulated the holy books to suit their agenda. Or maybe it proved how little they really knew about the Quran. Did he ever invite them over to view his forbidden prizes? Did they know how many he'd hidden from them? Did they care?

Nizari paused, his arms folded, his right hand curled under his chin in thought. Her nerves stretched taut, listening for another scream. Clenching one of the many veils of her ridiculous costume in her fingers, she planned Nizari's demise by strangulation. Maybe if she played along, she could seduce him enough he'd lower his guard. Once he drew close, she'd choke the life out of him. Then she'd escape and rescue Lee. This was just a waiting game. Maybe—

"The only thing I like better than a woman on her knees..." Nizari withdrew another item from the cabinet, "...is the fear in her eyes when she realizes no one can save her; that she'll soon give more of herself than she ever intended."

Tess stopped breathing. She couldn't make her lungs work. He'd lifted the object overhead like a prize and snapped his wrist forward. A serpentine crack of lightning bit the air, barely missing her ear. Her heart stuttered, her throat too dry to even whimper.

Nizari recoiled the wickedly long leather whip, its handle polished black. His upper lip lifted with a truly devious smile. "Shall we begin?"

After he cut the chains shackling his wrists, Lee dragged his pants on and loaded his pockets with all the weapons he could carry—knives, pliers, and road flares. The bolt cutters went into his rear pocket. The battery cables he draped over his neck. He left everything else behind.

Creeping barefooted toward the cell door, he heard his first victim grumbling. Bozo was on his way back. His sidekick might be on his heels, so Lee crouched low and waited, adrenaline hammering through his body. Killing these jokers might not be the smartest move, but he had to try. Doing nothing wasn't an option.

When Bozo bumped the door open with his foot, Lee exploded. His right arm snaked out and he stuck the fillet knife in Bozo's temple and left it there. Bozo dropped the battery with a small grunt and folded to the ground.

His sidekick must've thought he could accomplish what Bozo couldn't, but Lee entertained the upstart for all of three seconds. Sidekick suffered under the delusion he was invincible. He hefted his own dagger from hand to hand like the expert he wasn't. A kid should've known better. When he parried forward, Lee whipped the youngster's face with the metal clamp of the cable before tangling it with the knife. Disarmed and surprised, Sidekick never stood a chance. Lee left him on the floor beside Bozo, the cable around his neck and his tongue sticking out.

Retrieving the knife from Bozo's head, Lee wiped the blade on his thigh and pressed on. He shut the cell door and scanned the terrain. Same prison. Same bullshit. Different day. The evidence of the Corps' last assault remained. Bomb craters and debris littered the expansive field between this house of horrors and Hasim Nizari's *home*, if that was what you wanted to call a pigsty. Lights shone pleasantly golden from the windows, but none such pleasantry shone from the bullet-riddled wall of the prison cells.

Lee paused to listen. Taliban voices drifted through the night. The prisoners' building was long and narrow with multiple doors facing the house. Tess had to be in one of them. He shuddered to think of her stripped and tortured like he'd been. Lee hunkered low and prepared to meet the enemy. They wouldn't go easy, but they would go.

The first door yielded quietly, but there was no one inside, friend or foe. At the next Lee paused at the sound of groaning. Pressing the door open slowly, he caught sight of a young man hanging from the same type of hook and chains Lee had just escaped. A proud tattoo inked USMC across his bloodied, torn chest, and Lee saw red. The poor guy had been stripped down to his underwear, his chest lined with the precision cuts made by the master butcher, Nizari. A bearded man in a dirty tunic approached the poor guy with a lighted propane torch in his left hand, a pair of pliers in his right.

No fucking way.

Lee charged, opening a quick, gurgling smile below the enemy's chin. The sick bastard never saw who killed him.

"You gonna make it?" Lee asked the startled Marine as he hurriedly extinguished the torch and lowered this poor victim to the floor. "You okay?"

"Hell, yeah." The man crumbled, his nose to the dirt, his poor voice ragged and weak. "Ooh-rah. God bless America," he choked out, spitting blood.

"Whatever," Lee muttered as he cocked an ear for trouble. They could sing anthems later. Any minute now someone would discover the bodies he'd left behind. "Can you walk?"

"Yes," the man growled even though Lee suspected he couldn't stand much less walk. Nizari liked to break a man's feet, then run electrical cables around his toes to torture him while he stood back in the dark corner and watched his prisoner suffer.

This jarhead was in damned bad shape. Lee wanted to offer the same kindness that had been offered to him the night he'd been rescued. He wanted to tell this kid he was going home, but he couldn't. Not yet. He had to find Tess first.

"What's your name, Marine?" he asked gently as he crouched at the broken man's side.

"USMC... Lance Corporal... Ky Winchester, sir," Ky ground out. His face was swollen and bloodied. The poor kid couldn't see, much less assist.

"Damned good to meet you, Ky. I'm USMC Corporal Lee Hart, buddy." Lee pushed the knife handle into Ky's bloody fingers. "You kill the first bastard that lays a hand on you, understand? Gut him like a fish if you can, but end him. Make him pay for everything he did to you."

"Yes, sir," Ky declared bravely, but even in the dark, Lee saw the kid's lip quiver. Darkened blood smeared his face and chest, but there was nothing Lee could do for him.

"I've got another person to rescue. I'm coming back for you. You hear me?"

Ky nodded. It took Lee all the courage in the world to turn away. He offered the ex-prisoner one man-hug before he meant to stand. He never got to his feet. Ky grabbed him tight, clinging to him, shaking. "Sir," he growled, his tough voice shattering into sobs. "Please don't... don't leave me here."

Lee squeezed his eyes tight and pulled the man into his own bloody arms. The guy needed a moment, so Lee gave it to him. They held onto each other like only brothers in Hell could do, while Lee hugged some promise back into the kid. "How long you been in here, son?"

"F-five days, I think. Maybe more."

Lee sniffed his emotion back, biting his lip hard. Five days was an eternity, but he had to leave. "Marines never lie, do we?"

"N-no, sir," Ky responded, the top of his sweaty head pressed tight under Lee's chin and his fingers tight on his neck. "W-we never lie," he panted. "We never quit. We never f-f-fucking forget, either."

"Good answer. I'm not lying to you now, Ky. I will be back, but you gotta let me go. I've got more folks to save than just you." Lee pressed the knife handle into Ky's palm again. "Take this. There's others in this shithole who need my help. I can't leave them here any more than I'm gonna leave you. You understand?"

Ky sucked in a deep breath. "Yes, sir." His fingers relaxed and he pulled back, cradling the knife against his ragged chest, huffing for a full breath. God, the kid was a mess. It looked like someone had specifically targeted the USMC tattoo on his chest, turned him to hamburger, the edges of the eagle and globe all that was left. "Oohrah," Ky offered again, and Lee had to turn away. The kid might be scared, but he was alive.

Lee started for the door when the sad question reached him. "Sir? Was... was I... alone?"

What could he say? "Except for that dead guy with the torch, yeah. Why?"

The Marine's poor bloody lip quivered. "No... lady with green eyes?"

Lee jerked to vigilance, damn it. He might've arrived too late. This kid wasn't only half beat to death, he was losing his mind. Lee couldn't leave him sitting in the dark thinking he was crazy, though. He had to give Ky some kind of normal to hang onto, so he opted for guy talk. "I sure as hell hope not. Stop dreaming, kid. You've already got it made. Ladies like guys with scars. Now shut up and sit tight. I'll be right back."

The kid was tearing his heart out, but Lee had to get to Tess before time ran out. The next cell door revealed another man in chains, but seated on the ground and not in as bad shape. Petty Officer First Class Jack Snowden wanted payback, but Lee used the bolt cutters on the chain, then sent him to Ky with an order to clear out and get their asses to safety.

"Be careful," he warned Jack. "Ky's in rough shape, and he's got a knife. He's just inside the door so talk to him. Let him know who you are. He's scared to death, and he can't see. He will hurt you."

"Aye, Cap'n," Jack answered. "You can count on me. I'll take good care of 'im."

Two more doors to go. More Afghan voices, and Lee realized he'd stumbled on an interrogation. He paused to get his bearings. The person being questioned said nothing. Tess would be like that, stubborn and giving her abductors more trouble than they expected.

The thought of her alone in a room full of brutish soldiers triggered Lee's rage. He hefted his last knife in his right hand, the heavy bolt cutters in his left. Easing inside the cell without making a noise, he caught sight of two Taliban soldiers, their prisoner kneeling on the floor between them as they stood on the backs of his legs. It wasn't Tess, but damn…

The third Taliban soldier gripped the prisoner's hair, pulling his head too far back and berating him in one of the forty different languages of Afghanistan. The cruel man produced a long curved knife. This wasn't an interrogation; this was an execution.

The fool about to kill the prisoner looked up just in time to glimpse Lee's knife before it cleaved his forehead. He fell flat to his back with a strangled curse for all infidels on his lying lips.

Charging, Lee swung the bolt cutter from left to right, blasting its weight into the nearest soldier's temple while he landed a kick in the other's gut at the same time. The American prisoner collapsed to the floor. Lee relieved the first terrorist of the knife at his belt as he fell, and skewered his bearded friend straight through his heart with it. Neither offered much resistance after that. Three down and adrenaline pumped fast and hard through Lee.

"Who are you?" the man on the floor muttered through a mouthful of blood. "Superman?"

"USMC Corporal Lee Hart," Lee declared proudly. It felt good to hear it said correctly, expressed with courage instead of just stoic endurance in a place so bleak. He *was* a Marine; might as well be Superman. "Who are you, soldier?"

"Army Captain Ross Carter. I want to go home."

"Don't we all? Can you walk?" Lee asked, hating that he had to be tough on a man so battered.

"Yes, sir, I can." Tears and blood poured down Ross's face.

Lee gentled his voice as he helped the guy to his shaky feet. "I'm not gonna lie, Ross. It's just you and me and we're surrounded. Two other U.S. soldiers have been freed, but more Taliban are sneaking around this camp. Can I count on you to help me rescue the other prisoners? Can you see to do that?"

Ross nodded, and that was good enough for Lee. He grabbed one of the three AK-47s leaned against the wall, shouldered one of the others, and tossed the third to Ross. Together they relieved the dead men of their bandoliers and another pack of road flares. God only knew what they'd meant to do with them.

"You good?" Lee asked before they cleared the door.

"I'm damned good," Ross growled. "Let's kick some ass."

Nizari wanted her to cower, but Tess didn't have it in her. Still kneeling, she stiffened her spine and prepared for the lash. So far he'd just stalked and talked, explaining how filthy American women were, how weak and physically inferior to Afghan men. The man was a study in psychotic behavior, explaining how he preferred a woman's screams of pain to her screams of rapture. The bizarre thought of him ever pleasuring a woman enough to make her scream boggled Tess's mind. That he was evil was evident. That he'd break her? Another story entirely.

The whip cracked incredibly close to her leg, so close she felt its whisper of promised agony slither along her bare skin. It carved a sharp trail in the plush carpet as he pulled it back to his hand like a long, black snake. It hadn't hit her yet, but the lash would come, and once he started, he wouldn't stop. She might die, but she refused to cower to evil.

He flipped a switch on the cabinet and that odd gold cap in the middle of the floor moved, revealing a brass post beneath it. Swiftly, he grabbed her hands and secured her wrists through the ropes on the post before it finished rising. Her heart pounded. By the time the post stopped moving, her arms were stretched over her head. Tess couldn't breathe. This room wasn't a museum. It was Nizari's private torture chamber, complete with a whipping post.

"Hold on, Miss Culver," the real snake in the room hissed, snapping the whip again. "Your lesson is about to begin."

Ross was slowing Lee down as much as the Taliban who'd just arrived at Nizari's.

"Shhh," he cautioned Ross, watching Nizari's yard through the barely cracked door. He'd spotted three soldiers patrolling the place, another shadowing them. Too soon those guys would realize their prisoners had escaped and their buddies were dead. Lee needed to take the remaining guards out before they raised an alarm. The question was how. "You up for show and tell?"

Ross cocked a brow at him. "I'm up for anything that'll let me kill these bastards, sir."

"You know any Pashto? Arabic?" Lee asked as he laid both AK-47's in front of him.

"I speak some Urdu."

"Good." Lee knelt, his back to the door. "Put your rifle out of sight. I want you to scream the worst Urdu bullshit you can come up with. Berate me. Hit me. Make it convincing. Let's lure these last four assholes into this cell and finish them off."

Ross shook his head. "Sorry. I can't do that. I ain't hitting you, sir. Not after you just saved my life."

Lee put a stop to that foolish sentiment. They could cry later when they were singing anthems with Winchester. "Just do it, Carter. Let's kill them and get the hell out of here."

Ross nodded, sucked in a deep shaky breath, and bellowed a tirade of angry rhetoric that made Lee smile. Ross sounded like the real deal. He slapped his hands together, making it sound as if he'd struck Lee, then bellowed louder.

Boots crunched outside the final door. Someone called out. The hinges creaked as several men entered. All the enemy could see in the dark cell might be the light from the house on Ross's bloody back, maybe his upraised hand as he faked another slap. Lee grunted, feigning he'd been struck and hoping to hell all four of the guards were curious enough to fall for this act.

Ross ratcheted the nasty rhetoric up, ranting, his voice shrill and drawing the soldiers in closer. This farce would only work if all four Taliban believed. If all four of them were stupid enough to enter a darkened cell, and if they hadn't yet discovered their murdered cohorts. Lee's heart pounded at the incredible risk. The flare in his hand felt ready, but the knife in his other hand felt better. This dangerous ploy *had* to work.

At last, one of the guards called to Ross, not angry, more inquisitive, probably asking if he could join in the fun of beating an American to death. Nizari only collected the most depraved in his ranks.

Show time.

Lee jabbed the flare to the hard ground, igniting the pyrotechnic and blinding the hostiles with bright, orange light. Damn. Only three guards had foolishly entered the cell. They stopped dead in their tracks, blinded by the unexpected light, their hands splayed in front of their faces. The fight was on.

Ross barreled into the nearest guy and stabbed him in the chest. He opened the next guy's throat, while the last turned and ran. He didn't get far, probably because he couldn't see and ran into the wall by the door. With a startling burst of speed, Ross jumped on him and strangled him with his bare hands, twisting the guy's head to the left with a sharp crack. When the soldier collapsed, Ross grabbed a knife and stabbed him, and Lee let him. *Stab the son-of-a-bitch all you want. I've got to find Tess.*

Lee stood silent at the door for a moment, checking the way forward. Where the hell was that fourth guard? Bright lights still glowed from the house, but Lee knew he'd counted correctly. There was another guy out there. He cocked his head to listen, but couldn't hear with Ross grunting like a pig behind him. The man was panting. He'd gone all Chuck Norris on his victims, pumped full of adrenaline and revenge.

Lee didn't blame him. He hadn't had the opportunity to use even his knife, just let Ross do his thing, because he'd done it so quickly. So effectively. But this next infiltration had to be handled with care and precision. If this last guard was as good as Lee suspected, Chuck Norris needed to leave.

"Ross. Break cover. Hook up with Jack and Ky and retreat to safety, will you? They're both injured. They need someone to get them back to Eggers." Lee poured it on. "Can you do that?"

"Hell yeah." Ross huffed, his chest heaving. "Which way did they go?"

"Behind this row of prison cells. Keep your head up, and you'll see them," Lee ordered as he nodded the way Jack had gone, shoving the two rifles he carried at Ross. "They can't have gotten far. Here. Take all the rifles. You'll need them, I don't. Give one to Winchester. He's in rough condition, but he'll feel better once he's armed. Take all the ammo, too. Don't let me down, soldier. Get him back to Eggers alive."

"I'm not taking all the rifles." Ross pushed an AK back at Lee. "I can't leave you here unarmed. I don't know what you've got planned, but you'll need at least one."

"No, Ross. I don't." Lee fingered the grip on his knife. He didn't need the extra weight of rifle and ammo for work that needed to be done silently, as up close and as personal as he could make it. He was willing to bet Nizari was alone with Tess in that house, and if he was, the bastard didn't have long to live.

Ross balked. "You can't be serious." The light finally came on in his bloodshot eyes. "Shit. You're black ops, aren't you? That's why you're here. Now I get it. I'm out of here."

Lee turned away, not caring what Ross mistakenly thought. Lee wasn't black ops. He was just one pissed man going after the woman he loved, and he needed Ross out of his way. Ross was out of control and in worse shape and Lee just plain didn't need someone else to worry about. "Go now," he murmured, "while it's quiet."

Ross gathered two AKs, lifted the bandoliers over his neck, and situated the other rifle on his right arm. "Do me a favor and stay alive," he muttered as he headed out the door and around the prison cells. "I'd like to shake your hand some day, sir, and I'd like you to be alive when I do it."

Lee nodded, his eyes on Nizari's house while Ross faded into the night. It was now or never. Hefting the blade, he crept stealthily into the shadows along the house, his senses on high alert for any sound, sight, or scent of that other soldier, the one he knew damned well was still out there with him. The house seemed too quiet, but Lee couldn't waste time locating the missing guard. Unless Nizari had taken Tess somewhere else, the house was the only place left where she could be.

He sneaked up the steps on the south side. The lights were on, the room empty. Testing the latch, he found it unlocked. He went inside quickly, closing the door behind him. A sharp crack from the next room caught his attention. The next sound more so. Tess screamed.

Lee's rage exploded. He kicked the door off its hinges. The wretched sight of the whip raised over Nizari's head, and the bloody stripe twitching across Tess's bare back, blew through Lee like the shock wave of a nuclear bomb. He became all he was meant to be.

Muscle training took over. The knife in his hand flew from his fingers without thought or aim. Nizari's whip leapt out at him like sizzling black lightning, but Lee's blade pierced the slithering coils and hit true, shuddering upon impact, impaled deeply in Nizari's left chest. The bastard fell to one knee, not dead, only injured, but the hit was good. Solid. Lungs tended to fill with blood and suffocate a person before they died. Lee wanted that for Nizari.

"You hurt me!" Nizari shrieked, the whip dropping to his feet.

Lee would have finished the job, but Tess moaned. She needed him. Nizari would have to wait his turn.

Lee ran to Tess, but she was anchored to a post in the floor, sagging, her poor arms stretched tight and her head bowed. A nearby display of polished silver scimitars caught his eye. Shattering the glass display with his elbow, Lee grabbed a blade to cut the rope that held Tess and gently lifted her into his arms. With one eye on the whimpering Nizari, he dropped to the nearest couch to assess the damage done to the lady in his arms, the scimitar still at his side. Vicious welts curled over her soft sweet shoulders, her creamy skin torn deep and dripping blood. The clock was ticking. He needed her ready to travel before he finished Nizari off. Before that fourth guard returned.

"We've got to go, Tess," he explained. "I'm going to carry you, so hold on tight. It will hurt. I'm so sorry."

Too weak to hold her head up, Tess leaned heavily into his chest with the saddest whimper. "But I was coming to... rescue you," she whispered raggedly.

Lee groaned. How very like Tess to think she needed to rescue him. He cast his wrath at Nizari, wishing he had another knife to throw at the pig. There just wasn't time. Lee hefted the scimitar with one hand while he pressed Tess under his chin with the other and pushed to his feet. "Hang on to me. Don't let go."

Her slender arms circled his neck, but she was breathing hard and moaning.

"I always get what I want," Nizari taunted from across the room where he'd fallen, his voice hoarse, "and next time, you won't be around to stop me!"

"Shut the fuck up," Lee spat back at him, one arm at Tess's injured back, the other under her knees. For two cents, he'd march back to Nizari and cut his throat, but he had to make a choice. There was no option and little time. He chose to save Tess, to get her the hell out of there before he lost the advantage. "There won't be a next time, asshole, because you'll be dead."

Nizari seemed smaller than Lee remembered. More petite. Almost feminine. Certainly less frightening, kneeling like he was, whining and bleeding on his lovely carpet. Lee would've enjoyed it more if he hadn't felt the end of a gun barrel at the back of his head.

"Drop the weapon," a very British voice ordered, "and do take your seat, Agent Lee Hart."

Tess lifted her gaze over Lee's shoulder. The corners of her lips twitched with the barest smile. "Hello, Mohammed."

Chapter Twenty-Three

Mohammed seemed to have come out of nowhere. He looked as handsome as ever. And as deadly. He lifted the scimitar out of Lee's hand and set it out of reach. Still, Tess couldn't deny Mohammed was good-looking with those dark curls peeking out from under his checkered keffiyeh. That immaculately trimmed beard. Chocolate-drop eyes that sparkled, still fringed with decadently long lashes no man had a right to. He'd always been her weakness, masculine eye candy she hadn't been able to resist once upon a fairytale.

So gentlemanly. So much the lady's man, but so much a mindless minion of the fundamentalist purge sweeping through his country. Her heart ached to love him, at least as a brother again, but she despised all he stood for.

Reluctantly, Lee took a seat with a growl.

"Miss Culver," Mohammed said politely, almost as politely as when they'd dated during college. All he needed to do was tip his head, and she could've believed he was still the kindly, cavalier gentleman who'd courted her with wine, roses, and lies. The dapper hat he'd worn then had been replaced by the keffiyeh, a sign he really was an Afghan. Not British. Never American. His good heart had been replaced by terrorist ideals. *What a waste of a good man.*

Lee's gentle hand at her throat reminded her those silly, romantic days were over. Mohammed was just another Taliban soldier, come home from receiving a western education to terrorize the humble people of his native land, and rob them blind while he did it. That he'd once been a student of gentility and refinement appalled her. How could a man so well educated believe in the barbaric ways of the Taliban after knowing civility? He made no sense.

"You're... here," she accused, her voice weak.

"Kill them," Nizari ordered, still struggling to get to his feet, one knee raised to stand. "Kill them now!"

"I've been hunting you for days, Miss Culver," Mohammed said in the most proper King's English, ignoring Nizari. "You never cease to amaze me. At every turn, you've proven yourself my most worthy, although dangerous, adversary, quite possible even my better. I applaud you. Of course, now I shall have to kill you and your American friend, but I applaud your impeccable skill at thievery nonetheless. You've truly outdone yourself."

She offered her best evil brow for a woman whose back had just been laid open with a cruel whipping. The pain radiated long streaks of fire from her shoulders to her buttocks. Even Lee's gentle hands on her back hurt, but then, so did breathing. A tremble seized her. Soon, she wouldn't have to worry about the pain. She didn't think she could last much longer.

"You're looking... well, for a murderer," she offered weakly, grimacing at the effort her petty scorn cost.

His eyes skated over her barely covered body beneath the veils. "I'm afraid your host has been quite rude with you."

No shit. "He's not my... host," she wheezed.

Mohammed didn't reply, just strode to the nearest wall where an elegant gold tapestry hung. He ripped it down, and returned, draped it over her, his rifle still in his hand. The covering didn't stop the pain. It was nothing but the smallest token of his esteem for her, but—it was something.

"You fool!" Nizari hissed. "I'll have your head. Do you know what that is? It's priceless!"

Mohammed cut him short. "I don't care what it is. This woman is beyond priceless," he said evenly, eyeing Lee's arm. "I say, old man, tie that bloody thing up. Here. Make this work." He pulled the keffiyeh from his head, uncovering dark brown curls that added to the mystique he had going for him. An L-shaped scar nicked his cheekbone at the corner of one eye, but the man had always been Hollywood material. No wonder she'd gravitated toward him. What woman wouldn't?

Stiffly, Lee obeyed, but he pressed his mouth to her ear, his words only for her. "Hang in there, Tess. I will get you out of here."

She licked her dry lips. "I know you... will." He might as well believe that, but she didn't. Mohammed had killed everyone close to her, and she was the reason he was there now. Why would he let her walk away?

"Kill them, you fool," Nizari ordered. "Don't just stand there talking to them like you care. My men have gone after the reliquary. It will be back in my possession soon. I don't need either of them. Get it over with! Do it!"

"Silence. I've wanted to speak with Miss Culver for several days now," Mohammed answered patiently. "It seems only proper I do so before I take her life. Besides, I've just watched this single American soldier free all of your prisoners behind your back. You've nothing left to bargain with, Hasim. And your men, as you so eloquently term the pack of jackals you've chosen to surround yourself with, never left this abomination you call a home to do your bidding. Miss Culver might hold the secret to the treasure you covet so greedily, but she is not the one you should be afraid of here tonight."

Tess heard the blatant threat in her friend's steady voice, soothing but dark. Insinuating. Mohammed had changed. He was more powerful, instead of studious and playful. More intense. Stone cold serious.

Lee gazed down at her, his green eyes full of pain for her and questions she had no time left to answer. He curled her fingers to his lips, kissing them and pouring all of his love into that simple touch. Comfort flowed from him to her, offering his strength to endure. He blinked again through the sweat and blood glistening on his face; his gorgeous hair was sodden with it. "I love you, Tess."

She offered a weak smile, her eyes heavy with the utter exhaustion of pain. *I can die now. He loves me.*

"You've led me on quite a chase, Miss Culver," Mohammed interrupted the truest feelings of her heart. "That was an impressive backward dive off the palace the other night. Well done."

"Thank you," she whispered, her voice growing more faint, her heartbeat slower. Quieter.

"I must know," he persisted, like the arrogant cad that he was. "Did you find what you were looking for? Do you still believe you can pump the spirit of hope into this land, my dear Tess? Do you think someone out there can ever be as great as you've made Alexander in that foolish legend of yours?"

"Look..." she whispered, her voice fading and her strength along with it. Mohammed never understood her need to prove the legend of Alexander and Roxana. Could this foolish man not see that she was dying? Could he not see the stolen wealth displayed in this golden room of wicked deceit against his God, his country, and his countrymen? Could he not shut up for once in his arrogant life and listen? She stared up into Lee's sad face. *Oh yes, I found my Alexander. And more...*

"What?" Mohammed leaned forward, his head cocked and his handsome brows knitted in that endearing way of his, humoring her to the end. "I do say, speak up, Tess. You might've been beaten, but you're not dead yet. I've never known you to be so quiet or such a quitter. You're really not very good at it."

Lee's head jerked up to glare at Mohammed, and she knew he wanted to kill the man, but her time was running out. Before she died, Mohammed needed to understand. Only he could save Lee. She drew another labored breath. Speaking had become unbearably difficult. "Look... damn you. Look."

"I told you to kill them!" Nizari shrieked. "You work for me, not her. Do it now!"

"And I told you I will speak with Miss Culver first." Mohammed turned his back on Lee and Tess to face Nizari, his voice clipped and sharp and sounding more British than ever. "It will be quite difficult to speak with her once she's dead, don't you agree? And you are wrong. I am not one of your assassins to order around, nor have I ever worked for you. I work for the holy Imam. You would do well to remember that, brother." The word *brother* sizzled on his tongue.

That small distinction was good to know. At least it proved Mohammed wasn't in league with a despicable man like Nizari, for what that was worth. He had, after all, meant to kill her. He was still the best Taliban assassin, and apparently the ruling Imam wanted her dead.

Nizari glared. By now he'd sunk to his butt, Lee's knife on the floor beside him. The fool had pulled it out of his body, unleashing a trickle of bright red blood.

Tess dragged her eyes back to Lee. "I... love you," she said breathily, her voice infused with all the sincerity she could muster.

He nodded, those tender greens brimmed to overflowing. "I know," he rasped, kissing her knuckles with all the gentleness of his great heart. "And I love you. Don't—"

"He really does love you, you know," Mohammed interrupted again. "I wasn't lying. The bloody fool's just freed every prisoner in this compound, not to mention that he escaped his cell entirely on his own merit and killed every last one of Hasim's inept guards. This foolish American must love you deeply to have scoffed in the face of death the way he's done tonight."

She closed her eyes, content to die where she lay. *Lee loves me. He's all I've ever needed. All I've ever wanted.*

"Tess," Mohammed scolded. "You were quite scandalously dressed when I got here."

She would've chuckled if she'd had more strength. If she'd cared.

"What was it you wanted me to do?"

She rallied. "Look. Shut up, Mohammed, and... see."

"Look? See?" He grunted, amused. "What is this, a primary reading class for babies? What shall I do? See John run? Look at Judy? See Spot—" The breath whooshed out of him. "Oh. Now I see."

Even with her eyes closed, Tess sensed he had at last done what she'd requested. She let the world fade away.

"No!" Lee ground out as Tess went limp. She'd grown weaker with every word of this useless conversation, and now she'd relaxed entirely, lifeless. He cupped her head to his heart, like he could make her stay if he held her tight enough. "Please don't go, baby. Don't leave."

That bastard Turik set his rifle aside and had the nerve to crouch at Lee's knee. "Ah, Tess," he muttered, his hand to her forehead and his fingers to the pulse at her neck. "Don't frighten your American friend like this. I know you and you're too stubborn to die." He ran a hand over her face and peered at Lee. "May I take her, mate? I have something with me that may do the trick."

Lee couldn't believe his eyes. This was Turik, the murderous Taliban sniper suddenly on his knees and asking to help? "Don't hurt her," he growled, even as Turik didn't wait for permission to lift Tess out of his arms.

He seated himself on the same couch with Tess on his lap, the last place Lee wanted her to be. God, the man was arrogant. Lee would've made a grab for the rifle, but Tess's awful condition made him stay. If this was to be her last breath, he wanted to be there for her.

"My beautiful, stubborn Lady Tess," Turik muttered. "You've always been smarter than me and tonight, you've taught me yet another lesson. For that, I am most humbly in your debt."

Nothing the man said made sense. The world had shifted again, and Lee had no choice but to let this strange, cruel assassin help. Lee would've let Satan himself help if he could've saved Tess.

Turik produced a small metal flask no bigger than a perfume bottle from an inner pocket. "One nip should do the trick. I say, my good fellow, would you mind? My hands are a bit full." He tilted the bottle for Lee to open.

Turik didn't have to remind Lee how full his hands were. Lee uncapped the bottle quickly and Turik pressed the flask to her lips, tipping it barely enough for one drop of the coal-black liquid to drip forth.

"Come now," Turik whispered into Tess's ear. "Do be a good girl and drink up. We'll have none of these dramatics. Don't be a twit. Swallow. You're frightening your lover. You are lovers, aren't you?" he asked Lee pointedly.

Lee couldn't answer, not to this guy, not something so intimate. Turik knew damned well what Tess meant to Lee. He held his breath, his heart a gaping hole at the very real possibility she was already gone, that he'd lost his reason to live.

Turik pushed the bottle farther between her lips and tilted it upward. She coughed as her throat worked an automatic swallow. He placed a chaste kiss on her cheek, all the while eyeing Lee. "I must admit I didn't expect you to be such an honorable gentleman, Agent Hart. You're quite the fierce fighter, too. Duly noted. I'm impressed."

I don't give a shit what you think. Lee stared into the deep brown eyes of his enemy, an English-speaking, brown-skinned, native son of Afghanistan.

The man liked to talk. "Did you know Tess and I met in London?"

What the hell could Lee say to that? Why hadn't she told him?

"Ahh. I can see by the look in your eyes you didn't know. Tess is still keeping her secrets, is she?"

"I just barely met her." Defense for her came easily to his lips. Lee tamped down his panic. Tess would've gotten around to telling him all of her secrets.

"Yes, she was studying the history of her British forefathers and the Afghan lore of the other side of her family—I daresay the more romantic half. I was enthralled with world economics. Somehow, we found each other before we came to our senses. We parted friends and went our separate ways."

Tess moaned, and Lee wanted her back in his arms. Secrets or not, she belonged with him. "You're not her friend. You tried to kill her."

"Yes, I did, but we were once the truest friends. She's a treasure among women," Turik said reverently. He'd dropped his guard, gazing into her quiet face. She'd resumed breathing. Lee detected the lightest inhalations beneath that heavy wrap. His gaze drifted to the rifle at the other side of Turik.

Of course, Turik noticed. "We're not so different, Agent Hart," he said, his voice suddenly low, his gaze as filled with cunning as Lee's. "We're both in love with the same woman, but don't assume that just because I'm here, I don't also wage my own internal jihad at what my country asks of me. Surely you do the same?"

That sincere introspection was not expected. "You and your buddies are killing this country and you're ruining everything good in it," Lee countered, his jaw clenched tight. "Explain to me how terrorizing innocent people helps anyone."

"You will never understand our ways."

"You've got that right," Lee retorted, catching a glint of something else in Turik's eye. Something dark and deadly. He bit his tongue, remembering whose house he was still in. He and Tess weren't out of the woods yet. "It looks like you care for her. Why'd you take a shot at her at the palace?"

Turik framed the side of her face with his free hand, the bottle now stowed out of sight in some hidden pocket within his robe. "I never intended to kill her that night. She has given me too much to think about. Do what she said. Look around, Agent Hart. What do you see?"

Lee glanced around the fine art and décor of the gaudy room. All he saw was the bloodied prayer rug and the bastard who'd hurt Tess. His fists clenched with restrained rage. "We don't have time for this. She needs a doctor."

"Bloody hell," Turik muttered. "Look with your eyes, man, not your heart."

All Lee had was heart, damn it, only Turik was holding it. None of the ancient bullshit mattered. Not even Nizari's death mattered. Only Tess.

"My God, you're a worthless sot. You really are in love with her, aren't you?" Turik peered into Lee's brimming eyes. "Take her then, but trust me. Tess is strong. She needs rest and care, but she'll not die from these wicked stripes. Hold her while I have the supreme honor of telling you what I see."

With that, Turik relinquished Tess into Lee's waiting arms. Lee cradled her again, his heart breaking when she whimpered at the jostling. Pressing a kiss into her hair, he kept his eyes on the two murderers in the room. Only now, he wasn't so sure about the one. Turik had an air of dignity Lee hadn't expected for the cold-blooded assassin. The man acted as if he had nothing to fear from Lee or Nizari.

When Turik took hold of his weapon again, Lee noticed it was a modified, magazine-fed, gas-operated, semi-automatic M14 sniper rifle. The reverent way Turik handled it shot a wave of déjà vu through Lee. The man loved his weapon, and it showed. That friend he'd just tucked under his arm with a loving caress was American-made, accurate as hell, and effective at extremely long ranges with out-of-this-world takedown capability. Lee would know. It was his weapon of choice, too.

"Now I see what Miss Culver wanted me to see." Turik turned to Nizari, his brow spiked. "This is your home, my esteemed leader and noble friend? Your sanctuary from the world? I see now why you have kept it to yourself."

Turik toured the room, stopping in front of a glassed-in cabinet filled with shards of dingy carved ivory. "Ah, so this is where they really ended up." He stroked his chin and nodded at Lee. "Imagine that. We were told they'd been destroyed, but here they are. May I introduce you to the Begram Ivory panels of... what?" He turned back to Nizari, who'd grown exponentially paler and quieter now that Turik held his weapon again. "The first century? Earlier than that? Speak up, Hasim. I'm certain you have more lies to tell."

Nizari's shoulders sagged. His gaze dropped to the floor between his knees.

"Perhaps it is better you don't speak. Let this room speak for you and your less-than-noble deeds." Turik motioned to the tapestry covering Tess. "That priceless work of art belonged to Bayazid Roshan, if I'm not mistaken. Do you know your Afghan history, Agent Hart?"

Lee shook his head. This stupid conversation vexed him. He needed to get Tess to a doctor, not sit around and be forced to listen to an extreme trivia game.

"Ah, I see. You do not. And that is why your country shall fail to conquer mine," Turik said somberly. "For all your shock and awe, you American soldiers have not taken the time to truly study or understand the enemy you seek to destroy. No matter. We have time tonight, and I shall be glad to teach you. Bayazid Roshan was an enlightened intellectual who fought for independence in my country many years ago. In the sixteenth century, I believe. But wait..." Turik strode purposefully to an alcove tucked into the opposite wall. "I'm impressed, Hasim. You have the ancient Buddha of Nuristan. Amazing. I was told this alabaster statue was destroyed at the onset of the fatwa, but I see that is not the case. Interesting."

Turik marched from treasure to treasure, some ancient Afghan treasures and artifacts, some from far-off China and India. He spent a particularly long time at a round green plate with a gold-embossed face of what looked like Alexander the Great. His eyes suddenly turned cold and dark. "I think your time here is at an end, Agent Hart."

That didn't sound good. Lee's gut clenched at the ominous warning.

"See to it that you take extremely good care of our girl. Be gentle with Lady Tess. She'll make you angry enough to curse the day you met her, but she'll love you deeply and purely like none other." Turik's voice softened as he came back to Tess and knelt, his hand tunneled into her sweaty hair. He laid a gentle kiss on her forehead. "Love her," he admonished Lee quietly. "Love her as much as I do. Can you promise to do that?"

"If you loved her so much, you'd let me get her to a doctor," Lee growled, wanting to knock this pompous ass to his butt.

"You're right," Turik said softly, his eyes full of tender emotion, "but do love her. That's all I ask. Make her happy if you can. Dance with her in the morning and make love to her when the sun sets. Make babies. Many, many babies. She has a great love for children."

Lee nodded, his hands wrapped around Tess to lift her with him when he stood. If Turik was letting him go, he intended to seal the deal and split. But first...

Lee jerked his chin toward Nizari. "What will happen to him?"

"Ahh..." Turik turned to face the real devil in the room. His eyes narrowed. The soft smile left his lips. "The noble Hasim and I have much to talk about."

Lee caught the insinuation of what he hoped was more than just a friendly conversation in Nizari's near future. Rising to his feet, Lee turned his back on the Taliban's best assassin and banker. With Tess curled against his broad chest, Lee had what he'd come for.

He'd barely cleared the inner doorway when he heard footsteps on his heels. For one fraction of a second, he feared he'd been lied to, that Turik might kill him with a garrote. He kept walking.

The house had become eerily still. Angling Tess through the outer door, Lee paused for a second. The sleek, shiny BMW parked at the other side of the house had to be Nizari's. His gut told him Turik didn't travel in style. Good enough.

Lee didn't look a gift horse in the mouth. He rested Tess carefully in the passenger seat. The arrogant man had left the key in the ignition. Why not? Who would dare steal from a man who thought he was better than God?

Lee cranked the ignition, and drove away. He aimed the headlights toward Kabul. Behind the smoked glass of the devil's car, he was invincible. He just hoped the guards at Camp Eggers front gate gave him enough time to explain who he was before they shot him.

Chapter Twenty-Four

"I'm fine." Lee brushed Jordan's concern aside. He'd traded Turik's now bloodied scarf on his arm for a roll of white medical gauze, opting for real treatment only after Tess was taken care of. Jordan requisitioned a pair of scrubs for him, a welcome relief from his bloodied clothing. A shower would feel good, but for the moment he sat in a waiting room at Camp Eggers medical facility.

Tess had been loaded with antibiotics and painkillers, her three lash marks cleaned and treated. She rested blissfully unaware in a room one door down the hall. Hunter had a concussion from a near-fatal bullet to his hard head. Eric had a tidy hole through his left chest that had nicked a lung. Nothing critical. Both were shot full of drugs and resting in rooms a little farther down the hall.

Alex was the problem. He'd been in emergency surgery since Lee had returned to Eggers. In all the uproar of the Taliban ambush, he'd stepped on a dying sheep and shattered his right ankle when he fell. That didn't stop him from blowing more of the enemy away until they'd retreated, but it did set poor Seth and Jordan up for a royal dressing down when Alex finally got to his feet. He always came up fighting mad and spitting nails. Top that with the disaster of Lee and Tess's disappearance, and both Seth and Jordan were screwed just because they were the last men standing.

Jordan snickered. "I can hear it back at the office now. The boss lost a fight with a fluffy sheep."

"How long are they gonna keep him in there?" Seth asked. He looked like hell, his face covered with grime and sweat from the battle. But then, they all looked like hell.

Lee shot him a disbelieving look. Seth tended to talk too much when he was stressed. That was the third time he'd asked the same question. "Be glad he's still in there. The last thing I remember was you diving over the hood of our Humvee like Beau Duke sliding over General Lee. You want to tell me what happened?"

Seth dipped his head. "I don't exactly remember. I just thought, umm, they killed Eric. Made me mad."

"No shit. You charged into the night. I thought you went down with Eric. Scared the hell out of me."

"Yeah well," Seth mumbled. "I did kill a lot of sheep out there."

"Don't let him kid you," Jordan cut in. "Beau Duke nothing. Seth was a flaming Rambo on steroids. He took care of the whole west flank. How many'd you take out, Seth?"

"Sheep?" Seth asked.

"No," Jordan growled. "I don't care about the damned sheep. How many Taliban?"

Lee had to smile. Seth was still frazzled from the battle, dealing with the after-effects of its intense overload of adrenaline and fear. They all were. Lee had expected to find Eric dead for sure when he'd shown up at the hospital with Tess. That only sheep and Taliban had died was due to a freaking miracle called Seth. When he'd seen his buddy go down, he turned into an avenging angel, charged into the flock and ended the war. *Guess he'd gotten past his anxiety issues.*

"Seven," Seth answered. "I killed seven Taliban and eleven sheep. I feel bad about the sheep."

"Good on you," Jordan said proudly. "You saved Eric's life; mine, too. If you weren't just a civilian contractor, they'd be giving you a medal right now."

"I don't need a medal," Seth muttered.

"No, you don't," Lee said, "but I'm damned glad to know you, man."

Seth looked more confident than he had in months, his eyes clearer and his back straight. Just maybe he'd finally remembered the man he was. He nodded to Lee. "What's that bastard Turik like anyway?"

That was a tough one. How did you explain a privileged Afghan young man who'd been educated in England, loved a reckless American woman, and truly believed the divine law of Shari'a, but served his country in the same profession as the men on The TEAM?

"I guess I respect him," Lee said simply. "I don't like the guy, but he's not like any of the other Taliban I've met."

"Hey, a couple other American soldiers showed up here at the hospital. Some Marines found them when they were out on patrol," Jordan said. "Talk about Rambo. Those poor guys are singing your praises to anyone who'll listen to them. It sounds like you made up your mind to be a hero tonight, too."

Lee changed the subject. He was no hero. "How'd the Taliban get to me and Tess so fast? It's like they knew where we were in the convoy."

Jordan scrubbed a hand over his face. "Damned if I know. I saw a couple guys dragging you off through the sheep once I came to. There were so many explosions going off, I thought I was seeing things."

"They get the rig?"

"No, but they messed it up some. We'd a been in a world of shit if the guys from Eggers hadn't shown up."

"The reliquary's still safe?" Lee asked.

Seth blew out a tired sigh. "It's in the commander's safe, waiting for Tess to wake up. Alex was mad as a hornet because of the ambush."

Lee smiled. If Alex was mad, all must be right with the world.

A female orderly entered the small waiting room. "Excuse me, but we have a few empty beds at the moment. You'll have to give 'em up if we get casualties, but you're welcome to them if you'd like a place to sleep."

"I'm outta here." Seth rolled out the door behind the orderly. "Point me to a rack."

"You need to get that arm looked at," Jordan reminded Lee for the hundredth time.

"I'd rather wait, if you don't mind."

"Yeah right." Jordan thumped Lee's uninjured shoulder lightly. "Go give her a kiss and get some sleep. She isn't going anywhere, and the boss is still getting bolted back together. You've got time."

Lee eyed his big-mouthed friend. Jordan was right. He was beat, but the last thing he needed was an infection. He let out a deep sigh and pushed to his feet. It had been a long damn day, but kissing Tess was a good idea whether she was awake or not. He said his goodbyes and made his way to her room.

She lay on her side facing the door, sound asleep and her hair gathered in a ponytail. Lee was angry all over again that Nizari had struck her three times with that whip, but thankful it hadn't been more. He debated returning Nizari's BMW to

Turik, but decided against it. Spoils of war. Let Turik come and get it if he wanted it.

She looked a little better now, still pale but not as white. He traced her soft cheek with the backs of his fingers so as not to wake her. Tess had become everything to him. Silly woman had even said she was going to rescue him. Damn, she was a force to be reckoned with. He leaned down and kissed her sweet lips and told her so. "I love you, Tess. You're safe now. Sleep as long as you want. I'll be here when you wake up."

Of all things, she dreamed of Clint and sheep. They came in droves and the silly man sat among them, smoking a joint and looking as passive as they did. The smoke curled out of his twisted little cigarette into a wreath that circled his fat head.

All at once he was stranded up high on a mountaintop, so high. In her dream he was seven years old again, calling for her to save him. A thousand people stood gawking and watching, but no one took a step forward to help the frightened little boy. And in her dream she knew she was the only one who could. She climbed that rugged mountain, hand over hand and foot by foot. The handholds gave way to sheer rock that somehow she was still able to climb.

"Tessie! I'm scared!" he cried pitifully.

She had to save him, and only she could do it. Higher and higher she went until he was less than a few feet away. To save him, she had to climb beneath the lip of that mountain edge, exposing herself to the sheer drop below. With no place to fasten her feet, she pressed forward anyway because he was her baby brother, and that was what big sisters did.

The first handhold was the hardest. Suspended over nothing but a damn long way to fall, her heart pounded. This wasn't dangerous; it was suicide.

"I can't get down," he sobbed pathetically, tearing her heart apart. "I'm gonna fall. Help me, Tessie!"

"I'm almost there. I'm coming. Don't move." Her feet dangled beneath her, paddling nothing but frigid mountain air.

"I'm scared," he cried, and she cried with him.

Don't move, Clint. I'm coming. I'm scared, too, but I'll save you.

Her heart leapt up into her throat. The paralyzing fear of heights suffocated her. There was nothing else to hold onto. Her gallant act of bravery was futile. She couldn't reach him. Her fingers slipped, and she hung one-handed over a drop to earth that would surely kill her. She'd failed. No way forward. No way back. Only down.

"Tessie!" little boy Clint cried for his big sister.

Her grip weakened. Her fingernails etched the edge of the stone—and she fell.

No!

Tess woke up to her heart thundering in her chest and the plummet to earth fresh in her mind. She could barely swallow. Clint. Where was he? The terror of the nightmare persisted. He was in trouble. She knew it. Somehow, he'd reached out to her through time and space, and once again, she was his big sister and the only one who could save him. But how? Where?

She licked her dry lips and took stock of her clean hospital room. She wasn't exactly sure how she'd gotten there, but her path seemed obvious. There was only one person who could help her find her troublesome brother. As much as she despised the man, she needed his help.

Mohammed.

"Oops. Sorry."

Damn. The medic with the hypo of local anesthetic was doing a good job of pissing Lee off. One more stab in his bicep like that last one, and the dumbass would be picking himself off the deck.

Lee bit back his words and stared out the window. He hated hospitals. Tess was the only reason he'd stayed at this one. He needed to be close to her, his protective side on edge after their near-death encounter. If he could've gotten away with it, he would've crawled in bed with her.

While she slept, he intended to grab a few ZZZs, but then he and she were out of there. His mind was westward bound, and he wanted her beside him when he left the dirt and dust of this wretched country behind. He hadn't even asked her if she'd go with him yet. She might not want to leave, and he understood. She'd made a life of sorts in this third-world country, but a man could hope. After all, she had said she loved him when they both thought she was dying.

The miracle of walking out of there alive with Tess still amazed him, but the image of her on the floor in Nizari's house boiled Lee's blood all over again. If not for Turik, he would have killed Nizari before he'd left. *Still might go back and finish the job.*

He watched the medic clean and stitch the knife hole in his arm, then top it off with a topical antibiotic and a large bandage. Winchester, Snowden, and Carter were being treated in this same hospital. Some of their injuries were pretty serious, especially Winchester's. They'd be drugged and sleeping like Tess, so he couldn't visit with them, and he didn't plan on being around when Alex got out of recovery. That'd be a lot like a grizzly bear coming out of hibernation.

"You're good to go, Agent Hart," the medic said. "I can write you an order for pain pills if you'd like."

"No thanks." Lee didn't need pain pills. They had side effects. His whole life was one big side effect.

He settled a long, hot shower before he hit the clean sheets. Seth snored lightly in the next rack, already out cold. Knowing Tess laid only a couple doors away did the trick. Sleep had never felt so good or so hard.

Tess made her way quietly out of the hospital. It wasn't hard. Once she lifted a pair of scrubs from the hamper, she looked like she worked there. Well, almost. Lee had to be around there somewhere. He wouldn't approve, so she intended to make this visit to Mohammed quick.

Her dilemma struck the moment she hit the exit doors. She knew where Mohammed lived. The problem was getting there.

Glancing around the parking area, Nizari's BMW stuck out like a sore thumb amongst the olive drab. She remembered it vaguely from the previous night. She made yet another bold decision. She plucked up her courage and walked straight toward that BMW like she owned it.

Better yet, once she was safely inside and found the keys still in the ignition, she did own it. Feeling successful, she turned the ignition, and let the dark windows conceal her foolish decision.

She glanced back at the guarded gate as she drove out of Camp Eggers and into Kabul traffic. Would they let her back in? No matter. She'd cross that bridge when she got to it. It was imperative she chat with Mohammed, but first...

She pulled a hard left and swung onto Saint Raphael's open yard. Her heart ached to see the sweet little faces that meant more to her than all the riches of Afghanistan. This might be her last chance with Mina and Jamaal. She took it.

Saint Raphael's was nothing more than a rectangular concrete building that used to be a Catholic church. Where once rows of pews faced the sanctuary, now row after row of cots lined the floor. There were no statues in the sacristy, no holy pictures. Even the steeple was gone. Families too poor to help themselves lived there with the orphans. A woman she didn't recognize waved from the single concrete step at the two wooden doors. Tess waved back, but didn't dare leave the comfort of her air-conditioned ride.

There was a time she'd intended this work only as a cover for her real mission. No more. Somehow, the simple song she'd sung in Lee's shower changed everything. She hadn't realized just how lost she was until then. Until the kindest man pulled her out of harm's way and forced her to reevaluate her priorities. Until he made her see how poorly she'd chosen. Golden relics over the lives of people? Long dead ancient legends over the dearest little children on the face of the planet? Now Clint? How insanely stupid was she?

She nearly chuckled. The answer seemed pretty damn clear. She was stupid enough to ask the assassin who tried to kill her for help.

Tess rolled her window down as the woman approached. Dressed in flowing pants and a long shirt, only the crucifix at her neck gave her away. This had to be Sister Alison's replacement. "Can I help you?" she asked.

Tears welled up at the thought of her friend's death. Tess paused, not sure why she thought she could do this. Mina and Jamaal didn't need to see her looking like this. They needed that strong, vibrant woman who used to swing them up in to her arms and make them laugh, not a woman who could barely move. "Yes, please. I used to work here. I mean, I still work here, only I've been gone a couple days."

"You must be Tess Culver. Come in."

"I'm sorry. I can't. Are Mina and Jamaal still here? Are they well?" She bit her lip, hoping nothing had happened to those babies while she'd been busy being stupid. "Are they happy?"

The woman extended a slender hand through the window. "Yes, those little rascals are fine. I'm Sister Mary Joseph by the way It's good to meet you, Tess. Are you sure you don't have time? They're eating lunch, but I know they'd love to see you again. I'll make tea and we could visit."

That would have been the smart thing to do. Tess shook the nun's hand quickly. "Maybe tomorrow. Please tell them I was here and I'll be back."

Sister Mary Joseph offered a knowing smile. "Take care of yourself, Tess Culver."

Tess put the BMW into reverse and left Saint Raphael's behind, emotional beyond belief. Tears stung her eyes. Why couldn't the kids have been playing in the open yard? One glimpse of Mina and Jamaal was all she'd wanted. Was that too much to ask after the night she'd had?

Finally, on the outskirts of Kabul, her heart calmed. That Mohammed hadn't chosen to live in the wealthy neighborhood of Wazir Akbar Khan, where embassies were built and the elite lived, spoke volumes about his integrity. He practiced what he preached.

She pulled over alongside his humble home. A young boy sat in the front yard tinkering with a bicycle. Only when she stepped slowly out of the glamorous vehicle did a smile brighten his face. "Miss Culver!" Fahim ran to greet her.

Tess steeled herself for the enthusiastic welcome of Mohammed's eight-year-old son. They'd met before in kinder times. When he wrapped his arms around her waist, it took her breath. The lacerations on her back were waking up from the anesthetic.

"You have Mr. Nizari's car." Fahim seemed more impressed with the car than with her. "Did he give it to you? Can I ride in it?"

"Maybe later." Gritting her teeth against the pain, she put on her happy face and tousled his curly hair. Fahim was his father all over again, except for his pale blue eyes. Those he got from his American-born mother, Alessa. "Is your father home, Fahim?"

"Papa!" No sooner shouted than answered.

Mohammed stood at his door, one hand on his hip and surprise on his face. A simple gray baseball cap covered his head. He waved her forward, but one step and she faltered.

Mohammed rushed to her side. "Why are you here?" he asked, not unkindly. "You should be in your friend's care if not at the hospital. What are you thinking?"

And there he was, her ruggedly handsome desert warrior from the enthralling land of Alexander the Great. Tess sighed. What a fool she'd been to fall for this dusky-skinned Afghan idealist. The thickest lashes fringed his smoky amethyst eyes, so dark that a silly American girl living abroad could get lost in them. Could, nothing. Tess *had* gotten lost in the romance that was Mohammed—his country, too.

"We need to talk," she said, as he grasped her elbow firmly and steered her up the walk and into his home. Fresh, cool air met her at the door. He might live like everyone else in his neighborhood, but he had air-conditioning, a very welcome modern touch.

"Alessa," he called to his wife as he directed Tess to a couch. "Please bring my friend a glass of juice."

Tess would've preferred an introduction under different circumstances, preferably when she wasn't leaning against Alessa's husband's strong body. But one glance at Alessa, and Tess had to smile. She was exactly how Tess had pictured her. Blonde, beautiful, and American. She dressed in the simple garb of an Afghan woman at home: long pants, a knee-length tunic, and a hijab loose at her neck. How fitting.

Tess took the proffered drink and lifted it to her lips while Alessa crouched at the couch with her husband. "This is quite good. Thank you for your kindness, Alessa. I am in your debt."

Fahim stood nearby, fidgeting. "She has Mr. Nizari's car, Papa," he whispered into his father's ear. "Did you see it?"

Mohammed slanted a stern glance toward his son. "Don't you have lessons to finish?"

Fahim's brows furrowed. "Yes, Papa, but only math. Division is hard. I need your help"

"Go now. Do all you can, and I'll be in shortly." Mohammed sounded like any other father on the planet.

Fahim's fists curled at his side. "But Papa, it is the *silver* car. The pretty one. We could go for a short ride in it." His eyes gleamed.

Mohammed's brows furrowed. "We don't take what isn't ours, son."

"Just one little ride." Fahim wheedled, but he must've recognized the look in his father's eye. He pivoted on his heel without another word and obeyed.

"You have a handsome boy," Tess said, quietly locking gazes with Mohammed.

"Why are you here?"

Chapter Twenty-Five

Her heart stalled. "You know why."

Mohammed shot her a dark look, his cap in his hands. "I must speak to my friend alone," he said brusquely to his wife who still knelt at his side.

"Not now, my husband. Your friend isn't well," Alessa replied firmly. "She must rest while I'll fix something for her to eat, then you two may have your talk. What's your name?" she asked Tess.

"Tess Culver. I work at the orphanage. Saint Raphael's."

Alessa's eyes lit with recognition. "Ah, so you're the Lady Tess my Mohammed speaks so highly of. I've heard much about the work you've done with the children." She gave Tess's hand a gentle squeeze. "I'm Alessa. I must say, it's good to hear another American woman's voice. I'm so glad there are devoted workers like you in the orphanage. Mina and Jamaal are the sweetest, aren't they? I was so sad to hear their father abandoned them."

Tess relaxed, secretly relieved Mohammed shared her love of those special children with his wife. She and Alessa had a couple things in common, children and Mohammed. "I'd love to adopt them if I could," she confided another secret she had yet to tell Lee.

Mohammed rolled those dashing midnight eyes to the ceiling and shook his head, but Alessa's face brightened. "Oh,

I'm so glad to finally meet you, Tess. You're always welcome in our humble home. Please rest as long as you want. I'll run and prepare something that will go easy on your stomach."

A flash of tenderness lit Mohammed's face as he watched his wife walk away, and Tess relaxed. What an enigma. He might be a notorious assassin, but there at home, he was also a good husband, and he knew when to listen to his wife. He lifted to the couch beside Tess after Alessa left the room. "Talk," he ordered sternly but quietly, the brim of his cap twisted in his hands.

Tess kept her accusation low and calm. "Why are you killing all my friends?"

"Why are they robbing my country? What did you expect me to do—let them transfer every last Afghan treasure to the Paris Louvre right under my nose?"

"Sister Alison didn't steal anything. She was my friend."

Something dark and dangerous flashed across his face. "I don't kill women, Tess. The man who did that cowardly deed was not me."

"Liar. You tried to kill me," she exclaimed, her tone rising higher. "I know it. I've seen a video that shows—"

"Be careful, Tess," he warned, his perfect white teeth clenched together. "You know I do not lie. You're no better than your French ambassador, stealing Afghan trinkets and selling them on the—"

"Trinkets?" she nearly shrieked. "Those aren't trinkets. They're priceless artifacts, Mohammed. The only reason I've taken anything is to keep some small portion of this nation's history safe from your imam's ridiculous fatwa to destroy what is good in the world. I'll have you know I haven't made a single Afghani on what I've taken. Not one. If anything, this foolish quest is driving me to the poor house." She took a deep breath to steady her trembling. "Who do you think stole the Star of Persia back from that jerk in Darfur, you moron? Use your head, Mohammed. What I've stolen back from the Taliban hasn't even left the country, and it never will." She raked a hand through her thick hair, smoothing it behind her ear. "God, Mohammed. Who do you really think is selling your son's culture on the black market? It's not me. I'm trying to rescue it for Fahim. I happen to love this country, remember? Don't you get it? You were there. You saw Nizari's place. Do you think he cares about honoring your stupid fatwa?" Her fingers curled to fists just thinking of the evil man. How could Mohammed defend Nizari?

He ran a hand over his bearded chin, his dark eyes hooded. "Trust me. I saw, but... You're not getting rich on what you've stolen?"

Gah! This man was like all the others. He had a hard head and two ears that must have been painted on for as much as he listened. She wanted to deck him. "Look at me, Mohammed. Do you see any gold on my fingers or fine linens on my body? Am I wearing expensive cologne?" She touched her neck, searching for the only item of jewelry she owned, but her fingers came up empty. Even the crucifix Clint had given her was gone. Alexander and Roxana had finally taken everything. A swell of bitter recrimination lifted up from her battered heart. It was finally time to leave this country.

Mohammed looked at her through his brows, his chin nearly on his chest. The man was a study in culture all by himself—dark skinned, dark haired, and melted chocolate drops for eyes that at the moment seemed deep in thought. He let out a deliberately slow sigh. "I was given an order to kill you, yes, but I never intended to do it. If those bloody American snipers had minded their business, I might have winged you as I'd planned. As it was, I missed."

"You would've shot me just because someone told you to?" Her heart broke. This man had loved her once. She knew he did. How had he fallen so low?

The shadow darkening his brow lifted. Mohammed raised her fingers to his soft lips. "Dear Tess, listen to me. I could never kill you. You're the most exciting woman I've ever known when you're on one of your quests. I've watched you for years. Once you get a notion in your head, you run pell-mell into danger, and you take the bloodiest risks. At the worst, I would've sent you a warning only. If I'd winged you, Clint would've caught you with that ridiculous airbag in the back of his truck. You would've crawled off to lick your wounds for a month or two. Do you ever stop to think you could've been killed instead of just beaten that day?"

That day? She jerked her fingers away from his mouth, this newly revealed pain tearing her heart out all over again. "You were there?"

"Why do you think I visit the orphanage all the time? I've been running interference since you set foot in Kabul and decided to confront Nizari. He wanted more than your blood after you defied him in public. He'd gone to the Imam. It was all I could do to persuade him to let you live."

Her throat clamped shut. She had openly defied Nizari when she'd discovered he'd raped one of the teenage girls at the orphanage. It was a totally American response to an abhorrent crime that could not go unpunished. She'd gone to the police and pressed charges, but the criminal system in Afghanistan did not work like the one in the United States.

Nizari owned certain policemen. Certain judges. If they questioned him at all, she wasn't aware of it. The only way she'd known her charges were dismissed as frivolous was the day he'd shown up at the orphanage with his brutal lackeys to exact his revenge.

The memory of that beating on Nizari's order still lingered in heart-pounding nightmares. Sister Alison had wept while the local doctor tried to help after that beating. It was no small thing. Her jaw had been broken. Finally, only rest and Clint's sporadic care worked.

Tess no longer knew why she'd ever thought coming to Mohammed would help find her brother. Hell, she had no idea why she'd ever thought Clint needed help in the first place, or why she hadn't thought to call him before she'd stolen Nizari's car. Her brain was half numb from exhaustion, and she'd simply gone off half-cocked. Clearly, that dream she'd had was a product of the drugs she'd been given. But there she was, making an utter fool of herself once again. No wonder Mohammed thought he had to cover her back.

What was I thinking? Tess leaned forward to get to her feet. "I need to leave. I never should've come."

"No," he said kindly, pressing her easily into the cushion. "You came for knowledge, and you shall have it. Don't be a twit. Just because it isn't what you want to hear, doesn't make it any less true."

Another lost soul came to mind. "Omar?"

"Don't ask more about Omar." The ferocity of his answer startled Tess. He clutched her fingers tighter. "Too many of us have been misled by Nizari, the Imam included."

"Do you know where my brother is?" Tess asked, surprised at the sudden emotion in her voice. "He told you, didn't he?

That's how you knew I'd be at the palace that night. Clint sold me out. He told you where I'd be so you could—"

"No," Mohammed said quietly with a definite shake of his head. "Clint loves you. He'd never betray you. It was Nizari who set the trap. He knew if he moved the reliquary, he could bait the daring cat burglar of Kabul, he just didn't know that cat burglar was you. Imagine his surprise when he discovered he hadn't beaten the courage out of you. You've built quite a legend for yourself, but it would've been smarter if you'd stolen something besides just the artifacts he'd removed from the National Museum. You're brave, Tess, but you're not as clever as you think you are."

"But how did you know I'd be at the palace? You said you had an order to shoot me."

"I said I had a standing order to kill you as soon as I could locate you," he corrected. "Trust me. I was as surprised as Nizari to see you dancing on the edge of that wall. How could I kill you, woman? That was when I decided to injure you only. You more than anyone in this city needed to live."

Tess couldn't miss the anguish in his tone. She swallowed hard. An order meant he still needed to kill her. "I shouldn't have come, but I had no other way to find Clint, and I..." How could she tell Mohammed she'd run to him just because she'd had a dream? It seemed bizarre after all he'd told her, but she sighed and told him anyway. "I had a dream. He's in trouble, Mohammed. I need your help finding him." *I think.*

He growled low in his throat, running a hand through his hair. "You and your dreams. They get you into more trouble. I'll tell you what I know, my friend, but don't be angry. Your brother isn't you think he is."

"What do you mean?"

"My brothers and I might not have the resources of your American friends, Tess, but we are not without means. For instance, I know you belong to Worldwide Archeological Rescue, and for that, I'm thankful. You're one of the few who truly care for my country, its treasures, and its children. I respect that."

"Then why did you think I was selling the artifacts I've stolen?"

"Because that is what many archeologists have done."

"Then they must be the few unscrupulous ones in the field, because all the men and women I've known have been trying to save Afghanistan from people like you!"

Mohammed raked a quick hand through his hair, glancing toward the kitchen where his wife worked, clearly aggravated. "Will you keep your voice down?"

The paradox of a cold-blooded assassin afraid of his sweet little American wife would've made Tess chuckle on any other day. She crossed her arms, defiantly studying the puzzling man beside her. The memory of all they'd meant to each other still burned in her heart. Their problem had always been the same. They were idealists and dreamers, warriors off to save the world in their own ways. She'd met Jacque by the time she'd left England. She couldn't understand how Mohammed could join a group of fundamentalists who'd destroyed irreplaceable archeological wonders like the giant Buddhas at Bamiyan.

"Your brother also works for WAR."

"No, he doesn't," she said quickly and adamantly. That was one thing she knew for certain. Clint wasn't smart enough to work for WAR.

"Ah, my lovely Tess." Mohammed blew out a deep sigh, his arm behind her on the back of the couch. "You've always had your eyes so full of stars that you failed to see what was right in front of your nose. Why do you choose not to believe me? Why would I lie?"

The sparring match caught up with Tess. She leaned her head against the strong bicep behind her. It took too much energy to fight and, like it or not, Mohammed had many of the same qualities she admired in Lee. Strength. Devotion. Masculine confidence. Pride. A sense of honor.

"You believe with so much of your heart in the legend of your brave Alexander, but you do so at the risk of the real man standing in front of you. There was a day I would've given up everything I owned to follow you, but you couldn't see me, could you, Tess?"

She held her breath, trying to understand.

"And now you're so wrapped up in your fairytale legend that you cannot see Clint for the brave hero or the man he is." He kissed her knuckle again, his lips lingering and warm, his gaze on her.

Tears stung her eyes. "I didn't leave you to save the world. You left me. You were intent on returning to your country, a place I could never belong."

"And yet"—he offered a small shrug—"here you are."

The irony of his words didn't escape her. "But I'm only here because of the children and WAR and—"

He placed his index finger on her lips to shush her. "Precisely. You're here because you believe with all of your wild, crazy heart in something, Tess. It just isn't me. Admit it. When you believe in your dreams, you throw your heart and soul into it at the expense of everything and everyone else. There's no stopping you. This WAR you speak of has become an obsession you seem willing to die for." He traced the pad of this thumb to her chin. "What I wouldn't once have given to be that obsession. I saw the look on your friend's face last night when he thought you'd died. I can't help but feel sorry for Agent Hart."

"Why?" she breathed.

"Because he's me, my dear impetuous dreamer. Totally obsessed with you, and yet,"—Mohammed offered a sad smile—"here you are with me instead of where you belong with him. Why do you think that is?"

"Because I..." Had she really been so focused on her dreams that she'd walked away from Mohammed? Worse, was she making the same mistake again with Lee? Was she that blind?

"I shall tell you plainly what you have so miserably failed to deduce with your own two beautiful blue eyes." A gentle smile graced his lips as he cupped the back of her head and pulled her close. He leaned into her forehead, his breath soft on her cheek. "Clint is working deep undercover for WAR. He's used you, silly Tess, but only because it served both of your agendas, and I suspect, once you think about it, you'll see that I'm right. My sources have placed him high in the Hindu Kush of late, where he's in league with one of the few men in the country who can challenge us."

"What? Clint is challenging the Taliban?"

"Not exactly," Mohammed purred, "but he seems to be working closely with those who are. The next time you see him, tell him to be more careful. His helicopter flights have not gone unnoticed. The wrong people are watching."

"Are you sure he's working for WAR?" She couldn't wrap her head around that notion. Not Clint. Not her bumbling, pot-smoking, baby brother. No way.

But Mohammed didn't argue, and that made it—believable. It also explained why Clint had so easily turned her over to Lee that night. He hadn't betrayed her. Somehow, he'd already known she'd be safe with Lee. Agent Hart had some explaining to do.

Alex's words came back to her. *You'll be returned to America... You'll be placed in protective custody... Only then am I authorized to reveal who signed this contract for your safety.* Could Clint be that mysterious client? She'd been so angry with Alex and Lee, and things had happened so fast since that night at the palace that she hadn't taken the time to think clearly, but she was now. It was an unexpected brotherly intervention, but who the hell did Clint think he was?

Mohammed's eyes glistened with love for his foolish friend. "My beautiful Lady Tess, how many men like Agent Hart do you think will come along in your life? How many real warriors will you spurn on your quest for your legendary Alexander? Open your eyes. He's a thing of ancient history, Tess. Let him go. Clint isn't your son to raise. Let him go, too. And me?" He pressed his nose to the side of her head, drawing in a deep breath before he pressed a kiss in her hair. "You've already lost me. You must let me go as well."

His words pierced her soul. She would always love Mohammed, but not the way she loved Lee. Even under Nizari's lash, she'd only thought of Lee, and Lee needed to know that. She needed to make sure he knew. She swallowed hard. Mohammed was right. Lee wasn't her Alexander. He was better than that ancient legend. Lee was real.

"I have to go," she said quietly, pulling her fingers out of Mohammed's warm grasp.

"Not until Alessa says you may leave," he teased, casting a loving glance toward his kitchen. "My wife is on a mission, just like you. You'll be well fed and well rested before you're allowed to leave. It is our way of honoring strangers and celebrating friends."

"I'm afraid I've put you in great danger," she whispered. "If the Imam finds out I'm here…" She couldn't finish the thought.

He leaned in to plant a chaste kiss on her cheek. "A true believer is never in danger, Tess. The rest of the world is."

It had to be Seth.

"Wake up, man." He bumped Lee's leg a second time.

"You'd better have a damned good reason for bugging me," Lee grumbled, his bleary eyes barely cracked open enough to see Seth's grim face. "What's wrong?"

"It's Tess. She's gone."

"What?" Lee jumped to his feet.

"I went to check on the boss. On my way back, I stopped at her room."

"She can't be gone," Lee insisted as he barreled down the hall. Seth had to be wrong. Tess was too banged up to go anywhere. She was hurt. He flung her door open, but damn it. Her empty bed stared back at him. Lee turned on his buddy, his mind pinging to come up with any reason Tess would've left— or been taken. He instantly dismissed the notion of a kidnapping. "Maybe she's hungry. Where's the galley?"

"No, man." Seth placed his hand to Lee's forearm. "Jordan and me looked all over for her. She ain't here, but there's more."

"What?" Lee snarled. How could today possibly get any worse?

"Nizari's car's gone."

"Shit!" He raked one hand over his stupid damned head for sleeping too long and for thinking he could trust her. This was so like Tess. One minute she sounded believable, but the next...

He turned on his heel, determined to find her, but angry as hell she'd pull a stunt like this. Did she ever in her stubborn, pig-headed life think about anyone else? Hell, they were all beat-up and wounded. Was it too much to expect her to stay down like the rest of the guys and give him just one day of peace and quiet? No. Not Tess. She believed in legends and impossible things like dreams. *Stupid damned woman!*

"Where are you going?" Seth asked.

"Where do you think?" Lee snapped back at him.

Jordan had joined the posse. "Let's go get her. Weapons are still in the rig."

Lee didn't slow down. Knowing Tess, there could only be two places she would've gone—back to the orphanage or straight into the heart of Taliban country to confront Turik. *Jesus H. Christ! How many times will I have to save her sorry ass?*

Jordan beat him to the rig. It was in as rough a shape as they were, the front left wheel and axle crumpled and blackened from a grenade blast. Thank heavens for armor plating. Things could've gone a lot worse.

"You guys got some spare clothes?" he asked once he'd cleared the door. "I can't wear scrubs to battle."

"Yeah, man." Seth pointed to the rear of the rig. "Check the closet next to the last rack."

Lee tossed the scrubs he'd been wearing aside and helped himself to desert cammies, tops and pants. He grabbed a pair of clean socks and sand-colored boots. Today he was back in the Corps—might as well dress like it. Seth tossed him a tactical vest. Good thinking. He strapped it over his chest before he donned the rest of his uniform and buckled up.

Lee grabbed a double holster with matching pistols, a couple of extra magazines, and a gear bag full of the usual— grenades, flash-bangs, a sawed-off, and shotgun shells to go with it. He strapped on an ankle holster, the pistol that went with it, and stuck a knife in his boot. A man never knew what he'd run into.

"You ready?" Seth asked at the door. By the looks of these guys, they both thought they were going with him. He didn't argue. It might take both of them to keep him from wringing Tess's neck.

"Let's do this," Lee muttered, glancing to the empty stall where he'd left Nizari's BMW. "Shit, I should've taken the keys. I should've known she'd try something like this."

Scrambled to Alex's olive drab Humvee, Seth took shotgun and Jordan grabbed the backseat leaving Lee to drive. He wasted no time backing the vehicle away from the rig and exiting off the base.

"Where to?" Seth asked, gripping the suicide strap overhead.

"Saint Raphael's." It didn't take long to drive a half block and pull into the schoolyard of the orphanage. "Stay here. No sense all of us going in."

"We'll keep the doors open." Jordan already had one boot on the ground, his pistol drawn and ready. He tossed an earpiece at Lee. "Put this on before you go in."

"Seriously?" Lee snapped. "You think I need a comm link in this place?"

Jordan stared him down. "I think we're on an unauthorized op that could get us fired or dead. Put it on."

It was good someone was using his brain. Lee sure wasn't. He tucked the earpiece down deep where it wouldn't be seen.

"Comm check," Jordan growled.

Lee gave him the thumbs up and bailed out of the rig. His boots had no sooner hit the dirt than a tall, willowy woman holding a little boy with no legs in her arms headed his way. Several other children flocked at her knees, all of them brown-eyed, brown-skinned, and smiling. "I'm Sister Mary Joseph. I run this orphanage. May I help you?"

Lee offered a welcoming handshake and a sincere smile to remind himself that, despite his military gear and over-abundant weaponry, he was more than just a badassed soldier. "Morning, Sister. I don't suppose you've seen Tess Culver today, have you?"

"Tess?" Sister Mary Joseph's eyes brightened with concern, her grip gentle. "She was here over an hour ago. Why? Is she okay?"

"As far as I know she is," he answered, scanning the simple concrete building that looked more like an abandoned warehouse than a safe home for children. Two older girls approached with a smaller girl between them. A big smile split her face, but her eyes were blank and unseeing. Lee's heart faltered. If that was Tess's Mina, then the little guy in Sister Mary Joseph's arms was...

"Hey Jamaal," he said, taking a closer look at the poor little guy. One leg was taken off at the hip, the other at the knee, but damned if Jamaal didn't offer a toothy grin before he ducked his face into the kindly nun's shoulder.

"Would you like to hold him?" Sister Mary Joseph asked, even as she offloaded the little tyke to Lee's arms.

"No, I, umm..." Lee balked, but really had no choice. Marines had a reputation for being bigger, badder, and tougher than life, but right then? Jamaal was the only tough guy on scene. "How you doing?" he asked the boy.

Jamaal burrowed his backside into Lee's forearm, too shy to answer, or maybe he didn't understand English. Lee didn't care. The kid needed to feel safe so Lee obliged.

"You're a good man," Sister Mary Joseph said, her chin lifted appraisingly and her hands on her hips. "I can see it in your eyes, but tell me. Why is the Army looking for Tess?"

"We're not Army, ma'am." Lee glanced back at his rig. It sure looked Army. He gulped at his major indiscretion of the day. Alex would have his ass for this one. "We're just friends. I need to talk with her. That's all." He nodded at the girls. "Is that Mina?"

"Yes. Tess loves the little rascal."

Mina giggled at something one of her escorts whispered in her ear. Her friends were teasing her, but it was clear her handicap hadn't touched her heart. She looked like any other little girl. Shy smile. Innocent.

"May I talk with her?" he asked.

"Certainly." Sister Mary Joseph waved the girls to her. "Come here, girls. Bring Mina. This handsome man is Tess's friend."

Mina clapped her hands even as her friends steered her to join them. "Oh good! My sister Tess. Is she here?"

Damn. A shot straight to the heart. Lee could've bawled at the exuberance of that motherless child for the woman he loved. He knelt with Jamaal sitting snug on his forearm, his heart softened at Mina's trusting ways. Lee reached out his hand to Mina's shoulder so she'd know his exact location. "I can see why Tess loves you. She isn't here, Mina, but I can't wait to tell her I met you."

"Are you cute?" she whispered through her splayed fingers over her mouth. "I think you must be very strong and handsome."

"Why's that?" he asked, wishing he could offer more than just conversation to a child so in need.

"Because Mama Tess is the most beautiful lady in the world!" Mina twirled in a full circle while her little girlfriends giggled with her.

These kids were killing him. Sweet little Mina had probably never seen Tess. She'd judged her beauty based on everything but sight. Oh, if she only knew. "So if Tess is beautiful, that means I'm handsome?" he asked more tenderly.

"Of course," one of Mina's friends replied. "I have seen her. She's a beautiful princess. You must be her handsome prince like in the stories she reads to us. Do you ride a dashing stallion? Are you going to marry her?"

Another hit to his heart. His throat tightened. It was getting harder to speak. "For now I'd just like to find her."

"Is she lost?" Mina asked. "Did you lose her?"

"No." *I sure as hell hope not.* "Just need to talk to her."

"Did she lose a glass slipper? Is that why you're looking for her?" Those big beautiful brown eyes of Mina's blinked bright with pure innocence.

"Girls, shush now. That's a fairytale," Sister Mary Joseph intervened. "Run along."

And suddenly it was hard to let Jamaal go. Lee swallowed hard at the thought of the other side of the irrepressible woman he now knew a little better. He understood why she did what she did. These children were Afghanistan's future. It might not be as bright as it once was, but they deserved every last piece of their rich heritage, and Tess meant for them to have it. Wasn't that what mothers everywhere did?

"I'll tell her you've been here if I see her," Sister Mary Joseph said kindly, her hands outstretched to take Jamaal. "Please let me know when you locate her."

Lee sucked it up. He squeezed Jamaal before he handed him back, his heart stuck up high in his throat. "Yes, ma'am. Sure will. Is there anything you need?"

Sister Mary Joseph scanned her troupe of motherless children. "To be twins?" she offered with a weary smile. "I'll be fine. I have three others helping me. Take care of yourself, young man. You and Tess will be in my prayers."

"Thank you, Sister." He turned back to his vehicle, its doors flung open like some big bird of prey cooling itself in the sun.

"No word?" Seth asked as all doors slammed shut at the same time.

"She's not here."

"Where to?" Jordan asked.

Lee shot him a dark look. "Hell."

Chapter Twenty-Six

"Oh, shit."

Leave it to Seth to utter the world's biggest damned understatement. Lee's fist clenched on his rifle grip. They'd found Tess. It was easy for a man with a sniper scope to see her, only now it was trained on the woman who was ripping his heart out and stomping it into the ground.

"He's got a kid," Seth muttered, "or I'd take him out for you."

Lee didn't answer. He had eyes. Staring at Turik with his arm wrapped casually around Tess's shoulder didn't help the betrayal burning a hole in his gut. That there was a young boy involved in the deceit only made it worse. Who was he? Turik's son? Turik's and Tess's? They looked mighty friendly standing there beside Nizari's decadent ride.

"You knew where he lived all this time?" Lee ground out. "Did you know he had children, too? How many?"

"Course we knew," Seth admitted. "He's just got the one, but you know Alex's rules of engagement now that the war's supposedly over. We're not the Taliban and we're not military. We don't kill men in their homes in front of their families. We catch them in the act, somewhere else."

"You could've told me," Lee said, striving for a cool head while all of his worst fears slapped him in the face. He was a loser and there was the proof. She'd fled the hospital, damn her, and obviously, Tess preferred to heal in the arms of another man. Why did it have to be Turik? Hadn't the son-of-a-bitch just last night charged Lee with loving Tess and taking care of her? Yet there they stood, holding each other. Loving each other. The bearded liar leaned into Tess's hair, and Lee wanted to puke. So many lies and he'd fallen for every one of them.

"I thought you knew," Seth murmured, "It's in my reports."

And damn it to hell. This wasn't Seth's fault, it was Lee's, and he knew it. He'd made so many mistakes taking on this operation to guard Tess. If anyone shouldn't be on this mission, it was him. *Shit. Just shit.*

"The boss is awake," Jordan said calmly.

Sprawled a few hundred feet away in the dirt, all three men had the mighty Taliban assassin in their scopes. One shot could send him to hell, but three double taps would be better. Lee wanted to do just that. It took all of his common sense to not play the game the way the Taliban did. He'd never kill a guy in front of his family. Besides, that kid might be Tess's. It didn't feel right, but Lee didn't know what he knew anymore. His logic card had blown a fuse trying to keep up with her.

Tess looked happy with her arm wrapped around that bastard's waist. She smiled up at him, and Lee could plainly make out the light in those pretty eyes through his scope. He'd seen it before. Turik claimed they'd met at college in England, another secret Tess forgot to mention. What else had they studied? Chemistry? Biology? Classmates didn't look that chummy unless they'd been intimate with each other. Had they? His gut churned at the thought of Tess with that man— with any man. Lee rolled to his back to break the connection. Sick at heart and mad as hell. He couldn't watch.

"You seen enough?" Jordan asked politely, his finger at his ear and obviously listening to their very angry boss. Leave it to Alex to make a bad day worse.

Lee stared at the hot sky. Some kind of black birds circled high overhead. Looked like vultures, and there he was, laid out like a corpse on their menu. He felt like one, dead inside and thoroughly gutted, his heart torn out and his entrails spread for the feast. All those birds up there in the wild blue yonder needed was an invitation and a napkin.

I hate this son-of-a-bitchin' country. I need to leave. "Let's get back to Eggers."

"You... you don't want to go talk to her?" Seth asked.

"Nope." Lee pushed out of the dirt to his feet, his mind made up. Afghanistan was nothing but war and pain, and he'd had a gut full. Somewhere in the world an island was calling his name. Somewhere a man could hide until he got his head back in the game. It was damned past time to man up. Move out. Get the hell out of there.

"But you've come this far." Seth didn't get it. "We've got time and we're here. Go talk to her, man."

Lee shouldered his rifle and walked away. *You go talk to her.*

They stopped her at the Eggers' security gate, just like she knew they would.

"Step out of the car, ma'am," the very tense guard ordered, his weapon pointed at her while his buddy did the same. "Nice and slow. Don't make any sudden moves."

She showed them her hands. "May I unbuckle my seatbelt?"

"Yes, ma'am," he said, his chin pressed to the radio at his shoulder.

She snapped the buckle open and opened the door, one foot to the ground and her whole body shaking. These guys were just plain scary. "My name is—"

"Shut up! On the ground! One more move and I'll shoot."

She dropped to her hands and knees before lying facedown, not a simple feat for a woman whose back was torn, blood oozing from the stitches. This was her fault, though. She'd expected trouble when she'd turned Nizari's vehicle onto Camp Eggers. But everything would be okay. Once they checked her story, they'd know she was with Lee and Alex.

"This is Nizari's car," the other guard muttered. "Who the hell is she? His wife? His mistress?"

"More like his whore," the other growled.

Tess bit her lip. These guys were both young and hyped up on testosterone and adrenaline. They were capable of shooting her and asking questions later. She wasn't ready to die. At least, she was in the shade of the BMW.

A heavy truck rumbled behind her, blocking her from leaving, which seemed really absurd. It wasn't like she was going anywhere. More tense chatter she didn't understand, full of acronyms and military speak, and two booted feet stopped inches from her face.

"Get up," a woman's voice demanded.

Tess eyed this new person as she climbed slowly to her feet, her poor back muscles screaming with the simple movement. "I'm sorry. I'm with—"

"Shut up!" the woman bellowed, her face red. "No one said you could speak. Place your hands on top of your head."

Tess caught the female guard's nametag as she lifted her palms. George. Interesting name for a woman.

"I'm going to search you, and you *will* comply. Do you understand?" Officer George barked.

"Yes." Tess nodded quickly.

George directed Tess to the very hot and shiny BMW hood. "What's your name, rank, and serial number?" The woman had no volume control but loud and rude.

"Tess Culver. I'm not military," Tess answered truthfully, the tension more than she had strength to endure. Her knees shook. If she had to stand much longer, she'd fall on her face.

George stuck her palm in the middle of Tess's back, and Tess groaned, the pain of that harsh contact unbearable. "Ouch, you're—"

"Shut up!" The woman wouldn't listen. George strong-armed Tess, her elbow in Tess's back until she was facedown on the blazing hot hood of Nizari's BMW. "What makes you think you can enter a high security military base driving a vehicle that belongs to one of the highest Taliban officers, Miss Culver?"

Tess peeled her burning cheek away from the scorching metal, her eyes squeezed tight, confused if she should shut up or answer the question. The heat radiating off the metal sucked her last ounce of energy. George better get a clue or Tess was going down.

"Please," Tess muttered, her voice dry and far away. Shadows swarmed her peripheral vision. "Contact Lee Hart. He'll vouch for me. Or Alex Stewart."

George barked something, but Tess only half heard the words. The oven of Afghanistan baked her quickly. She passed out.

Alex looked pretty damned pale, but then, so did Seth. He kept glancing at Lee like he still had something to say about him not talking to Tess. First things first. They were still getting their butts reamed for taking the Hummer off base.

Like Jordan said, Alex was mostly mad that he'd tripped over a sheep in the fight and broken his ankle. To make everything worse, surgery in a foreign country would make traveling back to the States awkward. He was the kind of boss who never took a day off from being the biggest and baddest jerk on the planet. "Who owns this damn company?" he ground out.

Lee didn't answer because he knew Seth would. Sure enough, Seth opened his mouth, "You do, Boss."

Poor, dumb Seth. Predictably, Alex jumped down his throat. "You'd better damned well believe it!" he roared, but Lee saw the signs. Alex was weakening, his roar not so much anger as frustration combined with whatever drugs he'd been given. It was hard being mad when you're fighting the leftover anesthetic in your system. Alex scrubbed a hand over his face. He'd refused a bed and for now sat in a wheelchair, his bandage and booted foot raised in front of him. "Sit rep."

"On?" Jordan asked.

"On Miss Culver!" Alex snarled. "Who do you think?"

Lee blew out a long-suffering sigh and admitted defeat. The boss wanted this answer to come from him. "Last time we saw her, she was in the company of Mohammed Turik at his home with his kid."

"You're sure about that?"

Lee nodded. No sense answering. He had nothing nice to say.

"That doesn't seem right," Alex muttered. "Why would she do that? We've still got the reliquary."

To hell with the reliquary. Keep the damned thing for all I care.

"You get it on video?" Alex asked.

"Nope," Lee said tiredly. "We weren't wearing helmet cams."

He had a plane to catch, and Alex damned well knew it. This was his last op and it was over. It sucked that the operation was a bust, but Tess Culver had refused their protection. There wasn't much more they could do they hadn't already tried. She seemed hell-bent on getting herself killed. Let her.

"But she's injured," Alex insisted. The man was fading fast, and Lee wanted him to. "You talk to her?"

Damn. Those silver-blue lasers skewered Lee straight through the heart. Not fair. "What was I gonna do, Boss? Trot on down and shake hands with the happy couple?"

Pure disgust coursed over Alex's face. "You went all that way, but you didn't find out why she went there? Is she back yet?"

"Don't know if she's coming back. She looked pretty happy." Lee corrected himself, "I mean, *they* looked happy."

Alex dropped his head into his hand, his eyes closed and the stress of the last night etched on his face. "Find her," he ordered quietly. "Talk to her. At least, find out what she wants us to do with the reliquary. It's hers, not ours. I'll support her whichever way she wants to go."

"Yes, Boss," Seth answered promptly, the suck-up.

"Not you." Another dark look skewered Lee. "You."

And that was the straw that broke the camel's back. "No," he stated loudly and unequivocally. It wasn't often an agent told the boss no. Seth and Jordan stopped breathing. Lee, on the other hand... "You knew going in this was my last op. You want her, you go get her."

"But you care for her." Alex couldn't have landed a harder blow below the belt.

"Shit, Boss, that I care only proves I'm a friggin' moron!" Lee stifled his heart. What more could he say? Hell yes, he cared, but one out of two did not a decent relationship make, much less a marriage. And now there he was, everyone staring at him and discussing his failed forty-eight-hour-old nightmare. Another freaking fine day in paradise!

He turned his back on The TEAM. Let Alex figure out what to do next. Lee had a plane to catch, and despite the fact he hadn't scheduled it yet, he didn't plan to miss it.

"Where am I?" Tess asked. The fog in her head pressed her into the mattress. The heat had been replaced with cooling air, but some guy was bellowing in the hallway. He didn't sound happy. The noise hurt her eyes, the ones she had yet to open. *Please shut up, whoever you are. You're killing me here.*

No sooner wished than granted. The bellowing stopped. Footsteps approached her bed, and a gentle hand rested on her forehead. She peeled one eye open, but the soft light pillaged her retinas. She couldn't squeeze her eyes closed fast enough.

"Ma'am," a man said, his words like thunder in her skull. "On a scale of one to ten, how would you rate your pain?"

"Like hell," she squeaked. Worse than hell. More like a fiery migraine on steroids that stretched all the way to her toes. "What... happened?"

"Some moron at the front gate jumped to conclusions and tasered you." Careful hands smoothed along her arm. "You're in our medical wing. I'm Doctor Jackson. I'm still not sure why you were trying to enter Camp Eggers, but you shouldn't have been treated like that."

"Lee," she muttered an attempt to explain. "I'm with Lee Hart."

"Is this his duty station?"

"No," she whined. Her head felt ready to explode. Talking made everything worse. "He's with... Alex."

"I'm going to give you something to help you sleep," a faraway voice murmured.

"No, don't. Please. I just... want... Lee."

Chapter Twenty-Seven

"You need any help?" Seth asked.

"Sure don't," Lee answered with the same response he'd given the last ten times Seth asked.

They were in the parking lot of Eggers. He shouldered what was left of his gear. Nizari's men had taken his weapons, knife, and boots the night before. All he had left were the few borrowed clothes on his back, his bag, and one pistol that really belonged to The TEAM. He handed it grip-first to Seth. "Might need a ride though."

Seth accepted the weapon and secured it in his belt. He seemed stuck in a place he didn't want to be—the middle of a war between Lee and Alex. Lee let him off the hook and changed the subject. "How are the guys?"

"Hunter woke up. He can't remember the fight at all, and Eric's mad as hell that he took a hit. He wants to go back and kick some more Taliban ass."

Sounded like Eric, the feistiest medic Lee had ever run into. The man could save lives, but he wasn't against popping a few bad guys when they got in his way.

"Alex?"

Seth shrugged. "I ain't asking. I'm staying clear of him right now. When's your flight leaving?"

Lee grunted. "To tell you the truth, I don't have one yet. Thought I'd hang out at the airport for a while and see what comes in. I can always go stand-by."

That surprised Seth. "Stand-by sucks. I hate airports."

"Yeah, me too." *But I hate hanging around here worse.*

"You ready?"

Lee cast the military base behind him one last glance and climbed into the passenger seat of the Humvee. "Move out."

Seth obliged.

Traffic was light. Khwaja Rawash, the Kabul International Airport, was still a risky place for tourists. Lee planned to take stand-by on any flight that could get him out of the country. Dubai was close, and Ankara, Turkey, not much farther. He didn't care which airline he took. It was time he saw another part of the world. Any place else would do.

"I had a girl once," Seth muttered.

"Oh yeah?" Lee didn't know that about his buddy. "Sounds like that was a while ago."

Seth nodded. "It was. I, umm, I lost her."

"Sorry." The last thing Lee needed was a sad story about another woman who'd run off with someone else.

"It was the damnedest thing," Seth said quietly. "She was on her way to the airport to pick me up. I was home on a two-week leave. We were engaged. She planned to surprise me with our wedding the minute I stepped off the plane. Crazy woman. Had both of our families with her. Her maid-of-honor. My best man. My mom and dad. We'd waited so damned long..."

Lee glanced at Seth. His voice was far away.

"Katlynn was the prettiest girl this side of the Mississippi." He stopped there, and Lee waited, his gut clenched with foreboding. This wasn't a Dear John story. This was worse.

Seth blew out a small breath. "She was in her wedding dress when it happened, all white and pure and pretty. Her folks were driving because she was nervous, and she had these white, lacy three-inch heels."

Lee held his breath. Seth was actually on his way to get married at one time in his life?

"Anyway, a drunk driver hit their car just off the interstate. I could've seen it from the plane if I'd a known where to look when we were landing. The jet I was on flew over the scene of the accident, only..." His words trailed away.

"I'm sorry, man," Lee said.

"Yeah," Seth murmured. "Me too. Katlynn was the prettiest girl, and she loved me."

They drove in silence for a few minutes.

"That's why I was out drinking with my friends the night I shot that little girl. They thought they could cheer me up, and there was a band at some bar in downtown Chicago, and... anyway, that's why I was there. I was supposed to be drowning my sorrow only I ended up killing a teenager. Fate really sucks rocks sometimes."

Lee stared at the traffic. All he could see were Tess's violet blue eyes lit up with love that morning he'd awakened on the hotel floor in her arms. He'd had some feelings for her before then, but that day had changed everything. She got him like no one else. It was like she knew all about his private hell—she even knew the language that went with it. Singing "Amazing Grace" had cinched it. That was when he knew he had to have her, no matter what.

"I'm not asking for your pity," Seth interrupted Lee's hopeless thoughts. "Heck, I don't even care if anyone understands why I'm such a screwed-up mess today. I just want you to know that sometimes things happen, Lee, and we think they're really bad, and we get so mad we forget what's real, and we walk away from the very thing that can save us. We give up. We think we're too broke to ever be fixed again."

Lee couldn't have felt more like crap. *First Tess. Then Alex. Now Seth.*

"It's just that sometimes, when we're feeling like the whole damned world's crapping on us, we're not seeing what's real and what's not. We can't see through the shit to what's important. We got this little old ball of crap up against our eye, and the damned thing looks like the whole damned world, and I guess, in a way, at that moment it is. But it ain't, Lee. It's just a little piece of shit that's stuck in our eye. That's all it is."

Lee blew out a small sigh. Tess and Turik knew each other from their past lives. So what? He just wished he knew why she'd sought Turik out so soon after their very intimate profession of love. Hell, Lee had gone through hell to save her life, and the next thing he knew, she was hanging out with her Taliban assassin buddy. How messed up was that?

Seth didn't say another word until he pulled up to the curb at the domestic terminal at Kabul International. Plenty of NATO forces and military dominated the scene, but Lee just sat there. He no longer knew what to say. Or do.

"Guess this is goodbye," Seth muttered, his hand extended.

Lee obliged him with the traditional hand-to-wrist grip. He tugged his gear over the seat. The time had come to leave. The crazy woman he'd fallen in love with seemed determined to make something out of this stone-hard country. She saw diamonds where others saw nothing but dust and rocks. She saw hope. All Lee saw was that damned ball of crap.

Was she insane? Yes. Was she seeing things in Afghanistan that no one in their right mind saw? Definitely. Did he love her anyway? Hell, yeah. Could he forgive her for running to Turik? Lee just plain didn't know. She'd made that choice for the both of them, and Lee didn't know what to do with it.

He sat there with one foot in the Humvee, the other out. An orange and white airliner roared overhead, close enough he could see the heat waves coming off the jet engines. That would be him in a few hours, on his way to who knew where.

Seth sat there waiting, the engine idling while Lee stalled. Was this what he wanted to do? Leave? It felt a lot like running away. That was the real quandary. He wasn't a quitter, and yet he'd just quit The TEAM, but what the hell? What difference had he made? He'd done everything humanly possible to save Tess's life. Heck, he'd killed men with his bare hands to get to her. He'd saved three American soldiers in the process, but it had always been about her. It still was.

Ky, Jack, and Ross should be thanking her for their lives, not him. It was only because of Tess that he'd been so focused and so damned deadly. That the universe had complied with the unexpected alliance of Turik had helped, but not enough. The first moment Tess opened her eyes, she'd thrown Lee's gift of love back in his face like it meant nothing.

Enough was enough. Lee turned to Seth, thumped his bicep, and put both boots on the ground. "I'm tired of fighting the world, man. I've killed for my country, and what do I have to show for it? Squat. I get it now. I can't win. I'm gonna hitch a ride on a southbound current and spend some time adrift on the Atlantic. Maybe a year or two. Take care of yourself. See you around."

"Keep in touch," Seth muttered.

Lee turned away. *Not damned likely.*

Tess woke to a not-so-gentle pat on her cheek. At least her headache was gone.

When she opened her eyes, she about swallowed her tongue. Clint peered down at her, his pointy nose too close and his dark beard as scruffy as all get-out.

"Where have you been?" she croaked while she pushed herself to her elbows.

"Whoa. Listen to you." He chuckled at her raspy voice. "You sound like you need something to drink, Sis."

She punched his shoulder. "What I need is answers, you moron. Where the hell have you been, and how come you never told me you could fly? Where's your helicopter? Will you please raise this bed up so I can see you better?" She scooted her butt higher on the mattress as he elevated the bed. "And how could you leave me in the middle of one of the biggest heists we've ever attempted? Did you know Agent Hart before he bribed you with a fifth of whiskey? Were you expecting him? Huh? Answer me."

When Clint rolled his eyes, she wanted to smack him again. She'd had nightmares about him, and there he was all cavalier and smirky, the smartass. For a change he was in clean jeans and a simple white T-shirt. His cheeks weren't as sallow as they usually were, and he was smiling. He'd shaved. Gosh, he actually looked good beneath that mop of black hair.

He offered her a glass with a straw in it, and she couldn't refuse. Her throat was parched. After she swallowed a soothing sip of tepid water, she ordered again, "Answer me."

"Cease fire, why don't you?" He chuckled again as he rested his backside next to her. "I can't keep up with all your questions. You don't look your usual perky, bossy self. What's up, Sis?"

"Clint…" Tess gritted her teeth at his attempt at diversion, but the sight of him safe and sound was more than she could handle. "Damn you, Clint. It's so good to see you."

He grabbed her into his arms, and she bawled like a baby despite her anger. "So much has been going on." She gulped a breath before she sobbed again. "And I had a dream. You needed me, but I couldn't get to you. And where the hell have you been?"

"How about if I answer first questions first?' Clint was always the glib one, and now that Tess thought about it, he always could get around her. Even as mad as he made her, he had a charming, conniving way.

She leaned against her pillow, tired from her outburst. "Where the hell am I?"

"You, my dear sister, are in the Camp Eggers medical unit. Some guy named Jackson called to let me know you were here. They tasered you at the front gate, huh?"

"I don't remember that, but look at this." Lowering the shoulder of her hospital gown, which she just realized someone had changed her into, she showed her absentee brother the harsh whip marks.

Clint's eyes darkened. He lifted from the mattress to examine Tess's wounds more closely. "Nizari? The bastard."

"Yes, Nizari," she spat the words at Clint like he was to blame. "You should've been there. None of this would've happened!"

He frowned. "Give me a break. It ain't my fault. You know how you are. If you tangle with the wrong guys often enough, and they're going to catch up with you. For heck's sake, don't play on the freeway if you don't wanna get run over by a semi."

She didn't know why she'd ever worried about him. He sure didn't think twice about her. "You're an ass."

He grinned and waggled his brows. "And your point?"

Her point was she wanted to feel physically well enough to kick his butt. She crossed her arms and glared at him. "You traded me for a bottle of booze. Me. Your only sister."

"Not exactly. I mean, yeah, that is what Agent Hart gave me that night, but there's a little more to the story."

"Then spit it out. What aren't you telling me?"

He stared her down through a big sigh. "Only if you promise not to get mad."

"I'm already mad." Mad and feeling ill wasn't a good combination.

"Why don't I introduce you to a friend of mine first? That'll make everything crystal clear." He went to the door and motioned for someone to join them.

An Afghan man with the most amazing turquoise blue eyes entered her room. Dressed in the traditional shalwar kameez of his people, he nodded once to acknowledge her, and immediately, she pulled the blankets up to her neck. This was definitely a fundamentalist Muslim. She didn't want to offend him by exposing her bare shoulders and arms.

"Relax," Clint said. "He's a friend. I think you and he have needed to meet each other for a long time."

"Miss Culver." The man stretched his hand to hers. "I have been looking forward to this day. I am Iskandar Kadir."

"Very nice to meet you." Her hand trembled when he took it, and she didn't know why. She wasn't afraid of him. Something about this good-looking, bearded man seemed familiar. "Excuse me, but do I know you?"

Iskandar smiled. He had perfect teeth, a straight nose, and intelligent, smiling eyes. "You should. You have been searching for me for years."

His rich baritone rumbled between them, and she looked deeper. She didn't understand, and judging by Clint's big grin, she should. But why? What was going on that she didn't get?

"You see, Sis," Clint intervened, "I work for WAR just like you do, only I've been undercover."

"That's what Mohammed said." She settled into her pillow and listened mostly because Iskandar's presence made Clint's words seem more credible if not entirely palatable. But what was she missing?

"Who do you think hired your Agent Hart and his boss in the first place?" Clint asked, glancing around the room. "By the way, where is Agent Hart? You haven't sent him packing, have you?"

"No," she answered. "He's probably still sleeping. So who hired him? You?"

Clint didn't blink. "Hell no. How rich do you think I am? Guess again."

She hated guessing games, but the first name that came to her mind tripped off her tongue. It made sense. "Jacque?"

"You're getting warmer."

There was no one else who loved her enough to have her physically removed from this country. No one except... She swallowed hard. No. It couldn't be. "Mohammed?"

Clint winked at her. "Bingo. He had to do something to keep you safe."

"Mohammed did this?" Unbelievable. Incredibly unbelievable. She couldn't catch a breath. "To me? For me? You're wrong. He tried to shoot me." Only he didn't. Not really. He'd only meant to wound her, not kill her. She shook her head and placed both palms to the bed, the wind knocked out of her. "You talked with him? You know this for certain?"

Clint nodded. "He's a cocky son-of-a-bitch, all right."

She shook her head. "No, Clint. That's not right. Why would he hire Alex Stewart then? Why hire the very same man who was trying to kill him? My gosh…" She trailed her fingers through her hair, combing it back over her ear while she rubbed her scalp. None of this made sense. Mohammed definitely had an over-inflated male ego. He was smug, an Afghan male to his toes: autocratic, egotistical, and a bit of a windbag. She'd always known that, but this? To take on one of America's most elite covert teams, to contract Alex to guard her while they were trying to kill him at the same time? God, the man thought he was untouchable. Mindboggling. Simply mindboggling.

"Admit it. It was the only way to protect you, Sis. We knew you'd never give up this crazy quest you're on. Everything went south from the day you confronted Nizari. He had it bad for you anyway, which brings me to my friend here. Do you remember the legend of Alexander and Roxana, that nonsense you've been spouting, like forever?" His eyes glittered with some untold secret.

"Wait a minute…" She glared at her brother. She might have felt fairly crappy, and her head was pounding, but she'd heard that telling word. "Who exactly is we?"

His eyes narrowed. Clint shrugged like the little brother he would always be. "Okay, I give. Turik had a few run-ins with Alex Stewart before, and, don't ask me how, but he trusted the guy to get you home safely. Call me crazy, but I think Stewart likes this wacked out country more than you do. I also think he enjoyed the challenge Turik proposed."

Her brother simply would not answer a direct question. She pinned him down. "So you were in on this protection order with Mohammed?"

Clint reached over and tousled her hair, nodding. "Of course. I do love you, Sis."

She grabbed his hand to stop the playful gesture. "Then why didn't you tell me you were working for WAR? Why did you make me think you were drunk or doped up all the time? Damn it, you had me convinced."

"Because you…" he sighed deeply, "are a flaming ass to work with. Admit it, Tessie. You're pig-headed, overbearing, and once you get a notion in your head, you run over anyone and everyone in your way. You're secretive and for reals? I found I could accomplish more when you thought I was zoned out on drugs than I could working side-by-side with you. You tend to want to snap your fingers and expect everyone to fall in line behind you as if they don't have any brains." He glanced at Iskandar. "What say we table this brother-sister discussion until later?"

"Fine." she relented, perturbed he acted like he had the upper hand. Okay, so he was right about a couple of things, but she was pigheaded only because she was passionate about her missions. All of them.

"I'll wager you everything I own that this gentleman's DNA..." Clint nodded toward Iskandar, "matches the DNA of those fingers in the reliquary, as well as the mummies."

She forgot to breathe, her eyes shifting to Iskandar. The softest blue skies of Afghanistan smiled back at her. Could it be? Was this—him? "Are you sure?" she asked, her heart pounding.

Clint nudged Iskandar's elbow. "Told you she'd be shit-faced."

Iskandar came forward and knelt to one knee at her bedside. He latched onto her hand, and she was deeply embarrassed for her appearance. He was such a good-looking man, around thirty, his eyes clear, and his heart on his sleeve. Honesty stared back at her, and she was smitten.

"Miss Tess Culver," he said, his voice mellow and rich. "My people have guarded our ancient queen for centuries. Many of us can trace our lineage to her. We are in your debt for retrieving the sacred reliquary of Roxana from the evil warlords."

She honestly couldn't speak to save her life. "But... but..."

"I have submitted to the test your brother requested, but the legends are true. I am here to testify of what I know. It has been foretold. The descendants of Alexander will rule again. This country will be filled with peace and prosperity. The day will come when the Taliban will live no more."

"But... but..."

"And on the day the truth is declared to all the world, it would be my greatest honor if you would join me in my humble village for a celebration of rebirth. My people crave to meet the brave woman who dared believe in them."

Tess shut her mouth because nothing was coming out of it that made sense anyway. Clint still grinned like a Cheshire cat. Iskandar pressed his lips to the back of her hand, his sharp eyes beguiling her to her toes. "If you are still a single woman when that day comes, I will take you to be my fourth wife. It would bring me great joy."

Too much! She wished Lee was there to lend her some of his excellent strength. At last she remembered what she'd wanted to say. "But I saw the soldiers destroy the mummies. We watched it on satellite. Isn't Roxana gone?"

Iskandar shook his head. "The crypt where she and her son lay is dark within our mountain. Roxana rests there still, as do the precious artifacts you and your friend have returned to us."

Then she knew why Iskandar seemed so familiar. "You were there the day Jacque and I visited your village, weren't you? I've met you before, haven't I?"

His turquoise blue eyes twinkled. "Monsieur Favreau was my good friend. He will be missed. We have much need of good people like him and you in the world."

"Oh, wow," she declared, her silly heart doing back flips.

Clint winked at her. "You'll never guess what the English version of your new friend's name is."

Her mind was spinning, her head was pounding, and he wanted her to guess? "Just tell me. What?"

Clint reverted to her annoying baby brother. "Come on, Tess. Guess. Just once. Think about it."

"Will you just say it?" She spiked her evil big sister brow.

"Al... ex... an... der," Clint enunciated. "Iskandar *is* Alexander. I know you know that. You've done it, Sis. You found your Alexander."

She. Nearly. Squealed! She'd done it. If the DNA matched, she'd actually done it. She needed to tell Lee. She couldn't wait to see the pride glowing in his sexy emerald green eyes.

"Clint, do me a favor and find Lee for me. Wake him up if you have to, but he needs to hear this. Alex Stewart too, if you can find him. This is too incredible. I want them to meet Iskandar. Oh, wow. Lee will be thrilled. And Alex... Oh, Iskandar. I can't wait for you to meet Alex. You two have the same names." Not like that mattered, but Tess was so excited, it seemed important.

Clint bowed a short, insincere bow of brotherly respect. "At your service, Sis." He turned into the hall, leaving her with Iskandar.

"I'm so happy to meet you," she said as she squeezed his hands tight. "So happy. You don't know what this means."

"It is my pleasure. Your brother has done a great service for my people. We are in his debt."

Her heart soared. She was right. She just knew it! After all these years of worrying, wondering, and fighting the world, now she could throw it in their faces. Mina and Jamaal would live to see the day their country was restored to prosperity. Tess couldn't wait to tell them!

Clint appeared back at the door, but Seth and Jordan accompanied him instead of Lee and Alex. "Sis, there's something you need to—"

She cut him off and waved them into her room, her heart bursting with joy. "Wait until you guys hear this! Where's Lee? Is he still sleeping? And where's Alex? I want everyone to hear this." Only then did she catch Seth's stricken face. Jordan hadn't cracked a smile yet, either.

"Lee saw you with Turik and his kid," Seth muttered. "This morning. You went to Turik's house. We all saw you. What were you thinking?"

Her heart thudded to a dead stop. "I only went to ask if he knew where Clint was. I had a dream. I had… Oh never mind. I had to find my brother."

Seth looked at the floor. "He saw you kissing Turik. He said he's done fighting a war he can't win."

Tess sank back into her pillow. She couldn't breathe. "I didn't kiss Mohammed. Not that way. Where is he?"

"At the airport," Seth muttered. "I dropped him off an hour ago. He said he's taking his sailboat to the Atlantic for a few months, maybe a year."

She covered her face with her hands, ashamed and sad and sick. None of this tremendous good news meant anything without Lee.

Chapter Twenty-Eight

"Final call. Flight 3728 boarding for Dubai. Repeat..."

Lee kicked back in the molded plastic seat, his legs stretched long and straight in front of him, his boots worn and dusty. Cowboy boots, the most comfortable things he could find for the mangled feet Nizari had left him with. The bastard had won after all. Lee had lost Tess and his job all because of the damage inflicted years ago. And there he was, on the losing side of life, crawling off to hide for a few months on the Atlantic, not something he was proud to admit. His snap decision to leave rankled in his gut.

He pulled his long legs out of the aisle and leaned his elbows to his knees. Waiting on stand-by could take a while, especially with the military taking first available seating on all outbound flights. He wasn't about to step in line in front of an active duty soldier or Marine. Mostly, he was tired of the shadow of Nizari hovering over him day in and day out. Just tired, damn it.

People came and people went. Businessmen of all nationalities hurried by, briefcases in hand, some in business suits, some in flowing robes, some in military uniforms. Families disembarked. He fidgeted. Not ready to go. Not wanting to stay. Stuck somewhere in between. *Shit.*

He forced his mind to his favorite getaway, his sailboat. Still unnamed, she was a seaworthy craft. With stainless-steel ports and plenty of teak, she sported decent navigational lights and the traditional headsails. He'd already stocked the galley with enough canned food and dry goods for a party of one. He'd even plotted his course to the Med before he'd accepted this final mission. Hell, he might even name her on this cruise.

But the memory of Tess and Turik together kept poking at him, twisting a knife in his gut. One minute, Lee was sailing on the Atlantic with the wind in his face, the next, he was thinking of beating Turik's arrogant face to a bloody pulp.

Lee stared at his boots. The thing rankling deepest in his gut was that damned song. It linked him to Tess in a way Lee hadn't seen coming. For the first time in years, he'd truly believed he'd been saved. She made him feel like a man again, as if his scars and ugliness were nothing to her, like they didn't define him. He'd felt free to be himself with Tess. She'd made him feel alive.

The sun was setting low to the west, the sky filled with a steady orange glow, tinged with pink and offset by the cobalt blue of the upcoming night. Another jet rumbled outside the terminal windows. Lee didn't catch the airline logo splashed across the tail because the truth kept slapping around inside his hard USMC head, telling him he'd missed something. Telling him he couldn't leave yet.

"I'm not going back to her," he muttered quietly to himself. *She makes me crazy, and she lies, and I'm tired of the game and all of her secrets. Tess wants to chase her dreams? Let her.*

He swallowed hard, his chest a sucking hole of the deepest heartache he might not survive this time. Why the hell had she run to Turik? What was so important that she couldn't wait to heal first, or at least talk to him? Lee didn't know if he cared. But knowing Tess, it had something to do with that tribe up high in the Kush... or her brother, Clint... or Mina and Jamaal... or... *who cares?*

Lee scrubbed a quick hand over his face, tired of the puzzle that was Tess. He'd told her he loved her, and that hurt the worst. She might have been out cold when he said it, but he did love her. She'd had him by the balls and heart the first minute he'd laid eyes on her, and yeah, he was the dumbest ass on the planet to fall for a crazy, pretty woman. And she was crazy— crazy in love with... Turik? Nah. She did get kind of dreamy-eyed when she talked about the guy, but love didn't seem to fit. Enamored maybe. Not love.

Lee drummed his fingers on the armrest and stared at the sun, a deep orange ball of fire in the western sky, half visible as it kissed the day goodbye. But those two little kids? Mina and Jamaal were another bewildering facet to the puzzle. Now that was love. Lee had heard it in Mina's voice. The little girl believed in her Tess and her fairytale stories. What the hell was a man supposed to make of that? Lee didn't know. He couldn't fix Tess. Hell, he couldn't even fix himself.

"Is this seat taken?"

Lee looked up into the smirky face of one Clint Culver, not who he'd expected to see. Seth maybe. Not Tess's brother. He motioned to the vacant seat across from him. "It's all yours."

Clint could've passed for Tess's twin with the same dark hair and facial features. He had her nose, but not her eyes. No one had Tess's pretty eyes. Clint's were lively, but gray. He folded his lanky frame onto the molded plastic as casual as ever. "You catch a flight out of here yet?"

Lee shook his head, staring at his hands. Truth be known, he hadn't stepped up to the counter. "Still waiting."

"India Air's got one going to Sri Lanka if you're desperate to leave," Clint suggested. "It'll take a couple days, and it's headed in the wrong direction, but you'll get to the States eventually."

"No thanks. I'm good." Lee spared Clint a quick glance. He had time. He could wait.

An Afghan gentleman in traditional dress had taken the seat to Clint's left, a keffiyeh wrapped turban-style on his head, his unusually bright blue eyes dark and gentle. He nodded a wordless greeting at Lee.

"My sister's something, isn't she?" Clint offered, his gaze on the magnificent light show taking place in the western sky, one arm draped across the empty seat next to him. "Can you believe she thought I was a doper? I sure pulled one over on her this time. Sis always missed the forest for the trees."

He chuckled, and Lee wished he'd shut the hell up.

"I got into a fight one time when I was a kid. The guy was our neighbor. It was my fault, but Tess didn't know it. She came smoking out of the house. You'd have thought the place was on fire, but did she stop to think twice? Nosirree. She jumped into the fray like it was her fight. Bam, up she goes to the guy I'm scrapping with. He'd just kicked my ass, which I'd deserved, mind you, but there she was charging to the rescue. The thing is, he was big. You should've seen her. I mean really. There's this little Meerkat of a woman standing up to an adult male who outweighed her three to one and..." Clint tipped his head back and burst out laughing, the dumbass, tears rolling down his face. "You shoulda... you shoulda..."

The serene gentleman next to Clint offered up a quiet chuckle, nothing like the uproar Clint was making, though. The corners of Lee's mouth twitched. Clint had just described Tess to a T. She was a Meerkat of a woman, full of fight and determination and piss. Full of shit, too. His heart hurt for that independent woman. *God, I love her.*

Clint whined, twisting in the chair and pretty much making an ass of himself. People were looking. "Anyway..." he paused to draw in a deep breath and straightened, wiping his face with the back of his hand. "She didn't get hit, for which I'm eternally glad, but man, she did give that behemoth a piece of her mind. I can still see her standing there, spitting nails and glaring up at this big, red-faced, sweaty guy with picnic hams for fists, and he's glaring down at her, his bushy eyebrows twitching like he couldn't decide to hit her or not. She's yelling at him, '*You* would *hit a girl. I know you would, so do it, you big bully.*' Ahhhhh..." Clint dragged a hand over his teary eyes again. "I love that sister of mine, but damn, she can be a raging pain in the ass."

Lee kicked back in his seat. It felt good listening to this brotherly story, almost like Tess was there, laughing along with them.

"The thing is that whole mess was my fault." Clint sobered. "I picked the fight, but my sister was the one who finished it. She got so mad when I explained what really happened, then it was my turn in the barrel. Man, did she go off on me, screeching like a banshee, swearing and slapping my head and hands." He growled softly. "But then she started crying, because she'd made a fool of herself. Damn. Wind her up and she's an incredible force in the universe. Just don't get in her way."

Lee nodded, still seeing that incredible force in the universe, the one with violet sparks in her deep blue eyes. Still aching for Tess. That was her alright, defying bullies the world over and risking her sweet ass when she did it. Ready to die for her dreams. Ready to risk it all. And there he was—running away.

He changed the subject. "You ever met Mohammed Turik?"

Clint nodded. "The assassin? Once or twice."

Lee studied Clint, not sure if he could trust a Culver. These two Americans were a long ways from home and both up to their necks in intrigue and danger, Tess with her far-fetched dream for this godawful land, Clint with whatever was going on in the high Kush.

Clint took the pause in conversation for an opening. "I met him through Tess. She and Turik met in college in England."

Lee nodded. He knew that much. "And...?"

"And that's where their dreams collided," the somber Afghan gentleman at Clint's side offered. "Excuse me for interrupting, but I am Iskandar Kadir, a chieftain from the high mountains." He reached for Lee's hand, and Lee found it a firm grip. "I know Mohammed Turik. He is a good man, one of few who have braved the hard road to my village. One of the few who have come in peace."

Lee let him talk. The man's eyes were clear blue, the color of a spring sky without clouds, the color of a soul without guile. Clint brought his hands together, his fingers tip-to-tip, creating a temple of sorts through which he stared at the floor.

Iskandar beckoned Lee closer. "It is a hard road we all must walk, my friend, and there are so few lights along the way."

Lee didn't know where this line of chat was headed, but yeah. He understood the concept of lights along the way. That was what his self-therapy was about, restoring the fallen stars in the sky that Nizari had murdered.

"Always know this—there *are* lights, no matter how steep the road or how deep the darkness. No matter how high the mountains," Iskandar said with surety, "and when we are blessed to find one of those lights, we must hold close to it, for that is why it was given to us. Is not Allah the most wise?"

"Yes," Lee answered unequivocally. He'd long ago accepted God by all of His names and chosen peoples.

Iskandar curled his fingers into his palm as if showing Lee how to hold onto one of those lights. "Then keep that light close to you, Agent Lee Hart. Shelter it from the storms. Never be willing to settle for darkness again." His weathered face split into a smile. "I must say I do like your name. Hart. It is a strong name, and you are a strong man with a strong heart. Do not lose sight, my son. There is sufficient light for those who choose to believe."

He couldn't have spoken more directly to Lee's soul than with that last line, the wisdom of his mother come back to him. *Sufficient,* his mother's favorite word. Wow. His heart rate kicked up, and for no reason at all, he found it hard to breathe. The airport terminal swirled around him, then settled back to normal. "Who are you?" He had to know.

Iskandar blinked as if he didn't understand. "I am Iskandar Kadir of the most high Hindu Kush."

"No really," Lee persisted. "Have we ever met before?" Because this guy sure as hell seemed familiar in a weird way. Iskandar resembled one of the Three Wise Men with his checkered keffiyeh wrapped around his head like it was.

"No, my friend, we have not met before. Not in this sphere. Perhaps another."

Lee peered closer. That wasn't really an answer, was it?

"Who really knows? Tess and I believe he's Alexander's great, great, great..." Clint waved his fingers in a grandiose, circular motion over his head, "...grandson. We're running DNA tests now. Don't look so surprised. You might have met him in another lifetime, Lee. This is Afghanistan after all, a land of ancient legend and romance."

A bemused smile shifted over Iskandar's rugged face. For the first time, a glimmer of hope sparked to life in Lee's heart. There was just one fly in the ointment, one bully still blocking all that celestial light. Lee leveled a serious eye at Clint. "You fly a chopper?"

Clint nodded, one brow raised. "Once or twice, why? You need one?"

"You fly up to the Kush, do you?"

"I deliver supplies and... things."

"Guns? Ammo?"

Clint nodded. "Yes," he said without hesitation.

Lee deliberated for one split second. "You got any spares?"

Chapter Twenty-Nine

After Clint met him outside Kabul and armed him with two pistols, a sawed-off shotgun, and a short-stock AR, complete with enough ammo to take out an army, Lee felt more like himself again. He wasn't tucking in his tail and running away, not this Marine. Hell, no. He had his head on straight again and a job to do.

"I hope to see you again," Iskandar offered.

"Don't worry. You will," Lee promised as he hefted the AR strap to his shoulder. It seemed the right thing to say to the guy. Iskandar Kadir did have a mystical air about him, an ancient, wise way. Or something. Hell, maybe he was just one of those people who actually believed in this damned country. Like Alex. Like Tess. Like Lee was beginning to.

"Take care of your sister," Lee growled at Clint. *God knows she needs it.*

The masculine version of Tess smirked back at him. "Sorry, Agent Hart. I'm not *Ethan Hunt*. That's your job."

Maybe it was. Maybe it wasn't. Lee honestly didn't know at that moment, but for the first time since he'd seen Tess with Turik, he was willing to consider an alternative universe.

Clint and Iskandar went one way. Lee went the other. He couldn't trust Turik any more than Tess, but Lee needed to be sure Nizari was dead. He forfeited the smooth road for the stealth of shadows, the only company he needed aside from the cold steel on his hip. This wasn't a night for legal sanctions or rules of engagement. This was a night for a righteous kill, for vigilante justice. Lee might not live to talk about it. At the moment, he wasn't sure if he cared. Either way, he needed to make sure Nizari was dead.

The problem with walking was it gave a man too much time to dwell on things—like Tess. Like what the hell did he expect to find in this backward country—a loyal woman? Wasn't he the stupid ass? Still...

As much as her betrayal hurt, he recognized the attraction between them, and no, it wasn't just the sex. As good as sex with her was, as in hot-damned good, the real attraction that had drawn him to her was the enthusiasm for life within that athletically toned, running body of hers. The vigor. The way her eyes lit up. Her eagerness to touch him. Her greediness for his damaged body.

He clenched one fist to his massive chest, imagining her slender fingers fluttering over him. She'd never hesitated once she'd decided she'd wanted him. Not once. Just reached out and snagged him like one of her ancient treasures. Like she meant to save him, too.

And she had...

He flexed his fingers and scrubbed a wide palm over the ache in his heart, needing her out of there. He had a hard job to do. He needed to be a focused precision sniper, not some lovesick teenage boy. Hell, he needed to be the hand of God tonight, and, if Turik hadn't already taken care of business with Nizari like he should have, Lee needed to wipe Nizari's filthy stain off the face of the earth.

Lee's fingers brushed over the crucifix around his neck. Tess's crucifix. He'd hung it there when he'd found it in

Nizari's torture chamber—that night. *Shit. Last night.* He'd meant to give it back, but feeling it there under his shirt brought the audacious energy of that crazy woman back to him. A hint of coconut and lime came out of nowhere.

Suddenly, she was there. Walking with him. Teasing him. Revealing yet another secret to her wild and daring nature. Her free spirit. That was the difference between them. Lee still walked in shadow, perhaps because he'd spent more time with the Devil. But Tess Culver, the audacious cat burglar of Kabul, had risen above her pain. She'd put her near-death experience behind her, and she'd gone on to steal back from dishonorable men and despicable thieves the treasures of the country she loved. Better yet, she'd cracked the code to one tough-as-nails former Marine when she sang to him.

The words bubbled up from deep within. *"The Lord has promised good to me... As long as life endures..."* How many times had he sung it? Hummed it? Mentally prayed it? He honestly didn't know, but its message rang crystal clear tonight. Lee believed. There was a God who answered prayers, and tonight He'd sent Lee to be that answer.

He drew in a deep, soul-cleansing breath, then exhaled slowly, the weight lifting from his shoulders and away from his heart. He might not be the romantic hero of Tess's legends, but by the time the morning sun kissed the highest crest of the Hindu Kush, Tess and the rest of this country would be free of Nizari. She could live her impossible dreams and run her crazy schemes. Lee couldn't change who he was. He'd still be gone, but he could do this one thing before he left. He could prove he loved her enough to let her go. To let her live.

A light glimmered ahead. Nizari's compound. The infamous rows of torture cells stood a respectable distance to the east, bleak and dark. They looked more like a row of sheds lined up side-by-side. Respectable nothing. Vile. Wretched. Fifty shades of pure evil.

Hunkered low, Lee crept steadily toward the lighted window, needing to see inside. All five senses ranged far and wide to pull in the slightest sound from the distance, the hint of skulk within the shadows, or the scent and stink of the unwashed enemy he'd come to end.

He swung his AR off his shoulder and clenched the grip, his itchy finger on the trigger. Sideways at the window, he peered inside at the plush room where just hours earlier he'd found Tess stripped bare. The room had been cleared except for the whipping post. Her blood still marred the gold rug. Boxes stood stacked along one side of the room, scrolls, pictures, and larger boxes along the other.

What the hell? Nizari was still alive? Didn't it figure? Turik had given Lee false hope that he'd deal with Nizari. What'd he do—give the bastard a good talking to instead of putting a bullet in his head? Rage ignited an inferno in Lee's veins. Nizari first. Then the liar, Mohammed Turik.

Ducking out of sight, Lee circled the lavish home to the cells out back. All the doors stood ajar. No noises. No screams. Better yet, no American soldiers dangling from chains like sides of beef inside those cells. His heart settled to its normal rhythm. He meant to torch those cells before he left, but first...

He moved past the three trucks backed up to the concrete patio to the east and south of the house. Men's voices drifted to him. Maybe three. He closed in for the kill, needing it. Yearning for it. He came upon two—one loading the truck, the other handing up boxes. Both with their backs to him. It didn't take long. That was why the pistol. That was why the silencer. Two men down. Hopefully, just one more to go.

Lee scanned the quiet yard to his right, sensing another presence in the universe of wicked men, another like him who killed for his country. It had to be Turik out there laying for him. Well, hell. Lee ducked inside Nizari's southern door, the one he'd walked out of last night with Tess in his arms. Only one man would exit this building alive tonight. It wouldn't be Nizari, and it sure as hell wouldn't be Turik.

Lee was two-rooms deep into the house by the time he found who he was looking for. Nizari looked up from his packing. He shoved the gilded books in his hands hurriedly into a box and folded the flaps closed. Hiding more stolen artifacts. More deceit. The man just wouldn't quit.

"Going somewhere?" Lee taunted, the reticle of his AR on the lying bastard in the room. Ah, muscle memory. You've got to love the advantage it gave a guy. He'd trained for hours to become the steady, cool hand he was today. Course, he'd also gone through Nizari's brutal training camp, too. That had to count for something.

Lee rolled the righteous twinge out of his shoulder. A previously banked spike of self-righteousness slithered up his spine like a snake to take its place. It hissed for the kill. Demanded the blood of it. And somewhere down deep in Lee's gut, he needed it, too. He needed Nizari's screaming death to be able to lift his own head high again. Needed an end to this monster who'd delighted in torture to finally balance the universe. To make things right for Tess and all the women and children like her.

"You," Nizari hissed, but Lee caught the lie. Nizari might want to project contempt, but his trembling fingers gave him away.

"Me," Lee grunted, his scope on target—not that he needed the scope at this distance.

Nizari lifted his chin. He was still in dress slacks, the two top buttons on his cream-colored shirt open, his sleeves rolled to his elbows. The outline of the bandage on his upper-left chest covered the knife wound. It had to hurt what with all the packing. The pale tone of his shirt resonated against the deathly pallor of his normally dusky skin, no longer mocha so much as the hue of the belly of a desert lizard.

"You have no rights in my country," he declared, his voice tight. "You can't kill me. You're an American soldier. Your country operates on strict rules of engagement."

"Marine," Lee corrected the man at the business end of his weapon. "I'm not a soldier, I'm a Marine. Get it right. I do know the rules, but I doubt your Quran promotes the shit you've been doing."

"I've committed no crimes," he had the nerve to lie. "I merely ask for and then take what is offered, and eventually, everything is offered. Like you."

Lee tamped down his angst. He edged closer, the scent of sandalwood bringing every abhorrent crime committed against his body and soul back to the surface. "What the hell's that supposed to mean?"

Nizari's gaze narrowed. "Tell me you did not enjoy our time together. Tell me you are not a better man for the fire I put you through. Tell me you are not a god!"

A god? There were no words for the revulsion creeping up Lee's throat at Nizari's incredible gall to declare that his works of evil in any way resembled creative genius. Nizari had nothing to do with God, certainly not betterment. Unblinking, ice-cold insanity stared back at him, and Lee was done. His temper lifted its cloven wings, furled with deep, dark fury that his soul had suppressed for too long. It ached to be unleashed, to fill the sky now void of stars with the fire of revenge and justice.

"How?"

A nervous glitter raked Nizari's eyes. "How what?"

Lee shrugged as if he didn't care. "How do you want to die? Headshot? Gut shot? Cock shot? Trust me. I can't make you a god, but I can send you back to Hell where you belong."

When Nizari's nostrils flared, Lee added another option for good measure. "Or maybe you'd prefer your own brand of, what'd you call it? Taking what is offered? Yeah. Let's head out to your playhouse and see what you've got to offer when you're dangling by a hook. When you're the guy being sliced up like a deli tray." He let his gaze drift down to the man's zipper. "Not like I expect much from a little squirt like you."

Lee had the bastard good as gone, but damned if that crazy song didn't slide into the moment and throw him off balance. *"I once was lost, but now I'm found."* He blinked at the real message of the song. Forgiveness. *Shit.* Not why he was there.

Nizari, the perceptive snake that he was, must've picked up on the slight change in the universe. His tongue slithered over his lower lip. "I can make you rich."

Lee held perfectly still, struggling with his conscience, not the temptation of Nizari's offer. Thinking of Tess and the vile whipping at Nizari's hand. *"Was blind, but now I see..."* *Shit.*

That was the thing. Lee *could* see. He loved Tess and he always would. She'd saved him from himself just as he'd hoped he'd saved her from herself. The eternal yin and yang. The perfect balance of two hearts. The godawful rule that opposites attract. She deserved better than him, and he meant to see that she got it.

Nizari shifted his feet, his fingers nervously tapping the books, a glimmer of hope in his eyes. "There's more where these came from," he wheedled. "Gold. Jewels. Tell me what you want. I can make your dreams come true."

The final straw…

Lee fired one shot for every previously named target. Head. Gut. Cock. He put three in the man's balls for how Nizari used his manhood against women. For all those little girls and boys he'd molested. For the women he'd raped.

In twitching slow motion, Nizari crumpled to the floor, and *hell yeah!* The avenging angel in Lee lifted its glorious, purpled black wings and filled the room with righteous justice, damn it. With honor. With pride in a job well done. The bastard of Kabul was finally dead and accounted for. Game fucking over.

Lee knelt on one knee at the man's side, his darker nature released. For that single adrenaline-charged moment, he understood depraved indifference and the need to behead one's enemy. Every last filament of his warrior's soul begged to shout victory over evil to the world. To scream, "Homerun! Touchdown! Amen!" To raise Nizari's head so all could see the monster was no more.

But honor prevailed. Lee Hart was not Hasim Nizari. They'd never lived in the same universe, and that beastly evidence would only prove Lee's undoing at the most elemental level of a man. It was evidence. It was sin. He left the body intact. Collected his brass. Curled his nose at the job well done. And meant to fly out on the first available flight.

Too late, his sixth sense tingled up his spine. He jumped to his feet, his weapon instantly on target. On the Taliban assassin with his pistol dead center of Lee's head. Lee stilled his breathing. Focused his soul. This was the liar who'd kissed Tess only that morning. Now Turik could join Nizari in death.

Turik's gaze flitted to the dead body between them. "I see you have killed an important member of the Taliban leadership, Agent Hart. My Imam will not be pleased."

Lee nodded one slow affirmative. "I did," he growled, lest there be any mistake who'd ended Nizari's reign of terror. It should've been Turik, the coward. "Not like I give a damn what you or your Imam thinks. I thought you were going to take care of him last night. What the hell happened? He talk his way out of that one, too? Or are you the one who's been covering up for him all these years?"

The assassin of Kabul's gaze narrowed, his pistol never wavering, and that cocky British accent annoying as hell. "Why on earth do you think I'm here today, my good man?"

I'm not your good man. Lee had no answer for that, but his rifle did. Even then, he planned it. Measured the distance between Turik and him. He knew he could do it. The guy was Hollywood perfect, one of those natural-born handsome guys who got all the women. Not. This. Time.

"Why are you here?" Lee asked, his tone flat and deadly. Implacable. Turik was nothing but the enemy. He wasn't at home. There were no ROEs to stop Lee from fulfilling the contract Alex had signed. No wife or son in the immediate area. He could end this here and now.

Turik pursed his lips, not lowering his weapon. "If you must know, I needed Nizari to believe I trusted him, that he had time."

Damn, the guy almost sounded sincere, and Lee almost wanted to believe him. "Time for what?" *Spell it out, smart guy.* Lee took a sideways step toward the center of the room. Turik matched him, both predators sizing each other up, still dancing the slow tango of two assassins who could end each other and neither walk away. Caught in an Afghan version of a Mexican standoff.

"Time to think he could merely pack up his tent and fade into the desert. I needed him to disclose every last artifact and treasure he has stolen. I've been here since this morning watching him do just that. Drop your weapon, Agent Hart," Turik urged. "Tess deserves more than your dead body on her doorstep."

"Drop yours," Lee muttered, "and leave Tess out of this."

"Why the bloody hell do you think I'm here?"

Lee cocked his head, not understanding. "Don't know. Don't care. Lay your piece on the table and step away or so help me..."

Turik's lips thinned below that immaculately trimmed moustache. His dark eyes narrowed. "You really don't know, do you?"

There was no reason to answer, because Lee hadn't a clue what Turik was talking about, and he wasn't about to ask. His left eyelid narrowed, pushing more visual acuity to his right. His good eye. His strong eye. His right index finger stoked one miniscule loving caress to the curve of the metal trigger and—

"Okay. You win." Damned if Turik didn't lift his pistol to the ceiling, expelling a deep breath as he surrendered the moment. "You're not John Wayne, you know," he breathed, the weapon still in his hand, "and you're not taking my piece, as you so cleverly called it. You Americans. Do you all think you're cowboys?"

Lee kept his rifle on target, not trusting this trained assassin for one second. "Leave this place," he ordered. "Run back to your bloodthirsty friends, but don't think for one second I won't kill you the next time I see you."

Turik actually smirked while he stuck his pistol inside the folds of his flowing robe, a mix of brown, caramel, and vanilla-colored stripes with an intermittent slash of ruby red. God, the guy was arrogant. Well-dressed, but downright calm for a man about to die.

Turik extended an open palm in friendship. "Please, Agent Hart. I'm not here to kill you. I'm not even here to exact revenge for you ending Nizari, though my Imam will expect that of me. I'm simply here as an old friend of the woman you love."

Lee gritted his jaw, his back teeth grinding up a storm. He wasn't going to shake this guy's hand for anything. "I said leave Tess out of this."

"So you admit you love her?" Turik stated, amusement dancing over his face as he withdrew his hand. "I knew it the moment I saw you ride off in Clint Culver's truck that night. You really thought you were saving her, didn't you?" He allowed a small smile, his chin cupped in his hand. He winked. "How'd that work out for you? I'll wager Tess wasn't happy with the whole white-knight-in-shining-armor thing, was she?"

Lee refused to answer. His gaze drifted to Nizari's blood-soaked corpse.

"He deserved to die, Agent Hart," Turik muttered, his voice a guttural declaration without one speck of remorse. "A point in your favor. You got here first, but I do say, you went too easy on him. I would've tied him to his whipping post and used that tongue of Satan on him. I would've fed him that filthy male organ he has so callously used against the innocents of my country, and I would've made certain he choked on it."

Lee finally lowered his rifle, not exactly trusting the assassin in the crosshairs, but willing to listen. Anyone who hated Nizari as much as he did, couldn't be all bad.

Turik hadn't taken his eyes off the body, disgust simmering in his tone. "I would've cut out his lying eyes, Agent Hart. His ears. His fingers, knuckle by knuckle, and if his heart still beat after that feast, I would've cut it out of his chest and fed it to him as well. You showed extreme prejudice, but you Americans are all the same. You're too nice. Your military-style, pinpoint precision strikes offer more mercy than animals like Nizari deserve. I wouldn't have exercised that degree of gentlemanly restraint. To simply end a man's life does not exact adequate revenge. By the time I was done with him, Hasim would've begged for bloody mercy, and the world would've known a Taliban assassin ended him. But now..." He nodded toward the exit door behind him, "for this night only, we are not enemies. Let us talk."

Chapter Thirty

Lee shouldered his rifle and followed Turik, more to keep the guy within sight and range if this gambit proved to be another trick. He eyed the two dead men outside the door. His palm moved to the weapon at his hip, daring Turik to call him on those murders.

Turik said nothing, just cleared the concrete patio with an easy gait, and together they walked westward toward the gravel road, then crossed it. Lee came to a full stop at the nearest granite outcropping where the smell of blood and death didn't reach. "This is far enough. Talk."

Turik turned around to face him, one brow raised. "Yes. This is a sufficient distance for our needs. We are two reasonable men. Please. Sit." He squatted to his haunches in the manner of his people, an uncomfortable position Lee never intended to master.

Lee crouched to one knee, his pistol within reach. Kabul didn't glimmer with the brilliance of affluent cities in America, the United Arab Emirates, or Singapore. Its lights were fewer, limited to storefronts, streets, and those necessary for traffic. Only the airport, Camp Eggers, the presidential palace, and the important places were well lit, and not a hovel in between.

"It's a good night for revelation," Turik said simply, his head turned, his eyes on the city to the north. "Thank you for what you did for my country, Agent Hart. I know you did it more for Tess, but I do thank you."

"How could you cover for him?" Lee spat. "Surely you knew what he was doing."

"Many lies and half-truths are spoken in war..." Turik swallowed hard, "but yes. I knew."

Lee pushed to his feet, not willing to sit and chat with Nizari's heartless accomplice. "How could you? Innocent women and girls, little boys..." He couldn't come up with a word that fit Nizari's unfathomable depravity.

"I've heard worse lies about you Americans," Turik said softly. "Only when I corroborated the gossip with facts could I finally act."

It took all Lee's willpower not to strike Turik. "When the hell was that? Yesterday?"

"I've been watching Hasim for years." Turik glanced upward. "He was a powerful man with dangerous friends."

"Including your almighty Imam?"

Turik closed his eyes, his face devoid of emotion. "Yes," he said quietly. "I also believe my closest mentor, my Imam, has some explaining to do, but understand this. You must leave my country. You must let us tend to our problems in our way. As for the artifacts, not until I entered Nizari's home last night did I realize he hadn't destroyed what he'd taken."

"Yet you knew he dabbled in the black market."

"I knew Nizari was a man of shadows, not balls or fair games of cricket. The loss of our history is tragedy enough, but for a man to hoard the very items he declared he'd sold in the name of Allah..." A wistful tone breached Turik's voice. "*Ba mah nesheen mah shawe, ba deg nesheni siah shawe.*"

The sorrowful intonation hung between them. Turik could've just told him to go to hell, and Lee wouldn't have known the difference, but he flat didn't care.

The somber assassin nodded to the silvery crescent hung in the east like a Christmas ornament in a dark velvet sky. "It's an old Afghan proverb, Agent Hart. If you sit in the light of the moon, you'll become like the moon. But if you sit beside a cooking pot, you'll become as black as the pot."

Lee slanted a suspicious eye at the mumbo jumbo, but he caught the drift.

Turik drew in a long, deep lungful before his shoulders drooped with the gradual exhalation. "America. Afghanistan," he said quietly, "they are both the same—both overflowing with good people caught up in angry men's politics and wars. To be honest with you, I had no reason to visit Nizari's home until I caught word late yesterday of a trap set to recover the reliquary. Yes, I know Tess has it again. I'm not surprised that she stole it out of my safety deposit box. She has an uncanny instinct for putting herself in the wrong places at the worst possible times."

If you only knew, Lee thought. Walking on high palace walls, spitting in the face of the wind, that woman kept herself front and center of a showdown at all times. He swallowed hard. He couldn't fight it. The woman had done what Nizari had failed at. She'd driven him stark raving crazy.

"My country must seem a broken shambles to you, Agent Hart, and in many ways, it is," Turik said with a sigh, still talking at Kabul. "I can't condone the selling of our culture to wage war and terror, but neither can I condone the increase in poppy fields to satisfy the world's boundless appetite for heroin. It seems we will never be a united people again, that we will all die fighting, that we will end with nothing." He murmured as he shook his head. "*Jangal ked at greft, khusk o tar mesoza.* If the forest catches fire, both the dry and the wet will burn."

That one Lee understood. *We will all burn together.* But he had no words of encouragement. He wouldn't lie to the guy. Afghanistan did suck. Who the hell wanted to live in a perpetual warzone? He didn't. Hell, these fierce tribes had been fighting each other before any westerners showed up in their lands. Lee was tired of the wise old Afghan sayings, too.

"But it is my home," Turik continued calmly, "and I love it. I will fight for it the same as you will fight for your America and the woman you love."

Lee kept his mouth shut. Exactly how much did Turik know about him and Tess?

"She's a dreamer, Agent Hart. Know that. She's not like you and me. She sees stars in the sky, but when I look up, I only see the thief in the night, the bullet and the bomb, the rain that falls down like fire on my country. Where she sees romance and heat between the lovers on the dance floor, I see the assassin's blade and the cold, hard truth of the world we live in. But she..." He drew in a deep breath through his nose, "that damned woman sees the future that could be for my country."

"She sees what *should* be," Lee corrected, his tongue finally loosened. "No country deserves the violent history yours has had. You guys need to pull your heads out of your asses and strive for the common good. What the shit are you going to leave your sons and daughters if you don't?"

"I say, old chap, now you've got it." There was that British clip again, another clever ploy this Afghan warrior used and discarded as needed. Turik slapped his knee and lifted to his feet. "Which is why I fell in love with her a long time ago. I dare say, she loves my country more than some of us do. England was our time in Camelot, where everything and anything seemed possible between Tess and I. It just wasn't meant to be."

Lee didn't like the deep timbre in Turik's tone at the mention of Tess, nor the notion of Guinevere and Sir Lancelot that Turik had just summoned to mind. It fit, though, didn't it? Hadn't Guinevere cheated on King Arthur with Sir Lancelot? Wasn't that how women's betrayal went? They showed you their charm and grace, hooked you, and left you dangling. Your heart pierced and bleeding. Your dreams in a puddle at your feet.

"She loves you dearly, you know," Turik said to the night, his chin lifted toward those very same stars overhead and all of Lee's shattered dreams.

"Then why the hell were you kissing her?"

Turik met Lee's dark and loathsome gaze. "Because I do love her. I always will, but my dilemma is the same as every other man's in Lady Tess's universe. She doesn't love me," he said sadly, "not the way she loves you. I only kissed her cheek this morning, Agent Hart, not her sweet lips. I needed to tell her that I was not her Alexander, but it was clear she held no tender regard for me. Where once my reflection glimmered in her beautiful blue eyes, now stands the hero she's been searching for all of her life, her true Alexander."

Lee grunted. Turik sounded as hopelessly romantic as Tess. "Why'd she run to you then?"

"She was afraid for her brother, and she knew I could help her. Clint Culver has been consorting with a dangerous man. Tess should be worried."

Lee held his tongue. The stars were beginning to align. Tess would go off half-cocked like that, and Turik would certainly know Clint had located Iskandar. He had the same uncanny knack as Tess of getting into the right place at the wrong time. Damn, these two were kindred spirits, both fighting for the country they believed in, but both on opposites sides.

Turik offered a crooked smile. "Our fair lady loves you, Lee Hart. Don't ask me why she chose an American soldier over a scholar like me, but she did, and for that, I am grateful, because I have Alessa in my life. Rest assured, I love my wife more than I ever loved Tess."

His gaze drifted to Lee's feet. "I know you have suffered at Nizari's hand, but strive to put him in your past now that you've ended him. Tess is a rare woman who will take you places you never dreamed of going, and in the journey, she'll charm every logical reason for you not to follow her out of your mind. She'll flirt with you relentlessly, and she'll tease until she drives you crazy, but she'll love you just as deeply as she loves her causes. I'll tell you what I told your darling Tess. She's a dreamer. She tilts at windmills and thinks she has to spit in the eye of the devil to accomplish her goals. Are her goals noble and impossible? Absolutely. Is she a fool to love my country so deeply that she'll fight for it in her reckless way? Yes and no. Does she love you more than she ever loved me? You already know that answer."

Lee studied the liar in his midst more intently. Tess and Turik had certainly acted intimate. Cozy. But Lee could detect no deceit in the man's steady stare, and Turik's words rang true. Lee swallowed hard. Maybe he had jumped to the wrong conclusion.

"If I have one secret to share with you tonight it is simply this. Tess and I were never lovers." Turik didn't so much as blink or flare a nostril. "It is unfortunate, but true," he said softly, his open palm braced on Lee's shoulder. "I could lie to make you think I knew her that way, that I was her first, that I was a better man than you because of it, but I do believe that distinction goes to you and you alone. Besides, there are enough liars in my country. We don't need another."

Lee grunted. "There are enough liars in the whole damned world." But wait. Turik and Tess hadn't… Oh hell. Was it possible that Tess was a virgin until that afternoon in the hotel? Why hadn't she said anything? Why hadn't he detected that tender secret? That crazy damned secretive woman. She'd done it again!

"Which is why we are here, my friend"—Turik stuck his chin at the crime scene below—"and not there."

"I'm not leaving until I burn that shithole to the ground," Lee growled, his hatred for Nizari as strong as ever.

"Excellent. May I assist?"

You could've knocked Lee over with a feather at that offer. A really little downy feather. From a fluffy baby chick. He blew out a gut full of suspicion and finally accepted his assassin friend as a brother at arms. Kind of.

Together, they buried the two guards in shallow graves between the rows of cells and the house. They moved the last of the ancient treasures to the trucks, then drove them a safe distance from the house. Another surprise. Turik drove a sporty Land Rover, exactly like the one Lee had seen parked next to his Hummer in the hotel parking garage. Lee about choked at the sight of it.

He strode back to find Turik inside with Nizari facedown at the end of a rug, the dark still plenty dark "I say, Agent Hart, would you help me get my friend here into the back of my vehicle?"

"Why not let him burn with the house?" That bastard's dead body was the last thing Lee wanted to touch.

Turik rolled Nizari once, keeping him facedown. "Simple. The kill you made is clearly American. It's too clean. Too nice. Nizari's body must disappear so that evidence isn't used against you, or indirectly, Tess."

Plausible, but sketchy. Lee hesitated, not trusting that Turik had his back. He'd seen enough Taliban propaganda. The current regime had no trouble slandering American military or contractors. Why would Turik cover for an American murderer? Why not just abuse the corpse to make it look like torture and call it good?

Turik glanced up at him. "Trust me on this. I don't do this to protect you. Only Tess. Would I allow Hasim's shadow to stalk her for the rest of her life?"

Lee decided to trust. He dropped to one knee to assist. "That was you at my hotel?"

Turik shrugged. "I have been known to park at the Ambassador Hotel a time or two," he said slyly. "You drive one of those dastardly Hummers, right?"

"You know damned well I do." A chill skated up Lee's spine. This guy had gotten closer than he'd suspected, but not once had Turik made an attempt on his life. *That Lee knew of. Hmmm.* It seemed they had a lot in common. Protecting Tess.

Putting Nizari down. Torching his place, if that ten-gallon gas can in the back of that classy Land Rover was full.

"Would you care to know how Hasim came to be so evil?" Turik asked as he casually stuffed the rolled rug and the body within it deeper inside his rig, then tugged the can to the door and unscrewed the lid.

Lee shrugged, wiping his palms on his thighs. "Not sure if I care."

"You most certainly do." The clipped British accent was back. Turik leaned his hip to the tailgate and continued. "Hasim was not always evil. He was a decent man, a good husband, and an honest banker when he first moved from Syria. But he was not content with ordinary. He wanted power, and in wanting power, he fell to the same sin as Iblis, the sin of pride." Turik talked with his hands. He should've been Italian.

"Who the hell's Iblis?"

"You know. Iblis. Satan. The dark angel who refused to... Oh, never mind." Turik hefted the heavy can to his feet with a grunt. "The point is that Hasim went to great lengths to establish a reputation of fear and terror. He changed his name from Nafari, the name of his father and grandfather before him, to Nizari, the name of a cold-blooded murderer of ancient times. He wanted all who heard his name to cringe, so he sacrificed his family honor. You have heard of the Nizari Ismailies, the notorious Hashshashins of eleventh-century Syria, haven't you?"

"You mean the ruthless assassins of Hassan-I Sabbah?" Lee asked just as casually. Every sniper worth his salt knew the legend behind his profession. "The guys who threatened the Sunni Seljuk in ancient Persia? The legendary first assassins? Nah. Never heard of them."

Amusement bracketed the corners of Turik's mouth. "Well done, Agent Hart. You know your history." Lifting the can, he extended his other arm, counterbalancing the weight as he headed to Nizari's door. "The point is that Hasim became exactly what he wanted," he said, his voice strained. "He became the worst kind of man, a creature who preyed on the innocent and weak. He couldn't tolerate honorable men, which is why he sank to the depths of depravity that he did. Even then, I doubt he was satisfied with his work. Once he succumbed, his sin ruled him."

"He always wore clean linen shirts," Lee remembered out loud. "And sandalwood. Silk ties." *Shit.* The things he might never be able to forget. Lee shook his head to pull his mind out of the past. "What about you? How evil are you?"

Turik glanced sideways at him as he sloshed the first gulp of gasoline around the post that had once held Tess. "Surely you don't believe I'm anything like Nizari, Agent Hart. I'm more like you. An assassin for my country. A lover to my wife. A father to my son. And you? How evil are you?"

Stupid question. Lee never hesitated. "Evil, nothing. I'm a Marine." *And damned proud of it.*

In ten minutes, the cells and the interior of Nizari's brutal estate were doused with every last ounce of accelerant. The men stepped back from the gathering fumes. Turik unholstered his pistol and handed it grip-first to Lee. "It only seems sporting that you finish what you started. End the traitor's lair and the myth."

Lee hefted the pistol, a Sig Sauer like his own. He unholstered his own piece and handed it to Turik. "Let's finish this together. For Tess."

A genuine smile brightened Turik's face. "Yes. Let's do this."

Enough said. It took a second to sight the propane tank inside one of the open cells. Lee fired. Turik fired at the same time. Lee liked to think it was the spark off his round on metal that lit the inferno, but who could say? One thunderous whoosh pushed a shock wave of heat and fumes from the torture chambers to the house. In seconds, all was fully engaged in flames and lost. Or gained, depending on where a guy stood.

"How sweet the sound..." whispered off Lee's lips.

Turik slanted him a kind look, one brow lifted. He returned Lee's weapon and clasped his shoulder again. "I know you've suffered much in my country, and for that I am truly sorry. Go home, my brother. Marry that spirited woman we both love. Tame her. Leave a righteous posterity. Forget the trials and the things you've seen here. *Joyenda yabenda st.*"

Lee furrowed his brows intentionally. This son-of-a-bitch had certainly waxed poetic tonight. "You know damned well I don't know what you're saying."

Turik beamed, the light in his eyes genuinely tender. "The seeker is the finder, my friend," he whispered. "Seek love. Find joy. Marry Tess. Just don't return to my country. I will kill you the next time I see you."

Lee succumbed to the friendship offered him in the guise of a threat. "You can't kill a man if you're invited to his wedding."

Mischief sparked deep in Turik's eyes. "Ah, then I shall dance with the bride again."

"Only if you want to die." The banter felt good and honest, but Lee had one more jab to offer. It finally made sense, and he was going to kick Alex's butt the next time he saw him.

"You're the one," he ground out, Turik's hand still gripped firmly in his. He jerked the Taliban assassin in close until they were nose to nose. "You hired me and my boss to protect Tess, didn't you?"

Damned if something didn't glisten at the corners of Turik's dark eyes. He really did love Tess. "Please," he said quietly. "Let that be our little secret."

Chapter Thirty-One

Wow. When Alex Stewart offered protection, he meant it. Tess found herself guarded by more bodyguards than she could handle. Both Jordan Hannigan and Seth McCray kept steady watch, one at each side of her bed during the first few moments her meds allowed a bleary view of the world. She'd hoped to find Lee at her side, but he hadn't returned, so she embraced the power of the painkiller in the hypo.

Until she woke to the man himself. Alex Stewart was not a pleasant man to wake up to. He growled a lot. That grumbly noise was what awakened her from another mindless drift through dreamland. "Hmmm," she mumbled. Not exactly "hi there," but it got Alex's attention.

He leaned forward and took hold of her fingers. Not tightly, like Lee would've done if he'd been there, but tight enough. She tried to rouse herself again, the room coming into whirling, fuzzy focus. "Wm-m-m-m, Lm-m-m." Not the best vocalization for "Where's Lee?" but close enough for government work. Surely Alex got the drift. He was, after all, ex-military.

The effort of those poorly spoken words took her under for what felt like several more hours, but was probably only minutes since Alex was still holding her fingers when she lifted above the buzz again.

She wanted to go—*home.* A funny word that didn't describe her current habitation with Clint, her on-again, off-again brother, the guy who'd lied to her for years, apparently. Like Mohammed. Another liar. Her mind wandered to the only man who hadn't lied—the man who could've died rescuing her. The man she loved with every last beat of her foolish heart. "Lee," she said out loud, needing one word of hope that Lee Hart still lived in her universe.

"There, there," Alex offered. Like any man with a foolish woman on his hands, he sounded unapologetically firm. "It'll be all right."

"But how could he leave me?"

Alex grunted. "Because that's what guys do when they're hurt."

She thought she detected another hint. *Because you broke his heart.* "I did this to him," she admitted quickly. "I hurt him, and he's gone, and I'll never get to sail on his boat with him, and he's going to the Med, and... and..."

Right on cue, Alex offered a drink from her water bottle, most likely to silence the tragic ramblings of a woman at the edge of an emotional breakdown. "Here. You must be thirsty." He probably meant to say, *"Shut up. You talk too much."*

She took a long sip, then quickly agreed, "I talk too much." All she got was a grunt while Alex returned the bottle to her nightstand and shifted his position. She hadn't noticed until then. His right leg extended forward in a cast with shiny stainless-steel hardware breaching the plaster at his ankle. "You're in a wheelchair?"

He shrugged. "It's nothing. I'm good."

Wasn't that what all tough guys like him said?

Tess eased up slowly. Thanks to her pain meds, the stinging lashes on her back were quiet for the moment, but she had a mission. She couldn't let Lee leave the country without one final word. She snagged the sheet to her chin and straightened.

"Where do you think you're going?"

"To find Lee. This is my fault," she declared, wrapping the sheet toga-style around her, intending to slide out of bed, to get dressed and find that man before he did something stupid.

"You're damned right it's your fault, but you're not leaving. You've got guards outside your door."

Her brows narrowed. "I do?"

Tess stared Alex down. He didn't look so savvy sitting there in a rumpled button-up shirt, his elbow to the wheelchair armrest and his chin on his fist. The laugh lines she'd detected the morning he'd fixed breakfast were gone. No sparkle lit those tired blue eyes. He looked ragged. Weaker. She could take him.

"Don't you ever learn?" Alex scowled as if he'd read her mind.

"Did he... did he really leave me?" She hated the little girl tremor in her voice.

"He'll be back. Just wait. You'll see."

"How can you be sure?"

"I'm not blind, Miss Culver. That agent of mine has been studying you for months now. He's the one who collected every surveillance video, every wiretap, and every aerial reconnaissance on you and your brother. This was supposed to be his farewell tour, until he saw you. That was the first spark I'd seen in him since he came to work for me, but now I'm not sure he's smart enough to leave you the hell alone."

That revelation both enlightened and stung. "I made a mistake." *Sheesh.*

Alex huffed. "A mistake? You call this latest game of yours a mistake?"

If looks could kill. Her lashes dropped at his deadly parry and thrust. "It wasn't a game. Mohammed was my friend," she insisted. "We've known each other since—"

"Let me tell you something about your *friend.*" Sarcasm laced his words like barbed wire on a whip. "Mohammed Turik has intentionally killed everyone you know, but you don't seem to get the hint. Monsieur Jacque Favreau. Two assistant curators from the National Museum. Two Catholic nuns. And last but not least, he took a shot at you. He only missed because my men were hot on his ass. What will it take, Miss Culver? How many more have to die before you wake up and get the hell out of his country?"

Tess blinked at the death toll Alex spat at her. He was right. She'd caused nothing but pain and death for everyone who'd befriended her or believed in her cause. Her hands wrung in a tight tangle. She hadn't pulled the trigger, but she was the fool in the motive behind every murder. Five innocents... all dead because of her recklessness.

The truth hit her hard. How do you repent when you finally understand the depth of your sin? Mohammed was a killer, not a friend. But like the fool she was, she'd gone straight to him when she should've gone to Lee. She'd put her trust in her enemy instead of relying on the man she loved. Yes, loved. Her heart swelled with the terrible knowledge of all she'd lost, and all she'd thrown away. *God, what have I done?*

Suddenly there wasn't enough air in the room. Despair clamped down hard on her chest. Her over-the-top cat burglar persona deflated in the face of the betrayal she'd offered Lee when all he had ever done was protect her from herself.

She sucked in a choking sob before it got away from her. Nothing else mattered but that damaged man she'd fallen in love with. The gentle warrior who'd relied on a simple gospel song to get him through the worst time of his life, and there she was, his worst nemesis, a dreamer like Don Quixote, tilting at stupid windmills, running after a legend while Lee fought the real demons. She led with the only ace she had left. "But Lee loves me." *I know he does.*

"Well, I don't," Alex shot another mean volley, his lips thin and his temper up, "but I happen to love this country. I've got friends here I've known for years. Good friends who saved my life, not bastards who shot at me when my back was against the wall!"

Every word was a red-hot nail in her coffin of self-recrimination. There were no clever words to fire back at Alex, and Tess couldn't have used them if there were. The man had every right to hate her. All along, she'd been the loose cannon, reckless and throwing caution to the wind, endangering him and the others on his team. Maybe she'd taken worse risks these last two days because she'd known Alex and Lee had her back. That they were capable of holding off the devil if she needed them to. Not anymore. They didn't need the trouble of a headstrong woman and her impossible dreams. Eric, Seth, Hunter, or Jordan either.

God, what have I been thinking? I could've gotten everyone of these men killed.

"What do you want me to say?" she finally asked, her nerves shot and her meds getting the best of her. "You're right—is that what you want to hear? Because you are, Alex.

I've been a fool, and I admit it. I took you and Lee for granted, but honestly, you knew what I was when you signed up for this. It's not like I was a nun who needed help crossing the border."

He glared at her. She glared right back. She was in the wrong, but she would only apologize so much.

Alex raked his fingers over his scalp, flipping his dark hair on end only to smooth it down again. The man was one hundred percent pegged, yet there he sat, trying his damnedest to reason with her. "Let me tell you something about Lee Hart," he ground out. "You're not the only one with dreams. The man joined the Corps because he believed in America, and what she stood for. He's the real deal, one of the damned few proud men left in my country. After what that bastard Nizari put him through, I'm not sure America deserves him any more than you do."

Tess held her breath. Alex had no trouble hitting below the belt, a testament to the depth of his feelings for his junior agent. She understood loyalty, but Tess had never had a friend like Alex, someone who'd take on all comers and defend her behind your back. She wanted one now. "I'm not *Suzy Homemaker*, Alex. You have to believe that I do love Lee, and yes, what I did to him this morning was beyond stupid, but what do you want me to say?"

"Goddamn it, Tess, say yes! That's what I want you to say! The second he asks, you jump up out of that bed, and you say yes, damn it. Don't you dare break his heart."

So not what she'd expected. "Excuse me?"

Alex had to be on some pretty stout meds too. He made no sense, but he did chuckle. "Trust me. I know my men. Lee's strung as tight as I've ever seen him, and it's all because of you. You're the one holding the bow, playing him like a goddamned fiddle. Don't toy with him if you're not serious."

She flexed her sore fingers and faced her sad reality. "It's not like he's going to ask me to go home with him now. Not anymore."

The door burst open and there stood one angry Lee Hart, breathing hard, his palm spread wide to the open door, his chin stuck out in sheer male dominance and a ferocious sneer. "Why the hell didn't you tell me you were a virgin, woman?" he bellowed at Tess right before he lashed out at his boss. "And you! Turik's behind this contract, isn't he, Boss? You've had us chasing our tails when you—you!—were the man he was paying? God damn you, Alex. We need to talk, but not now. Get out!"

Alex about choked. Lee hadn't meant to lead with that line straight out of *Caveman Etiquette,* but damn it, this woman drove him ten ways of crazy! Alex wasn't much help either, not accepting a contract with a Taliban assassin no less. What was the world coming to?

"You're here," Tess choked, her violet blues shimmering and her lips pinched tight. Damned if she didn't look like a little girl, her eyes too big for her pale face.

Lee glared at his boss. "The next time you sign me up for one of your goddamned missions, I want to be front and center of every last contract negotiation, do you hear me? Now get out. Tess and I need to talk."

Alex had the nerve to smirk on his way out the door. "She's all yours."

In two long-legged strides, Lee was at Tess's side, one knee to the floor and not sure if he meant to kiss her or kill her. "Why didn't you tell me that was your first time making love?" he asked through gritted teeth. "It was, wasn't it? Why didn't you tell me you were a virgin?"

She ran a warm palm over his sweaty cheek. "You're really here."

He clutched her fingers to end the sensual distraction before he caved in and fell for her tender touch. "Why, why—*why!*—didn't you tell me? God, Tess. I could've hurt you. I could've been gentler. Why don't you open up and tell me who you really are? Why all the secrets all the time?" He ached to kiss those pouting lips, but the poor woman had dark circles under her eyes. She wasn't up for this stormy confrontation, well too damned bad. Some things couldn't wait.

"You love me," she stated, those damned tears still threatening, changing the violet in her stormy blues to glimmering amethyst fire.

The woman wouldn't answer a direct question, but what could he say? "Yes," he hissed the truth that failed all understanding. "I've loved you since the first time I video-taped you running on the desert. You looked like the wind, Tess. You're wild and free and full of life. You're everything I'm not. When Alex offered this last mission to me, I couldn't get here fast enough, damn you."

"Damn me?" she asked meekly, a chuckle caught in her throat.

"Damn me, too," he muttered, lifting her knuckles to his lips. "I saw you and Turik together."

"I didn't kiss Mohammed," she offered meekly. "Not like that. It was friendship only."

Lee grunted. "Yeah, I know. Where do you think I've been?"

"At the airport?"

He shook his head. "Try Nizari's place."

The color, what there was of it, drained from her face. "Why?"

A scowl pinched his lips. "I had business with the bastard."

"You..." She lowered her chin, looking at him through her thick lashes. "You killed him?"

Lee ran a hand over his face. "Burned his son-of-a-bitchin' house to the ground, too. All of it. I talked with your buddy, Turik. He helped me torch the place. For a Taliban assassin, he's not so bad."

Now Tess's brows really furrowed. "Not so bad? Mohammed's a cold-blooded murderer. Don't ever meet with him again."

"You're telling *me* what to do?" *The nerve of this woman.* "So tell me. Why didn't you let me know that was your first time?"

Tess gulped, her neck muscles contracting with the effort. "You'll think I'm foolish."

"I already know that," Lee muttered, "but Tess, we have to be honest with each other. No more secrets. No more half-truths or subterfuge. I fell in love with you, only I'm not exactly sure who you are. Start now. Were you a virgin before I touched you or not?"

Her lashes fell as she nodded. "Yes, but…" Another gulp. "I was waiting until I found my Alexander."

Lee had to cock his head at that one. "Why? Were you planning on, what? Marrying the guy once you found him? Living a life of dirt and drudgery in the mountains of Afghanistan for the rest of your life?"

Her shoulders lifted. "I told you it was foolish, but honestly, yes. I knew deep in my soul that I wanted to give myself to one man in my life, and he had to be braver than most. Fearless. Reckless. He had to be like Alexander, someone strong enough to throw stars back into the sky."

Now it was Lee's turn to gulp.

"I've been waiting for you, Lee," she whispered, her eyes shining. "You're my Alexander. My hero. And I'm sorry. I've been talking with your boss and..." she nearly whimpered. "He's so mad at me, but he's right. I've done nothing but put you and everyone else at risk."

Lee had to blink to get his eyes to see straight. Tess apologized? For being her? What else did Alex say? *Never mind.* Lee got down to business. He'd been thinking how to resolve this prickly situation with Tess on the ride back to town with the Taliban's best sniper. The night had gotten pretty bizarre with Turik chatting away while Nizari's dead body bumped around in the back of his Land Rover, but there Lee was, on one knee and not about to let this opportunity get away from him again. "Marry me, damn it."

She giggled.

"Marry me, Tess Culver," he demanded, so damned serious his teeth hurt. "Damn it, you're mine and you always have been. Admit it. Say yes and marry me and brush the dust of this crazy country off your backside and—"

"Kiss me," she ordered in that sultry, sexy way she had that ensured she got what she wanted. "Kiss me, Lee."

The girl had the nerve to tug him close to her mouth—without answering the damned question. What could he do but close the distance and plant a wet one on her? He was a red-blooded male after all. "Is this a yes?" he mumbled around her lips, his stupid heart on fire all over again.

She chewed on his bottom lip, breathing life back into him with a heated, "Yes, Lee Hart. I'll marry you, and I'll leave this country on the next flight with you, and I'll have all of your children, and—"

"And you'll leave the reliquary with your friend, Iskandar."

She never hesitated, never asked how he knew Iskandar, or how she knew about him throwing stars back into the sky, just moaned while her silky tongue breached his thin hold on restraint. "Whatever you say, my love."

Epilogue

Turik lay low, his belly flat to the polished wooden parquet floor of one Ashley Fellows' Washington D.C. penthouse apartment, the business end of his high-powered rifle pointed out the open patio window, not exposed, just aimed where no one could detect it. He'd leveled his M14 on its tripod and kept his right index finger light on the trigger guard, his keffiyeh stuffed in his pocket for the time being. He hadn't acquired his target yet, but he would.

Today was a day for patience. He'd chosen a suitable location for the day's business as his line of work often took an inordinate amount of time. He'd also chosen comfort while he waited. The wealthy in America were not so different from the wealthy in Afghanistan. They all aspired to the finer things in life, the comfortable things. Fine silk tapestries from the Orient adorned Ashley Fellows' walls. Fine antique furniture throughout the place, possibly early American. The Federal period, if Turik wasn't mistaken. A cut-crystal glass of purified water at his elbow for when he got thirsty. All of it fine. *Just fine.*

Omar let out a deep sigh from where he sat cross-legged beside him. It must've been the breeze from the open patio door toying with the Irish crystal chandelier overhead that had finally soothed his frazzled nerves. Yes, *that* Omar. The boy Tess thought Nizari had ordered tortured and killed, never to be seen again. Not so. Turik made sure Omar escaped the evil Nizari had in store for him. The boy was now an American citizen, attending one of the finer universities in the D.C. area, and thrilled to assist with this one, last mission.

There was that word again. *Fine.* It rankled in the deepest pocket of Turik's gut like a stone he'd accidently chewed and swallowed. Maybe the rancid pit of a sour plum. He'd come to America for one purpose only—to ensure Tess Culver, now the deliriously happy Mrs. Lee Hart, lived a *fine* life. But somehow, that equated with him living a less-than-fine life. He would no longer have her in it, would he? Not if he succeeded tonight, and to be perfectly truthful, a future without Tess could only be less than—*fine.*

"Have you seen him yet?" Omar asked quietly. This young man must never go into covert work. He simply wasn't cut out to be an assassin. He hadn't the patience, but he was devoted to Turik. That was what truly mattered.

"Not yet," Turik breathed, his attention riveted to the spectacle in the distance, still quartering the happy crowd a good mile away on the steps of the very open Jefferson Monument. What a lovely, awful location for the small reception taking place. It wasn't boisterous or rowdy, just unprotected. *Foolish decision, Lady Tess,* he admonished silently, *to dance like a free spirit in the open where any mad man could take a potshot at you or send an RPG into the middle of those impressive, marble columns behind you.*

But then...

This was America, the land of the brave and the home of the free. Not perfectly safe, but safe enough that terrorist attacks didn't happen often. Children cried here, but generally not for the same reasons they cried in Afghanistan. How strange that capricious fate would consign one child to a *fine* life in the land of liberty while another suffered a lesser life in a war zone.

It ate at him, that word, with tiny, razor-sharp bites, reminding him he'd never watch Tess run in the desert again. That their time was finally ending. Manfully, Turik reminded himself he had the better woman in his life, his dear, sweet Alessa. Hadn't she given up her country out of love for him? Hadn't she proved that love time and time again? And yet...

His excellent scope instantly brought Tess up close and personal one more time. What he wouldn't give for another day with her. One last kiss. It wouldn't really be a sin against Alessa, not if it was only a goodbye kiss. Would it?

He knew better.

Fine.

The pink cherry blossom haze of April in Washington D.C. conflicted his view, making the upcoming shot difficult, but not impossible. Any sniper worth his salt knew how to solve that mathematical dilemma. Turik had adjusted his reticle for the distance. Made the necessary ocular alteration. The parallax, too. He'd accounted for the effect of the warmer breeze in the city to the cooler breeze coming off the Tidal Basin to the west of his target. A sniper knew how to use the forces of nature to accomplish his goal. He might have to aim farther to the left to hit the man he'd come to kill, but he'd had enough practice over the years. He could make the hit.

Night had fallen, requiring further refinement to his settings, but Turik had the time to be thorough. Ashley Fellows was away on business in Tampa, Florida. She'd never know her pristine home had served as a sniper hide on this, Tess Culver's wedding day.

"How can you see him all the way over there?" Omar asked quietly.

"I have an excellent scope," Turik murmured, his eye intent on the bride. Tess truly looked happy, her eyes aglow while she danced with her husband. Today she'd promised to love, honor, and obey. A pinch of jealousy stabbed Turik's proud, manly heart at the thought of that wedding bed, but he brushed it quickly away. Alessa owned his soul now. Tess was a thing of the past. He let her go—again.

She'd found her Alexander twice by the time she'd moved back home to America. Once in the tribal chieftain, Iskandar Kadir, a proven descendant of the legendary Alexander the Great if the DNA test could be trusted. The second time was in Lee Hart, the rakishly good-looking American Marine who held her against his muscular body like she meant everything to him. Lucky sot.

Turik blinked, the pinpoint of his laser centered on the back of Lee's head. He lowered the crosshairs to the bride in Lee's powerful arms, his heart suddenly stuck in the back of his throat, making it harder to breathe. There was a time when Tess had looked adoringly up at Turik. Just. Like. That. Her midnight blue eyes full of stars. Her tangled ebony locks a dark, magical halo that never failed to draw his focus to her lush red lips. Sinfully full and lusciously wet. Plump and sweet. Still as tempting as ever.

He ran his tongue over his bottom lip, remembering the day he'd bruised those tender ruby reds in the middle of Trafalgar Square. London. It was raining. She'd squealed about something or other. He honestly couldn't recall what she'd been ecstatic about that time. He could barely remember his name after she'd grabbed him by his jacket collar and kissed the hell out of him with those lips. With that sassy tongue. With every last ounce of her passionate heart.

The wildfire named Tess had stolen his heart at that precise moment in time, the wickedly sinful taste of Irish coffee still on her tongue, on her breath. Her mouth had been on his, breathing a wild and crazy kind of life into him.

He'd kissed her back, the door to his passionate soul breached and the fierce lion in his Pashtun heart unleashed. The world had stopped spinning. He hadn't been able to catch his breath, and he, Mohammed Turik, would have renounced his family, his country, and his god if it meant Tess would have loved him then the way she loved Lee Hart now.

But she didn't.

Turik faced the truth. He swallowed hard. *She'll be—fine. Just fine.*

Scanning the other dancers at the reception, he withdrew from the world with all its memories and calmed his soul, still determined to fulfill his mission. Sadly, it had to be done.

Tess had proved Iskandar's noble lineage. The treasures she'd stolen didn't make it to the Louvre as she'd originally planned, but to this day remained in the safe-keeping of the ancient Queen Roxana and her son, Alexander IV, alongside the loot Turik had recovered before he and Lee reduced Nizari's place to ashes.

Nizari's body was never found. *Tsk. Tsk. A shame that.*

Tonight's shot would raise an alarm, but by the time the local authorities covered the body and estimated the killing shot's trajectory, Turik and Omar would be gone. Ashley Fellows' patio door would be closed and locked up tight, every last fingerprint wiped. The scent of the pink dahlias in the fine crystal vase in the center of her dining table would cover the slightest out-of-place odor, and no doubt, she would wonder who'd left them. He'd never tell.

"They're dancing now." Omar kept vigilant watch through the high-powered binoculars Turik had loaned him. "Oh, look. There. I see him."

I see him, too, the lucky bastard. Damn Lee Hart for being all Tess wanted and needed. For being so tall that his muscular body overshadowed her so much that she had to look up at him like a little girl with adoration in her eyes. So broad-shouldered that his body easily encompassed her delicate, feminine curves, that he held her in his big, manly hands like the rarest treasure in his world. So dashing and handsome in that black tux that he looked better than all the princes of Arabia. *Damn him.*

What was not to like about the gentle giant staring down into Tess's blue eyes like a lover? Lee Hart possessed uncommon virtues. Incredible resilience. Honor. Humility too. The man was what American soldiers call *badassed*. Turik had to wonder, had Lee always been this noble? But of course. That was what heroes were made of, and there they were. The woman who would always haunt his dreams was finally married to the only hero in the world for her.

Like it or not, Lee would do Tess proud. Turik knew that for a fact. He'd worked his fingers to the bone to pull off another impossible dream—that of getting adoption papers through the bureaucratic nightmare of his government. Lee had done his share of bartering and working his side of the system, but it was done. The adoptions were cleared. Tess just had to sign the papers and she would have what she wanted. Mina and Jamaal.

Just. Not. Me.

Turik blew out an exasperated breath at the lovely apparition in his sights. What he wouldn't give to be a fly on the wall when Lee told her about Mina and Jamaal. Would she cry? Would she wrap her slender arms around that strong man's neck and cover him in kisses? Would that tender embrace lead to Lee taking hold of Tess and making mad, passionate love to—?

Let her go, Turik commanded himself sternly. *Alessa. I only love Alessa.*

"What are you waiting for?" Omar groused impatiently. "Do you not see him? Is that not him at the north side coming up from the basement? See?"

Chagrined at his apprentice's scolding, Turik panned to his left and—there he was. Finally alone. The last assassin. Creeping in the shadows like the coward he was. Disguised as a waiter, passing champagne on a tray that possibly concealed a blade or pistol beneath its crisp, white napkin. Come to wreak Hasim Nizari's brand of havoc one last time. Come to destroy something beautiful and noble and pure. Come to kill Tess and Lee.

By Allah, no more. It ended tonight.

Ballistics. Elevation. The breeze tossing Tess's curls to reveal the blush on her cheeks was just enough to also determine wind speed. Turik bowed to the precision sniper of his soul. His pure gift from Allah. His wedding gift now to Tess.

He calmed, the universe at last in league with the blessed duty of the night. He inhaled, then exhaled with deliberate slowness and held. Even the cherry blossoms between him and his target parted.

He squeezed the trigger slowly and precisely and held it as the round launched through space and time to its intended kill.

Omar jumped at the report, but Turik didn't move a muscle. Didn't take a breath. Didn't even blink. He needed to see the impact. The hit. The back spray when the round plowed through skull and brain matter. The shock in that dead man's eyes when he met his end. Turik needed to know for certain the last of Nizari's tentacles was finally severed.

The round hit true.

Allah be praised. Abdul Sherazi, the last Hashshashin of Hasim Nizari, was dead.

Turik stilled to watch the ensuing chaos through his scope. Lee had taken Tess to ground, the poor thing, wedding dress and all. Turik could no longer see her sweet face, not with Lee's massive body crouched over her like he was. God, the fierce rage in that man's eyes. Alarmingly savage. Amazingly passionate. Magnificent was what Lee was. A true warrior. Precisely what a recklessly daring woman like Tess needed in her perfect mate. Someone who was tough enough to take on the world and willing to do it alone—for her.

Of course every other TEAM agent sprang to Lee's defense, a murderous quantity of pistols now bristled in Turik's direction. Wouldn't you know? Alex Stewart stood on point, a short stock automatic rifle stuck in his shoulder, his eye to another excellent scope. Where on earth had he hidden that on his person? If Turik hadn't known better, he would've sworn Alex looked straight at him. Daring him. Eye to eye. Assassin to assassin.

But that just wasn't physically possible, was it? Turik eased to his knees, a small smile tugging at his lips, and his heart at peace with the world again. The deed was done. He could go home to his Alessa now and trust that he loved her as much as she loved him. He could teach Fahim the better paths of his people, the enlightened teachings of wiser, more levelheaded clerics and imams.

Likewise, Tess and Lee would now live a long life unfettered by the devil who had once sorely tested them both. They would make lots of babies. They would live in a free country where those little babies of theirs would never know hunger or fear or war.

They would be—*fine*.

THE END

Sneak Preview of Ky

Book 13

In the Company of Snipers

A man without hope will pray to die.

Lance Corporal Ky Winchester had.

It was five days since Coalition Forces had sent him and his squad to track down Hasim Nizari and bring him to justice. The United States Army wanted the monster dead or alive for his crimes against Afghan women and military prisoners. The ANA, the Afghan National Army wanted him, too. They'd hunted him for months, but the Teflon-coated degenerate had managed to stay one step ahead of the game. Until a couple of ANA soldiers had betrayed Ky and his men, leading him and his RTO, his radio tech officer, down a dead end and straight into hell.

Now Ky knew exactly where the bastard was.

Ky had taken one round to his body armor, just enough to knock him down. Not kill him, damn it. He didn't recall how he'd gotten from that stinking alley to this modern day pit of despair. He only knew that since he'd come to, torment visited him daily in the ways of cruel men. Fists. Leather belts with sharp buckles. Metal rods. Knives for sport. And worse.

Nizari. The treacherous, cold-blooded banker to the Taliban commandeered his own torture chamber. He was always dressed in a business suit, a linen shirt, and a clean silk tie when he soiled his victims. He always retained cool, aloof control while he worked his dark designs on human flesh. He never lost his composure that Ky could recall. Not once.

God, the depravity of man.

Nizari had yet to make his appearance for the day, but that didn't mean Ky hadn't been sorely tried. Hell, no. Nizari had plenty of soldiers in his band of merry men. They'd left Ky hanging so long he'd lost track of all feeling in his arms. He hadn't eaten in days—was made to endure at the edge of death until he broke.

"Ky." The single word came to him softly, too quiet to be real, but too loud to be imaginary. He strained to hear it one more time. Dared to believe. His broken nose twitched, and despite the dried clots stuffing it closed, the poor thing still detected a cooling hint of menthol. His nostrils flared, drawing the scent in along with another that was—good. Distinctly female. No man in this hellhole smelled like that.

"Ky."

His name again. He had heard it. He had! The shiver of hope raced up his spine and over his sweaty scalp. Was this his descent into delirium or the onset of death?

A vision materialized that would've made his eyes water if he could've opened them. An angel, more blur than shadow, more light than darkness. A hazy halo of gold. Cool, green eyes. Not Kelly green. Not emerald. But a clear, mint green that refreshed like the brisk bite of wintergreen in cold December. He *did* see her. He did. *Maybe...*

She drifted toward him, those green eyes too big for her face, and that was the cruelest nightmare of all, because he could—not—see. His heart thumped at the awful paradox he was caught in. His eyes were too swollen and bruised to work. If seeing was believing, what was she? Another nightmare?

Torture would drive a man crazy. But then...

That same drift of menthol and camphor filtered up through his tender nostrils and into his throbbing sinus cavities. He sniffed it in, as painful as the effort was, relishing the calming scent of eucalyptus as it soothed the damaged membranes in his skull. That he knew the distinctive fragrance only proved how close he was to losing his mind. But then...

She. Touched. Him.

Silky, soft fingertips traced his broken orbital bone. Warm palms cupped his bloody chin. *Impossible.* He swallowed hard, not ready to believe the end had come, that his brain was shutting down, offering hallucinations during his transition from life to death. *Just wait. There'll be a tunnel of light. The pain will cease. My time will end, and I'll be free, and...*

The light-as-breath brush of delicate arms encompassed his ragged, sweaty body. Another heartbeat echoed against his as if this gentle apparition cradled his head to her breasts, his ear to her heart, and God! This hallucination felt so good. He would've cried if he could have.

Perhaps it was merely the onset of his dying heart begging to be set free from torment, but it seemed so real. Greedily, he turned his face into the softness and warmth of that imaginary female body, seeking the comfort she offered. Wanting so much to believe. Needing her to—please, God! Be more than a wish and a prayer.

Her warm breath caressed the curl of his ear. He didn't understand how it worked; he only knew that his dream whispered loud enough he could no longer doubt her. *"I'm here, Ky. I'm not leaving you."*

She'd no more than stopped speaking when the wooden door to his sweatbox banged open. The sharp metallic tang of a lighted propane torch struck his nostrils. Oh, God. Another twist to the torture.

"Hold onto me," she commanded, her grip tighter.

God, he wanted to, but frantic panic crawled up his spine like a living thing, a sinister ice-cold dragon with serrated talons, an icicle tail that wrapped around his neck and choked him. It came with the despair of reality, the shuddering fear of the living damned. He clenched the chain instead of his imaginary angel and prepared to meet his maker.

"You talk now?" Nizari's brutal lackey asked, smacking something against his open palm with an intimidating *thwack, thwack, thwack.*

That was why his angel asked him to hold on. Somehow she'd known. This was it. His last moment on earth.

His soon-to-be murderer landed a sharp fist to his gut. The unexpected impact sent him spinning into the wall.

Ky wouldn't cry out, not to this bastard, but he did want to tell that patient angel, who lingered at the edge of his mind, *"Thanks for trying. Leave now. Never look back. Save yourself."*

Instead, the menthol scent grew stronger. Her hands grew tighter. *"I won't let you go."*

Yes. You will.

His captor muttered a bizarre gurgling curse. It sounded as if someone had joined the guy with the torch, no doubt both licking their chops for the despicable pleasure they derived from torturing Americans. *Bastards. Every last one of them.*

Ky bowed his chin to his chest and prepared to die. He didn't dare guess which appendage this bastard would burn first. Toes. Hair. His face. His balls. It didn't friggin' matter. He could take no more. *Just get it the fuck over with! Kill me!*

But then a hand steadied Ky's trembling body. A big hand. A kind hand. "You gonna make it?" a gentler voice asked. Strong and clear. American.

The chain lowered Ky to the floor, but his feet couldn't support his own weight. He collapsed even as his ears strained for another word, needing to know for certain this was no trick or dream, that this person was not Afghan. Not Mideastern. Not even from this part of the goddamned world.

"You okay?" The man spoke again, softer this time. Tenderly. Definite West Coast accent.

Thank God. Ky groaned a raspy, "Hell, yeah."

Careful fingers travelled over his neck and shoulders, down his arms and across his ribs, physically checking without leaving pain in their wake. How odd that he flinched anyway. That it took the last of his willpower *not* to scream after all— that.

Freedom hurt so damned good.

He gave West Coast the best answer a jarhead knew. "Ooh-rah," he choked, his tongue parched, his lips swollen and ragged. "God bless... America."

"Whatever," the guy muttered. "Can you walk?"

"Yes," Ky ground out through clenched teeth. *I can run, just get me the hell out of here!*

But rolling to his side took his breath. His mouth filled with blood. Drawing his arms down to his sides hurt like a mother. He wasn't going anywhere.

"What's your name, Marine?"

Ky faced his rescuer like a man. "USMC Lance Corporal Ky Winchester, sir." Damn, he'd mumbled like he had a mouth full of marbles.

West Coast didn't seem to notice. "Damned good to meet you, Ky. I'm USMC Corporal Lee Hart, buddy." Lee pushed a knife handle into Ky's bloody fingers. "You kill the first bastard that lays a hand on you, understand? Gut him like a fish. Make him pay for everything he did to you."

"Yes, sir." Ky clutched the knife, but he shook so hard. Every bone and muscle screamed that he was no longer forced to stand on his toes. No longer stretched to the point of breaking.

"I've got another person to rescue. I'm coming back for you. You hear me?"

The knife slipped to the floor. His heart spoke before his brain could rein it in. "Sir." Shit, he was bawling like a baby. "Please don't... don't leave me here."

And there in the dark, USMC Corporal Lee Hart did what any brother would do for another brother. He lifted Ky off the filth of rotgut Afghanistan and gathered him into his strong arms like a damned kid. Lee's fingers spread wide. He cupped the back of Ky's bobbing head to hold him still against his chest, as if Ky was the weaker, baby brother. As if Lee wasn't going to leave.

Ky fought for self-control and lost it. He pressed his forehead to Lee's collarbone, shaking and breathing hard. Nothing felt as good as this American-born shoulder. *Don't go!*

He dug his shredded fingernails into this brother's bare arms and struggled to hang onto what little dignity he had left. Not much. A guy who'd been made to dance on the short end of a rusted, iron chain was a damned humble man. *Please don't leave me!*

"How long you been in here, son?" Lee Hart, God bless him, had the rumbling voice of an older, wiser angel. Brought tears to a guy's eyes, not that Ky knew for certain what dripped down his cheeks. Could've been blood.

"F-five days, I think. Maybe more." *Seems like forever.*

A growl rumbled deep in Lee's chest. "Marines never lie, do we?"

Damned sneaky question. *Get me to feel valiant and brave when I'm—not.* "N-no, sir. W-we never lie. We never quit. We never f-f-fucking forget, either."

"Good answer. I'm not lying to you now, Ky. I will be back, but you gotta let me go. I've got more folks to save than just you." He pressed the knife handle back into Ky's palm and made sure his worthless fingers wrapped around it. "Hang onto this. There's others in this shithole who need my help. I can't leave them here any more than I'm gonna leave you. You understand?"

"Y-y-yes, sir," he replied, an obedient jarhead to the bitter end. Hell, he wanted to bawl like a baby. Instead, he sucked up a deep breath of freedom and remembered who he really was. What he stood for. Nizari couldn't take that.

"Ooh-rah," he growled from the depths of his American-born soul. He willed his fingernails to release his rescuer. He clasped the knife handle to his chest, his bloody little finger snug against the finger guard, his crushed thumb stroking the butt-end like it was a long-lost friend. The next murderer through that door would die, and Ky meant to die with him rather than endure another round of fun and games.

Lee Hart got him situated upright with his back to the wall beside the door.

"Sir?" Ky asked, not sure whether he wanted to know or not. "Was I... was I... alone?"

Lee grunted. "Except for that dead guy with the torch over there, yeah. Why?"

Ky shook his head, working his throat muscles to drum up enough saliva to swallow. "No lady with green eyes?" He hated the hopeful quaver in his voice.

Lee's solid hand gripped Ky's shoulder. "I sure as hell hope not. Stop dreaming. You've already got it made. Ladies like guys with scars. Now shut up and sit tight. I'll be right back."

Something lethal in his tone brooked no further discussion. Ky reached for him, but he was gone, and Ky was alone again.

Marines didn't lie and that was the gospel truth. But sometimes, they cries. Sometimes, the darkness got the best of them. Ky shook when his savior left. Tears oozed like molten lead between his mashed eyelids. They ran down his face, and he let them. There was no woman. No angel. None of this was real. He was all by himself. Blind. Scared. And losing his friggin' mind.

But just when the night seemed blackest...

Just when Nizari's evil spirit whispered that Lee wouldn't return...

That all was lost...

Ky cursed at the darkness. He sucked up the last of his courage and he chose to believe, damn it. He *had* seen a green-eyed woman. Okay, so he was blind, but she *was* there. And Lee *would* return. He would.

The cooling breath of menthol wafted into Ky's poor wrecked nose. She hadn't left. He wasn't crazy. *"Ky,"* she breathed life into him once more.

"I... I tried to hold onto you," he choked out unashamedly.

The peace that surpassed all understanding invaded his wrecked soul. He couldn't explain how it worked. Didn't even try. Just leaned into the warmth of her heart and thanked God for angels.

And hope.

Thank you for reading Lee!

Be sure to check out the rest of the guys and gals of Irish Winters' series: *In the Company of Snipers*

Other Irish Winters' books:

King of Hearts, Deuces Wild Series, *#1*

Joker Joker, Deuces Wild Series, *#2*

Smoke, Hearts and Ashes Series, *#1*

Ash, Hearts and Ashes Series, *#2*

Coming soon!

Seth, In the Company of Snipers, *#17*

One-Eyed Jack, Deuces Wild Series, *#3*

YOU are the key to this book's success!

Please tell other readers why you liked Lee and Tess's story by leaving an honest review at the retail site where you purchased it.
Recommend it to your friends. Lend it.
Most of all, enjoy it!

The best way to keep up with my new releases, giveaways, and actionable intel is to sign up for my spam-free newsletter at IrishWinters.com.

About the Author

Irish Winters is an award winning, Amazon best-selling author who, when she isn't writing, dabbles in poetry, grandchildren, and rarely (as in extremely rarely) the kitchen. More prone to be outdoors than in, she grew up the quintessential tomboy on a dairy farm in rural Wisconsin, spent her teenage years in the Pacific Northwest, but calls the Wasatch Mountains of Northern Utah home. For now.

She believes in making every day count for something, and follows the wise admonition of her mother to, "Look out the window and see something!"

Connect with Irish!
On Facebook: https://www.facebook.com/author.irishwinters
On Twitter: https://twitter.com/irishwinters1
Or at www. IrishWinters.com

www.ingramcontent.com/pod-product-compliance
Lightning Source LLC
Chambersburg PA
CBHW021322110726
47900CB00005B/1319